THE ALLEGATIONS

Also by Mark Lawson

BLOODY MARGARET
Three Political Fantasies

THE BATTLE FOR ROOM SERVICE
Journeys to all the Safe Places

IDLEWILD

GOING OUT LIVE

ENOUGH IS ENOUGH

THE DEATHS

MARK LAWSON

THE ALLEGATIONS

PICADOR

First published 2016 by Picador
an imprint of Pan Macmillan
20 New Wharf Road, London N1 9RR
Associated companies throughout the world
www.panmacmillan.com

ISBN 978-1-5098-2088-7

A CIP catalogue record for this book is available from the British Library.

Printed and bound by CPI Group (UK) Ltd, Croydon, CR0 4YY

V   it was a pleasure once to send to us and to all our
books and to   You will also find   author interviews and
news of any author events, and you can sign up for e-newsletters
so that you're always first to hear about our new releases.

For

MRD, *who gave me the idea*

DDR, *who gave me the time*

And To

FD and HB, *who gave me the example*

AA and AS, *who kept me alive*

and

SWAB, MF and F, *for knowing the truth*

Is the accuser always holy now?   Arthur Miller, *The Crucible*

'You are presumably very surprised at the events of this morning?'
asked the Inspector

Franz Kafka, *The Trial*

Whereof we cannot speak except with prurience, sanctimony or
inspired retrospective wisdom, thereof we must not say a word

Blake Morrison, 'It Was Good While It Lasted'

On the back page he saw that the News had transformed his statement that Katharina was intelligent, cool, and level-headed into
'ice-cold and calculating,' and his general observations on crime
now read that she was 'entirely capable of committing a crime'.

Heinrich Böll, *The Lost Honour of Katharina Blum*

The student–teacher dynamic has been re-envisioned along a line
that's simultaneously consumerist and hyper-protective, giving
each and every student the ability to claim Grievous Harm in
nearly any circumstance, after any affront, and a teacher's formal
ability to respond to these claims is limited at best.

'Edward Schlosser'
'I am a Liberal professor, and my liberal students terrify me'

CONTENTS

PART ONE

FALLS

Burning Names

He set down the letters carefully, handwriting feeling unnatural after decades of typing. The unfamiliarity was amplified because, even before the death of the pen, he had never used dipped ink on vellum. An unrecognizable signature resulted, neater and more elaborate than it was on cheques and contracts, the N, D and final paired Ts looped and curlicued, giving him a stranger's name. He raised the candle and angled it towards the paper, first drying the ink, then pressing the document towards the flame, watching the blaze until dropping the last ember to spare his fingers. Looking directly at the camera, he said: 'In the days of the witch-hunts, writing someone's name and then burning it was believed to be a way of bringing destruction down on them.'

The Centre

Appreciating its clients' desperation for discretion, the business made vagueness an art form. The bi-annual reminders by e-mail read simply: *Dear Mr Marriott* – he had dropped his professional title in this context – *your next appointment is scheduled for* . . . In this case, July 16th. On credit card bills, the charge line was *The Centre, W1*, a deliberate contraction, designed to thwart search engines, of the actual trading title. *Using the boxes below, indicate if you wish to accept this appointment.* He placed his cursor over the *Yes* box and clicked.

Pedantry

Sir – Although I am an historian of American politics rather than a specialist in English language, I feel qualified to express concern at the increasing use, by police and media, of the word 'historic' to describe events that occurred – or, more often, allegedly occurred – in the past.

To be clear: 'historic' properly denotes something or someone unique, or otherwise of particular note. The correct word for what happened in the past is 'historical'.

Some of those celebrities accused or arrested in connection with sexual offences – who seem to form such a large part of the target group of Operation Yewtree and now the related investigation Operation Millpond – may arguably be regarded as historic for their achievements in various fields. However, any crimes they may have committed in the past could and should only be described as historical.

Yours faithfully,
Dr Tom Pimm
Senior Lecturer in Modern American History
University of Middle England
Aylesbury Campus
Bucks

DID

NM: When I started out as an historian – I know that *an* doesn't sound quite right these days but I have a colleague who beats me up if I don't say it – there was quite a stark divide. One school – the 'Great Man' theory of history, or 'Great Person' we should say now – held that things happen because of certain persuasive or invasive personalities. Although, in the case of Suez, it would be the *Weak* Man Theory. The other version – in shorthand, Marxist – avers that events occur because of inevitable forces. Without sounding too much like a fence sitter, I suppose I'm sort of half-Marxist, half-Great Person. The virtues or flaws of individuals are important. But they affect – or are affected by – shifts in society or culture. Some believe that the English temperament would instinctively resist a Hitler. I would say that the question hasn't yet been tested here in circumstances akin to Germany's in the 1930s. I suppose what I'm arguing is that, in a country in which every woman were a lesbian, there could be no Don Giovanni. But might there arise a *Donna* Giovanni? And, if you want to go on, would there be a great opera about her? I tell my students to remain alive to the mystery of history.

KY: Although you yourself are a natural contrarian?

NM: No. I couldn't possibly agree with that.

KY: Well, there you . . . oh, I see. You've got me.

NM: Sorry, Kirsty. I can never resist it.

KY: Okay, Ned Marriott, your second record?

NM: Well, I said that the *Don Giovanni* was the first LP I ever owned but I sort of liberated that from my dad's collection when he was ill. You know a lot of those quizzes you get in magazines want to know the first record you ever *bought* because it's such a significant rite of passage? In my case, it was the winter of 1968, when I was thirteen and – I can see the paper sleeve now – it was 'Delilah' by Tom Jones.

The Problem With History

'The problem with history,' Tom Pimm began his introductory lecture every September, 'is that we know what came next. But – to understand the subject best – we must always remember that the people involved aren't living in our past, they're living in *their* present. King Henry VIII knew that Anne Boleyn was his second wife but not – at that time – that she was the second of six. Our retrospective perspective tells us that she was a transient infatuation but, by viewing her as such, we miss the much more interesting possibility that the King was truly in love with her and believed, as serial spouses often do, that this one was a keeper. And so always try to see *then* as a *now*. People knew that the Second World War was the second but not that the First was the first. We know that the original Millennialists were wrong to think that the world would end in 1000 AD but our job is not to sneer at their naivety – it's to appreciate how and why they thought that. However distant their lives and their beliefs may seem, historical figures are in one crucial sense like us. They don't know what's going to happen next, they don't know the ending.'

A Study in Evil

When disgrace and disaster arrived in his life, Ned Marriott was terrified – by the threat to his profession, reputation, family and health – but not surprised. As a teenager, it had struck him that those involved in devastating news stories always seemed astonished by what had happened. 'It came out of nowhere,' they told reporters. Or, even, bluntly: 'I never saw that coming!'

And so he adopted a strategy of insuring against ruin by expecting it. With his first girlfriends, he assumed (often sensibly) that each date was the last. Getting married, he thought about the divorce statistics. Once divorced, he avoided a recurrence by not remarrying. Becoming rich, he put more than half of his after-tax earnings into savings, though always in a wide range of banks in case of a financial crash.

If every twitch in a limb was bound to be cancer, each e-mail from an employer undoubtedly the sack and any knock on the door assuredly brought news that one of his children had been killed, then it followed that such outcomes, because anticipated, would not occur.

These precautions worked for sixty years. Exactly that, in fact, as the catastrophe began on the morning after his landmark birthday party. Afterwards, Ned wondered if he had fatally relaxed. Having completed six mainly fortunate decades, what – except for the scheduled horror of eventual death – was the worst thing that could happen to him? Was it this thought that let bad luck in?

Although Emma and the girls had been told that there must in no circumstances be a surprise party, Ned accepted the inevitability of one and knew that this was an eventuality in which expectation would not prove preventative.

Emma had booked a car so that they could all drink. The driver knew who Ned was, or at least gave him the sort of recognition he suffered: 'I seen you? History Channel. Hitler!'

Ned wearily smiled agreement. There had been a time when one of his stock anecdotes was the frequency with which he answered to the name of the twentieth century's most-reviled figure, but it was a long time since he had found the confusion amusing. *Adolf: A Study in Evil* had been an American co-production that he only undertook because of the procreative misfortune of having two daughters simultaneously at college. However, this oddity among his dozens of documentaries now seemed to be screened on a loop by the worryingly numerous UK channels devoted to the achievements of the Third Reich. Once, two telephone engineers, waist deep in a hole in the road, had raised their right arms in salute and shouted 'Heil!' as he walked past. He wondered what unknowing shoppers must have thought.

As normal, there were paps outside the restaurant, trawling for a bigger catch than him but happy to get a tiddler in their net until then. Ned agreed that the family would pose for one picture. He understood that the snappers were covering themselves in case you died or got caught with a lover (unless, even better, you killed her or vice versa) the following day, giving the papers a snap that now transmitted tragic poignancy or puritanical irony. But, if you refused to let them shoot you, they would capture your shying heads and ducking backs in an image to be printed in the event of your infamy.

Each of the foursome performed to type under photographic obligation. Ned tightened and lowered his jaw to reduce double chin, while Emma, an accidental and unwilling public figure, gripped his hand so tightly that his fingers tingled. His daughters were just as predictable. Dee glowed towards the flash storm, like a supermodel selling eye gloss, as Phee stared glumly down and sideways in the manner of a scandalous defendant hustled up the courtroom steps.

'Cheers, Ned,' piped one of the paps, the dark varnish of his tan suggesting warmer and more glamorous assignments just before this one. 'And happy birthday, mate!'

Though delivered as lightly as it might be from one civilian to another, the greeting, in this context, flashed the warning that they knew what he was doing.

In acknowledgement of his family's efforts in arranging the surprise party, Ned sportingly acted bafflement when, giving his name for the supposed table for four at Piero, the maître d' fawningly apologized for a mix-up over bookings and directed their group, with a politeness always fighting a wink, to the adjacent private dining annexe, and from there to the top floor which housed the large rooms where launches had been held for some of the books and TV series.

As a teenager, Ned had fantasized about being the guest on *This is Your Life*, but that show had gone the eventual way of all broadcasting, and, even if it were still running, he was not quite famous enough to qualify. He had been offered *Who Do You Think You Are?*, but was too frightened of either crying when talking about his father or of discovering something terrible about him.

But tonight, he knew, would be a sort of *This is Your Life*. He noticed Dee sending a sneaky text as they walked towards the Attenborough Room and assumed that was the cause of the sudden reduction in the noise from behind the oaken double doors. He wondered which faces from his past would be revealed.

The first image as they walked in was of dozens of people standing in a semicircle three or four deep. Seeing him, they raggedly began to sing 'Happy Birthday!' He spotted his mother and her husband, the Pimms, Professor Hannah Smith and, less happily, Dominic Ogg, whom he knew would have been invited but hoped might have been too busy to attend. His once fellow Rhodes Scholar and now publisher, Jack Beane, looked as sleek and lean as Ned had hoped to be at sixty. Behind the ad hoc choir, in the centre of the room, were white-clothed tables laid with heavy silver cutlery that bounced spikes of light from electric chandeliers lining the ceiling.

'Christ! How much did this cost?' he whispered to Emma.

'Oh, pooh! Just enjoy it. You deserve it!'

In a sudden rush of love and desire, he had a pleasant flash of their private celebration later.

During the applause that followed the final *you* – or *yous*, the timings staggered by some singing *Edmund* and others *Ned – Dee*, too near to his ear, made that piercing whooping sound that was the sonic signature of his daughters' generation in the way that whistling had marked his grandfather's. A waiter handed Ned a flute of champagne or a cheaper equivalent, fizzing so much that it spat bubbles on his hand. He took a sip – a rather metallic Prosecco – and raised it vaguely in the direction of the guests.

'Thank you,' he muttered to his family.

'You said no but we knew you meant yes,' said Phee. Dee threw her a disapproving look.

A waft of his mother's night-out scent, instantly flashing-back scenes from his life. He turned to embrace her.

'There you are,' she said. 'I told you so!'

During his near-breakdown a decade and a half before, which his friends had called a midlife crisis but was, in fact, an end-life crisis – convinced that he would die at the same age as his dad – she had predicted that she would say those words at his fiftieth and sixtieth birthdays, a prophecy now fulfilled. Ned had a momentary panic that this maternal charm expired at midnight and that he or she, or both, were now doomed.

'Many of the best!' boomed his mother's husband. 'And many more of them!'

Ned toured the loud, yapping groups into which the guests had rearranged themselves. Dominic Ogg wrapped him in the man-hug that now seemed to be obligatory in any encounter with a television executive.

'Mate,' he said. 'You're History now and I mean that in the nicest possible way!'

Ogg mentioned three of the incredibly famous people he had most recently met and then said, in a busily self-important person's learned tone of dismissal: 'Give Perce a bell about finding a slot to see me. We should talk about what you want to do next.'

A half-dozen historians – what would the collective noun be? *Court*? *Sphere*? – were laughing at a story Antonia Fraser was telling. Ned was going over to them, rehearsing a joke about *The Birthday Party*, when he noticed Tom Pimm standing alone in a corner, beckoning and calling: 'Nod! Nod!'

The two men did the half-embrace and back-pat – as if each were a baby with wind – that was their compromise with the new tactility of masculinity.

'Can I ring you tomorrow?'

'Yes, sure. You can talk to me tonight if . . .'

'Not here.'

'Christ. Is something wrong with . . . ?'

'It isn't cancer.'

'Christ! Well, I'm glad. You mean you've had tests and . . .'

'No. I mean it isn't illness at all. No one's sick. When people say they want to tell you something, you always think it's – I suppose because it's the thing that we most – so I'm just saying that it isn't. It's a work thing.'

Ned guessed that Tom must have fucked – or, which was little different these days, been accused of fucking – a student. But he said: 'Are you worried about the cuts?'

'The *what*? I can't hear a thing at parties now. The doctor says it's completely normal.'

'Everyone's worried about another round of redundancies.'

'What? Well, hopefully it won't come to that.'

'Tom, what the fuck's happened?'

'I've had a message from Special, asking me to see him tomorrow. He hasn't asked to see you?'

'What? No. Not that I know of.'

The quacking babble of the gathering suddenly rose in intensity and Ned, already stooped to reduce the difference in their heights, only partly caught what Tom said next. Something something *trail*. Had there been a trailer for something on TV? But there was no new series due and the channels didn't generally advertise repeats. Ned bent even lower but could only make out something again *trail* and then, as the din dipped, more clearly: 'I'm just worried about Daggers.'

'Oh, don't worry about Daggers,' Ned reassured his colleague. 'Harmless enough old nut. As long as no one expects us to be his student or his carer. I've always been more concerned about Quatermass. If we ever come in to find the department roped off by a hostage siege team, it will be Prof Q in the AJP Taylor Lecture Theatre with a grenade strapped to his goolies.'

'Ha! But Special definitely hasn't sent for you?'

'No.'

Tom made a pained face but, as the background soundtrack gave another swoop fuelled by Italian effervescence, Ned lost the next sentence. It felt weirdly as if a face-to-face encounter were aping a mobile phone conversation from a train.

Shrugging surrender, Tom made the ring-you gesture with finger and thumb. 'I'll . . . tomorrow, okay? And don't tell Hells I'm worried. Which I'm not really.'

The sound levels fell as serving staff urged the guests to sit down. Reaching the top table, Ned saw that a place setting and name card were being removed and the gaps between the chairs on that side widened. Tom flicked his eyes to the close-up strip of his bifocals and read the folded cardboard as it was placed on a tray.

'Oh, no great loss,' he said. 'It's Fumo.'

Smiling, Helen asked: 'And, in your cast list of nicknames, which is . . . ?'

'The Vice Chancellor.'

'Yes, he's had to cancel,' said Emma, coming up behind them. 'Another of their beloved crises, apparently.'

'Oh? I expect LGBT Soc is trying to no-platform the Macaulay Memorial Lecturer. After I've gone, Hells, don't ever let them put a statue of me up on campus, however hard they ask.'

Personal History

Teaching is a kind of public speaking, but thirty years of lecturing seemed to be no help with other forms of oration. Tom Pimm had been almost breathless with terror before each of his three best man's speeches (two of these, anti-romantically, for the same groom), three funeral eulogies, four fortieth birthday party tributes, three fiftieth bashes (the number reduced by one of the eulogies), and, now, his first attempt at summing up sixty years.

'As *an* historian,' he began, lightly stressing the indefinite article for the pleasure of pedantic and therefore almost certainly older guests, 'Ned Marriott has dealt in centuries, even millennia.' Pausing to let the same constituency be thrilled by the correct plural. 'But – tonight – we focus on six very special decades.'

At these cue words, earlier confided to a youth in a booth, the electric candelabras dimmed. On all four walls, screens, which would once have been regarded as large but were now smaller than most domestic televisions, filled with images.

Ned as an infant, gummily grinning, held upright astride the laps of his parents, from whom, it became clear in a series of pictures taking him from nappy-fattened dungarees to baggy grow-into primary school blazer, he had inherited his mother's large, dark eyes and his father's lankiness, broad brow and wide nose. These were scenes from a childhood in the decade that had featured in Ned's first TV series and non-academic book, called, with the consensus-denting that would become his signature: *The Fabulous Fifties – Defending a Demonized Decade*.

12

Next, in early adolescence, huddled on a beach (windswept, Norfolk or sort-of) with his mum. In old photos, from before timers and selfies, there was always the unseen sub-plot of who took them. Was the unseen photographer Ned's dad, whose early death had made him a shadowy but sanctified figure for his son? Or the stepfather, who was at the top table tonight, but to whom Ned had pointedly never dedicated a book, excluding him even when *Elizabeth I – Elizabeth II: Who Wins?* had been ascribed: 'To Mum, at 80'.

A professional ceremonial photographer was clearly responsible for the one of Ned in his King's London graduation robes, with a beginner's beard that had grown to only a smudge on his upper lip. Then a dark thick moustache was the only facial hair as Dr Ned Marriott, circa 1985, stood in front of a blackboard chalked with the question *Was Churchill A War Criminal?*, a breakthrough book and (though banned by the BBC governors under pressure from Margaret Thatcher and not screened until twenty years later) TV documentary that had been the thirty-one-year-old historian's breakthrough into newsworthiness. That same moustached snap would have been on the back of the dust jackets flashing up from *The Fabulous Fifties* (1990) to *Fawlty Britain – How TV Punchlined Britain* (2000), although he was clean-shaven by the time of Tony Blair's second election victory in 2001.

And here now was the former prime minister, boyishly thin and honey-tanned, squinting into the sun under a palm tree by a pool, with golden minarets in the distance. 'Ned,' he said. 'I'm caught up in a bi' of history here myself.' Tom had hoped that Blair, once out of office, might stop the dropping of t-sounds that had presumably been an egalitarian tactic. 'Bu' the happiest of birthdays, okay, May? And, look, hundreds of thousands of students have benefi'ed from the work you did as History National Curriculum Adviser. Look, people say I'm history now but *you* will always be part of the history of teaching and of broadcasting. Listen, Cherie and the kids send their love to

Emma, Phee, Dee and Toby. Wish I could raise a glass to you there, bu' I'll do it here. Happy Birthday, Professor Marriott!'

Just in time, the ex-premier hit a T, indeed two together, as he lifted a glass of what looked like white wine. Behind him, a camel jerked past. The room filled with applause, except for one yell of 'War criminal!' that Tom thought came from Dee.

A freeze-frame of Blair's Middle Eastern refuge dissolved into a clip reel of Ned's television career. On a steel-and-leather chair in a *Late Show* discussion apparently filmed during a power cut, Dr Marriott hairily declares: 'The saviour of this nation was Emperor Hirohito, not Churchill. If it hadn't been for Pearl Harbor, this discussion would be in German.' Cutaway to Sir Winston's Churchill's grandson, whose colour suggested that he was near to a seizure as he tried to catch the attention of a worried-looking presenter, who would later run unsuccessfully to become Prime Minister of Canada. 'People say the Fifties were just dull, fumbling foreplay before the ecstatic orgasm of the 1960s,' Ned projects above a howling gale on the site of the 1851 Great Exhibition. 'But people are *wrong*. In this series, I want to make a forgotten decade *memorable*.'

Now, captioned as Professor Ned Marriott, he stands, hair clipped short in a man's first bulwark against baldness, holding a candle in the prow of a boat on the Thames, St Paul's floodlit in the background. 'No longer an international Empire,' he says, 'Britain still hoped to be an international Umpire. But Blighty was still trying to apply the rules of cricket to what had become – in the American century – a game of baseball.' This was a clip from *UK 2000: The Story of Our History*, which, a cruel TV reviewer had said, 'puts the "um" into Millennium.'

On a drawbridge with a sunlit castle in the background, a summer day's sweat not quite disguised by make-up, Ned, in an extract from *The English Witch Hunts*, noticeably more demonstrative as his TV career proceeds, booms: 'If they did not conform to the beliefs of the day, burn them! If they might be trouble, burn them! If polls showed that the public liked bonfires, light more! Although she didn't know this, Jane Wenham was already as good as dead. To be called a witch was to be christened a corpse!'

Seeing the sequence now, Tom was surprised by the angle of the presenter's head, an extreme profile favouring one cheek, which he attributed to the whim of one of those directors whom his friend would shudderingly describe as imaginative. And Ned, he noticed, grimaced and looked away when that piece to camera came on screen.

Now, on juddery Skype, like pictures from the moon landings, Barbie Tim, in a living room bright with daylight, said: 'Birthday greetings from Sydney, little Bro! Don't worry, I'm not going to tell anyone what you did with the Subbuteo Arsenal goalkeeper that afternoon with Karen Jones. You know, people often say to me: "Has your brother become stuck-up and full of himself since he started being on television?" And I always say: "Absolutely not . . . he was always like that!" But seriously, little Bro, I want to say the words that I know will mean the most to you: Dad would have been very proud of you.'

A speedy sequence of clips from other shows included several cutaways of the over-enthusiastic agreement with speakers that had spawned Tom's epithet for his friend. Then, finally, electronic trickery inserts a miniaturized Ned between Basil and the guest's breasts he is about to accidentally grope in the scene from *Fawlty Britain* that was shown at the BAFTA awards when it took the prize for Best Factual Series. 'Just as *Dad's Army* surreptitiously satirized the futility of Britain's nuclear defences,' the shrunken pundit told the audience, 'so *Fawlty Towers*, in the disguise of sit-com, presented British industry as the consumer-hostile farce that, in the Seventies, it largely was.'

Now the film shifted from slick television pictures to home-shot stills. Ned with an arm around Phee and Dee, in a quick-cut succession of images which, from the numbered cakes in front of them, seemed to have been taken on birthdays through their teenage years. With these photos, the identity of the unseen photographer was a matter of particular speculation. The earlier shots had almost certainly been taken by the twins' mother,

Jenny, who had been Stalined out of the montage, while, from the way the early and later pictures were framed against the walls of two distinct family homes, the more recent pictures had been posed for Emma, who soon appeared in a sequence of cuddles with Ned, first as a couple on white sand beside dazzling sea and then with Toby between them as a baby, a toddler and the seven-or-whatever he was now. Two family albums, BD and AD, caused by the divorce.

Ned in the main lecture hall at UME, the heads of the front rows of students jolting as they laughed at his jokes; as part of the enhanced service to justify the teaching fees, every lecture was now filmed and posted online.

Television again – the professor asking, 'Which other head of state has been called great for never saying anything and staying out of politics?' in the infamous *Newsnight* Diamond Jubilee debate – and then phone-footage of Ned's mother's eightieth, with a protective wedge of relatives, including the brother Tom had never met, separating Ned from the mother's second husband.

Now a clip that had become the most familiar, through use in trails and screening at the BAFTA awards, as Ned kissed the side of Emma's head and buttoned up his tuxedo on the way to the stage: the moment in *The English Witch Hunts* when Ned writes his name on vellum, then burns it with a candle to show how a curse was cast.

A final piece of TV from *The British People*: Ned, a long red scarf wound raffishly around him in Highgate Cemetery, saying: 'Britons learn the stories of their kings and queens but in this series, I'll be exploring the stories of ordinary Britons and the *object* lessons that rulers could have learned from their *subjects*' – and then the screens wiped to white, the lights brightened and Tom Pimm, fighting stage fright greater than for any of his previous public speeches, had to stand and speak again, feeling like a politician as he raised a hand to staunch the applause for the biopic.

'Thanks to Dominic Ogg and all the staff at Ogglebox TV

– who produced most of the series from which those extracts came – for their highly generous and professional work on that tribute film.'

Allowing another round of clapping for the TV people, Tom went on: 'Those were scenes from the life of one of the few people who has been able to call King Henry VIII a subject, but who has also made famous many ordinary Britons. And, although no one who is lucky enough to know him would ever call him ordinary, we are here tonight to celebrate the personal history of Ned, or, as I call him, for reasons you may have deduced from some of those shots of him listening, Nod.'

The butt of this insult lifted his finger in Tom's direction, while, with instinctive maternal loyalty, Daphne Marriott-Starling threw a disapproving look.

'As you all know, Ned always expects the worst.' From the top table especially, a loving chuckle about his legendary pessimism. 'But – tonight – he should expect to hear only the best. I've reflected for a long time on what to say about the man I have known for more than forty years, since we were students together in London, and with whom I have worked at UME for almost thirty, and what I want to say is this . . .'

Professor Perverse

Tom had apparently been the best man when Daddy married Mummy and so Dee had been expecting that sort of speech from him here: sentimentality with an edge of ribaldry. But she was astonished to hear him say – actually couldn't at first believe that she had heard it – 'Professor Ned Marriott is one of my worst enemies.'

Tom had one of those drawling deliveries that make everything sound a bit like a joke and so a laugh began that the speaker cut off by continuing, sternly: 'Ned Marriott began his life sixty years ago as he meant to go on, by being a notoriously uncaring son.'

Granny, skitter-eyed, whisperingly ruled out sudden-onset Alzheimer's with Grandpa Jack, then looked appealingly at Dee, who shrugged.

'He has been a faithless husband,' the eulogist continued, causing Helen Pimm to turn her startled glance into the flash-eyed semaphore of wifely social warning. 'And a disastrous father.'

Granny and Helen stared with protective concern at Dee, who tried to catch her sister's eye across the table, but Phee seemed not to be listening, her head bowed, probably nervous about their own turn. Helen, a domestic detective, checked the level in her husband's wine glass. Phee turned towards Emma for facial guidance, but their stepmother was gazing urgently at Daddy. However, the target of this unexpected prosecution, with the amateur actor's knack that had served him so well in TV, held an entirely level expression, waiting for the situation to be explained.

'His books,' Tom went on, 'are filled with pithy and clever sentences – unfortunately, most of them are stolen from the work of Geoffrey Elton, Barbara Tuchman, Antonia Fraser, David Starkey, David Reynolds and many others! It would be wrong, though, to see him only as a plagiarist of work that has taken others a lifetime to research. He is also an opportunistic broadcaster, who will spout any bollocks the producer wants if it means the possibility of another TV series, tie-in book and box set.'

Dee saw on the face of Emma, who was now tightly holding Ned's hand, a numbed, puzzled expression that she was sure mirrored her own. Helen was leaning towards Tom, glowering, as if she hoped to silence him by telepathy. Then the chilly silence in the room was broken by the happy, crackly cackle of Daddy.

'This is a career that has taught us above all,' Tom said, raising his voice to indicate the peroration, 'that the best way to gain an audience's attention is to say the exact opposite of what most people feel about a person.'

Dee realized the conceit at the same time as several others in the audience, sending a rippling giggle around the room that made even Phee raise her head to see what was going on. Emma was affectionately patting Ned's arm, while Helen Pimm brought her hands together in an almost-clap of comprehension and forgiveness. Grandpa Jack muttered at Granny, who smiled uncertainly, but with relief.

Without looking down, Tom located his wine glass on the table and fingered the stem, ready for a toast.

'The *Daily Telegraph* TV critic,' he said, 'dubbed him Professor Perverse. We in this room know him as a loyal friend, warm companion, loving son, red-hot lover – oh God, sorry, he asked me not to tell you about us – and, above all, devoted father. But, in his own profitable spirit of wilful revisionism, let's raise our glasses to the humourless egotist, Oedipal weirdo, serial child-abuser, wife-beater and woman-hater, repetitive plagiarist and dumbed-down television Autocutie who is Professor Ned Marriott!'

By now either in on the joke, or at least aware that catastrophic embarrassment seemed to have been averted, all the guests stood and echoed the name. *Follow that*, thought Dee, aiming an encouraging smile at her sister.

Rhyming Couplets

Although the plan had been for a collaboration – and the texts and e-mails between them always referred to the secret project as 'our' – Dee had been lead writer and more or less sole director and producer, which had been no surprise to Phee.

Advice-sites about twins that Phee had consulted – as a teenager feeling oppressed by the condition – had generally made three recommendations to the parents of double births: treat them completely equally, in everything from pocket money to inheritances; be wary of matching outfits and haircuts; and try to avoid them ever being referred to, by you or anyone else, as 'the twins'.

Although the question of bequests was thankfully yet to be tested, their parents seemed to have followed the first and third instructions: even after the divorce, Daddy, when spoil-bribing them, was careful to offer identical inducements to both daughters, and friends and relatives, even now, were rebuked for referring to them as a single unit. At their one-form entry primary school, they had been in the same class, but seated several rows apart, and, once there were two or more groups, educated separately, although Mummy had agonized over Phee being ranked higher in streamed subjects.

On the issue of lookalikes, their mother had been prone, early on, to take two pieces of clothing off the same peg and brush their hair with matching strokes, Phee sitting on one knee and Dee on the other. However, from the perspective of twenty-six, Phee could see that the standard rules for bringing up twinned siblings contained a contradiction. Selecting two different dresses and back-combing one head and front-combing the other would, by definition, break the rule of exactly equal treatment. A childcare expert (especially, as many seemed to be, a childless one) might advise letting the girls decide but, in practice, that would have led to Dee going to primary school in a clown suit with her hair in a tricolour Mohican.

From the age of around eleven, the sisters had differentiated themselves: Dee chopping and tinting her hair short and blondish, while Phee copied Mummy's shoulder-length, dark (now dye-assisted) locks. Jeans or dresses, cardigans v sweaters, heels not Converse, nipple-ridge rather than custom-fitted bra – it was an increasing statistical improbability that anyone except their parents would reckon them identical. When Phee, at fourteen, turned vegetarian, they could no longer even be served the same meals. Chat from boys moved from 'Are you *completely* identical?' (with its slavering innuendo) to: 'Did you meet your friend at school?', which was doubly funny because they more or less hated each other by then.

Yet, though the avoidance of a double-act had been a driving motivation in their lives, it would have seemed strange, even to them, to make separate speeches at Daddy's landmark birthday, where 'my father' sounded divisive and possessive but 'our father' had an odd religious echo. Once they had decided to do something together, Phee came up with the idea of a mock history exam paper on Daddy's life – the sisters alternating Qs and As – but Dee had suggested a poem in which they took successive lines, resulting in a brief discussion about why her idea was the best.

Tom Pimm, 'Uncle Tom', who was always good fun, as long as you weren't on the end of too many of his jokes, rode the applause that followed the toasts, and then said: 'Toby, with school tomorrow, was considered a bit young for tonight, and, with someone called Edmund, you don't want three kids telling their dad what they think of him.' The age of those in the room who got the joke was a mini-history of the British education system. 'Though Tobes will, of course, be at the private family lunch, to which the bastards haven't invited us, or at least me, next Sunday. But now Phee and Dee, to whom I will certainly not refer as the twins' – cheery jeering from those in on the joke – 'would like to pay their own tribute.'

They both stood, Phee in her black Monsoon cocktail dress, Dee wearing a pillar box-red '40s evening frock with plunging bust-line and pussy-bow, bought from a Vintage site.

Even their adjustments of the table microphone were individual, because of Dee's heels and Phee's flats.

It was the elder (by seventeen minutes) sister who did the introduction: 'Phee and me – don't worry, Uncle Tom, that's not a "grammatical howler", it's a rhyme, for reasons you'll hear – felt that, as we come from one ovum – Daddy, please don't do the *un oeuf is enough* joke again – we were being egged on to do something together. So . . .'

Dee paused and looked across the table at Phee, like a conductor, her nodded head the baton.

'Daddy,' she began, 'sisters born together are a certain type of rhyme.'

'So couplets seem the way to praise you at this special time,' Phee added, tapping out the rhythm for safety on the under-edge of the table, but relieved that her voice wasn't squeaking.

There was a hum of soppy pleasure in the room that Phee hadn't heard since they put on little plays as kids, but she also sensed less sentimental notes of approval at the punning structure.

Dee was swinging like a dancer to the beat as she spoke her next line – 'Especially, as with Phee and Dee, you gave us chiming names' – to which Phee matched hers – 'Although such diminutions often fly above the brains' – until they were confidently alternating sentences.

'Of people who don't realize that from the Bard they're spun'

'Does brother Toby know yet he's a belch-related pun?'

A big laugh and, although a stand-up comedian was the thing that Phee was least likely to become, she had a glimpse of the hit for which they did it. Strictly, Tobes was their half-brother, but that felt mean and the kinder form also saved them a syllable. Her sister looked directly at Daddy, who was wiping his brow, and possibly eyes, with a napkin.

'A lot of folk don't comprehend your own name is a part,' she said, with Phee replying: 'In that play about the king who drives his daughters from his heart.'

'You, though, have always had a different effect on us.'

'Which is why we're thrilled that everyone is making such a fuss . . .'

'Of all you've said and done in your own history.'

Dee had to say it *hist-or-ee*, like in Abba's 'Waterloo'.

'We sometimes wish to switch you off, like when you're on TV.'

That reference to Daddy's argumentativeness went down almost as well as the play on Belch. Dee surely can't have planned to give Phee the biggest laugh lines.

'But, generally, we want to see a never-ending run . . .'

'Repeating back-to-back those sixty years of love and fun.'

'So hugs from Emma, Toby, Granny, Grandpa Jack and Dee!'

Daddy hated them calling his stepfather Grandpa Jack but it was necessary for the scansion.

'And kisses from Uncle Timon, "Uncle" Tom, Dom Ogg and Phee!'

Daddy's high-pitched snigger at the mention of his TV boss, spotting the gag about Ogg's reputation for dropping his name into everything.

'Daddy, thanks for stopping people ever calling us "the twins".'

This was the tricky bit, where they started dividing lines.

'Because we're very different,' said Phee.

'Dee smiles,' said Dee, flashing her teeth as illustration.

'Phee never grins,' Phee completed the couplet, a line that her sister may have intended as cruel, winning the target another *Comedy at the Apollo* response.

'But, for once, we have a subject on which we can agree.'

'You've been a perfect Dad for me . . .'

'And also, Dad, for me!' added Dee, characteristically claiming the last word. They had almost never called him 'Dad' before, except in a period when Dee said it to be different from Phee, but that was what happened in a form in which metre came before meaning.

When Dee bowed to emphasize the end, there was the sort of applause that would make a theatre cast look happy and abashed. Emma was openly weeping, using the bright pink napkin as an emergency hankie, and Granny, sniffing back her own emotions, was rocking her head slowly in approval. 'Brava!' Grandpa Jack shouted, stressing the final letter to demonstrate his sophistication. 'Brava!'

Daddy was on Phee's side of the top table so it was simply logistical that he embraced her first. 'Brilliant!' his winey breath whispered, '*history* didn't quite scan but . . .' which was very him, so she didn't let it upset her, but told him: 'Dee basically wrote it.' And he had to lean awkwardly across the table, over-turning a microphone, to reach her sister, which also felt pleasing, although she knew that the thought broke their truce for tonight.

Good Morning

Too much alcohol – a welcome sedative when they had gone to bed at 2 a.m. – proved an equally effective diuretic by – she blindly tapped the clock's indented top and stickily squinted at the numbers – five o'clock. Ned always said you didn't get a hangover if the booze was good enough, a theory they both frequently contradicted, and, anyway, the bladder couldn't dis-tinguish between vintages.

When Emma got back from the bathroom – while washing her hands, she swilled around her after-party mouth some tap water which, this humid night, was not as cold as hoped – Ned had rolled onto his back, arms splayed like a shot soldier, though advertising vitality with snores that made his jaw jerk as if punched. She jarred an elbow against his arm – one of the acquired reflexes of two people who have long shared a bed – causing him to roll onto his side, where the noise was more muffled by pillows.

Groggy annoyance at being awake after only three hours was heightened by the bright light through the curtains as the year approached its shortest border between night and day. Desperately though she needed sleep, there might be no more this morning. The only benefit of midsummer was that she could try to read herself asleep without a row about the light being on. Emma fumbled her glasses off the top of the Donna Tartt, which was split halfway through its bulk by the Mother's Day bookmark Toby had made at school.

'Em, you awake?'

'Go back to sleep.' She patted her partner's arm through the flimsy summer duvet. 'You blokes of sixty need your kip.'

'Fuck off!' he said, using the expression's friendly form, rolling to face her, shaping his body into a half-hug to be completed. 'Are you worrying about something?'

'No.'

She moved onto her back, compromising short of an embrace.

'Ah. You hesitated before answering.'

A career explaining the events of history had made him an amateur psychologist, her smallest shifts in mood analysed as if they were the diaries of Anne Boleyn.

'I was trying to remember how to speak. I've had three hours' sleep, Ned.'

'Why are you awake, then?'

'One, probably two, flutes of fizz. A different wine with every course, including pudding. More bubbles for the toasts. I may be much younger than you, love, but I'm too old to do that on a weekday. So I've had a wee and now I'm trying to knock myself out with a novel.'

He tapped the hardback that was awkwardly resting on her belly, increasingly conscious of the weight of the book's almost-Biblical thickness. 'How about a cock instead of a goldfinch?'

Happiness at his interest in her reading tastes was cancelled by his sometimes depressingly adolescent attitude to sex.

'Grow up, you'd think it was thirteen you've just been.'

They slept naked in the summer. She knew, if she looked, that the bedclothes would be tented by his erection. She had thought she'd got away with it the night before; he had briefly pressed against her when they went to bed, but then had fallen asleep. And, if he started now, the night was over; older men are naturally slower and, after that much drink, he could be stabbing away for hours.

Now she felt the familiar pressure against her thigh. In their long-established rituals of intimacy, she was supposed to turn and face him. But she remained on her back and felt his shuffling adjustment against her, his penis trembling against her thigh as he edged it towards the goal.

'Good morning,' he said, in the throaty loaded tone that he used as a prelude to sex.

'Not now, Sweet, please? I need to go back to sleep.'

'Meanie.' The voice he used was borrowed – another feature of his foreplay – from that duck that used to sing on television. 'I want my birthday present.'

'Well, if you're promising you'll only have to have it once a year, okay.'

'Ha ha. Remember I've written a book about the wives of Henry VIII. Don't be like this, Em. We've always done it on my birthday. I think of it as a present even if . . .'

'Well, sometimes it's nice to open . . .'

She abandoned the image, fearing the sort of joke it might provoke. Using his elbow for awkward support, like a picnicker trying to eat while lying on the grass, he was half leaning across her now. She felt him against the cleft of her legs and then a raindrop of glop against her thigh, which she briefly hoped might be the end but knew was the beginning.

'Please, Em. Perfect end to a perfect day and all that?'

'It's *next* day. Five in the morning.'

He shifted again, until almost in a press-up position above her, then tried a kiss, which she met with closed lips, less from rejection than fear of morning breath.

'You'd have more fun tonight, Sweet, when I'm less shattered.'

'You're a cruel woman, Emma Jane Humpage.' The whole maiden name was generally scolding, but in this case the surname that had caused so much trouble at school was also slick with innuendo. 'Take it while it's going. After sixty, they say, it's . . .' He laughed. 'Up and down.'

'Doesn't feel as if you've got any problem there.'

Emma had hoped that this tribute to his virility might appease him – she was feeling mildly mean about not letting him – but he took it as permission to circle the object of the compliment, like a vibrator, until it pushed against her.

'Ned, I love you but . . . I haven't got my cap in. You don't want to be paying tuition fees at . . .'

She decided it would be unwise to speak aloud his projected age when a second child would go through college.

'It's okay. We'll do what the Pope does.'

The first time he made that joke, she had laughed.

'Ugh. That's so messy.'

He was edging inside her now, swirling the tip around, one of his favourite foreplay moves. Her slight regret at denying him was boosted by sensations of pleasure and, although she felt habitual irritation at the human animal's surrender to programmed appetite, her body began to smooth his route.

'You will pull out?'

'You always say . . .' – his wheezy sex voice – 'it's sad for Toby to be an only child.'

She raised her hand and air-slapped him, but he intercepted the gesture and sucked on the end of her fingers, a clue to how he really wished to finish, although he would be bloody lucky this time; there were limits to her conciliatory nature.

While she was annoyed by his insistence, and disappointed by having given in, the sex was not unpleasant – eventually or reluctantly consensual, she would have described it, his kissing of her nipples always irresistible – because she was with someone she loved and with whom, in most other circumstances, she was happy, even eager, to make love.

Despite her exhaustion, she felt an orgasm starting, and exaggerated the sounds and movements in the hope of quickening him up. But he seemed lost in private pleasure and didn't take the hint.

'Ned, it's nice but I'm nearly asleep.'

She reached down and gently stroked his testicles, a proven trigger, and, as she groaned encouragement, he gasped, lurched backwards and his penis briefly beat time on her belly. Ungallantly moving away from the mess he had made, he rolled away, pulled up the kicked-down duvet and wiped himself drier. More washing. Great.

'Thank you,' he said.

'Is that better?' she replied, as if to a child who had been sick.

'Mooom. Happy birthday.'

His voice was sleepy. She hit his arm. 'Oi, now you've *woken me up*, don't . . .'

At first, in her confusion, she thought the ringing was an alarm clock or the bedside telephone, and turned, flinching at the sticky dripping from her stomach, towards them. But the noise was down the corridor: the entryphone.

'Ned?'

'The fuck is that?' he yawn-talked, unwillingly alert.

'Someone at the . . .'

'Pissed kids pissing about. Or a minicab mix-up . . .'

But, if so, it was persistent pranksters, or a stubbornly mis-informed driver. The doorbell's shrill single note kept repeating, like a modernist composition.

'There'll be another note under the door from that dragon in Flat D,' worried Emma. 'You'll have to go down.'

'I can't. I've still got half a hard-on.'

'And I'm all covered in gunk.'

In the hay fever season, she always kept a box of tissues on the bedside table. Drying herself as best she could, she pulled from the floor the faded sarong from their Australasian honey-moon and gathered it around her as she went to the window and pulled back the curtain.

In the peeled and faded painting that her distance vision had become without glasses, she made out that the sloping road on their side of the square was double-parked with cars, their lights on and engines running, which would have signalled taxis, except that there were three in a row. Two of them were dark saloons but the other white and with a flashing light. She let the curtain drop and, from a ridiculous instinct, whispered, as she told Ned: 'It's the police!'

The words had the effect of a wire instantly pulling Ned out of bed and into a standing position.

'Oh Christ, no! It must be Phee or Dee!'

Naked, he pouched his hands, from some reflex of shock or shame, across his lap. Emma noticed, with the intensity of attention that adrenaline brings, that his penis had instantly shrivelled.

'Do you want me to go, Sweet?'

'No, Em, I've got to . . .'

Emma felt the smug relief of knowing that her partner was here and her child was safe in Winslow with Maddy. If anything were up with Toby, the child-minder would have called her. Unless they had both died in a fire. She consoled herself with the odds against such a conflagration, then shifted to worrying about her mother or brother, until that fear too was relieved by the thought that, however bad the news might be about them, she would be able to cope in a way that could not be the case if it involved Toby or Ned.

Three nights a week, even if they were at the London flat, Ned laid across the bedroom armchair his running clothes for next morning. The more he had drunk, the longer he ran, a TV critic having made him sensitive about his silhouette. Emma watched – the slow-motion vision that people described at such moments must be due to heightened, frightened concentration – as her husband stumbled into boxer shorts and struggled with a University of Middle England sweatshirt, the name of his employer blurred and faded by perspiration and washing.

As he went to pass her, she blocked him and kissed him on the chest, noticing the bath-salt smell of cleaned clothes.

'You hear about these . . . the police are drama queens . . . it's probably . . .'

He was out of the room before she could say *nothing*.

Emma knew people who were suddenly forced to wipe a birthday or wedding anniversary from the calendar because the day had become twinned with bereavement or catastrophe, and she imagined this happening to Ned who, however long he lived beyond sixty, would be unable to celebrate again a date overshadowed by the death of one of his daughters, as she now assumed the revelation would be, although her pessimism was partly a mental tactic, learned from Ned, in which predicting the worst was insurance against it ever occurring. She had always thought that, if they had been her daughters, she would have been too superstitious to give them such tragically weighted names as Ophelia and Cordelia.

Ophelia, she knew, had drowned. She was less clear on *King Lear*, never sure exactly which date to fear for Dee or, tending to mix up Edmund and Edgar, for Ned.

Seemingly satisfied by the movement at the window that some response would be forthcoming, the callers had stopped ringing the doorbell for the last few minutes. But, in the early morning quiet, their buzzer would have been audible in the other flats. The neighbours – and the houses around, woken by the revving engines and slamming doors – would soon be peering out, just as Emma and Ned had done when the former cabinet minister who lived in the square was doorstepped for several mornings over his expenses claims.

Fear made her need to pee again. The wet mess on the floor and cistern told her that Ned had been affected in the same way. She cleaned up without complaint; a lesson in priorities. Through the open door of the bathroom came the sounds of scraping and rattling as Ned deactivated the array of bolts and dead-locks that protected these wealthy residents of Kensington, as law-abiding citizens, from burglars, journalists and other potential intruders.

Ned had left the door on the latch. Emma pushed it and went out onto the landing. She could hear the retired teacher in D moving around, doubtless looking for paper to write a letter about being woken by the noise.

Feeling too exposed to face the police with only a post-coital wrap thrown round her, Emma stood on the stairs, just before the bend, listening, like a child in a movie about divorce.

'Good morning, sir,' she heard a deep male voice, poshed-up Cockney, say.

'Can you just tell me what's happened, please?' Ned pleaded, throaty, cold.

'Are you Edmund Horatio Marriott . . . ?'

Because they had never married, her only exposure to his full name had been from mortgage forms and their will.

'Please just . . .' Ned asked.

'He nodded,' the voice of a youngish woman said.

'Professionally known as Ned Marriott?'

'Look. What . . . ?'

'He nodded again, Guv.'

'Mr Marriott, I am Detective Inspector Richard Dent of the Metropolitan Police's Sexual Offences Investigation Unit. And this is my colleague DS Heather Walters.'

Oh my God, Emma thought: one of the girls has been raped. She would go to the station with him.

'Edmund Horatio Marriott,' the male policeman began, in the tones of slow solemnity familiar from TV cop series. 'I am arresting you on suspicion of a sexual offence.'

The Traill Inquiry

Emeritus Professor Padraig Allison was an energetic Ulsterman who had been recruited to UME from the University of Belfast in the late 1960s on the strength of a reputation created by a revelatory biography of de Valera. Allison had dissipated this early promise through a diligent tasting of all available malts and the easy temptation of becoming a television rent-a-gob on the Troubles.

By the Millennium, the professor's drinking and ubiquitous presence in documentaries about the prospect of peace in Northern Ireland began to concern the Dean at a time when every member of staff was under pressure to prove value for money. Allison's high visibility on TV usefully accumulated the impact points that had been introduced as a measure of academic performance, but, in teaching situations, both his presences and absences caused different problems and, in 2001, he was persuaded to take his pension, an Emeritus professorship and an office in which to work on his long-delayed 'big book' on Ireland, while giving occasional lectures on Bloody Sunday or the hunger strikes. His successor as head of department was Ellie Remgard, a star of the fashionable new discipline of post-imperial independence and conflict resolution.

Then, arm-twisted, during Professor Remgard's breast cancer treatment in 2012, into taking over her module on the peace process, Allison had been accused of forcing his hand between the legs and buttock cleft of a twenty-year-old female student as she stretched for a book he had asked her to retrieve from the top of the shelves in his office. Although (a fact that caused great discomfort to the university when it emerged during the trial) Allison had been barred from individual tuition of women after a series of complaints in the 1980s, it had been the misfortune of this second-year to arrive early and first for the seminar.

UME People (previously Human Resources and, before that, Personnel) had tried to resolve the case with an apology and Allison's forced final retirement, but reports in the campus newspapers, *Fume* and *Um . . . er*, encouraged other current woman students to raise complaints of being made to feel uneasy by the teacher's vocabulary and body-language in classes. A small story sold by the editor of *Fume* to a Sunday newspaper (You're History, Girls Tell Grope Prof) caused two of the women involved in the hushed-up cases three decades earlier to go to the police with complaints of rape. During a six-day trial at Birmingham Crown Court, the prosecution alleged that Allison had operated a sort of droit de seigneur over female History undergraduates for several decades. Defence counsel argued that consensual sex between staff and students had been possible and even commonplace on campus at the time of the most serious cases, implying a lesser offence of abusing a position of power, but the judge's summing up warned that counsel could not rewrite the charge sheet.

The jury of six women and five men (one male had been dismissed for trying to contact a plaintiff through Facebook) took eleven hours to find him guilty of one historic allegation of rape and six historic and one contemporary charges of sexual assault. The seventy-four-year-old Allison was given a six-year prison sentence.

The local Conservative MP argued in a speech that the campus had become a 'taxpayer-funded sexual sewer', and multiple compensation claims were received from victims for failure of duty of care. As a result, the Dean (now re-titled the Executive Dean, as part of the reorganization of the institution on corporate lines) and the Director of History submitted to a series of press conferences and media interviews in which they resorted frequently to what, Professor Ned Marriott told TV producers during a break from filming, were the institution's two default responses when caught in grievous error: 'The University is learning hard lessons from this' and 'I can see why you would think that.'

More practically, UME removed Allison's books from the *Ireland 1916–93* section of the library and formulated rules of teacher conduct so strict that Tom Pimm, the faculty wag, suggested that it would be safest in future to lecture from behind the sort of protective screen used by the witnesses in the Allison trial. And, after a meeting with a delegation from the National Union of Students, Kevan Neades, Director of History, also set up an inquiry into the 'conduct and culture of staff in the History department (now Directorate), both retrospectively and contemporaneously'.

Neades asked ('tasked', as his e-mail to staff put it) Dr Andrea Traill, an Urban Development specialist in the Geography department, to lead the investigation (UME guidelines now advised that potentially disciplinary inquiries should be conducted by an outsider).

On the top floor of the abandoned Faith (previously Theology) faculty, Traill set up an office, in which, over the course of several weeks, she spoke to staff and students who had either offered themselves in response to a global e-mail announcing the investigation or, in some cases, were summoned to her now godless premises, presumably as a result of being mentioned in someone else's evidence. All had been warned not to discuss their evidence with anyone else, although Tom felt safe talking to Ned, who said that he had been in the room for less than ten minutes under questioning that seemed friendly enough.

Corinthians

Ned noticed, with the sharpened senses crises trigger, that the rising sun had cast on the floor a bright half-moon reflection of the door's curved top panel. As the charge was read, he briefly feared he would vomit over the officers. An instant of relief that his daughters were safe was crushed by an understanding of the trouble he was in.

'Could we talk about this upstairs?' he managed to say. It was a hopeless instinct, from concern about prying neighbours and lurking photographers, to keep the ignominy hidden for a few more moments.

'Under certain conditions, yes.'

He led the detectives up. Just before they turned the curve in the stairway, he heard a whimpering he knew was Emma and now they found her standing in front of the flat's open door, hugging herself in a gesture that lifted her sarong and exposed her thighs and higher. Ned looked away and sensed that Dent had just made the same swivel.

Inside, Emma reached round the bedroom door and found her dressing gown. The senior detective repeated that Edmund Horatio Marriott was being arrested under suspicion of sexual assault. He need not be handcuffed at this stage if he agreed to accompany them to the police station selected for interrogation and as long as he showed no sign of resistance or flight. He could request that a solicitor of his own choice be present during the questioning, or representation could be arranged for him. Did he understand?

'I've just got up,' he said. 'I don't suppose I'd be allowed to shower, shave and change?'

He heard the pitch of wryly reasonable educated politeness that he employed with traffic wardens.

The cops moved to a corner of the corridor and muttered at each other.

'We're allowing that,' the male detective said, turning round. 'But I'm afraid you'll have to keep the bathroom door open. At least more than half ajar. Due to your gender, I will be the one standing outside.'

The sentinel, he assumed, would listen for noises suggestive of suicide or escape through a window, while also watching him pissing or shitting in case he tried surreptitiously to flush away his VIP key-card to a boys' home.

'DS Walters,' explained the detective, 'will stay with your wife, is it?' Rather than explain their status, Ned nodded. 'Are there any other people in the house?'

'No, we have a son but he's at our . . .'

His intended ending of the sentence – *at our main house with the nanny* – would probably guarantee, in these inequality-conscious times, execution without trial.

'He's staying with someone,' Ned revised his explanation.

'Which room would you like to be in, madam?' the female officer asked.

Emma gestured towards the main bedroom. She was pale and shaking. Ned pulled her towards him. Their escorts didn't intervene but, like boxing referees, scrutinized the clinch from side on, alert for words or items being exchanged.

'It's all gone mad since Savile,' he whispered. 'I haven't done anything.'

'Ring me as soon as . . .'

Sobbing into the usefully absorbent shoulder of his running shirt, she was unable to complete the sentence.

Ned turned towards the man and asked quietly: 'Where should my solicitor come to?'

'We're taking . . .' The detective's voice was loud and Ned gestured at the floor and ceiling with a finger he then put to his lips. Though visibly irritated at the admonition, the DI breath-spoke: 'We're taking you to Paddington Green, tell him.'

'Her.'

Ned relished the power of this second correction. He embraced Emma again and said gently: 'Can you ring and tell Claire what's happened and, er, Paddington Green?'

The station was familiar from news reports as the one at which terrorists, *suspected* terrorists, were questioned.

Emma's head trembled a yes against his neck. He asked the woman: 'Do I need to bring anything?'

'Just any medications you may need in the course of the day.'

He was cheered by the apparent confirmation that he would be back that night. The DS said, 'Madam, show me where you want to go to make that call,' and, when Ned eased Emma away from him, after a final squeeze of bewildered mutual support, she led the woman cop into the bedroom.

Ned pulled the bathroom door almost latched, but Dent pushed it until it filled only half the frame. Although his bowels were groaning with rich party food, now agitated by panic, he restricted himself to a quick piss, conscious of being watched. Washing his hands, he was startled, in the shaving mirror, to see his face as a plaster death-mask.

Moving behind the door, Ned pulled off his shorts and top, which had stuck slightly to his belly hair, and threw them back-wards into the strip of light from the half-open door, like a satirical striptease.

Noticing, in the shower, that he was washing away peels of dried semen from his groin and stomach, Ned understood what the cops had been discussing downstairs; someone arrested at home might still be carrying evidence. But, unless the world had become even madder than recent events suggested, it could not have been Emma who reported him.

She was required to leave the bedroom, with her guard, before Ned could enter it to dress, hearing Dent's breathing beyond the angled door. In the corridor, the DI checked the items in the small shoulder-bag that Ned had packed. Choosing a book for in-cell entertainment had been tricky. The Jeremy Thorpe biography that he was actually reading might be incriminating and so he chose the life of Roy Jenkins that was next on the pile by the bed.

Dent lifted out the book and shook the pages, then shuffled the packets of Atorvastatin, Ramipril, and baby aspirin with a rapidity that suggested he was familiar with the chemical support systems of late-middle-aged men. Finding the can of hairspray, he lifted it out and examined it for long enough to make Ned embarrassed of his vanity.

The detectives allowed the couple another policed cuddle in the hall. Ned noticed that Emma had put on the sky blue cashmere roll neck he had bought her for Christmas, even though it was too warm for this weather. He took it as a gesture of comfort and was touched. But, as he held her, the collar was already damp from crying.

'This is all just rubbish,' he whispered. 'I love you.'

But she was too upset to reply.

'Don't ring the girls yet,' he said. 'It might still all blow over quite quickly. And obviously not Tobes.'

When the entry phone sizzled, Ned's first thought was: *the press*. Already at home in someone else's house, Walters answered and exchanged grunts and uh-huhs, then latched the door open again. A plump Asian man entered, leading in a group of younger people, who were carrying white boxes and bags.

Literate enough in TV cop shows to know what this meant, Ned thought of the stories of the Mafia sending hearses to the doors of people who weren't dead yet; this was like the removers arriving when you hadn't put your house on the market.

'We have a warrant to search these premises,' said Walters. 'And others of interest.'

That new investigative ritual: the removal of the computers. In the way that penitents examine their souls for sin, the arrested now mentally checked their hard drive for stain. Ned could not immediately think of any files that could trigger suspicion.

A small woman in a blouse and skirt combo of dark and light blue – giving an effect somewhere between uniform and plain clothes – came and stood at the edge of the group. She was young or unlucky enough still to have serious acne.

'DC Pearson will stay with you while the search is done, Mrs Marriott,' Dent said, again marrying them. 'You okay with that?'

Emma mutely moved her head up and down, sending a wet-dog-shake of tears into the air.

'Stay here till I call you,' Ned told her. 'Maddy's doing both pick-ups today, anyway?'

A shudder of Emma's torso gave confirmation.

Leaving the house between the two detectives – what Americans called the 'perp walk' – Ned tried to look as if he had booked a minicab from a firm whose drivers worked in pairs. But there were no flashing snappers or gawking dog-walkers.

Dent drove, with Walters in the back seat beside Ned. He speculated that, if he had been a proper dangerous criminal, the roles would have been reversed or there would have been more officers. This felt like a genteel sort of arrest.

'Okay,' said the female detective. 'I've got to do this now. Rules.' She had taken a pair of cuffs from her pocket. 'Even though we've seen you on the telly.'

She gave the final word a sardonic wobble. He was unsure if it was flattery or an attempt to put him down; he would mention it to Claire in case it indicated victimization.

He endured the cuffing by thinking of it as a sort of dental procedure, closing his eyes as he always did in Dr Rashid's chair.

Each of them looked out of the window on their side. As they turned out of the square, Walters said, 'So someone's died?'

He turned to her. 'What?'

Although he had read *The Trial*, they surely couldn't just introduce a murder charge in this way.

'All the flowers there.'

'Oh. No, not recently. That's where Freddie Mercury lived. People still lay flowers. Even more on his birthday, the anniversary.'

He was surprised by how normal his voice sounded; a benefit of the presenter's experience in dissembling pressure.

'Right, wow,' the DS said. 'That's fame for you.'

He wasn't sure if she was being sympathetic or belittling to him.

From the front, Dent spoke for the first time on the journey. 'Don't worry. This isn't kiddies.'

Don't worry: although these words were unusually prone to misleading application, they could rarely have been spoken as inappropriately as this.

We are troubled on every side, Ned thought. Many people, in extreme moments, are surprised by lines from prayers or poems learned in childhood. But a broadcaster, like an actor, also carries around fragments of scripts ineradicably remembered. As if a tape had been activated in his brain, Ned heard himself speaking some verses from, he thought, Corinthians. *We are troubled on every side, yet not distressed; we are perplexed, but not in despair.*

He saw himself – though unsure whether from a memory of the recording or of watching it broadcast – crouching beside the Dead Sea, during his Easter Special *The Bible – History or Myth?*, delivering a link on the canniness of Christianity in turning suffering into a virtue. It was the only one of his programmes that had not been followed by a proud phone call from his mother. He remembered an argument with the producer, who had wanted to use, instead of the bass cadences of the King James, a modern American translation – something like, *we are down, but not out; worried, but not depressed* – that the viewers were judged more likely to 'get'.

Ned repeated the ancient consolations in his head, but they

had no calming effect, as they would have done for his mother. He *was* distressed, he *was* in despair.

'When we're there, we'll get you settled in,' Walters said, sounding like the courtesy driver for a luxury hotel. 'But nothing will happen until your brief turns up.'

Ned smiled, tension in the muscles making his face hurt as he did so, and stared out of the window, trying to remember every woman he had ever – it seemed wrong even to think *fucked* – known.

He had once read an interview with an elderly writer who admitted that he spent much of his twilight time remembering sexual pleasures from the past. But, except when away on long filming trips (in the great divide between masturbators, he favoured factual scenes over fantasy ones), he had never expected to be doing it at sixty and still less in an unmarked police car.

Some men, he supposed, must think, as they are driven to the station, *oh, fuck, that kid in Scarborough in 70 something*, or understand that a dread at the edge of their dreams for decades – modern western democracies' version of the dawn knock on the door by the secret police – has finally arrived. But no guilt – only fear – was triggered in Ned.

Starting with Nicky Harper – 1972, freshers' week, eighteen, a virgin, as was he, but potentially more reluctant, as a woman of that time, to have sex – he began to play back his mental porn collection.

The Director of History

Reminded of waiting for the headmaster's door to open fifty years before, Tom Pimm tried to guess how much trouble he was in from the tone and expressions of, Eileen-was-it?, his line manager's personal assistant.

The e-mail had dropped at 2.30pm the previous afternoon, when he was wondering how early he could reasonably leave to prepare for Ned Marriott's party; the days when a member of the department could spend months or even years 'reading at home' were over. With 'customers' now paying for their tuition, 'absenteeism' had become a disciplinary matter.

'Tom', the message began. Although some departmental relics of the letter-writing era employed even electronically a Victorian 'Dear', and the younger and looser used 'Hi', management traditionally dispensed with any preface, presumably in fear of being accused of over-familiarity or misleading the recipient with a friendly tone.

Tom,

Following receipt of the Traill Report, the Director of History would like to see you tomorrow (Friday) at 3.45pm in his office.

Elaine Benham,
executive assistant to Kevan Neades (Director of History
– Deputy Executive Dean of Humanities)

No 'yours', neither faithful nor sincere. Like judges nervous of being overturned on appeal, Neades always tried to be as noncommittal as possible in all communications, and his team seemed to follow his example. But Tom's suddenly charging heart understood, before his mind formulated the thought, that he was unlikely to have been summoned to be asked his opinion of the report's pagination.

Only almost a bottle of red wine, speedily downed in relief at completing his tribute to Ned without being struck dumb or punched by the subject of the speech, had allowed him to sleep at all: for two hours until he woke with a dry, sour mouth and lay awake until the unnecessary 6.45am alarm, scripting the most positive possibilities for their conversation. *Look, Tom, it's no big deal, but, with the students going bankrupt to be here, we need to give premium service: a couple of freshers have found your comments on their essays a bit robust. You know the drill these days: here's an idea that might help you to make*

*your work even better. I'm really sorry to have to do this –
you're one of our best teachers – but these are the times!*

A warning it would be, at worst. Or, if worse, what? *Dr
Pimm, I'm afraid I have to tell you that a number of the women
in the department have raised concerns that some of what you
say – jokes, anecdotes, banter though you and I know them to
be – may be capable of misinterpretation in the modern workplace. Dial them down a bit, eh, maybe?*

Except that the real Neades didn't speak in anything like the
voice he had in those consoling fantasies. His language was that
of the career bureaucrat, calculatedly drained of detail and
meaning. The passive – passive-aggressive voice – *Offence has
been given, steps will be taken* – was more in the line of what
he might say. And, if Tom asked what those steps might be:
There is a range of views.

It couldn't be anything actually physically sexual, he
thought; turning away from Helen's warm, sleeping form, as if
to emphasize his virtue even within the marital bed. Tom was
one of the few university teachers he knew in his generation
who had never screwed a student – when there were numerous
rumours about Ned Marriott and many others – and so at least
that was one bullet he would duck.

For an hour, he conducted one of the gruelling, looping self-
interviews with which insomniacs ensure the impossibility of
sleep. Sometimes the questions were helpful to his cause. *Why
do you assume you're the only one? Marriott might have been
summoned on a charge of fucking freshers.* But when I mentioned the meeting with Special last night, Ned showed no
recognition. *But he's a TV presenter, which is virtually an actor.*
Yeah, yeah, but I know him well enough to be able to tell.

Elsewhere, the interrogation challenged even his consolations. *You say there won't be sexual accusations, but what if
people have lied in their evidence?* Well, why would they do
that? *Are you serious? You've worked in that department for
thirty years: to call it a nest of vipers is defamatory to snakes.
The managers all turned a blind eye to Allison for three decades*

and are now spinning this fiction they didn't know anything about him. And everybody thinks they should have the job one rung above theirs, and so conspires against whoever's got it. They get through gossip like Formula One uses gasoline.

Then, at 05.50 by the red-eyed clock, in a moment of ecstatic clarity, he understood that Neades had asked to see him as a witness to the conduct of others – he had made some observations to the investigation – and experienced a moment of almost-calm until he began to fret about being pressured to give evidence against Ned and other friends in the department.

Just before quarter to seven, he switched off the alarm before it sounded, but the cancelling click was enough to half-wake Helen. She drowsily rubbed her feet against the back of his legs, toenails always sharper than she thought.

'You had a restless night,' she yawn-talked. 'You okay?'

'Yeah. My friend red wine is now my enemy, apparently.'

'You're not . . .' – another loving rake from the talons – '. . . worried about something?'

'No.'

Luckily, 'The Past Roots and Present Consequences of America's Fear of Communism' was a lecture he could have delivered in his sleep, a theory almost tested that morning. Tom conducted a seminar on a favourite presidential paradox: Nixon avoiding impeachment but resigning, Clinton being impeached but remaining in office. It worried him that so many of the students seemed to view Nixon as strong and wronged (because of his frozen head in *Futurama*, he was the president they knew best) and Clinton as weak and sleazy, his treatment of Monica Lewinsky 'gross'. 'But isn't there a case,' Tom asked, 'that what Clinton didn't quite do to Ms Lewinsky, Nixon actually did to Cambodia? And which, we might ask, matters more?' But he had been too oblique – the joke only working with the word *fucked* – and they didn't get it. 'Monica was a vulnerable young woman and he was President, *plus* married,' said Milly Morton-King, sounding, morally if not linguistically, more nineteenth century than nineteen, to much nodding from the other women and silent stillness from the men.

He set them for a fortnight's time 'Did Teddy Kennedy or Jack Kennedy achieve most in American politics?', adding: 'And, by the way, don't follow the mistake of a previous student in thinking that one of those Kennedys was called Nigel' – and then tried to eat at his desk a tuna sandwich that he threw away after chewing out a half-moon from one crust.

'Tom Pimm. For the Director,' he announced himself at 3.40pm.

He was mumbling slightly, worried that his breath was still boozy from the birthday party.

The Director's assistant didn't look up.

'If you wait over there.' Her voice was as blank as her message had been. 'He'll pop out.'

Tom suppressed a smile at the hideous unbidden image of Special exposing himself. Eileen-was-it? – early thirties, extremely pregnant – had a working area that was partly private, with a right-angled partition bracketed to the front of her boss's office but one wall missing, as in a stage-set. Opposite this gap was a red sofa and a low table that, until the most recent round of spending cuts, would have held the week's editions of the *THES* and other educational publications.

His first flashback was to school, trying to guess the severity of the misdemeanour from the manner of the secretary, but with no more success now than then. The second memory was from February, waiting on a shabby banquette to be called for his evidence to the Traill Inquiry.

Remove Belts and Shoes

An unexpected effect of the high level of terrorist threat to the western world had been to make the process of arrest feel less alien to novices in a police station's custody suite.

Ned rattled his coins and keys into a plastic bowl, was pat-searched by a man with body odour and halitosis, pressed his index finger and thumb onto an under-lit glass rectangle and aligned his shoes with foot-prints on the floor (too small for his size 14s) until he faced a camera lens that flashed at him. This check-in procedure at least, he thought, was no worse than you would endure to fly to Florence for the weekend. The only departure from terminal protocol was the collection of cheek cells with a swab-bud and that, according to some articles, would be introduced at airports soon.

But this consoling comparison soon collapsed. Here, shoes, belts and phones were not returned. And he felt more shivery, dizzy and arrhythmic than at Stansted because his destination, after being printed and pictured, was not the Euro-Traveller Lounge.

Escorting him to the cell, one of the custody officers asked: 'Do I know you from somewhere?'

If the notorious penalty of celebrity was harassment, the drawback of being slightly known was half-recognition. In a restaurant once, Ned, after being stared at by the occupants of another table, felt flattered by the apparent rise in his status as a TV face. When one of the party strode over, red-faced and Merlot-lipped, Ned was bracing himself for the gracious granting of an autograph when the man asked him if he could settle a bet that was driving them mad: had he once sat next to them on an Easy Jet flight to Faro? When he answered, 'I don't think so,' the man replied menacingly: 'Are you sure?'

'I don't think so,' he said again to the policeman.

'Okey-doke. Just something a bit familiar somehow.'

Ned doubted that the cop-shop escort fitted the demographics for his channels, although some of the series had also been screened or repeated on digital history networks, which drew a broader audience because they showed so many programmes about Nazis. And, in this instance, there was the additional risk he had not been clocked as an historian but mistaken for an habitual offender. He imagined the humiliation of the potential exchange: 'Well, you might have seen *Suez – Britain's Vietnam*?'

/ 'Yer what? Listen, you didn't do a ten-year for that Heathrow blag?'

The cell was about the size of the downstairs loo in Winslow, although the lavatory contained in this cramped rectangle was a stainless-steel cone with no seat. Ned guessed that this was to prevent it being used as a weapon of resistance or (as a sort of hanging harness) against yourself. He feared that he would soon need to puke into the already ominously-stained bowl. There appeared to be no loo roll either. Was that an attempt at degradation or because the tissue might be twisted into a noose? The pressure in his bowels was more fierce than his worst experience of live broadcasting nerves and, in this squalid lack of privacy, he was equally determined to ignore the command.

Being imprisoned for the first time was like an initial sight of New York: a series of moments known from movies. The hollow knock on the steel door and the viewing panel clattering back were expected, almost welcome. A hand extending from an institutional blue cuff passed through a cardboard beaker with steam rising from it.

'Tea?' asked the voice of the guy who had known him.

'Oh, that's so kind. Thank-you very much.'

A conversation in a Cheltenham tea-shop.

When Ned took the drink, the policeman stooped to the window. 'How you feeling? You can see a doctor if you . . .?'

Even standing and crossing the tiny space to take the cup had left him feeling faint – he couldn't remember if he had taken his statins at the flat – but Ned said: 'No. I think I'm fine.'

Not since football matches in the '70s had he sipped a drink that smelled so strongly of piss and tasted as he assumed that urine would. He had managed half an inch of the liquid without being sick when there was another bang on the door and the warder-waiter spoke through the pulled-back portal: 'Ms' – the feminist prefix elongated like a mosquito's whine – 'Ellen is here to see you.'

In the past, Claire had handled his divorce, various contractual disputes with broadcasters and the plagiarism case. She strode through the jail door with an air of brisk but casual purpose that could only have been professional bravado but served to relax and relieve Ned, who stood and shook hands – it had never seemed appropriate to kiss her, and still less so now – with his solicitor. The custody officer backed out of the doorway but kept a line of sight and entry. Ned's historian's eye for patterns noted the recurrence of half-open doors in his descent through the justice system.

Positioning her back against the gap, Claire handed across a small wrap of paper, dazzlingly white against her hands. He began to unravel it to find out what was inside but found that the gift was simply several sheets of Andrex. Claire inclined her head slightly towards the steel latrine and winked. Watching the door, Ned slipped the paper into his pocket.

Gesturing for them to sit on the edge of the hard bench bed, Claire said: 'So. I could spin you with the ratio of arrests to charges but you'd still think you'd be in the exceptions. They say you've declined a medical assessment?'

'Yeah. There was a moment I thought I was going to die on the spot. But I just have to get through this now.'

'Ned, how much have they told you?'

'A charge of sexual assault.'

'Charge? Singular?'

'Yeah. That's good, I mean, better than, isn't it . . . ?'

'Let's see what they think they've got.'

'I have – I suppose all clients do – an urge to tell you that I didn't do anything. But . . .'

'No. You probably know the drill from telly, like most people now. Two of them will ask you questions in a room with a tape running. You don't have to give any answers at all but, if you don't, that could be an issue were there ever to be a trial. I'll be there and you can take my advice. Now, I warn you, I've done a fair few of these and there's a sort of working assumption that it's fishy if you can't actually remember what you had for breakfast on a given Thursday in 1969. So, in as much as you can, be ready for *Mastermind*: Specialist subject – yourself. Now, if you're okay for the moment, I said I'd ring Emma when I'd seen you.'

It was one of those speeches that certain professionals – doctors, teachers, lawyers – needed to have in their repertoire, delivered with a calming confidence that made you want to applaud like a theatre-goer. He felt an impulse to hug Claire but had already come to the conclusion that he might never touch a woman again.

Deposition

Tom had reluctantly volunteered to meet the Inquiry, on the grounds that, in the snake pit of History, he couldn't be sure what others might be saying about him. He had Googled Dr Traill in advance, but found only links to joint-authored research papers and one foggy photograph from the schedule of a Belgrade symposium in 2002, showing someone who looked no closer than a younger sister to the serious, soft-voiced fortyish woman, with fluff-cut grey hair, who, when she stood to shake Tom's hand, proved to be a willowy six-footer, triggering his small-man neuroses by looming over him.

'Dr Pimm, I'm Andrea Traill,' she greeted him, then angled her freed hand towards an Asian woman who, rising to be introduced, proved reassuringly small.

'Jani Goswani,' she said, although he had to glance at the printed card in front of her to compute the names. 'Senior Leader, WH.'

'WH?' queried Tom, who had missed this addition to the campus acronyms.

'Workplace Harmony,' she explained. 'We used to be People.'

'Many of your employees would feel the same.'

'I'm sorry?'

Both women sat down, in front of opened laptops, at a wide glass desk. Disconcertingly, they continuously typed, like court reporters, whenever Tom was speaking, stopping only for questions, which, at first, were always asked by Traill.

She began with general inquiries about the department. Was it a good place to work? Tom riffed about the definition of *good*, resisting the temptation to discourse on some of his colleagues' interpretation of *work*. Had he ever experienced difficult relationships with colleagues and / or customers?

'The artists formerly known as students?' he checked. The guardian of Harmony stiffly nodded.

Here was the biggest dilemma of his testimony. He heard, as clearly as if it had been spoken in the room, his long-dead father's warning, when he had attempted to indict his brother for some infringement of the table football rules, *don't tell tales.* And a memory from prep school, informing the house master of the rude words that Felix Gonzales (an embassy kid, a rare exotic foreigner in those days) had used in dorm, and Dr Gore-Balls replying: *Maybe leave the policing to the teachers, Pimm.* Tom Pimm the snitch and, by contemporary standards, possibly a racist one as well.

'Well, look, I'm not really comfortable about dobbing people in.'

The tapping fingers paused at the participle and the two women glanced at each other and then entered their best guess. Tom imagined the transcript holding a sudden equine reference: *Dobbin.*

'Everything said in this room is confidential.'

'Er, yeah.'

Although the snort was intended to be sceptical, it came out more dismissively than he intended.

'I am giving you my word on that,' Traill said.

'I don't doubt it. But, at roughly the time they rebranded HR as People, the joke in our quarters was that History should be renamed' – Tom's actual gag had been Bitchery – '*Hissed Stories.* If I say anything to you about anyone, you presumably then raise that with him or her and then he or she immediately thinks: *that fucker Pimm has snitched on me.*'

They flinched at the expletive and Tom wondered if they typed it in full or, as in the Watergate tapes, put *[expletive deleted]*.

Traill switched again from stenographer to inquisitor. 'So you would say that you have quite a combative relationship with colleagues, then?'

He thought of the stories he could tell. Daggers, with his unstoppable bonkers monologues in that batty vernacular. Quatermass's refusal to make eye contact or, since the advent of electronic communication, any human contact at all, conversing only by e-mail even with people sharing his office or sitting next to him in meetings. And Horny, whose escalating mental-health problems and the medication prescribed for them had caused a fogging of knowledge that resulted in students being taught a timeline of English history in which royal children were born before their parents, or battles were fought long after all the combatants were dead. As Tom had once commented to Ned, becoming vague about dates may be a common trait of ageing but can be a more serious symptom in a professor of history. And, then, the unfathomable mystery of the constant expansion in the responsibilities and income of Special, who, outside of the department, would surely struggle to hold down a paper round.

In this quasi-legal setting, though, such complaints felt petty, anecdotal, standard office politics. 'Look,' Tom said, 'stuff happens. But has there ever been a work-place where it doesn't? My mate Professor Ned Marriott – as seen on TV – is a left . . . a Catholic and he was saying the other day that the first thing this new Pope pledged to do was sort out the Vatican bureaucracy. I mean, *first*, even before the paedophilia.'

Tom inadvertently reproduced the ironic smile with which Ned had made the comment.

'Do you find child abuse amusing?' Goswani asked.

'*What?* No, of course I don't. I was making the point that even Il Papa has bad days at the office. Look, my colleagues drive me berserk sometimes, and I'm sure that I do them. I've screamed at them occasionally; they've screamed at me. But, as my teenage daughter likes to say, sometimes you just have to grow a pair.'

Goswani looked bemused – Tom imagined the word being recorded as *pear* – while Traill's expression was disapproving.

'Could you look at this please?' she asked, sliding a small piece of laminated card across the table. His first assumption was that, in another parody of legal process, it was some sort of oath.

In antiquated capitals, a digital echo of the laborious ink marks of mediaeval monks, were printed the words: 'We respect and are courteous at all times to all our colleagues and customers, regardless of who they are and what they say or do. We aim at all times to avoid giving offence to anyone by words, by silence, by action, by inaction, by confrontation, by avoidance, by unwanted intervention or by failing to intervene to meet their needs.'

The rhythms and repetitions of the words held a distant reverberation of the prayers – *if I have offended You by my thoughts, by my words, or by my deeds*, a memory from school chapel – for which they were a humanist substitute. Once the prospect of eternal damnation kept people in line; now it was the threat of a formal disciplinary letter.

'What do you think of that?' asked the Snitchfinder General.

Tom censored his thoughts considerably, though not completely. 'Well, I suppose, for me, the key word is *aim.*'

'Do you want to say more about that?' asked Traill.

'Well, they're admirable ideals but perhaps a little impractical and contradictory in an actual working environment.'

Goswani intervened with a sharpness of tone that startled him. 'In what way?'

'Look, I see where you're going with all those sentiments. And obviously colleagues should be respected regardless of *who they are*. But regardless of *what they say or do*? I mean, what if they call you a fat Jewish queer?' The fingers of both women froze above the keyboard, then, after a nervous shared glance, played a short chord. 'What if they give a Nazi salute or rape a student?' Another stutter in the transcription. 'Under a strict reading of that varnished sheet of card, the university was right to let Professor Allison carry on being a rapist for so long and would have been wrong to intervene because he presumably didn't want them to. And, for example, Ms Goswani' – she seemed to flinch at the prefix, but what else could he have risked? – 'just intervened to ask me a question. But how can she possibly know whether her intervention was unwanted or was meeting my needs?'

'I think we probably don't want to get trapped in semantics,' said Dr Traill.

'But the mission statement on manners you just showed me is an exercise in semantic acrobatics. You print a list of antonyms and then tell people to avoid all of them.' He stopped and breathed deeply, suddenly worried that they were trying to trap him into losing his temper. 'And you talk of giving offence by silence. But I have a colleague who will only communicate by e-mail, even if you're sitting next to them.'

'Really?' queried the deputy interrogator. 'Who is this?'

'No, I'm not going to tell you. Because I'm not trying to lose anyone their job. That's why, although I resolutely disapprove of the unisex pronoun *them*, I used it. And, as I said, sometimes, you just have to' – this time, he self-censored the genital reference – 'get on with it.'

'How well did you know Padraig Allison?' Traill asked him.

He noted the loaded premise of the question and was concerned that the phonetic pronunciation of the jailed professor's first name (to rhyme with *mad taig*, Christ, don't say that out loud) rather than the correct *porrick* might reflect a lack of preparation, suggesting that she knew about the Allison case only from last-minute printed or online references.

'We were members of the same department,' Tom said, 'but weren't friends and never taught on the same course.'

Goswani made a puzzled face. 'Oh, but surely there must be an overlap between the American and Irish syllabuses? I mean, given the historical links.'

Pimm laughed. 'Well, I don't know what it's like in Geography.' Traill looked offended. 'But, in our building, every course has fiercely defended borders. The American and Irish modules are more like, well, the Irish Civil War than Ireland and America.'

'So cooperation with colleagues isn't a high priority for you?'

Too late, he realized he had rolled his eyes at Traill. 'It takes two not to tango, as I often say.'

'Often?' echoed Goswani, then asked: 'You described Professor Edmund Marriott as your *mate*. Do you commonly divide your colleagues into those who are friends and those who are not?'

'Doesn't everyone?'

'What I asked was whether you do.'

'I think History is like any other business. Some people in the office like some people more than they like others. There are groups who go to the pub together, or to Pilates or to book group, or to Sicily. There are people who sleep together . . .'

'That's a serious allegation,' said Traill.

'*Is* it?' Tom replied.

'Or a serious admission,' the deputy interrogator added.

'Isn't it just *life*?'

'Are you prepared to name names?'

'Of who is sleeping with who? Sorry, *whom*.'

They did not seem to type the grammatical correction.

'If people are alleging misconduct, I am asking them to name names,' said Traill. 'Under the protection of anonymity, of course.'

What? 'I'm sorry, am I being thick? But you know who I am . . . Oh, I see. The alleged offenders are named but the accusers are anonymous?'

'Yes. Would you be prepared to identify individuals under that protocol?'

'No. No, I won't.'

'Do you want to tell us why?'

'You say I was making an accusation. But I was describing a situation. It's a little bit, Sharia law, isn't it, the naming of adulterers?'

Goswani typed one entry – presumably the Islamophobia – with a shivery frisson, then glanced at an A4 sheet beside the laptop. 'How close are you and Professor Ned Marriott?'

'What? Well, we've never slept together, if that's what you're asking.'

'I strongly advise you to take this process seriously, Dr Pimm.'

'I am certainly trying to, Ms Goswani.'

'I'm pleased to hear that. Would you describe yourself and Professor Marriott as a clique?'

'Well, I'm not completely sure you can have a clique of two. But, as Dr Traill said, let's not get hung up on semantics. I think Ned and I are colleagues of the same generation who probably wouldn't have met, except through education, but, because of it, did. I'd describe us as friends, friends through work. Of which there are many other examples in the department.'

'So you are saying that History is a cliquey place?'

He thought of deliberately confusing the department's subject with the entire past of the world but regretfully conceded that his joke reflex was probably not helping him. 'No, Ms Goswani, I'm saying that it's a place where – because it probably isn't practicable for everyone to have a picnic and a softball tournament together every day – people form into smaller, more manageable groups.'

'Which some might see as cliques?'

'If they do, they kept me out of the loop on it.'

He would die for his jokes, his wife often told him. His interrogators surlily conferred.

After whispering briefly to her colleague, who nodded, Traill said: 'Well, Professor Pimm, that's everything we wanted to cover. Is there anything you want to ask either about today or the process in general?'

'Well, though I know it's not your intention, the mere existence of the investigation is making the department an un-pleasant place to work. People are suspicious and twitchy, wondering who's saying what about whom.'

'Yes.' Dr Traill moved her chin up and down twice. 'I hesitate to invoke McCarthyism to a teacher of American history. But, yes, we see that risk.'

He elected not to mention that his daughter was taking a production of *The Crucible* to the Edinburgh Fringe.

'Less Senator McCarthy than the Stasi,' he suggested. 'Everyone wondering if their neighbour is a secret informer.'

At the mention of the East German secret police, Goswani made a mouth-twist of seeming disapproval and crisply touch-typed for a few seconds.

Traill continued: 'That's why we plan to report as quickly as possible. Until then, I remind you that everything said in this room is considered confidential.'

But the weakness in this secrecy agreement was that the inquisition, through either time pressure or naivety, had not scheduled gaps between sessions, so that witnesses, as they left, crossed over in the waiting area with the next testifier.

Weary and depleted from the effort and menacing ambiguity of the proceedings, Tom fumbled the door open to reveal Daggers, who said, from the waiting bench, with a wide-eyed clown's grin: 'Wotcher, Cocker!' His adopted accent, on this occasion, was somewhere between Cockney and Cornish. 'I felt me old ears burning! Now I knows why!'

Tom levered his lips into a smile. His colleague's chainsaw guffaw rang across the otherwise empty floor. As Tom retreated down the corridor, he passed posters, peeling from the walls where union reps had stuck them, protesting against planned cuts in teaching staff, and then a board holding yellowing, curling-edged notices from the building's earlier purpose, advertising talks and debates – 'A Sermon and a Salmon Sandwich' and 'Controversy in the Crypt' – on subjects including *The Sex Factor – Pastoral Counselling in the Age of Eros.* And *Get Over It – Has Offence Become An Industry?*

Walking back to History, he was struck by the peculiarity that the word 'deposition' covered both a legal submission and the removal of someone from office.

Sexual History

On the anti-erotic bed in his cell, failing to find a sitting or lying position that didn't send sciatic spikes down his spine, Ned completed his mental list of sexual partners. Seventeen women. Although, without getting too Clintonian, it depended on what your meaning of sex was.

He had never penetrated (flinching at even thinking the word) Marie Finch for religious reasons and Alex Crumley-Smith because (or so she said) of menstruation. But Ned had read enough of the Operation Yewtree or related trials to know that definitions had broadened to include, for instance, 'sexual assault by touching' and he had certainly touched Marie sexually during his schooldays and also Alex after that Freshers' Week party. But those had been (how silly and childish the word sounded) *snogs* and would a woman suddenly call in the cops about some (this word not much better) cuddle after forty years or more? (In Ned's mind, a voice – a paranoid and misogynistic tone he had not heard before – answered *yes*.)

That left fifteen. His four longest relationships (but wasn't the charge most likely to have arisen from a brief liaison?) were Emma (fourteen years so far), Jenny (twenty-one years married, lovers for four years before that, although not the final two before the divorce), Lucia (three years, including college and after), and Kathy (eighteen months).

He immediately ruled out Lucia, one of the nicest and kindest women he had ever known; they had attended each other's weddings, were mutually god-parents, and Toby's dog, Aguero, was the son of Lucia's Fred. He was sure they would have married if they had met later. (And if she had not found out that he had slept with Kathy.)

The most obvious suspect, he supposed, was Jenny, who had a clear psychological motive for getting back at the husband who had left her, and for using poisoned sex to do so. Not, however, a financial inducement: damaging his earnings, an obvious risk of such an allegation, would reduce his ability to meet his obligations to her and their daughters.

Kathy, then. Apart from Jenny, Kathy was the woman whom he had most consciously hurt because, ironically, he had left her for Jenny. But Kathy he remembered as gentle, clever, diffident; he might have married her if it had not been for the thunder-strike of love for Jenny. He remembered – now that he was forcing himself to do so – that sex with Kathy – both frequency and, what word to use, variety – had been more of an issue than with others, but surely he had never forced her, and that was 19 . . . 1980 (he remembered watching Reagan's election on television with her in the Brixton flat) and so why wait until now to complain? (Because, the sniping voice in Ned's head said, since the post-Savile sexual witch hunt, people were being encouraged to reinterpret heartbreak as violation.)

There had also been (if it was possible to think in a whisper, then he did so now) a number of one-night or few-week flings and (so far under the breath as to be soundless) one longer involvement.

It was not the first time he had constructed this catalogue, or at least large parts of it. But he had always previously done so in the service of congratulatory nostalgia or / and orgasm. Never had it occurred to him that he would one day revisit these memories to completely detumescent effect.

People questioned on fraud charges, Ned thought, are presumably still able to spend money. But could someone whose sex-life was criminalized ever have sex again?

He stopped his self-interrogation, deciding to wait until a name was mentioned. Because he suspected, feeling like a character in a spy thriller, the most dangerous enemies were those who could not easily be guessed.

Emma's alleged tendency to read novels autobiographically – and to buy them, both professionally and personally, on that basis – was one of the things that Ned enjoyed teasing her about. When asked for an opinion on a particular publicized or popular book, her answer, she freely admitted, would often be along the lines of, 'I'm still trying to decide if *I* would have slept with a concentration camp commandant to save the life of *my* child,' or, 'If *I* found a diary under Toby's bed revealing his plot to assassinate the American president, I'd jolly well say something, not follow him at a distance to the White House on the day.'

Ned accused her of 'over-identifying' and lectured her, in his domestic-professorial way, that *The Curious Incident of the Dog in the Night-Time* was a technical exercise in unreliable narration rather than, as Emma and her first Thursday of the month Winslow literati seemed to think, a multiple-choice paper on how you would bring up a child with an autism-type disorder.

But Emma held her ground, both at the group and also to some extent with Ned. After all, he made his living from the belief that History, which was only a posh form of fiction, was a handbook for the future behaviour of leaders and nations. Well, she believed that novels were a psychological rehearsal room. Readers of fiction were trying out other lives and putting themselves interactively (long before gaming) into crises and dilemmas. And it was the same, she privately felt, with the news. Looking at pictures of those killed by terrorism, accident, tsunami or flu virus, she thought not, as humans surely should, *poor them*, but, *could that be poor me?* If Emma wore a motivational wristband, it would ask not, as those of American Jesus-freaks did, WWJD? but WWID?

In a world so written-about and filmed, she doubted that anything now happened without the victim having already imagined it. Entertainment and journalism had prepped us for the footsteps running up behind, the sudden plummet of the plane, the bang in the next-door carriage, the shopper in the mall pulling a sub-machine gun from a shoulder bag, the dawn raid that drags your lover from your bed to a police cell. Our reactions had evolved from *what is happening?* to: *so this is how it happens.*

During the frequent recent stories of the arrests of elderly DJs and veteran children's TV presenters, she had speculated what it might be like for the partner or child of someone whose life and personality were reinterpreted by an accusation. What would I do?

So this was how it happened. She was familiar with the symptoms of catastrophic shock from a motorway pile-up in fog years before and so the alternating shivering and fever, the tension about whether the next eruption would be from the gullet or bowels, were no surprise to her.

Dressing, while the female cop peeped through the door-frame like a creepy gym mistress, she was shaking so much that, even though the forecast was hot, she put on a thick jumper. It was one that she had never worn much because Ned – loyally, incompetently or pointedly – had bought a size slightly too small. The trembling of her hands meant that buckling her watch-strap took several attempts.

The junior detective with bad skin solemnly followed Emma wherever she went. Like brazen but well-mannered burglars, the police teams stepped aside for her when she passed them in the flat or on the stairs, laden with boxes and transparent bags, in two of which she saw the laptop and iPad they kept in the flat.

For the moment, they had not taken her iPhone. Which now flashed and played the theme from *Ski Sunday*. Caller ID: *Maddy.*

Succumbing already to the subservience of a hostage, she looked to the cop for approval to answer.

'Do you know who it is?'

'Our, er, nanny.'

'Go on. I'll stop you if I have to.'

Maddy spoke in such a slushy rush that, for a moment,

Emma thought that, in some impossible coincidence, something terrible had happened to Toby on the same morning. It turned out, though, to be a continuation of the bad news she already knew.

'Emma!' the teenage Australian blurted, 'the police are here! They say they have to search the house! What do I do?'

'Stay there. I'll just check something.'

She asked her new minder: 'Apparently, they're at our other . . . at our house in Buckinghamshire?'

'A warrant may list several addresses of interest.'

Emma resumed her conversation with an occupant of one of them: 'Maddy, I think you'd better let them in.'

'Okay? Do you want to tell me what's going on?'

'Yeah. Look. I'll explain later but what it basically is . . .' – a tight throat and rising bile made speaking painful – 'is that someone has made a completely stupid allegation against Ned' – no reaction from the watcher – 'and until he can disprove it . . . is Toby up?'

'No. You know Tobes. He'd sleep through anything. What'll I say when . . . ?'

She panicked at how much lying there would be from now on. 'Keep him . . .' Her voice like Brando in *The Godfather*. 'Sorry . . .' She tried to cough her clogged throat clear. 'Keep him out of their way as much as you can. But tell him they're a film crew – Daddy's recording some links in the house later on . . .'

Was there the slightest of smiles from her minder at that? But the invention was credible: as TV budgets were squeezed, the Winslow house had often been used for filming to cut costs. And, if Ned were unable to come home that night, she could say that he was shooting some last-minute 'stand-ups' (the family had become fluent in the vocabulary of film-making) on location.

After reassuring Maddy that she hoped to be back by the time Toby came home from school, Emma checked with the cop that she was free to go when she wanted.

'As long as you feel good to drive.'

'No, I'd get the train. Leave the car for my . . .'

She asked if it was all right to make a cup of tea. The young cop nodded but, offered one herself, unsmilingly declined and stood at the kitchen door watching, so that Emma felt like someone taking an examination in refreshment.

Waiting for the kettle, she considered what to tell their son later. Should she flexi-board him to buy some time? Or tell him – rehearsing a speech of baby-talk vagueness – that 'a silly person says Daddy did something bad and the police have had to take our things away to prove that he didn't.'

Yes, that had to be the best approach, casting the family as victims whom the police were doctorishly trying to help. But, soon, it would presumably be all over online and, while the only bonus of the raids was that Toby would have no devices on which to see his father demonized, schoolmates would quickly update him from their screens. That was an argument against letting him sleep over at school.

And *had* Daddy done something bad? Watching the staunch wives, daughters and girlfriends standing at the gate while the statement of denial was read, or being helped up or down the court steps, Emma had thought, *Can they really be so sure of his innocence?* She suspected that it was just a social instinct, of the sort some wives of philanderers developed, to hold the family together.

So it may have been merely that impulse – and a lover's blurred vision – that made her certain, when she heard the charge, that Ned was the victim of persecution. This must be a misunderstanding. But, if so, based on nothing or on something?

In her worst moments, she thought that letting ageing men teach large groups of women who were not only over the age of consent but also living away from home for the first time was like locking alcoholics in a wine cellar. Although universities had cracked down on droit de seminar – an English professor had taken hasty early retirement during Emma's time at Manchester – the taboo on screwing students was seen as contractual

rather than criminal, and men were weak while women, presumably, sometimes came on strong.

And Ned not only liked sex but to have it when he liked –
their encounter just that morning would find many indicters on
Mumsnet – and so it was possible – an unsisterly thought that,
even unvoiced, made her feel guilty – that some *silly bitch* had
got the wrong end of the . . . no, don't go there.

She also knew that he was capable of adultery; he was getting divorced when they met, but had admitted to a 'wild spell'
as his marriage failed. Would an allegation from a woman with
whom he was cheating on her be worse than a complaint
involving a relationship that pre-dated their meeting? If the
accusation could not completely go away, then she prayed that
it would come from the time before she knew him.

One of the removal team came into the living room and told
their solemn colleague: 'We're done here.'

Emma declined the cop's offer to leave her with what she
first heard as 'a flow', but which turned out to be FLO (Family
Liaison Officer), lying that her sister (non-existent) was on the
way. She walked around the ransacked main bedroom and the
spare, cracking the bitter internal joke, as so many of the war-
rant-searched must have done before her, that one's first instinct
was to call the police: desks and tables stood empty, dust out-
lines showing where objects had been; drawers gaped open. The
box-files on the shelves above Ned's work-desk in the second
bedroom had mainly gone. She imagined his horror, and was
only relieved that he was not at the moment writing a book.

Most of the stuff had been taken away from the flat un-
bagged and in un-gloved hands, which probably meant, she
knew enough from *Lewis*, that the interest lay not in possible
fingerprints but potential content. She thought of the husband
of one of the agency's writers, who had been suspected of fraud,
cleared without charge but then convicted of having indecent
images of children on his hard-drive. As Ned had to be more or
less bribed to spend time alone with Toby until their son was
old enough to have proper conversations about football – and

he was not one of those creepy dads who slobber all over their daughters – she had little fear that he suffered an unhealthy interest in children, but, if the newspapers and occasional conversations with work-friends were to be believed, men's computers were a storage depot for porn. Would that matter? She decided it would be a blessing in comparison with the alternatives.

For distraction, she wiped and polished the newly uncluttered surfaces. It reminded her of trying to fill time in the house when Mummy was having her operation. Toby had chess club on a Friday and so would be home at 6pm. If Ned wasn't *free* – the word alarmed her – by then, it would surely be better to tell him a holding lie.

While she cleaned, the house phone had rung several times but the numbers on caller ID – which they had to have, in case of hacks and trolls, because of Ned being on TV – were unfamiliar. There were also repeated unknown numbers on her mobile. Was the notoriety beginning already?

She was drinking tea without tasting it when the landline trilled and the security panel identified: *Ned Office*. She was thrown by his having gone back to the university, but that must be good news.

Grabbing the receiver, she answered: 'Darling!'

B & H

'I called you to see you this afternoon, Professor Pimm . . .'

'Actually, it's only Dr Pimm.'

'Dr Pimm, following my receipt of the completed Traill Report into the conduct and culture of the History department . . .'

As the assistant showed Tom into the room, the Director had made no eye contact, which was standard manners for him, but, with more than usual dysfunction, he continued to look down while pointing blindly towards a chair, and kept his shaved head low over the desk even as he began speaking. Tom saw that Special was reading from typed sheets of foolscap, on which could be read upside down, scrawled in big capitals at the head of the first sheet: SPEAK SLOWLY.

'You have been found guilty by your colleagues,' Neades read, at GCSE French Comprehension pace, 'of contraventions of the University of Middle England's "Respect" policy.'

The Director was morbidly, almost internet-freak-site obese. Massive man-tits wobbled against the fabric of his vainly under-sized shirt each time he moved, although, perhaps to restrict these spasms, he most often opted to sit in gigantic stillness. There was no more motion on his pale slab of a face, which remained, seemingly regardless of the import of what he was saying or hearing, almost always impassive.

Some of his detractors on the campus claimed that it was this dour inscrutability that had raised Neades far above the position to which they felt his capabilities would naturally have taken him. By almost completely avoiding comment and reaction, he left it to others to assume his approval or infer a rebuke. The recipients of this unreadable stolidity then attempted to retain or gain his approbation by promoting him to a succession of posts from which more voluble participation in meetings might have disqualified him.

'The findings are that you have committed multiple breaches of the disciplinary code over a period of twenty-two years. And, in the light of these findings, I am today setting out for you the steps that will now follow in this process.'

Tom stared at the bristled dome. Neades had succumbed to the common delusion of bald English men that shaving disguised the condition, which, in combination with his body-shape, meant that he resembled the stereotype of a football hooligan in all except the fact that he received an annual salary far bigger than the prime minister's.

'It is my judgement that these multiple offences constitute a breach of contract under the clause relating to the bringing of the academic institution into disrepute.'

64

Neades licked dry lips with a tongue furred yellow-white. By now, he was pausing for so long between sentences, and sometimes words, that an observer would have assumed that he was relearning speech after a stroke. The scribbled reminder to go slowly was presumably a warning from the legal department – a precaution against Tom later claiming not to have understood what he was being told – which the Director had followed with the meticulous obedience he showed to whichever regime was in place.

'As a result – if you accept the findings – your contract of employment will be terminated with immediate effect. As you are in breach of contract, you will not be eligible for any severance compensation. However, your accumulated pension contributions and associated rights will remain unaffected.'

Tom's chest and left upper arm were trembling from the rate at which his heart was racing. He was aware, as remotely as a doctor noting perspiration on a patient, of a slick of sweat rolling down the inside of his left leg until dammed by the top of his sock. The left side. An image of heart and stroke posters at the surgery. Left-sided-weakness. He was going to have a fatal thrombosis. His final sight would be the face of his immense nemesis talking in slow motion.

'I understand that you are hearing some hard things today.' For the first time, the Director stopped reading and resumed a more ordinarily ponderous speed of speech, but then, glancing at his crib sheet again, seemed to confirm that these theoretically human platitudes were scripted as well. 'So do please take as much time now as you want to reflect on what I have just told you.'

But the accused wanted to speak at once. 'You.' The word emerged as the weakened squeak of a stricken animal. Tom tried to cough away the film of phlegm and refluxed bile that felt stuck in his throat. 'You say . . .' After a second paroxysm of raw hawking, he was finally able to ask: 'You say I have been found guilty?' His voice sounded like Tom Pimm as played by a frightened child. 'But I seem to have missed the trial.'

For a period that felt considerably longer than the few seconds it probably was, Neades' face and torso were stonily immobile. Then he stared down at the fan of foolscap on the desk, presumably attempting, like a Scrabble player mentally shuffling the line of letters, to construct an answer from the legally pre-agreed phrases in front of him.

'These findings were the result of charges formulated from evidence received by the Traill Inquiry.'

Tom had an instant saving instinct that to lose his temper would serve to confirm whatever the charges were. But the calm voice he attempted had the sound of the thin whisper he had used to convince his mother that he was too unwell to go back to school yet.

'But . . . but I am not aware of any charges ever being put to me.'

'As I have stated, Dr Traill's assessment of the evidence put to her was that a substantial number of breaches of the University code of conduct had occurred and that charges should result.'

Forcing down the impulse to scream the words, Tom asked: 'But what *are* the charges?'

Neades again searched the typed sheets for a prompt. 'If your decision is to appeal, then the formal complaints will be sent to you by letter or by e-mail.'

'If I . . . ? But . . .' He thought, but also saw in his mind in flashing form, like an Accident Stop sign, the word *Kafkaesque*. 'But doesn't an appeal usually follow the trial which, as I say, I seem to have missed? Although clearly . . .' The word was belied by its delivery, and Tom growled away another plug of gunge. 'Cuh-cur-clearly and obviously I *will* be appealing.'

The Director blinked slowly several times, then slid his highest stack of pages aside to expose a single sheet of heavier, yellow paper holding short numbered paragraphs that looked professionally rather than home-printed. After studying the document for a moment, he kept his head down as he spoke. 'If you agree to the termination of your contract today, you will immediately be eligible to activate your pension. In these circumstances, the University would guarantee to say nothing in public about the circumstances of your departure, which would be stated as having been by mutual consent.'

Neades looked up and, the rougher, faster speech confirming that he was now ad-libbing, concluded: 'Of course, any settlement would be on the understanding that you never publicly discuss what has happened.'

'But I don't know what *has* happened yet.'

The deputy executive dean twisted his mouth and noisily kissed his lips together as if he had just finished a particularly delicious snack.

Tom was beginning to feel faint from the banging of his startled heart. He was not sure if, when he left, he would be able to stand. All except the most arrogant employees have imagined being sacked but, as a professional with thirty years' service, he had foreseen a process involving merging of posts, notice periods, payoffs and a fancy printed pack (passed across the desk by someone like the George Clooney character in *Up in the Air*) outlining possible retraining schemes. Two weeks somewhere with Helen in the heat by the sea, making notes for *Watergate to Whitewater: the Pathology of Presidential Scandals*, and then lunches with old chums to discuss a clutch of visiting professorships. But now it seemed that he would leave as terminally, mysteriously and shamefully as a Soviet era leader.

'Take your time,' said Neades, in a bad *karaoke* of compassion. 'This is a lot to take in.'

Confirming accounts that Tom had read about victims of attack or accident finding a final kick of energy to resist or summon help, he experienced, even as his circulatory system threatened to split, an impulse to fight and survive. He did not suffer the impression, much reported in ordeals, that this could not be taking place – it too obviously fucking was – but knew that he had to stop it.

'Is this actually legal?' he managed to ask.

At considerable risk to the fabric of his shirt, Neades raised both arms. 'I didn't run this process! The new rubric demands that the investigation must be independent from the department involved. But I think you can assume, Dr Pimm, that the University will have thought this through thoroughly.'

What Tom hoped was bile but was possibly vomit scorched the back of his tongue. He swallowed it down, fighting through a sore scratchiness like laryngitis to say: 'I am giving immediate notice of my intention to appeal. This is without prejudice to any separate legal action I may take.'

The recourse to formal language in moments of fear. A customer at the returns desk: *I will be consulting my solicitor.* Patients in the oncologist's office: *I have been advised of an experimental treatment in Bavaria with very impressive initial outcomes.*

'Look,' said Neades. 'These are very serious findings. I strongly advise you to consider the offer we have made you.'

'BUT I DON'T KNOW WHAT THE CHARGES ARE!'

He had no control over the shout coming out – a purging bursting like blood or pus.

Neades made the quick, defensive blinks of someone splashed by lemon juice. 'I had hoped we knew each other well enough to discuss this calmly. That is why I made no arrangement for an observer from WH to be present.'

'*But . . .*' Like a singer botching the opening note, he paused and started again, softer. 'But you're asking me to resign without my even knowing what I've been accused of.'

Tom congratulated himself on remembering a gerund in these circumstances.

'I have only read Dr Traill's executive summary. As I say, I didn't run this process. But it's my understanding that the charges relate to the Respect code – mainly under the B & H section . . .'

Ridiculously, the image of a crumpled cigarette packet from his smoking days.

'Benson & Hedges?'

'Bullying & Harassment.'

Fuck. So, hitting and hitting-*on* people. But Tom had never done the first and, though sometimes tempted, in a primitive masculine way, towards the second, was convinced that, unlike some colleagues, he had always avoided it.

'Although, in your case, I understand, only B,' said Neades.

'Eh?' queried Tom.

The Director looked alphabetically confused for a moment. 'Er, B – Bullying.'

Tom flinched at the punching ugliness of the word, but had a rush of optimism that the allegations, whatever they were, did not involve sex or expenses – the standard destructions of an academic career – and so this was almost certainly survivable.

'There is also, I am led to believe,' Neades continued, 'at least one charge of Insubordination.'

'What is this, Dr Neades? *Mutiny on the Bounty*?'

Tom's anger, again, was an unstoppable spasm. Picking up an already unsheathed Sharpie, Neades made an illegible scribble in the margin, perhaps adding a degree of aggravation to the charge involving disobedience.

'Professor, er, Dr Pimm,' the deputy executive dean said. 'I appreciate this is a big decision to make today. Can I suggest that you sleep on it . . . ?'

Involuntarily, Tom released an asthmatic gasp. He already knew that there would be no hope of sleeping tonight, or potentially ever again.

'Sorry? I . . .' Neades faltered. 'Can I suggest that you sleep on it and come back to see me tomorrow with your decision.' Placed geometrically in parallel to his keyboard was a printed business card, which he slid across the desk towards Tom. 'These are the contact details for David Wellington, Group WH Leader in Humanities. He can talk you through the pension situation and the confidentiality arrangements.'

'And will he be able to tell me what the charges actually are?'

'He's sitting across the situation. He knows that you might call for support.'

'Ke-*van* . . .' The formality of 'Dr Neades' having failed to penetrate the managerial iciness, Tom now attempted intimacy, although sounding the counterintuitive second syllable of his superior's name with the fussy articulation of a Victorian actor. 'This is bonkers, isn't it? I'm being asked to leave without even being told what I'm supposed to have done wrong.'

'As you know, I have indicated the category of the allegations.'

'You've mentioned two initials, one of which I haven't done, and a word last applied to Captain Bligh.'

'Dr Pimm, I'm afraid we have to take allegations of abuse seriously.'

'Abuse? But I thought you said . . .'

'Verbal impropriety – comments, jokes, *argumentativeness* – is, as I understand it, the basis of the case against you.' The spread arms again, an arthritic magician's reveal. 'Although I am not running this process.'

'Right. So actually you're abusing the word "abuse"?'

There was movement from no part of Neades, except, eventually, his eyes, which slowly widened, like an opening flower filmed in time-lapse photography.

'Dr Pimm, I'd strongly advise you not to be clever. From my knowledge of the findings, there's a view that that may be one of the things that got you into trouble.'

Tom failed to stop himself laughing, but didn't care. 'Does it worry you that you run a university in which staff are being warned not to be clever?'

Neades' shoulders shook violently in a way reminiscent, for Tom's generation, of Edward Heath, whose upper torso always trembled when he laughed, although the former prime minister always wore a jacket, presumably to obscure the knocker-wobble that now disrupted Special's shirt. In repose again, he spoke in a plaintive tenor tone that Tom had never heard before. 'So are we agreed that you should come back tomorrow when all this has had time to settle? I'm pretty jammed all day but I'll instruct Elaine to juggle if necessary.'

'I've already decided what I'm doing. I want to appeal and will be taking immediate legal advice.'

The Director sighed so violently that a waft of rotten breath reached Tom. Locating the relevant sheet of paper, Neades recited widely spaced typed lines: 'Following your request to challenge the disciplinary findings against you, arrangements will be made for an appeal hearing before senior managers from an external department. You are requested to provide a secure e-mail address on which you are happy to be sent the time and location of this meeting, along with a formal presentation of the charges. Before the appeal hearing, you will be invited to examine – after signing a confidentiality agreement – witness statements and other supporting documentation.'

Neades was audibly wheezing now, his unhealthy bulk making sustained oration a struggle. He stopped and puffed noisily, releasing another rancid breeze, before resuming. 'Because the University appreciates that this process may be daunting, you are permitted to bring with you to both the documentation stage and the hearing stage a supporter or observer, who must not be a qualified lawyer or someone who is herself or himself involved in any disciplinary proceedings at this University; and whose suitability to attend must be agreed in advance with your designated representative from Workplace Harmony. Pending the completion of this process, you will immediately be suspended on full pay. You are permitted one hour from this time to make any necessary removals from your office and to leave the premises. To protect the confidentiality of the process, you will not be required to be supervised during this time. However, if you are subsequently found to have made any physical alteration to or intervention in the premises, or to have made verbal or electronic contact with any representative of the University, especially but not exclusively anyone whom you may believe to be a witness or complainant, your contract will immediately be terminated with no possibility of appeal. After leaving the premises, you will have no contact with col-leagues or customers . . .'

Tom knew what the word meant but was made even more than usually furious by hearing it in this context. 'Customers?'

'With colleagues or *customers*. This stipulation will include – but not be limited to – the attendance at any events taking place on premises owned, leased or in use on an ad hoc basis, however temporary, by the University of Middle England. Can I check one thing, Dr Pimm? You are not a member of any of the teachers' unions?'

A member for more than thirty years, Tom had left over the insistence of Quatermass (as father of chapel) on defending a policy of jobs for life, even if the posts were held by such incompetents as Daggers and Horny.

'No. No, not now.'

For the first time, Neades seemed briefly to smile, then posed with face and body frozen. Tom wondered if he should wait for the manager to stand, but the Director seemed to be doing 'statue' in a game of charades. Perhaps, like FDR, who would be lifted out from behind the Oval Office desk when the photographers had gone away, he was now winched in and out of the office when no one was looking.

Stupidly, Englishly, Tom extended his hand in farewell, but the other man was fixedly examining his script, checking that he had delivered the sentences correctly.

The only lavatory in the Administration block that Tom could reach in time was the Disabled cubicle on the second floor. Lowering his boxers agonizingly late, Tom dropped litres of acidic diarrhoea into the bowl while leaning forward over the floor in case the simultaneous retching became productive.

When he came out, Professor Ironsides was inevitably waiting, hands impatiently holding his wheel-brakes and focusing a disapproving rictus that Tom at first attributed to a stench left in the cubicle, until he realized that he had just broken another rule of the university.

With hands not quite perfumed enough by soap from their earlier purpose, Tom tremblingly selected from the contacts in his phone the name that he had always known he would call in such a catastrophe: *Ned*.

Historic

Although Ned, like many viewers, had often lamented TV's devotion to crime dramas, one beneficial consequence was that Britons were now familiarized with the processes of police interrogation in the way that schoolchildren once knew poems by heart.

The forgettably decorated room with the table, two chairs on either side, the angled cameras above and a recording machine on the desk. A glance at the clock from the top cop and then: 'It's, uh, 13.15 on Friday May 18th. This is an interview under caution as part of the Operation Millpond investigation. I am DI Richard Dent; also present are DS Heather Walters; the defendant Edmund Horatio Marriott and Ms Claire Ellen, his solicitor. The alleged offence is of an historic nature. Edmund Horatio Marriott, you are under arrest for an alleged sexual offence in or around March to October 1976 against Wilhelmina – known as "Billy" – Dawson Hessendon, now known as Mrs Hessendon Castle.'

During the hours in the cell, the eventual moment of disclosure had grown in Ned's mind until it felt like it would be spoken by an angel clothed in fire. But the actual revelation brought confusion and bemusement. Billy H! As he remembered, they had *fu*—, slept together a few times in London when he was doing his MPhil. He had met her, he thought, through friends, or possibly his brother. Jolly and jolly posh.

'Unless Ms Ellen has any objections,' Dent said, 'my intention is that DS Walters will read the victim's . . .'

'Complainant?' Claire queried.

'Victim,' Dent insisted. 'Will read the victim's statement into the record.'

'I'm sorry for the delay, Mr Marriott,' said Walters. 'There was a development on another case.'

Ned thought, *Who else are you persecuting as well?*, but, already learning the manners of a defendant, nodded his thanks for her courtesy. Although he felt far from normal – the stamping of his heart and churning of his guts unnervingly palpable – Ned was reassured by the fact that the ghost from his past took the form not of an inevitable avenging angel – as must surely be the case with so many of the accused – but as a bizarre ambush that he expected at any moment to be revealed as a prank. Although, even in modern culture, he doubted that there could yet be a TV game show in which people faced hoax arrest.

The detective sergeant shuffled two foolscap sheets, coughed and took on the role of Ned's old girlfriend. 'I am Wilhelmina Dawson Hessendon Castle, often known as "Billy".' *Castle*, which must be her married name, was news to Ned, as was *Dawson*, probably what her mother was called before marriage, but you only discovered someone's middle name by attending their wedding, seeing their passport or being arrested and questioned about them.

'During the summer of 1976, when I was known by my maiden name of Wilhelmina Dawson Hessendon, though commonly "Billy", I was working in a secretarial capacity for a publishing company in London. I was twenty-one years old at the time.'

Although Ned had only rough recall of the woman's actual voice – he thought of a generic southern posh girl – it was incongruous to hear her speaking in the Scouse accent of DS Walters, like Shakespeare acted by Americans.

'During my time at Exeter University, I had become acquainted with Timon Edgar Marriott.' The detective pronounced it *Timmon*; Ned saw that Dent had noted his startled reaction to his brother's appearance in the story. 'Commonly known as Tim. At a party to which I was invited by Tim Marriott, I was introduced to his brother Edmund Horatio Marriott, commonly known as Ned.'

The world of thirty-eight years before, already hazy through the cataracts of time, was even less recognizable because everyone, as in a Russian novel, used their full family names. Nor did he remember Billy H. talking like a copper giving evidence in court, but knew that this was a quirk of the judicial system. His only previous involvement with the police, apart from nine speeding points tried and sentenced by post, was as the near-victim of a veering speeding driver while out running near what was then his country home in Sussex. He had learned from this experience that police statements were not verbatim but written by officers after interview. His own testimony had begun, *It is my custom of a late Sunday morning to take exercise in the West Sussex countryside*, a formula that made him sound like an Edwardian jogger who had got badly lost.

'After that party, at which some consensual intimacy occurred, I agreed to have lunch with Ned Marriott and we subsequently had consensual sexual intercourse.'

Immediately after lunch? Ned's mental defence counsel sceptically challenged. *Actually in the restaurant? In a cupboard like that tennis player?*

'It is my recollection that the first occasion took place at my flat in Earl's Court and we also later had sexual intercourse on a few other occasions there or at Ned Marriott's flat in Redbourne Avenue, in Finchley, North London. I was not involved in any other sexual relationship at the time, although I strongly suspected that Ned Marriott was. While he on occasion pressured me to perform sexual acts with which I felt uncomfortable' – Ned made an amazed-face at the detectives and then Claire, who had not reacted – 'our encounters were generally consensual. But, on one occasion, which I believe to have been at Ned Marriott's flat in Redbourne Avenue, Finchley, North London, he raped me.'

The word was like a bomb blast in the room. Understanding the impact, Walters had paused to let the allegation settle. When the moment unfroze, Ned turned to his solicitor, with his mouth open and hands spread wide, like a footballer protesting to a referee. But Claire showed nothing. Surgeons, he supposed, allowed as little reaction when a victim of motorway carnage was wheeled into theatre.

'I had consented to sexual intercourse,' the woman detective resumed reading. 'But, knowing from my awareness of my menstrual cycle that I was at high risk of becoming pregnant, I warned Edmund Horatio Marriott that I was not contraceptively protected and asked him to withdraw before ejaculation.'

Even in his horror at what was happening, Ned had to stifle laughter at the dialogue, like a badly-dubbed porn film, that was created by police reported speech, a kissing mouth pulling away to gasp: *Edmund Horatio Marriott, I know from my awareness . . .*

'However, he ignored me and pushed harder, continuing until ejaculation. Afterwards, he laughed and said: "That was amazing, the best ever."' To Ned's ear, Walters adopted a sort of thuggish bluster for his alleged post-coital remark. 'I could not understand why he was laughing. Although I was extremely upset and worried, I hoped that I would not become pregnant. Subsequently, however, I discovered that I was pregnant and, after consultation with my General Practitioner, underwent a termination.'

Claire scribbled something, which Ned, glancing across, saw was: *medical notes?* He nodded, then thought that, if all this came out, it was the abortion that would appal his mother more than the sexual allegation.

Walters turned over a page, which showed that only one paragraph remained: 'I did not inform Ned Marriott of the termination because we were no longer in contact and I had no need of financial assistance from him. Because our relationship was intermittent and we had sexual intercourse on a number of occasions, I cannot be certain of the date. But to the best of my recollection, the rape occurred between the months of March and October in the year of 1976.'

Ned's in-head attorney jeered: *Well, you can't have been*

very traumatized then! Someone wouldn't say that they remembered being stabbed at some point during 1976!

'At the time, I told no one, feeling that I would be disbelieved because the assault occurred during a previously consensual encounter. In fact, it was only during recent publicity about changing understanding of what can constitute sexual assault and rape' – *well, which was this?*, wrote Claire – 'that I came to understand that I had been raped by Ned Marriott and to contact the police. Statement ends.'

'So,' said the detective inspector. 'Do you want time to discuss with your solicitor or are you prepared to answer questions on the statement now?'

In mime, Ned and Claire debated the question and agreed to continue.

'The allegation relates to 1976,' DI Dent resumed. 'As this date is now distant, I am going to mention three events that happened in that year within the range of dates given by the victim.'

For Ned, 1976 meant Harold Wilson resigning mysteriously and being replaced by James Callaghan, and Viv Richards blasting England's bowlers across and over outfields parched brownish-yellow by an infernal summer.

'These events may provide a context for your memories,' DI Dent said. 'Do you understand what I mean?'

'Yeah. I think.'

'1976 was the year,' the detective began, sounding like the voice-over on a documentary (*The Rock n Roll Years: Operation Millpond Special*), 'when the teenage gymnast Nadia Comăneci became a star of the Montreal Olympics, Princess Margaret announced her separation from Lord Snowdon, and twenty thousand women took part in a peace march in Northern Ireland.'

He must ask Claire afterwards if they always used such prompts, or only for historians. Perhaps, if the accused were a lorry driver, they read out fuel prices from the year in question.

77

'Mr Marriott, did you live in 1976 at Redbourne Avenue, Finchley, North London?'

'Er, yeah. That would be the year I came down to London. I was there, I think, until I finished my second degree two years later.'

'Which number did you live at?' asked Walters, very casually.

Ned was about to answer when Claire raised her hand. 'Because my client is a public figure, about whom a great deal of information exists in the public domain, the origin of knowledge may become an issue at a later stage.' His solicitor smiled and addressed Dent. 'Why don't you ask the complainant which number it was and then we'll tell you if she got it right?'

With a little *oof* of amusement, Dent conceded the point. Ned was impressed by Claire's sharpness; once mentioned, it seemed striking that the complainant knew the road but not the number.

'Mr Marriott,' Dent said. 'Were you, during 1976, involved in a sexual relationship with Wilhelmina "Billy" Hessendon.'

'Um, yes. I think people still said "going out" then, not "seeing". We went out for a bit.'

'What are your memories of the victim?'

Ned looked at Claire. 'Well, obviously, that isn't how I think of her.'

'Can we settle on "alleged victim"?' Claire asked.

'We're following agreed protocols.'

'Can we just use her name, then, okay, Rich?' his solicitor asked the DI. The first name gave Ned a sense of being an outsider in a club.

Dent sighed. 'What are your memories of Ms Hessendon?'

'She was a really nice girl. Young woman, I think we have to say now. Look, I was single, she was single; it was – don't lock me up for saying this – no big deal.'

'Is she right to think it wasn't an exclusive relationship?' asked Walters.

Before the final vowel, Claire interrupted. 'Come on, this isn't Iran or the Vatican. I didn't know Millpond was investigating infidelity.'

Ned guessed that the question was an attempt to find character assassination evidence for use in any – he still could not believe that it would ever come to this – trial.

Dent removed his spectacles, as if to emphasize that he was looking Ned in the eye, for this question. 'What is your memory of the specific sexual encounter described by the, by Ms Hessendon?'

'Oh, look. I'm not suggesting that I was any kind of stud or anything. But I had the sort of sex-life of the average man of my time. My generation missed the '60s but we were just before Aids.' He had unconsciously dropped into the tone of a Radio 4 discussion programme. 'But, I mean, can *you* remember in detail what you did in bed thirty-eight years ago? Yeah, I know, before you say it, that you'd have been six or so and DS Walters hadn't been born, but you understand what I'm saying?'

Unsmiling, Walters asked him, 'Would you have been in the habit of having unprotected sex?'

Fact cop / sleaze cop seemed to be their agreed teaming.

'As I've said, this was pre-Aids. Most girls, women, were on the Pill.'

'Do you ever remember using protection with Ms Hessendon?'

'It was a very short relationship. We weren't, you know, going to a Family Planning clinic or anything. Thinking back, I think I would probably have left it up to her.'

DS Walters gave what he took as a disapproving look. 'Because of the nature of the allegation, we have to ask some pretty, er, graphic questions. The alleged victim says that she asked you to, um, pull out and you didn't?'

'Yeah.' Claire tapped a pen on the table in a code he thought he cracked. 'By which I mean that, yes, she does say that. But I have absolutely no memory of that happening.'

'It's sometimes not easy to stop,' Walters followed up. 'Is it possible that you just couldn't?'

Forcibly developing the instincts of a criminal, Ned saw a trap: an admission that he had inadvertently been unable to obey her instructions involved an acknowledgement that she had given them.

'I have absolutely no memory of ever being asked to stop,' he said.

Dent joined in again. 'And can you recall cases – in other relationships – when you were asked and did so?'

'Come on, Rich,' said Claire. 'Why don't you re-name it Operation Angler? You've got one woman. Let's stick to what supposedly happened to her.'

Dent dipped his nose towards Walters; like players in a string quartet, they seemed to have agreed signals.

'You're a very big guy, Mr Marriott,' the woman detective said. 'Tall, broad. You look like you work out . . .'

'Thank you,' he stupidly interrupted.

'A woman of even average size might find you frightening? Certainly would be unable to stop you?'

'I admit I've been on holiday recently,' Claire cut in. 'But I seem to have missed the introduction into the legal system of guilt by *build*?'

'Look, this is bonkers,' Ned said. 'If we were all fitted with erotic black boxes – like the recorders aeroplanes have – then we could play back every shag we'd ever had' – he wished he hadn't said shag – 'and the porn industry would collapse' – he wished he hadn't mentioned pornography, but his punditry impulse had switched on – 'but we haven't and the average man, woman, can't fill in a questionnaire on who did what to whom on a random night when Margaret Thatcher was leader of the opposition!'

At the start of his speech, he had felt his solicitor's warning fingers on his arm but the pressure lessened as he went on, as if she were approving anger as a tactic. Refusing to answer, he suspected, was the riskiest tactic in this room.

'I appreciate this is stressful for you,' Dent said. 'But we have to take these allegations seriously. We're almost done here. But can I just ask you to cast your mind back to 1976 and tell me if there is anything else at all you can recall that might be helpful?'

Ned almost physically closed his eyes but then felt self-conscious and stared at the floor in the corner of the room as he searched his memory files.

Richards smashing Underwood back for six over his head at the Oval. An Olympic commentator (Ron Pickering? No, someone Weeks, Alec?, Alan?) shouting: *Gold for little Nadia!* And then sex, though not Billy H at all, but Vicky Atkinson, curtain of long black hair as she crouched over his. No, no, no. Did all men reach the point where they wished they had cut off their cock long ago and gone into a monastery?

'Because you have no memory of the events,' said Walters, 'then you can't be sure that they did not take place?'

Ned thought of mentioning Kafka but was finding the giving of evidence like writing for a tabloid newspaper, constantly worrying whether the references would be got. As he hesitated, Claire spoke: 'Oh, stop this! Does the fact that one of DI Dent's hands is under the table at the moment mean he might be playing with himself?' The detective instinctively lifted his arm clear. 'Come on, Rich, I think it's time my client had a break.' She turned to Ned: 'You are denying any knowledge of the *alleged* offences?'

Looking directly at the detectives, he said: 'Yes. I do not recognize this account of my brief relationship with Miss Hessendon. And I am not – and have never been – a . . .' He found it impossible to voice the word, even in denial, and worried that this would be taken as guilt. He eventually succeeded in saying: 'a . . . a . . . rapist.'

But the word was muffled by a burp of bile that burned his throat.

Three times, Tom chose HOME on speed dial, the tremor in his fingers a preview of the Parkinson's to come if he lived long enough to get it. But, as he tried to script the conversation with his wife, the lines he gave himself consisted of false chronology ('There's a bit of an investigation going on in the department'), optimistic euphemism ('I think it will be fine, but I may be in a bit of trouble') or gangsterish bravado: 'You know I've told you about Special and Daggers and Horny? Well, the bastards have kippered me up.'

His attempts to give the dialogue more detail failed because, while it was possible to imagine saying 'insubordination' with a mocking laugh, he could not bring himself to spell out the meaning of the letters 'b & h', and the allegations were so vague that, even if he told Helen everything he knew, she would surely assume he was holding something back. What had happened to him that afternoon was so odd and astonishing that it would be like coming home with a dent in his head and claiming that a rainbow had fallen on him. So he decided that he would tell Helen only when he knew what the charges were.

It was Ned that he had tried first from outside the Adapted Lavatory – but the mobile, uncharacteristically, had been turned off completely – and so he moved the cursor over NOD and pressed again. Still dead. Tom looked into the glossy, younger features of his friend: a promotional poster from *The Fabulous Fifties* was Blu-tacked among the framed degree certificates and book covers in the middle of the ego wall opposite.

On the desk was a big, boxy office telephone, its black plastic sun-dulled and chipped: equipment had been one of the first costs the university had cut during the 'efficiency savings'. Beside the receiver, ten horizontal panels held paper strips, on which Ned had typed words including HOME, MUM, TOM, DEAN, OGGLE. Taking satisfaction in being ranked third, Tom thought, *Special can pay for this call*, and pressed HOME. Listening to the drilling of the dialling tone, he was preparing an opening comment, something like: 'Nod, you thought Senator McCarthy was an essay topic. Turns out he's running the fucking department!'

But it was Emma who answered, and she said: 'Darling!'

Though no less prone than most men to the delusion that his friends' wives were secretly plotting to seduce him, Tom was still startled by the greeting.

'Er, hi. This is Tom. Tom Pimm.'

'Oh, God, I'm sorry. It came up on the creep screen, for some reason, as Ned's office.' Her voice sounded tired and strained. 'I'll have to get someone to . . .'

'No, no. That's where I am.'

'Oh, God! Is he okay? Has something happened? Is he there with you?'

'Whoo, Em, take it easy. I don't think there's anything to worry about. I needed a safe phone to call him about some . . . some office gossip. His thought-pod was empty and so, as he wasn't here and his mobile's off, I thought he must be nursing a birthday head . . .'

'Oh-kay. Don't you have an office?'

'Shared. Only big potatoes like Nod get their own.' He was trying to sound like himself, but could hear the distortion from the tension in his neck and face. 'Okay, so he isn't with you and his moby's off. Any clues to when and where he might . . . ?'

'I . . . I'm not sure I can help you, Tom. He did say he was busy, telly meetings I think. Is it anything I . . . is it urgent?'

'No, no, no. Just tell him to ring me if . . . oh, and great party last night . . .'

'Yes. Yes, it was . . .'

She seemed to be choking on the words and Tom was yet again envious of the passion in a second marriage. Until a second explanation occurred to him: his mobile off, Emma having no idea where he was and sounding as if she might have been crying. Ned, Tom became convinced, was with another woman.

Short Game / Long Game

London reacted to the first warm evenings of the year with a panicked impression of Paris. Long stretches of pavement were narrowed by hastily-placed tables, smokers winning the bonus of sun, tan-addicts paying the penalty of the fumes now outlawed indoors.

Coming down the Paddington Green steps, Claire had made to hail a taxi, but Ned stopped her, from an atavistic instinct to breathe free air. An image came to him of chemo-bald patients sitting in hospital grounds, basking in breeze and warmth, the everyday suddenly cherished because of its imminent perishability.

Leaving home in a supervised hurry that morning, Ned had scrambled wallet and phone into his pockets but had no time to find the baseball cap he wore when a series was going out or there was a person or place that he preferred not to be Instagrammed or Tweeted. So his only defence against recognition was to avoid eye contact when he sensed he had been spotted. His stare-radar bleeped repeatedly but he accepted that the settings might be affected by paranoia.

He had started several sentences, but Claire raised a hand that she then pointed in warning towards the lines of people queuing to edge past the outside diners. Ned and Claire forced their way down another crowded side-street. Barbecue smells of grilled meat and fish rose from plates but, although Ned had drunk two half-cups of police tea and eaten nothing that day, the meals made him nauseous rather than hungry.

His phone repeatedly vibrated in the jacket slung over his shoulder. Convinced that there would already be journalists calling, he was terrified to check for messages. The scroll of missed calls when Ned's phone was returned by the custody sergeant had been filled with *Em* and *Tom P*, the almost quarter-hourly persistence of the latter convincing him that the story must already be out, either online or, only marginally better, the departmental intranet. He had phoned neither Emma nor Tom, finding it impossible at the moment – and perhaps ever – to imagine the conversations he might have.

At the end of the interrogation, he had been released on police bail until September 1, on condition of surrendering his passport, although he might be permitted to travel outside the UK on request. In addition to the search of the Kensington flat and the Winslow house that had already taken place, the detectives advised that they were also seeking warrants for the Cotswolds cottage and the offices of both Emma's agency and the television production company Ogglebox. *Everyone is going to know*, he appreciated stupidly late.

Eventually, after a series of turns from the High Street, they reached a side-road of closed or closed-down offices and factories.

'You okay?' asked Claire. 'You absolutely have to tell me if you're not. I'm no doctor but I know people who are.'

'It's . . . I hate the way everything these days gets called *surreal*.' His mouth was so dry that he felt he was gouging the words out of his throat one by one. 'But . . . I'll be okay . . .'

They took a short-cut across an industrial estate, deserted by workers drawn out early by the sun. On chained gates, sealed with rusted padlocks, notices warned of dog patrols. This distance from the main road, Claire's deep throaty laugh rang loudly.

'Hessendon Castle – she sounds more like a tourist attraction than a complainant!'

'The stuff she said about sex acts that she found – all she meant was . . .'

'Hold it there, partner! This isn't an episode of *Girls*.'

'Storming into buildings after all these years, and taking away files and computers, presumably, like something you see . . .' In a reversal of his previous concern about not being famous enough, he reassured himself that he was not enough of a celebrity for there to be much publicity. 'What the fuck do they think they'll find after thirty-eight years?' He tried to pump saliva across his palate. '*The Rough Guide to . . .*' He couldn't say the word. '*Non-Consensual Sex* stuck down the back of a sofa?'

'I know. Everyone always reacts like that.'

'So you've done these before?'

'Have I? You wouldn't want me discussing *your* case with others. Look, if you don't know where the mouse is – or even whether there is a mouse – you put traps down in as many corners as possible. And it's a kind of cop motto these days that, if you don't have very much, you'll always find more on a hard-drive. E-mails, diaries, searches . . .'

Ned wondered if the list was a question. 'Look, I . . . I suppose every man . . .'

'Woh, no thank you!' his solicitor cut in. 'If you want to make a confession, find a priest, or an IT specialist. If stuff comes up, we'll deal with it. But not until.'

They passed an L-plated car, joltingly attempting turns in an empty factory car park. As if sensing that the temperature was wrong for England, the evening was suddenly getting colder. Ned optimistically picked up on her earlier comment. 'So you don't think they've got very much?'

'Well, to put it in a kind of perspective, I actually wasn't born when this thing allegedly happened. So the trail is sort of cold? Which leads to their working assumption that there's something suspicious in not remembering exactly what you were doing when you first heard Abba's "Dancing Queen". But, at the bottom of their socks, Millpond know that life doesn't actually work like that and no jury is going to conclude that it does.'

He swallowed, suffering the sensation of choking on a lump of meat. 'Jury? You think it will get to that?'

'It shouldn't. But the law is sort of off-piste here. In most cases, the allegation comes at the end of the investigation. But, in this kind of thing, it's the start. Look, we've got two choices – the long game and the short game. Short means we bombard them with evidence – dates, data, inconsistencies, your character, *hers* – until that claim has so many holes in it, they can only use it for crazy golf. Long means we just lodge a complete denial of the allegation and sit it out. If – *if* – they can get it to court, that's when we shoot her – *it* – full of holes. Your choice.'

Ned had once faced the prospect of standing in the witness box – when the spin-off book from the Henry VIII series was accused of plagiarism – but had never envisaged being in the dock, except possibly for his anarchistic attitude to speed cameras.

'Okay. Well, which way are we more likely to win?'

'Here's the thing . . .' The impact of American screenplays on English speech. 'If we go short, we're in effect giving them leads, clues they can use to either firm up Tourist Attraction's story or, in the worst case, to find others. But, when this comes out – and it will come out, whatever they promise, you know that?' He reluctantly nodded. 'There's a risk anyway that others will have a pop.'

After their earlier exchange, Ned decided not to see the comment as an invitation to confess. 'So you're saying it makes no difference what we do?'

'I think, whatever happens, they don't have enough on you, as it stands. But recently the CPS have been going to court without enough, so that the jury takes the rap if people get off. If that's where we end up, they'd be trying to convince women jurors that you're a menace to the gender. So a standard piece of advice would be to get a chick solicitor, but you've got that already. I'd also strongly suggest that we go for a lady QC as well. A star one.'

He began the desperate financial calculations of a tourist who has picked the wrong restaurant. 'So, what you're saying is that short is risky but cheap, while long is risky but crippling?'

Her happy cackle. 'Bad for business to say this, obviously. But, in the end, it probably comes down to how much you want to go on living in your house. *Houses.*'

'Okay, I'm going to say short.'

Even on her habitual high heels, she still had to peer up at him. 'Careful what you say or I'll have you for discriminatory language.'

When he laughed, his throat hurt. 'How, er, soon do you think people are going to start knowing?'

'I think we have to assume more leaks than a bed-sit heater. Of course, there are limits to what they could print. But they don't apply to the trolls. What I think is that the feds know this isn't cooked enough yet. If they'd had the courage of their, um, potential convictions, they'd have knocked on your door this morning with a couple of Murdoch's finest popping flash guns in your face. It's good news that didn't happen.'

Ned breathed out noisily. 'I'm struggling to adjust to a situation in which that counts as good news.'

'Yeah, well. That's the world we're in now.'

They shook hands and, as Ned walked home to tell his family of his potential ignominy, he was glad, for the first time ever, that his father was dead, and would have been even happier if his mother were as well. He had become a thought-orphan.

Bad People

'Mummy! I can't find my PS4 and iPad in the bedroom! Oh, Daddy, you're back.'

'Yes, Tobes. Sit down. We need to talk to you.'

'And put your phone down on the table as well.'

Their son's face crumpled. Emma had not intended to sound so like a detective.

'No, no, you haven't done anything wrong, muffin.'

'Then why have you taken away my stuff?'

He assumed they were imposing game-time restrictions, like after his Year 3 report.

'That's what we're . . .'

'And you can go back on your phone in a minute. You just need to concentrate.'

A liquid glint in his eyes, then a deadpan manner, and perhaps even a line, learned from television: 'You guys are getting divorced?'

Grasping Ned's hand to dramatize their togetherness, Emma said: 'No. No, of course not . . .'

'Well, we're not actually married so we couldn't even if we wanted to.'

'Ned, stop it!'

'Which we don't.'

'Toby, you probably know from school that sometimes bad people spread stories about other people.'

The eyes brimming again, now within a scarlet face. 'Oscar's just really annoying sometimes.'

'What? No. This isn't about school. A bad person has said some things about Daddy that aren't true.' Emma paused for Ned to add details but he just nodded. 'And, for the police to be able to prove that what they said is wrong, they've had to take some things away from the house for a while.'

'Can I get new ones?'

Emma was uncertain whether to be annoyed or relieved that Toby had pursued his own selfish concerns rather than seeking more details.

'Yes. We'll go shopping,' she said, feeling Ned flinch, presumably financially, which he confirmed by adding: 'To get some stuff. Not all of it because the other things will come back . . .' A pause while she thought what he now spoke aloud. 'Eventually.'

Because

Each September, since the installation of PowerPoint, Tom, in his introductory lecture, played the clip from the movie of *The History Boys* in which Deakin complains that history 'is one fucking thing after another.' After the laughter of the freshers had died down, Tom would say: 'You'll all have days when you feel that. So do I. But he's wrong. The reason we study this subject is that History is one fucking thing *because* of another. Our job is to spot the becauses.'

PART TWO

FINDINGS

Weaving

People often congratulated Ned on the fullness and darkness of his hair. On the night of his sixtieth, it had attracted the usual tributes from envious baldies and grey-heads of his generation. Such admirers presumably suspected that the thick black coif was a cosmetic illusion and probably commented in the hope of detecting some guilt in his acceptance of their compliments.

He could not deny that his expensive reversal of nature was vanity, but argued in his defence a practical motivation. Until very recently, when presenters could claim youth credibility by shaving their heads as a fashion choice, a TV broadcaster who went bald was soon heard on radio. So from the first flash of scalp in the mirror after a shower or swim – and then the paranoid conviction that a silver-locked intruder had been sleeping on his pillow during the day – Ned had taken precautions against his genetic fate.

For more than twenty years, strands – he had been too squeamish to ask if they were synthetic or, as urban legend said, from the dead or poor – had been woven with his own, then tinted and dyed to match the publicity photograph of Ned at thirty-seven that he had given The Centre as a reference.

But, if the effort and expense were intended to keep him on television, should he continue them while he was not? A folk instinct that the exiled ceased to care about their hair – like straggly Timon, for whom his brother was named – merged with a feeling that, with money shorter, he should not be spending it on defying time. He suddenly wondered if the documented phenomenon of men in the public eye going grey during crises was due not to stress but to economizing or no longer bothering.

He searched his in-box for the e-mail from The Centre confirming his July 16 appointment.

What Minds Do

Knowing that he had three hours before Helen came home, Tom folded a blanket lengthways and laid it on the floor, in the way that the websites demonstrated. The spot he had chosen was between the twin beds in the spare room. He added a second doubled-up blanket because the carpet seemed to have little effect on the hard coldness of the wooden boards. From what he took to be a combination of psychological and orthopaedic wisdoms, the booklet advised against lying on a bed, recommending bedding on the floor. Flashbacks of crashing on people's floors as a student.

He had bought online a bolster of the type you only saw in boutique hotels these days, and a padded rectangle, like a shrunken bean bag or, with its lavender smell, a scented sanitary towel.

Tom settled the bolster under his head, sculpted the duvet into a cocoon and, self-mothering, tucked himself in. Balancing the iPhone on his chest, with thoughts of paramedics' equipment, he fumbled the earphones into position, avoiding the thick crusted scab on the right lobe, a result of shaky shaving.

There was a single toll of a church bell. *Meditation 1: Mindfulness of Body and Breath*, said the voice, so soft that Tom had to blindly fumble with the volume control. *Finding a position where you're comfortable: if you're lying down, allowing your legs to be uncrossed with your feet falling away from each other and your arms slightly away from your body. Allowing your eyes to close, if that feels comfortable.*

It did. Oxymoronically a powerful murmur, the tones were those that English middle-class believers would attribute to the voice of God. *Being fully aware of the sensations of breathing, for the completion of the in-breath and the completion of the out-breath*. Or, Tom thought, the recording that the UK government had made during the Cold War, spoken by a Shakespearean actor, that would be broadcast in the moments before the Russian nuclear missiles struck.

Spookily, these soothing tones seemed somehow even to know that Tom had become distracted by thoughts of total conflagration.

Sooner or later, God / Armageddon said, *you'll probably find that the mind wanders away from the breath: to thinking, planning, remembering. And, if so, don't worry or blame yourself. That's just what minds do. Call it back.*

A cartoon image of concentration as a dog. With his wandering consciousness settled, Tom listened to the soothing instructions to focus on each part of his body, from the feet to the head in turn, and *focus on the sensations you can feel there.* At first most aware of an inner trembling that he ascribed to adrenaline ('your adrenals are very buzzy,' an osteopath had once said), he felt himself loosen until the doubled blanket underneath seemed as supportively plump as a lilo.

Focus now on the sensation of the breath in your abdomen.

He was woken up by Helen, lifting the silent plugs from his ears. Told what he was doing, she asked why he needed it. Tom told her he was stressed at work because of the threat of redundancies.

K, I, C, B, M, M, R, R

Just as new lovers turn to certain poems to express what they are feeling, there were particular books that Ned was driven to revisit or, alerted to the ironies of the storyline by a friend or an article, to read for the first time. Unnervingly, he discovered that some of the most relevant texts were waiting on his shelves, bought years ago but never opened, as if he had somehow known that denunciation would one day come.

In his workroom, searching the not-quite-alphabetical lines

of spines and the random stacks of volumes waiting to be arranged, Ned suddenly had a powerful sense of how he must look in front of the book-case, standing on the polished half-ladder that Emma had given him one Christmas. But this was not the 'depersonalization' identified on his antidepressant packet as a possible side effect. A favoured piece of background footage ('B-roll' or 'wallpaper' in broadcasting argot) for news interviews with professionals – sacked cabinet ministers, judges appointed to run public inquiries – showed them peering along the shiny titles in their libraries. The pictures were supposed to be un-distracting, running under commentary, but Ned often found himself ignoring the voice-over, inclining his head side-ways to see what the worthy had on their shelves. As one of the final questions on *Desert Island Discs* acknowledged, reading tastes were revealing. (Ned had chosen G. K. Chesterton's *The Man Who Was Thursday*, his dad's favourite book.)

Ned's versions of this mime had run under a correspondent saying, for example: 'The government today appointed the his-torian and broadcaster Professor Ned Marriott to chair a commission on what British schoolchildren should be taught about their nation's past.' He tried – and failed – to avoid visual-izing the footage being re-used under a correspondent saying: 'He enjoyed a glittering career as an author and broadcaster and confidant of politicians. But the prosecution told another story and today the jury of ten women and two men concluded . . .'

Neatly where it should have been between Berger and Boyd, the Böll was a Penguin paperback bearing a sticker from the University book shop, the £1.95 price an astonishment now, the decimalization a novelty at the time. An edition of the Kafka, from around the same time, had somehow, probably during a house move, ended up on the wrong side of Stephen King and Milan Kundera, but Ned discovered the book he wanted, took it and shuffled the others into order. The Coetzee, however, was in perfect surname sequence, between three Jonathan Coes and the *Collected Lyrics* of Leonard Cohen, and the Philip Roths were bookended by a Joseph Roth, which might have pleased him, and a J. K. Rowling, which probably would not.

The drama bookcase had been pilfered during the period of Dee's fevered desire to be an actress. He found the Mamet as a Royal Court programme-playscript and a Miller *Plays: One*, with marginal notes ('Sexual subtext!') in his more histrionic daughter's large, looping purple-inked script, so she must have returned that one, although she seemed to have filched his Ibsen, which he ordered in a Very Good edition from Amazon's Used and New. Finding the Rattigan, he felt sad.

He created a file and typed the list of novels and plays, realizing that, a suspended professor, he was compiling a reading list for a course on which he would be both tutor and student. 'Summer Seminar: The Literature of False Accusation', he thought. Or: 'Reputation 101'.

The Contents of This E-Mail

To: tkpimm@chatter.co.uk
From: d.j.wellington@ume.ac.uk

THE CONTENTS OF THIS E-MAIL ARE HIGHLY CONFIDENTIAL AND INTENDED ONLY FOR THE SPECIFIED RECIPIENT

Dr Tom Pimm,

As you are aware, you have been charged with offences under the university codes of Bullying & Harassment (incorporating Insubordination).

At this stage of the process, I am formally informing you of the charges against you. These include:

— Sarcastic and undermining comments to colleagues and to customers.

— Undermining the confidence of customers by persistent negative feedback and under-marking.

— Offensive and personal remarks to third parties about colleagues and customers.

— Using sexually explicit and offensive language in teaching situations.

— Displaying favouritist behaviour to some colleagues and customers, through actions such as divisive social invitations and preferential marking practices.

— Sighing – or, on other occasions, seeming to stifle a sigh – during departmental meetings, thereby displaying verbal Insubordination towards senior management.

— Exhibiting dismissive and undermining body language during departmental meetings, thereby displaying visual Insubordination towards senior management.

— Failure fully to cooperate – including dismissive and undermining spoken language and body language – with the Traill Inquiry into the Culture and Conduct of the Department of History.

As these are extremely serious charges, you should be aware that, if even one of them is upheld, your contract with the university is likely to be terminated immediately.

You have chosen to appeal against the charges and I can now inform you that this process will consist of two stages: the Documentation Stage (during which you will be permitted to inspect victim and witness statements and other supporting material) and the Hearing Stage, in which you will be allowed to answer the charges in front of a senior manager from another department.

In order to protect the anonymity of the victims, you will not be able to call victims or witnesses for cross-examination, nor is there any facility for provision of witnesses (to either incidents or character) in your own defence. However, as we understand that the process can be daunting, you are invited to bring with you to both the Documentation Stage and the

Hearing Stage one supporter, who must not be a qualified lawyer but may be the official of a union or other trade organization. In order to protect the integrity of the process, the identity of this supporter must be stated in advance for approval by UME WH.

Although the victims will remain anonymous throughout the process – and their identities will be anonymized or redacted in all documentation – you may believe, from circumstantial evidence, that you are able to make an identification. But, if so, you must not attempt any form of contact with a victim or witness or to disseminate names or complaints in any way. Such actions would be treated as an extremely serious breach of contract and could lead to immediate dismissal before the completion of the process, and without the possibility of appeal.

As you have already been informed, you will, until the completion of the process, be suspended on full pay and with the terms of your contract intact. However, during this period, you must have no contact with any colleagues or customers of UME, including in the latter case (but not restricted to) receiving or returning academic work, taking part in any teaching situations (undergraduate or postgraduate) or granting verbal or written references. You will not – without formal written invitation from the Director of History or a designated representative – enter any premises owned by (or, at that time, occupied by) UME.

In respect of the latter provision, UME WH, as deputed by the Director of History, formally invites you to attend the following two appointments:

For completion of the Documentation Stage, you and one supporter if desired (subject to the conditions above) are invited to attend Conference Room 1 at the Aylesbury Motel (location and directions on Attachment A) between 2.30 and 4.30pm on Friday June 7. You may take written notes but no photographic record will be allowed. A representative of WH will be in attendance.

For completion of the Hearing Stage, you and one supporter if desired (subject to the conditions above) are invited to attend the Ground Floor Meeting Room at the Marlow Motor Inn (location and directions on Attachment B) between 2.30 and 4.30pm on Friday June 14. The hearing will be chaired by Professor Henry Gibson, Professor of Creative Writing at UME. A representative of UME WH will also be in attendance.

Please contact me immediately to confirm these arrangements or express any observations that you may have. Unless otherwise advised by you, we will continue to use this e-mail address as the primary means of communication.

With best wishes,

David Wellington

WH Group Leader, Humanities

House Arrest

Academic historians were the unknown studying the unforgotten. But TV dons were given a little glimpse into what happened to monarchs and politicians. The dilemma of celebrity, Ned had concluded, during the period when he became The Hitler Man, was that it involved alternating irritation at both recognition and the lack of it.

Before his fall, a few days without public acknowledgement (though this generally consisted of people saying that they ought to know who he was, rather than that they did) would have left him fearing that his lucrative spell in the moonlight of TV would soon be over. Now, he hoped to go unnoticed.

And this risk was reduced by a tactic thrown up by his roiling mind. On the first day of disgrace, home from the interrogation suite, he had suffered an agoraphobic panic and sentenced himself, from a reflex that even the pedantic Tom Pimm would surely accept as an irony, to house arrest. Emma, told everything, declared an unconditional belief in his innocence that would have made him weep in loving gratitude if he were the kind of man who could. She e-mailed History to say that he was down with a virus for a while; the secretary, wishing him better, advised that they would require a sick-note after three days' absence. Toby, knowing only that a bad person had been telling tales about Daddy like sometimes happened at school, was baffled and anguished but seemed satisfied with his mother's assurance that the lying toad would be made to pay for this, and gave Ned a tight, silent hug that forced him to sniff away a lurking tear-burst.

What sense could there be in leaving this place of safety and trust? Until, in the early hours of that first sleepless night, he suffered a trembling, sweating, breathless fit of such intensity – his jerking jaw making speech impossible for some minutes – that he feared his heart was failing him. For forty-eight years since he had woken to be told of his father's death, Ned had visualized dying in the night like this and wanted an ambulance calling at once, but Emma phoned the out-of-hours service and provided enough negative answers (to questions about pains, pallor and pre-existing conditions) and personal context (her husband had received some *unexpected bad news* that day, *no not of a medical kind*) to be diagnosed with shock, prescribed deep breathing exercises and camomile tea and advised to see his GP as soon as possible.

Emma drove him there, after he had asked her to put his name into Google to check if there was any mention of his infamy. Despite Claire's reassurance that nothing would break soon, he suffered the common delusion of the humiliated that everyone knew everything.

His concentration shattered by distractions, he had written down his ten main physical problems on an index card. Coughing away throat phlegm (one of the symptoms), he read them to Dr Rafi, who listened without the visible concern that Ned felt was merited by this description of imminent physical collapse, then asked him if he had recently suffered any major shock or trauma.

Ned cleared his throat again. 'Anything I say here – even if it isn't medical – is confidential?'

'Yes, of course. Well, I should say, unless you inform me of your direct intention to kill anyone . . .'

'Oh, no, no, not at the moment.'

'And, even then, I have to check with the General Medical Council.'

'Okay.' When Ned spoke, it was as if a tumour filled his throat. 'I was – I find this almost impossible to say . . .'

'You know, doctors have heard most things.'

'Yesterday, I was . . . arrested . . . a woman I knew – a former girlfriend – has made a claim . . .'

True to his promise, the GP looked no more alarmed than if Ned had mentioned that he had a bug he couldn't seem to throw off.

'She was, I should say, an adult at the time and, of course, I completely . . .'

Dr Rafi raised a hand. 'My friend, all I need to know is what effect this, this . . . *event* has had on you. This has obviously been a huge shock for you. And what you describe – the difficulty sleeping, the digestive issues, extremes of temperature, the muscular spasms and loss of concentration – these, though obviously no fun at all to go through, are classic symptoms of sudden trauma, leading to what we call mixed anxiety and depression disorder. Now, I need to ask you a couple of questions. Do you have people who are supporting you?'

An image of Emma and Toby at the breakfast table. 'Yes.'

'Are there ways in which you fear the situation becoming worse?'

This question, he guessed, was designed to identify potentially unbearable pressure points: a loan becoming due, a court appearance, a tragic anniversary. 'Telling my daughters, I suppose. And, of course, if, probably when to be honest, it all becomes public.'

'And – please do answer honestly, there is a lot of help we can give you – have you had any thoughts at all of harming yourself?'

Yes. 'No.'

'Okay, I know you're a bit iffy about pills.' Ned had followed an intricate regime of diet and exercise for a year before reluctantly submitting to the middle-aged male panacea of statins. 'But I really think you need a little help at the moment to settle you down. I recommend two treatments in particular.'

'And these are – what? – Antidepressants? Antipsychotics? Sleeping pills?'

'Oh, my friend, I don't know how helpful these labels are. Will you try these and then come back to see me in a week? Do you need me to sign you off work?'

Ned had been dreading the call to Neades and now saw a way of delaying the explanation. 'Oh, er, can you? That would . . .'

The doctor reached for a pad, on which Ned could read upside down the words *medical* and *absence*. A counterfoil strip showed that only two or three sign-off chits were left. Ned pictured a Britain in which the workforce divided between those depressed by unemployment and employees too depressed to do their jobs.

'I've given you a month,' said Dr Rafi. 'We can always top-up if need be.'

The dispensary manager, handing him the white crinkly bag with a stapled top, said: 'So, will we be seeing you back on the box soon?'

Ned's scalp instantly pricked hot. The nurse, who would surely know what the drugs were for, must have guessed that he had suffered a breakdown and / or been sacked.

'Oh, I'm, er, having a bit of a break.'

Emma, in the car, asked: 'Are you okay?'

'That's like asking someone coming back from the butchers

if they're vegetarian. I've got a bagful of Swiss marching powder here.'

'Ned, I'm trying to help.'

Ecstatic to find no paparazzi outside the house, he vowed that he would never go out again, except to be bailed, jailed, cleared or buried. But, that lunchtime, his mobile rang and it was a number that he could see no excuse to go on ignoring.

'Nod!'

'Oh, er, Tom. Hi.'

'Look, are you okay? Someone told me – and not one of the nutters – that there's a rumour you're off sick. I said, sure, it's Puligny-Montrachet Syndrome. I saw him going down with a case of it – or possibly two cases – the other night.'

'I'm fine. It's just a bug I can't throw off.'

'Yeah, yeah. Scorch marks at both ends of the candle will be all, I said. Look, Noddy, I need to talk to you . . .'

'Sure. Go on.'

'Ideally, alone and not on the phone. Can I meet you some-where?'

'Do you want to come here?'

'Lads' night out, I thought. I take it you're not actually housebound with this bug, mate?'

'Are you all right, Tom? You sound a bit manic.'

Eating with a Towel

Ned was almost permanently aware of a dampness on back, hands, and scalp. The *cold sweat*, previously a cliché of thriller fiction, was his natural body temperature. The *damp handshake*, until now a detail from campus anecdotes about despised col-leagues, became a daily social obstacle.

But it was when he tried to sleep or eat that his internal engine really went to work. Startled awake, an hour into his first night of shame, by the clammy wetness of the pillow, he first suspected tears – this would have been no surprise, the way he was feeling – in his uneasy sleep. But, if so, then his whole body, from ears to feet, had found a way to weep because every limb and ligament was slicked. After the last, short, pill-induced, deep but bad-dreaming blackout after dawn, reluctantly accepting that he could not force himself under again, he would stand in the bathroom and wring out his pillow-case and UME sweatshirt (the name-claim of the garment never so tested) into the sink, liquid spilling as if they had been soaked in the bath overnight.

Meals released a sauna-drench of warmer sweat. Fantasizing an appetite, he forced down some milk-soaked cereal and coffee at breakfast and slurps or chews of adult baby-food – a gloopy soup, a fluffed risotto – at roughly the times he would once have eaten lunch and supper.

But, as soon as he consumed even lukewarm food or drink, he felt his temperature rising and perspiration blurred his eyes, until he was dabbing them and then his forehead with a napkin that rapidly became soaked. After two days of this, he began to take to the table a hand-towel from the bathroom, staunching the cascade between bites and eventually tying the cloth round his head as an emergency turban.

'Is it – have you asked Dr Rafi – the pills?' said Emma.

'It's the Disgrace Diet,' Ned replied, failing to stop another drop of salty seasoning falling from his face to the plate. 'Apparently, shock either makes you unable to eat or unable to stop eating. And I'm sure most people would rather have the thin version. The health sites say it's quite normal – normal if you're falling apart, that is.'

'You're not falling apart,' Emma said.

The Literature of False Accusation

Summary: On the day of his thirtieth birthday, Josef K., the chief financial officer of a bank, is puzzled by his landlady's failure to bring his usual breakfast. Shortly after 8am, he is surprised in his bedroom by two men in dark suits who tell him that he is under arrest for an unspecified crime. The boss of the arresting agency arrives and holds an impromptu hearing in the room of K's fellow lodger, Fräulein Bürstner, whom the suspect impulsively kisses.

Confined under house arrest, K is subpoenaed on a Sunday to an address where his trial will apparently take place. In the attic of a tenement building, he locates the proceedings but is unable to discover the nature of the charges or even the identity of the judges. K delivers a lengthy denunciation of his situation and the court. Later, K returns to the building, hoping to catch the court unawares, but its sessions have been suspended, although he meets a young woman who seduces him.

Returning to work at the bank, he enters a store room, where he finds that the agents who arrested him are being tortured, apparently for trying to bribe K. The suspect is visited by his Uncle Karl, who urges him to employ Huld, a lawyer, to write a brief for the court, although Huld acknowledges that the document will be tough to construct without knowledge of the crime or the jurisdiction.

A client at the bank suggests that K should consult a man called Titorelli, who turns out to be the official court painter. The artist confides that no defendant has ever won a case and advises K to prolong the hearing for as long as possible.

On the eve of his thirty-first birthday, two men again arrive at K's lodging although, this time, he seems unsurprised and almost welcomes them. They walk to the edge of a quarry, where the men kill K.

Reader Review: While it is complicated to talk of Kafka's intentions – given that his wish, ignored by his executor, Max Brod, was for *The Trial* to be burned and never published – he had presumably planned that any reader would assume K to be completely innocent and falsely accused. And this was fine in 1925 and for most of the book's library life. But those encountering the novel for the first time since 2008 would think that K, being a banker, was guilty of at least something, and possibly everything.

This Penguin Classics edition was dated 1976 which, as the publication history showed a reprint every year at that time, suggested that Ned must have bought the paperback around the time of his life now under suspicion. But, in contrast to some of the other set-texts on Reputation 101, he had no memory of reading it on a holiday or another particular occasion.

Encountered again now, the unexpected police raid induced such lurid visions of his own arrest that it took Ned more than an hour, repeatedly forcing himself to re-read the same paragraphs, to complete the opening pages. But, whatever your doubts about the methods of Operation Millpond, you were at least told upfront what you were supposed to have done, although with the drawback that the media were informed simultaneously.

He recalled the broad details of the obscure prosecution – possibly helped by the film scripted by Pinter with that guy from *Twin Peaks* as the suspect – but had forgotten the weird detail that the state's one mistake – which leads to K finally finding out what little information he obtains – is to have wanted their secret business recorded by a painter. He must ask Tom if anyone had ever made the connection with Nixon and his ruinous tapes.

And it was the 'process' Tom was going through – *Der Prozess* was the original German title – of which the book most reminded him: the opacity of the charges and the difficulty of mounting a defence. But, when he asked his friend if he had ever read or was re-reading *The Trial*, Tom replied that he had just finished it but had come to the conclusion that 'the point about what I am going through is that it is specifically *not* Kafkaesque.'

Snap!

Acceding to Tom's pleas to meet, Ned had tried to calculate the venue where he was least likely to be known. He settled on The Best Cafe, as the premises claimed to be in flaking green and yellow paint above a door that carried no reviews or tourist board rosettes in support of the naming.

A twenty-minute walk from the middle of Winslow, on the edge of an estate, it was on the head-clearing route that Ned took when blocked on a book or script, and he had occasionally come in for lunch or tea, excusing it as thinking time.

Around a hatched serving counter were discoloured photographs of burgers, pizzas, pastas, curries, salads and breakfasts of escalating cholesterol: Big, Super, Monster, All-Day, the latter adding chips to the traditional British morning feast. A laminated poster, with handwritten amendments stuck on, listed these and other options. Curling away at the edges as it became unstuck, a poster on the inside of the door appealed for information about a student who had gone missing in the area two years previously. Ned felt a flash of anger against the police for not focusing their resources on the disappeared rather than an ejaculation from when Harold Wilson was prime minister.

At several tables were groups of four or five men, apartheid-divided by race. They wore the colours of physical labour: the blue cloth of overalls, the yellow shine and grey reflector stripes of Hi-Vis, although the fabric of some of these jackets was now orange, possibly due to the finding that eyes had become so used to the original safety shade that they now screened it out. The men were heavy-set, their chins unshaven and hands smeared with oil or grease, teasing each other in languages that sounded Slavic and African. The throaty shouts suggested the universal man-banter of sex and sport. This business would mainly rely, Ned guessed, on road-gangs and house-builders. Even on this early summer evening, they were chasing down piled carbohydrate – pies, chips, at least one All-Day Breakfast – with, in one concession to the temperature, frequent swigs from chilled cans of beer, empties Stonehenged around each plate. But these were Ned's preferred people now: he doubted that they would have seen even his Hitler programme.

He was trying to decide between water and Diet Coke when the bell-ping of the door made him turn to see Tom, giving an eyebrow-raising sweep of the premises.

'Christ, Nod! Is your next book a history of working-class England?'

'Ha. No, there's something I need to say.' A questioning face from his friend. 'And I got the sense there was something up with you as well?' A grimace of confirmation. 'And, even if we were overheard here, we wouldn't be understood. They do wine but it's almost certainly sub-Lidl. The beer's fine. I'm sticking to water, though.'

'Golly. The old liver took a kicking at the sixtieth?'

'No. It's these pills I'm on. I'll tell you in a minute. They do Budvar or another more generic Eastern European brew?'

'No, no. Water's fine.'

'Tom, I haven't gone AA or anything. You don't have to jump on the wagon just because . . .'

'No. Snap. Doc's bollocking.'

'Really? Jesus, I hope you haven't got what I've got,' Ned said.

His friend looked concerned. 'Ditto.'

'Two bottles of still water, please,' Ned asked the matriarch of the managing clan, which he had classified, without inquiry or evidence, as Albanian. Despite many years of service, she still required him to point to the requested bottles in the fridge behind her.

'Glarse?' she asked gutturally, sounding as if she were cursing them.

'What? Oh, er, no, no thanks.'

Ned paid, aware, as he picked the coins from the pocket change pooled in his palm, that, for the first time in years, he was registering how much things cost. There was a set of empty tables in the furthest corner of the room. As they walked towards them, Tom inspected the wet plastic bottle.

'*English River Water*. I'd be happier knowing which one. What if it's the Thames?'

As they sat down, Ned noticed that builders were looking over at them and laughing, but he remained calm. Being seen with Tom was an imperfect test of conspicuousness. Even before Ned's TV career, people had tended to stare at them because of the huge disparity in their heights. In their early days as lecturers, they had been known as Little & Large, until the tag lapsed, first because younger staff were unfamiliar with the comedy act and then due to the modern terror of drawing attention to a colleague's appearance in any way.

Because of the length of Ned's legs, it was more comfortable, at small tables such as this, for them to sit diagonally rather than opposite each other. Each took a swig of the geographically unspecified freshwater.

'Hwæt?' said Tom. Since a newspaper debate over whether this Anglo-Saxon exclamation was the root of the contemporary 'So', Tom often adopted it to open conversations. 'Who goes first?'

Happy to postpone his own revelation – still unsure of the words he would use – Ned said: 'Well, it was you who asked to meet.'

'Yep. Okay.'

Cancer, divorce, a pregnant or suicidal student, Ned thought, during a pause in which Tom reached into an inside pocket of the linen jacket he had placed on the back of the chair. Ned, in his new default condition of paranoia, stupidly feared for a moment that he was going to be shot or stabbed, until Tom took out two folded sheets of foolscap and shunted them across the table top – plastic but stained to look like wood – where they snagged on some dripped fridge-sweat from Ned's drink.

Opening and straightening the document, Ned expected the first page to be headed by the crest of a hospital or law firm, but it was a smudgy print-out of an e-mail. He recognized the college web-address, although not the name of the sender. At the end of the introductory paragraph, Ned said, 'Christ!', and then, following the list of allegations, 'God!' and, after Wellington's sign-off, 'Fuck!'

'Yes,' said Tom. 'That adaptable little expression pretty much covers it. We're the opposite of Eskimos and snow. One word for the thing we most want and the things we most don't.'

'Did you know all this was going on?'

'Well, I told you at the party that Special had asked to see me . . .'

'Fuck, er, yes.'

'And you remember the Traill hearings? You gave evidence?'

Unsure how much he had told Tom at the time, Ned thought before saying: 'Oh, yeah. But I was in and out in ten minutes. My line was that Special was an unimaginative bag-carrier who had got himself over-promoted by being willing to carry out whatever new madness the management spouted. I threw in a couple of the most famous anecdotes about Daggers and Savlon. Who, I'm assuming, are among your anonymous accusers?'

'Well, I suppose so. And Horny. And probably Rafferty. I'd be amazed if I haven't sighed during those endless meetings and *presentations* of hers and, if I apparently *stifled a sigh* on one occasion, then they ought, in my opinion, to be congratulating me for holding it in, rather than trying to sack me. But the rest of it. It's like getting your passport back with someone else's photo in it. I just don't *know* this potty-mouthed bigot who has apparently been taking my classes. Until now, I thought "What did I say?" was something you said when someone you were talking to went a bit moody. But now I actually sit there for hours, going back over everything I might possibly have said, ever, like Krapp with his tapes. Some of it is just bonkers. I mean, I am absolutely one hundred and ten per cent, as the tennis play-ers say, certain that I have never made *offensive comments on sensitive topics, including disability, religion, and sexuality* or, indeed used *sexually explicit and offensive language in teaching situations*. In a way, it's reassuring because it means that it isn't,

111

like, they've got Watergate tapes or anything. This is just nutters venting and, indeed, *inventing*.'

'Yes, it's pretty vague stuff. This feels like a fishing trip, a witch hunt.' Ned caught himself sounding like a lawyer and recognized that this must be what happens to the accused, forcibly schooled in prosecution and defence. He tapped his finger down the list of alleged offences. 'So. There are . . . *eight* charges.'

'Yes, though over twenty-two years. So, statistically, I have long spells of pleasantness. The student ones, I'm assuming, are darlings who'd grown up being told they were Einstein and then found themselves staring at a ballet skirt . . .'

Even though used to simultaneously translating Tom, Ned was thrown: 'At a . . . ? Oh, a 2:2. When they say the charges *include*, do you think they're using the term properly or loosely?'

'Properly, I'm gambling, and not just as a notorious pedant. Later on, there's an *including but not restricted to*. Hwæt . . .'

Ned re-scanned the e-mail. 'Favouritism? I never really think of that as one of the proper sins like sexism or racism. I mean, not liking someone because they're thick or tricky has to be different from not liking them because they're black or female.'

Tom frowned. 'You'd hope. But these times are mighty strange. And Savlon is thick, tricky *and* female, so she may have played the gender card. At least none of my enemies is black.' Ned glanced across at the nearest non-white diners to check eavesdropping distance. 'Although I suppose that might be seen as discriminatory!'

Ned was fighting an uncomfortable feeling of pleasure that someone else was in trouble as well.

'Have they seized your hard drive?' he asked.

'Lines unlikely to be spoken in the nineteenth century. No, of course, they haven't. You make me sound like a children's television presenter.'

Ned was taking offence until he remembered that his friend didn't know.

'Nod, I want to ask a favour. If you say no, you'll burn in hell for ever but it won't affect our friendship.'

A reference? You won't want one when I've had my turn in the confessional.

'This sort of boxing second I can take along to the stages,' Tom said. 'With a bottle of water and a spare pair of pants, presumably. I'd like to take you.'

'Look, Tom, there's something I should tell *you* first.' They were sweating from the stored heat of the sunny day and the blast from the ovens. Their water bottles had long been empty. 'Shall we graduate to the harder stuff?'

'No. Really. I can't . . .'

'Trust me.'

Slightly resenting Tom for not standing this round – but they had abandoned Dutch rules when Ned's television career made him the richer of the pair – he bought two more frosted bottles. Coca-Cola was running a summer promotion in which the drinks had a name stamped on the side. Ned's Diet Coke was personalized to Debbie, Tom's to Pete. Ned imagined the new religion of significance that must already have been constructed around someone being served a bottle with their own name on it, or the one that was soppily stamped Love.

'Do you think it's a globally customized promotion?' Tom asked. 'Are there Austrians riffling through the chiller cabinet for the Adolf and Eva ones?'

From his new instinct, Ned checked the room for lederhosen or dirndl skirts. He took a sip from his bottle of Debbie, the fizz tickling his throat into a cough. 'So what pills have they got you on?'

'Diazepam, 5mg.'

'Snap. Well, almost, I'm on 10.'

'Get him! Competitive even in anti-anxiety treatments. And another one – 50mg, beat that! – of Sert, Sert something . . .'

'Sertraline?'

'Yeah.'

'It's two-nil, Tom. Dr Rafi's got me on 100 mils of that.'

'Bugger. So you must be twice as fucked-up as I am? Better tell me why, Nod.'

So much of his time now, Ned realized, would be spent trying to delay saying what had happened. In his head, he rehearsed a euphemistic introduction, then staged it. 'You'll doubtless be familiar with the work of Operations Yewtree and Millpond?'

'Christ! You were fucked by Jimmy Savile? I always knew the swots would pay a price for writing to *Jim'll Fix It.*'

'It's not a joke, Tom!' His voice came out louder than he had intended and most of the customers turned in their direction.

'Steady, Nod. They'll think they're witnessing one of Britain's first gay divorces.'

'That's what I mean.' Though his speech was quieter, Ned felt a sob building, almost unstoppably. 'Not everything's a feed for a punch-line, Tom.' As close to a whisper as he could go. 'Two days ago – the morning after the party – I was arrested and charged with a . . .' – scarcely more than mouthing now – 'a sexual offence.'

'Denmark!'

Over the years, in Tom's personal patois, 'No way!' had become 'Norway!' and then, progressively, other Scandinavian nations.

'Fin bloody Land!' Tom emphasized his shock, then moved a hand across the table to find Ned's, which he squeezed. Though his generation's instinctive resistance to potential effeminacy told him to pull away, Ned held on and returned the pressure, moved nearly to weeping by the gesture.

From one of the Balkan foursomes rose a roar that developed into wolf whistles.

'Well, whatever's happened to us,' said Tom, 'it would be worse being a queer in Slovenia.'

Ned breathed out theatrically. 'Do you ever think the trouble – *your* trouble – might come from the sort of stuff you say?'

'You tink I haven't taught that?' Spoken, for some reason, in a parody Al Capone accent. 'And that's what Hells will say when I tell her.' Back to Chicago gangsterese. 'But I never meant nottin by it, Boss.'

'Helen doesn't know yet?'

'No.'

'Wow. Hasn't she noticed . . . Oh, Christ, you're not one of those guys who still pretends to go to work, spinning out cups of tea in a cafe near the station all day . . .'

'No, no. I've told her I'm rush-writing an article to steroid my REF score. Less distraction at the old homestead.'

'Why haven't you told her the truth?'

'Because it's like . . . what *is* it like? Telling your mother you've shat yourself? Telling your *wife* you've shat yourself. Telling your wife you've got chlamydia and she'll have to be tested. Telling your *mother* you've got chlamydia and she'll have to be tested. But worse than all of the above. You've told Emma?'

'Of course.'

'And how was that?'

'Your comparisons are pretty spot on. Except that, look, suppose you have to tell your partner that you've lost all the savings on a one-legged donkey at Uttoxeter – at least horse betting wasn't something you did together. But when you're accused of . . . something like this . . . it's like infidelity but with . . . with . . .'

'Knobs on!'

'Oh, Thomas, please.'

'I'm sorry. I'm sorry. You haven't said what sort of sexual offence? Demonstrate with the salt and sugar cellars if it helps.'

'I'm pleased you find this all so amusing.'

'Nod, *Nod*, there's nothing remotely funny about what you're going through. But I don't take the *charges* seriously. If I'm making light of it, it's because I don't think for one moment that you did it.'

Ned blinked away the sudden blurring of his vision. Emma had to believe in his innocence – or to say that she did – but his friend's confidence – because optional – was more touching.

'So what are you supposed to have done?' Tom asked, with a tenderness that Ned had only experienced from him during the divorce. 'Talking? Touching? Or . . . more.'

'More.' He mentally translated the allegation into words that he felt able to speak. '*Sex*. Sex that started as consensual but then became not so. According to her.'

Tom's face twisted in pain but Ned imagined him feeling the comparative consolation of a below-knee amputee who meets someone who has lost both legs.

'Historic, as the illiterates say?'

'Virtually prehistoric.'

'What? You shagged a pterodactyl?'

'*Tom.*'

'Sorry. What date?'

'1976.'

'Ya have the name of the dame?'

'They sort of tell you not to tell anyone.' A do-me-a-favour face from Tom. 'Okay. Chatham House rules. Billy Hessendon.'

'Silly Billy! But I never thought she was more for you than someone walking across a desert looking for . . . I won't finish that metaphor.'

'Nor did I. In the cell, before they told me, when I was doing a version of Leporello's list, I'm not sure I even included her. You remember the '70s! Although obviously I won't be saying that in court.'

'This isn't going anywhere near a court.'

'You promise? I missed your appointment to head the CPS.'

'Nod, I know it won't be any consolation but you're standing in a big tent and it's crowded. The word in the fields is that Tinky Winky is worried about a knock on the Teletubbies' burrow. The weird thing is that I've looked at guys at conferences – the Juan Dons, you'll know the ones I mean – and thought: you must lie awake worrying about the knock on the door at dawn?' Ned flinched at his memory of the detectives' arrival. 'Some student you screwed in the '70s, who got a Crookback in their finals and now sees the chance to make a point and a few grand. Especially since Prof Allison. But we've kept our Y-fronts clean on that one and now they've come for us with this other stuff. It's just what's in the water. Some countries have typhoid; we have moral fever. What does the Uni-perversity say?'

'I haven't told them yet. What about you?'

'Full-pay suspension.'

'Then I guess I'll get the same.'

'But it – the thing – didn't even happen on campus?'

'I don't think that matters much these days. Claire – my solicitor – says that, with historic victims now, it's guilty until proven innocent.'

'Yeah, I think I've come across that somewhere. What about t' Telly?'

'I've got to see Ogg tomorrow.'

'And, from what we know of old *Odd*, he'll do whatever brings him most money . . .'

'Yeah. Or least trouble. And I think I know which way he'll go on this.'

Tom laughed. 'At least, the job we're in, this doesn't come as a surprise. History repeats itself, the second time as faeces. It's like the days of Savlon-arola!'

'Savlon-arola!'

Ned raised his Diet Coke in a toast and, in that moment, was struck by the twinge of intellectual conception that he had never expected to feel again. Aware that one of the symptoms of his depression was forgetfulness, he made a mental note as literally as he could, seeing a pen writing the key word on the squashy grey cauliflower of his brain.

'So that,' he told Tom, 'is why you won't want me to hold your coat during the Inquisition. And that's fine. I fully under-stand.'

'Bollocks, Nod. You're the even more perfect choice now. The buddy they give you at AA is another drunk, not a life-time abstainer. Do you think I'm guilty?'

Ned tried not to hesitate. 'No.'

'And I don't think *you* are.'

Overwhelmed by this declaration, Ned was worried that he would blub.

'Okay. If you're sure. But if you change your mind . . . is there anything else we can do?'

'I've thought of getting people to write. The thing is, I actually broke up a – Christ, I can barely say this word now – *bullying* thing at Teddy's by going to the beaks. But I don't suppose Gore-Balls – he was the housemaster – is with us any longer . . .'

'He wasn't really called Gore-Balls, was he?'

'Of course he fucking wasn't. Even at Teddy's. He was called McTavish, which became Gorbals, which became . . .'

Tom shuffled his jacket from the back of the chair and hugged the fabric around him, even though at least two of the builders now had bare shoulders, the tunic of their overalls lowered and tied like a cummerbund.

'Thermostat buggered?' Ned asked. 'I've had that.'

'Yeah. From summer to winter in a minute. It's weird. The quack says it's all quite normal, although presumably using the word loosely. Some of his stuff, though . . . apparently counting sheep – counting anything, in fact – for insomnia is a no-no. Apparently it's too stimulating. Who knew? He suggested visualizing every room in your childhood home one by one . . .'

'Really? Well, fine if you grew up in a house with a hundred and eighty-four rooms like you . . .'

'Yeah yeah. Pass me the laughing gas. It does work, though. I'm usually flat out by the back dining room.'

'Okay. I'll try it with our Kentish hovel. Might have to go round twice.'

Tom, presumably warmer now, ended his self-embrace and lifted his empty bottle. 'Should we go on drinking these until we get our own names or a Billy or Daggers?'

'I'd better go. If I'm even slightly late, Emma worries I'm under a train.'

'Ah, yes. Did the quack ask you if you've had suicidal thoughts?'

'Yep.'

'And what did you say?'

'No.'

'And have you had them?'

'*Yes.* What about you?'

'Triple ditto. I think you'd have to have Asperger's not to. Nod, I think we should make a pact.'

'Steady on, Tom. I didn't say I was actually . . .'

'No, you quarter-wit. A *non*-suicide pact. If you ever think you're going to, you tell me. And Vicky Verka.'

'Let's hope it won't come to that.'

'Christ, what I'd give for a big chilled glass of Sav Blank!'

'Rafi said the warning isn't better not, it's don't.'

Tom knocked his empty plastic bottle against Ned's. 'The tranquillizer twins!'

Office Politics

After two days of failing to tell Helen, Tom had phoned her at the magazine from their shared office at home, where he was supposed to be finishing his comparison of the dynastic ambitions and achievements of the Kennedys, Clintons and Bushes.

It was Thursday afternoon, the brief lull in weekly production between the publication of one edition and the preparation of the next. He suggested she found a corner where she wouldn't be surrounded, less from concern for privacy than to soften her to hear something shocking.

The ruse worked. Through the booming acoustic of a stairwell, his wife, slightly breathless – not just, he guessed, from rushing – asked: 'What's happened? Are you okay?'

He knew what she was imagining and found it shamefully useful. Almost any bad news could be broken to a loved one through strategic use of the ABCC tactic: anything but cancer or the children.

'Tom, just *tell* me. Becky or Theo?'

119

It upset him that she was concerned for their kids ahead of him, but would have had the same priorities if the conversation were reversed.

'They're fine. Or, if they're not, they haven't posted it on Facebook yet. Look, Hells, I'm in trouble at t' Mill.'

'What? The cuts?' Her voice lowered in volume but rose in pitch. 'They've *sacked* you?'

ABCCC – children, cancer, or career.

'No, no, no. A "customer" has made a complaint . . .'

Again, he let her fall into an assumption from which he could save her. 'Oh, God! You mean a girl has . . .'

'Women plural . . .'

'Tom!'

'And merry men as well.'

'What!'

A wheezing breathing as she contemplated her husband the sex criminal, the bi-sex criminal. He pitied Ned, for whom the revelation had turned out to be what Emma would most have feared.

'I've been accused of . . . "insubordination" . . . and what they call "bullying" . . .'

'What? . . . Wait, sweetheart . . .'

An echoey conversation with an Australian woman about ad pages in the Weekend Breaks supplement. Heavy heels retreating on stone steps.

'Sorry, I'm back. So they're saying you've – what? Thumped people, threatened them . . . ?'

'Basta! Does that sound like me? This is the problem: everyone thinks it's hitting people or hitting *on* them. But, as far as I can tell, it's stuff in seminars and meetings. Challenging Savlon's idiosyncratic grasp of historical chronology, visibly losing consciousness during bonkers monologues from Daggers in departmentals and so on. And these days, I suppose, failing to tell every student-sorry-client that they've got the best grasp of history since Simon Schama.'

120

'Right. This is crazy, Tom. You're an argumentative smart-arse but you're no bully!'

'Thanks. We'll let you know if we want that as a formal witness statement.'

'How did you find out?'

'From Special.'

'He told you all this on the phone?'

'No, no. I was summoned to the Special Zone.'

'What? But you're on study leave?'

Shit, yes. An improvised lie: 'He sent one of those Aspergery e-mails asking me to come in.'

'Have you told anyone there?'

'One of the Special requests is that I can't. So only Nod.'

'And what does he think?'

'He's . . . sympathetic. *Empathetic* even.'

'That's good. Have they done him for shagging his students?'

'How dare you, Hells! The word is *customer*. No, anyway, I think that's mainly rumour.'

'And they wouldn't touch him because he's their trophy professor.'

Tom didn't react to insult by implication. Helen asked: 'So what happens?'

'Suspension. Which is like study-leave, except you're too terrified to read or write anything. There's an appeal next month.'

'Oh, right. Well, that's when you'll knock – not knock, whatever – sense into them.'

'Remember what I do for a living, Hells. McCarthy, Stalin – the really smart ones have show appeals as well as show trials.'

'Oh, you poor thing. Look, I've got a routine with Marketing at 4pm, but I'll bunk off early and come home.'

'You don't have to.'

'Actually, I do.'

Ned was sure that he would haemorrhage to death. He pressed a towel against the cut but when he pulled it away, blood gushed like an oil-geyser and, in the mirror, the cut showed deep edges that refused to stick together. In a flash of hypochondriac understanding, it struck him that the violent flow was due to heightened blood pressure. Dr Rafi, diagnosing his break-down, had mentioned that his 'bp and pulse are up but not surprisingly in the circumstances' and that they should treat the other anxiety symptoms first.

However, Ned had read about haemophiliacs and patients on blood thinners who die from shaving cuts. Presumably an over-pumping heart could have the same result. In the past, his worst razor-damage had always come on the days of TV recordings – when a combination of fear and the desire to be a screen smoothie led to him pressing too hard – and, as trembling hands were one of the physical effects of his crisis, he had contemplated growing a beard until he was cleared.

But if he walked into the production company office with grey stubble, Dominic Ogg's first reaction would be that despair and disgrace had made Ned careless of his appearance and that, even if he were exonerated, it might be time to try more youthfully telegenic presenters. So he decided to shave and almost accidentally killed himself by slitting his chin.

The thick streaks of blood on the peaks of shaving foam in the basin made the bathroom resemble a scene from *Fargo*. Seeing no way to tie a tourniquet on a jowl, Ned lay on his back on the mat beside the bath, hoping that gravity might reverse the spurting, while he held a clean piece of towel hard against the gash. When he dared to stand and peeled the emergency bandage away, the slight adhesion surely a good sign, only a few drops splooshed onto the bloody snowscape. Reaching across, he tore off four squares of toilet tissue and folded them into a pad that he pressed gently against the sliced skin. The red line remained wet but no longer pouring and, when he pushed, the loo-roll stuck there, a bright outline of the laceration showing through, but with no dripping on his shirt. When he walked, the paper stayed in place.

'Oh dear, you are losing it,' said Emma when he went into her study to say goodbye. 'That stuff's supposed to be for wiping your bum.'

'Ha ha. The jokes are a bonus of you working at home.'

She stayed here most days now, in what he took as a suicide watch. Getting up from the desk – the manuscript of a Monégasque crime novelist for whom she had high hopes, splayed, with several lines yellow-Highlighted – she crossed to kiss him carefully on the lips above the bloody wedge.

'Do you think you ought to take a spare shirt just in case?'

'It's pretty much stopped. And even Ogg wouldn't hit me. He's just going to sack me.'

'He isn't going to sack you.'

'My sort of historian connects narrative with character.'

'He can't. You haven't done anything.'

Self-conscious about his grooming-wound and fearful of being spotted on the train, he drove to London, using Emma's new Golf, the number plates of which were unlikely to have reached newspaper files. He could have parked outside the flat, but convinced himself photographers would be waiting. In the underground NCP just off the slip road from the M40, he paid so much for three hours that he decided, if his TV and teaching careers proved to be over, he would diversify into car parking. Tilting the rear-view mirror, he pulled away the patch, which smarted like the sticking plaster it was imitating. Poppies of dried blood stained the paper. But the cut had closed, though in a thick and crusted line, which gave the impression that he had been in a fight or an accident.

The offices of Ogglebox were in a granite-and-glass new-build in Paddington Basin, just across the canal from the roll-up bridge. In a condition where he was constantly alive to possibilities of catastrophe, Ned imagined Heatherwick's elegant white caterpillar mistakenly curling up and crushing him to death.

In the converted warehouse that the production company occupied, reception was decorated with silk-screen prints of stills from hit series, including several of Ned's. In the past, he had been flattered by this but it now felt like mockery of his disintegrating condition. Giving his name, which seemed to mean nothing to the receptionist, Ned elaborately kept his eye-line from her cleavage, in exchange for her attempt not to be caught staring at the scarlet-and-black scab on his face.

The boss's latest assistant – an unusually tall and thin man whose black suit and matching bob of hair gave an impression of an exclamation mark – showed Ned into the office, a massive rectangle with polished wood floors and ethnic rugs hanging on the walls.

At the long glass desk, Ogg was speaking aloud and ahead, like a newsreader, looking as if he was rehearsing a speech until you saw the flashing phone on the desk.

Waving Ned to one of the navy overstuffed sofas, Ogg continued to speak on hands-free. 'Listen, compadre, if you pass, you pass and I'll have a deal with Four or Sky by sun-down. I'm just frankly surprised because, from what Tony said at the dinner in Edinburgh, this is exactly the sort of project he's looking for.'

During the silence at the other end of the line, Ogg winked at his guest. When the answer came, Ned knew the voice of a genre commissioner, his mournful northern tones further distorted by technology and a concern that he might be failing to enact the Director General's vision.

'So, Oggy, I'll tell you what,' crackled the reply. 'If you give us another day on this, we'll have another meeting here.'

Ogg smirked at Ned and bent closer to the phone. 'I think that's the right call. Would it help if I texted Tony myself?'

'No, no, no. Leave it with me.'

'Great. Same time tomorrow, then. Ciao for now.'

Ogg came over and gave Ned the usual air-hug and back-pat, although stretching the distance between them when he saw the facial injury.

'Bugger! You do that blading?'

The tycoon subtitled his question with a glance to the side of his desk, where a pair of Inline roller skates was neatly placed. For some years, Ogg had been engaged with rival broadcasting barons in a contest to travel with the highest possible degree of modish environmental responsibility. A BBC senior's use of increasingly collapsible bikes – culminating in one so tiny that it could be carried like a Picasso handbag – had provoked Ogg to under-feet wheels, which, characteristically, he now assumed everyone used.

'From Winslow, Dom? Even you wouldn't,' Ned said.

'Gotcha!'

He was also prone to the assumption that the world lived in West London.

'Even so, whoah! Look after yourself, won't you?'

Once Ogg's challengers switched to trundling shoes, Ned assumed, the next step would be to explore teleportation. The assistant entered with a glass tray, perilously hoist, that held the makings of hot drinks. The coffee cups had no handles but, given the executive's enthusiastic embrace of each new design fad, it could be considered lucky that they retained sides and a base.

After a sip and lip-smack, Ogg's face became grave. 'So, what can I say, mate? I'm shocked, concerned, supportive. Everyone here is.'

Finding himself unable to endure the thought of the phone call, Ned had asked Claire to send an explanatory e-mail the day before and to arrange this meeting.

'Before anything else, what can we do for you? Are you sure you have all the support you need – legally and medically? I have to say, if your lawyer lady's half as good with coppers as she is at negotiating TV fees, you'll be fine. Arf Arf.'

One of Ogg's oddities, charming twenty-five years ago, was signalling amusement in the manner of a cartoon character.

'I . . . the hardest thing is to get out of saying: *I'm fine*. Obviously, I'm not. I don't recommend it.'

'You poor thing,' said Ogg, although the words sounded false and self-conscious, like a politician or priest using slang.

'Did Claire also tell you she's convinced this will come to nothing?'

'In terms. Yes, she did. And we all are.'

'You ask what you can do for me? I'd really like to keep on working. Otherwise, I think I'll go mad. I've actually had an idea for a series. I know there probably couldn't be any filming until the charges are dropped but I could get on with the research and the scripting if they'd commission . . .'

'Listen,' Ogg cut in. 'I spoke to the network this morning and they are absolutely clear that they want another Ned Marriott.'

Ned's in-head translator, fluent in paranoia, flashed up a subtitle. He asked: 'What? They're talking about replacing me already?'

'Whoah! No, no, no, Prof. What they mean is that they want another Marriott project . . .'

'Right. Great!'

'Well. But. But they are minded to put a hold on future commissions for the moment until the dust has settled.'

'Okay . . . and . . . what, what *pan* and *brush* would they use to come to that conclusion?'

'My sense of that is they want to see what happens.'

'So if, as I am convinced will be the case, this whole thing is thrown out, then I can go back?'

Ogg seemed to be trying to swallow his lips, the delaying mechanism of someone who always liked to keep two roads open as long as possible.

'I, um, think they'd be looking to see if, whatever the outcome, there had been any brand-damage.'

The obscure threat that had lain almost hidden behind the more solidly obvious fears now took appalling form. Even if the case against him collapsed, the publicity of the suspicion might have an effect indistinguishable from guilt.

'But the archive will be fine. They'll still repeat *The English Witch Hunts* in September?'

'Well, you know, there's a feeling that might also be a distraction in these circumstances.'

'Pulling the programme, though? Doesn't that assume guilt?'

'I don't think anyone is saying or thinking that for one single moment, Ned.' It had been his experience of media executives that the more emphatically they denied something the more likely it was to be the truth. 'And, in any case, it wouldn't strictly have been pulled as the schedule hasn't actually been published. Mate, I know what a nightmare this must be for you and, er, Emma. But the jails are filling up with guys who stood on their doorsteps roaring about lynch mobs when their name came up.'

'Is that what you . . . ? *Fuck* you . . .'

'Whoah! Professor, I'm not saying that *I* don't believe you. But the point is that the network has a moral and legal duty not to be seen to take sides until we have finality on this. They and we also, of course, have a duty of care to you and you must tell me if there is anything you need. Now, please don't get shouty at me again but our legal eagles have asked me to ask you to confirm that you have no reason to believe that any further allegations may be forthcoming from any of the work that you did with Ogglebox?'

Did. Past-tense. 'Jesus. What were you saying about witch hunts?'

'Listen, Ned. We don't think anything's coming but we need to *know* it's not. What happens on location stays on location – until it doesn't – is all I'm saying. At the, er, bottom of this is people suddenly remembering things and so . . .'

'You want me to search other people's memories? The memories of everyone I ever worked with?'

'I understand that this is difficult for you.'

'Tell your briefs . . .' He was halted by the strangeness of the phrase, like something Bart Simpson might say. 'Tell them that I am confident that I have never had sex with anyone against their will, either on your time or on anyone else's.'

Ogg spotted that the response allowed for the possibility that sex had happened during shoots, and considered a rejoinder but then let it go. He softened his voice: 'Claire told me that you understand that this is bound to come out one way or the other?'

Understand but still can't imagine. 'Yes.'

'Okay. This is the pack drill. There will be no pro-active ex-cons . . .'

'Ex-cons. What have criminals . . . ?'

'Whoa! Ex-*comms*. External Communications? Neither we nor the network will ex-comm pro-actively. But in the event of media contacts, network will refer the caller to us, where Press will hold a statement against inquiry. That statement will say that they do not have you under contract at the moment but would not rule out doing so again in future.'

Driving north, Ned squeezed the wheel tightly whenever the radio presenter said *breaking news*, sure that it would turn out to be his fall. He had been too afraid to Google his name that morning, but would do so when he got home.

The Twins

Phee texted: what do you think it is? Px Although she now finally managed not to start with a capital letter, Phee still refused to stoop to abbreviations and misspellings and only added more than one kiss when a boyfriend made an issue of it. Obvs ES sprogging DXXXXX came Dee's swift reply, her own communication rules inevitably antithetical. As Daddy often said, if they really came from one egg, it must have been double-yolked.

Explaining that Toby was going to a Wycombe game with a friend, Daddy had e-mailed on the Tuesday night to ask if he and E (as he always called her in writing) could give his daughters lunch at the flat on Saturday. Fleetingly at the time – and more concretely on reflection – three things struck Phee as strange about this invitation: that he hadn't phoned, that they were eating at home (a disappointment, as he always took them to restaurants far above those she could afford herself) and that the visit to London came so soon after the birthday party.

Until her sister's prediction, it had never occurred to Phee that Emma (ES, for Evil Stepmother, in Dee's formulation) might be pregnant again. She was not sure how to deal with this, not due to the further dilution of her father's affections and assets but because of how the annunciation would have resulted. The tactful desire for their parents to be celibate (the prince's plea to his mother in the play from which her name came) is less easily available to children whose father lives with a much younger partner.

Oh? Phee replied. I was worried it was divorce. The swift reply: Y worry? Result! lol Xxxxx Then, immediately, at the speed of speech. PS If wuz that, he tell us aloan, not with ES. OMG, D not ill????? Xxxx Once raised, this possibility became the only one. She sent a text to her father, D you're not ill are you?, and, after two distracted hours in which she had to keep nudging back the time bar while watching *The Great British Bake Off* on iPlayer, unable to remember for more than a few seconds which patisserie had actually been that week's technical challenge, he replied: No no no. Just boring admin. Tell all on Sat XX

From this reply, Phee divined that Daddy was going to show them, or ask them to witness, a will, or living will: many friends of her generation had reported such morbid parental conversations. When she confided in Andy, he reassured her by saying that he was certain she was right and, against all precedent, even Dee eventually agreed, and the assumption seemed to be confirmed when she checked if she could / should bring Andy to the lunch and got the response: Do you mind if only family biz for moment? No offence. So, intermittently, until Saturday came,

Phee war-gamed the future in which they would have to decide whether to switch off Daddy's machine. As the sisters had historically disagreed on everything, she envisaged a decision reached by the UK Supreme Court eventually being referred to the European Court of Human Rights.

As one of their contests in adulthood involved attempting to arrive first for any social engagement with their father, Phee found herself falling in step beside her unalike double passing the Commonwealth Institute at 12:35.

'Oh, hello,' said Phee, trying to disguise her frustration that their besting schedules had matched.

'Howsa, Little Sis. You still think Living Will?'

'Or just Will. But that'll be fine because he's always had that complete equality thing.'

'Ish.'

They turned down a street where offices and warehouses had been converted into apartment blocks with balconies, the Americanization of London accelerating. Couples in fluffy towelling robes, the sort bought or stolen from hotels, were drinking Buck's Fizz with their feet up on the railings, overlooking joggers jostling past tubby men in blazers and straw-hats heading to the cricket. Phee had thought Daddy was going to the Test match, but he had texted that he didn't fancy the weather forecast.

She asked her sister dutifully: 'How's . . . ?'

One male name had appeared more than others on her sister's recent texts, and she had tried to commit it to a memory from which it had now infuriatingly dropped out.

'Jacob,' Dee helped her. 'Jay-cob.' Phee assumed the second pronunciation was some sort of dirty joke. 'Can't find the dishwasher but knows where a clitoris is. Blokes are a compromise.'

Phee hated the fact that her sister's frankness still made her blush.

'And Andy?' Dee asked.

'Fine.'

An inquiring glance invited more detail, but Phee said nothing.

Like sprinters at the finish, they both speeded up on the steps but Dee pressed the doorbell first, gave her name and was buzzed in.

'Oh, you're *both* here,' said Emma, admitting them to the flat. She seemed to have lost several pounds in the week since the party, which must finally rule out pregnancy. Perhaps it was their stepmother who was ill, which, Phee guiltily thought, would be the easiest of all the potential revelations.

In their childhood, Daddy had perfected a mathematically equal welcome, ducking his head between theirs, placing a hand gently on their hair and pulling them towards one cheek each. But he held them there for much longer than usual, which worried her.

Emma came in from the kitchen and placed one of her signature quiches, browned broccoli breaking the surface like rocks, alongside a bowl of salad leaves, a basket of crusty bread and a plate of salmon fillets steamed almost white. Daddy handed them each a glass of Prosecco but she noticed that he poured water for himself. So he was the one who was sick. She saw him smiling bravely from white sheets, steroid-bloated, baby-bald.

While serving food and picking at it, they swapped bland anecdotes about what Toby, Jacob and Andy had been doing, then compared notes on post-party hangovers and TV binge-watches, but all four knew that this was only a prologue to the troubling discussion to come.

In the silence that followed their exhaustion of the subjects they had in common, Daddy and Emma communicated in blink-Morse before she said: 'There's something we have to tell you.'

We means a kid, Phee was thinking, and the tight line of Dee's lips suggested that she had reached the same conclusion.

'A . . . *woman* – I'm tempted to call her something else – has made an accusation against your dad . . .'

An affair. So another couple of days of rubbish in the papers, with columnists and bloggers ridiculing the names they had been given.

'This was long ago, before you and I were even around . . .'

Emma's tone was so positive that Phee was slower than her sister to understand the implications.

'Christ! You mean like Jimmy Savile?' Dee blurted.

Blood rushed to their father's face. 'No. Absolutely not like, like *him*,' he snarled. 'This, this *woman* was in her twenties at the time . . .'

'So that's . . .'

But the sentence remained unfinished. Indestructible Dee – always called by most observers the 'confident one' of the two women who must never be referred to as 'the twins' – bumped herself up from the table and stumbled towards the bathroom door, one hand flapping towards her eyes to catch tears while the other was cupped in front of her mouth against another gush.

The Press

Fearing the newspapers was a familiar sensation for Ned. The publication of books, the screening of TV series, the reporting of the plagiarism case and the divorce had all brought days of anticipatory belly-ache and nights of churning wakefulness waiting for the smack of rolled newsprint on the mat, or, in London, the drive to Victoria or St Pancras late at night to buy a wet-inked first printing from the bundles unloaded to be transported north.

The outcomes of these vigils varied. Because books might be reviewed within a period of weeks or ignored completely, publication dates brought moments of giddy reprieve, the relief of not having to face a hostile notice overcoming disappointment at the missed possibility of a good one. In contrast, TV critiques and court reports always appeared, if they were going to, on the day or at latest Sunday after they occurred.

But such waits for execution had been changed, like so much else, by the Internet. As part of a mystifying mission to give their content free of charge to readers who in many cases hated the paper, some publications posted book and TV reviews long in advance of the doorstep or bookstall drops, forcing the subjects of judgement either to set up alerts for their own name or risk a tip-off text from a pleased or consoling friend. And as the publications released their web editions during a span of several hours around midnight, the sleepless nights of those under editorial threat were punctuated by surfing to see if any reports had yet appeared. For the most recent TV series and books, he had alternated between staying up until 00:00 to check if any stuff was on the web or going down to the study in the early hours, when he could be sure that all the dailies or weeklies would be up. But if the reviews were good, the composition of prize acceptance speeches kept him from sleeping, and, if bad, bile had the same effect.

In this case, though, the only possibilities were no news or bad news. His pattern became that at 3am – he usually managed a couple of hour-long Diazepam-assisted naps between 9pm (the earliest Emma would let him go to bed) and around 2am – he went down to the study and Googled himself.

As the iBook, iPads and desk iMac were still retained by the police – his impressive loyalty to one brand, it struck him, was now unlikely to result in any more gifted products or the sponsorship deal of which he had long dreamed – he was using a Samsung Chromebook, one of the instinctive economies to which fears for his future earnings and legal fees had driven him. He had sent Emma to buy it, citing fear of being noticed, although his real concern was being spotted in an act of infidelity to Apple. She used a credit card that bore only her name.

To Ned's horror, the second of his pre-dawn trawls threw up

Ned Marriott rapist among the search terms, but, his galloping pulse making his fingers shake on the keys, this turned out to refer to a blog by someone in the History Department of the University of Portsmouth who had moaned that Ned operated as a 'rapist and plagiarist of the work of historians who are far more original and formidable but don't have any mates in the media.'

Ned had accidentally uncovered this sentence many times in the digital swamp but had never previously been pleased to see it. And, for six days, it was the same. There was the generalized brutal abuse that any slightly public figure now had to expect in the online stocks – *Nazi cunt, Blair-fucker, Channel Whore, BBC cock-sucker, fat cunt, Professor Pervert, stupid cunt, paedo cunt, Tory cunt, Marxist cock-fucker, Biased Broadcasting Cunts* – but there was no suggestion that he had done anything wrong except earning money in public. And while the standard cyber-catch was not ideal reading in his paranoid, insomniac condition, he knew that the abuse would be much worse if he were a woman.

So he thought, each morning: *Good.* But returning to bed for the mumbled exchange with a mostly comatose Emma – '*Anything?*' / '*No.*' / '*Good. Sleep then.*' – he was always unable to obey her instruction, dramatizing the time when this nocturnal search would be productive.

Bad People (2)

Although football in England was now almost a year-round sport, there were, even in a World Cup summer, still a few Saturday afternoons that fell empty for Ned and Toby. Usually they played penalty shoot-outs in the mini-goal in the garden, which Ned enjoyed. He had been warned that the major drawback for older or second-time fathers was the impact on the knees of kickabouts but his joints were holding up fine; his only football-related difficulty was being old enough to have seen England win the World Cup, an event that seemed science-fictional to his son.

But, when Ned's post-arrest agoraphobia made him terrified of playing outside – imagining paparazzi behind the hedgerow – he pretended to have a tender patella and suggested that they play *FIFA 2014* in the games room: a Champions League final, with Ned as Liverpool (his dad's home team and now, by adoption, his) and Toby controlling Manchester City, a team based in a place with which he had no personal links but had adopted, in the opportunistic stock-market way of young fans now, in the season that Man City won the Premiership.

Toby's avatar – a six-foot-six-inch striker – had just completed a hat-trick, from another Aguero assist, when Ned's iPhone vibrated and then sounded (his ringtone Stephen Sondheim's 'Into the Woods') on the window-sill that was one of the places with a consistent signal.

Abandoning his defence of a free kick just outside the box – Toby Marriott and Ya Ya Toure standing over the ball – Ned uncurled himself with arthritic inelegance from his semi-lotus crouch in front of the flat-screen TV and grabbed the trembling rectangle. It was a call from a mobile that failed to link to a name in his contacts. Advice from Claire had confirmed his psychotic instinct that, while waiting for exposure, he should be wary of taking calls from *unknown numbers*, fearing the excitedly coiled voice of a newspaper reporter.

'Gooooooalllllllllllllll!!!!' shouted Toby as the call rang out and went to voicemail. An elaborate goal celebration was going on in the corner of the room, the lampstand a corner flag, as the 901 alert came on and Ned accepted it.

He knew the helium-squeak Ulster tones immediately. 'Kevan Neades on Saturday afternoon, 16:15. Professor Marriott, would you be able to give me a call at your earliest convenience?'

The mobile number given and repeated. Toby made the L-sign with his fingers. 'Loser! Loser! 5–1 to the Blues!'

'Tobes, do you want to go and get a couple of Diet Cokes? I've just got to take this call.'

As the back of Toby's light blue replica shirt vanished from the door frame, the last number redialled was answered: 'Neades.'

There was a foreign echo on the line, a hint of insect chirrup in the background. The Director of History had a weekend place in France. Ned identified himself.

'Ah, yes. Thanks for calling back so swiftly.' The voice was as clear and cold as in the office. Ned, abroad for the weekend, would be half-tanked by now, pre-Diazepam at least, but Neades was teetotal, for reasons of either health or Presbyterianism. 'First off, I should ask you: are you bearing up under all this, Ned?'

Unable to face cold-calling Neades with news of his notoriety, Ned had asked Claire to send a letter.

'Well, I wouldn't wish it on you.' Because so few people knew yet what had happened, Ned was rarely asked how he was coping but already had a scripted response: 'Luckily, I've got good family, friends, doctors, lawyers.'

'It's good that you have the support you need,' Neades replied, the sentence as lacking in inflection as a foreign language student parroting sample phrases.

'And my mate Pimm is going through something similar, which helps in a funny sort of way.'

One of the director's signature long silences was filled with insect noise. 'I couldn't speak to that.' Another pause to underline his discretion. 'As I will be informing your legal representative by letter, you will be suspended on full pay. This is a precautionary suspension, under established protocols. The University makes – and intends – no judgement on the situation in which you find yourself and will make no decision until its outcome.'

Was Neades reading from a brief or did he now speak effortless bureaucratese? 'The business is winding down for the summer. But, internally, for the moment, your customers will be advised that you are on a leave of absence for "personal reasons". Externally, the University will make no statement pro-actively. Against inquiry, we will advise of the advice given to your customers.'

Toby, prone in front of the television, was fiddling with in-game tactics screens, switching to his favoured 1–1–8 formation. A picture came to Ned of his son struggling through a rolling maul of reporters and photographers outside the door.

'And if . . . if . . .' He ignored the apocalyptic prompter whispering *when*. 'If the actual . . . reason . . . becomes known . . . then . . .'

After lengthily exploring his trademark option of not talking at all, Neades answered: 'Then, not pro-actively but against inquiry, Ex Comms would advise of your precautionary suspension.' More dead air with a cicada soundtrack. 'As I am required to do, I've passed the details on a confidential basis to WH. You should expect a call to see if we can offer any support during what we are aware must be a very stressful time for you and for your family.'

In the final sentence, the English pupil reached vocabulary and meanings so far beyond his comprehension and delivery that it had the sat-nav staccato of a phrase generated from a digital word-bank, as did: 'Is there anything that I have said to you today that requires clarification?'

'No.' Ned hated himself for the inculcated manners that made him finish the call: 'Thank you.'

Through the window, he could see Emma, kneeling beside a flower bed, doing some of whatever it was that people who liked gardening did. As he watched, she put down the trowel, wiped her hands on her gardening jeans, leaned back and kneaded tension from her neck and shoulders.

Ned looked back to where Toby was practising penalties, scoring every time to either side.

'Sorry,' he said, then, with forced jauntiness: 'So. How many minutes have I got to score five?'

'Yeah, that's so going to happen.' Solemnity descended over Toby's gap-toothed grin. 'Was that one of the bad people, Daddy?'

The Literature of False Accusation (2)

Summary: In a Norwegian town, mainly dependent for employment and wealth on the curative legend of the local spa, the medical officer, Dr Tomas Stockmann, comes to suspect – from the numbers of bathers suffering a gastric bug – that the healing waters are diseased. Confirming this with the most modern scientific tests, he believes that what would now be called his 'duty of care' is to close down the baths, while a completely new water supply system is installed, and expects to be thanked for saving lives. Instead, he is accused by the local newspaper and the business community – led by the mayor, his brother Peter – of ruining livelihoods by destroying tourism. Dr Stockmann has his house stoned, is denounced at a public meeting and is driven out of town with his family.

Reader Review: The version of *An Enemy of the People* on Ned's shelves was the script of the production he saw at the Playhouse Theatre in London in late 1988. From the dates, Cordelia and Ophelia must just have been born but he had no memory of whether he had taken Jenny to the theatre or someone else. This adaptation had been written by Arthur Miller in 1950 and, three years later, heavily influenced Miller's own consideration of a wrongheaded mob, *The Crucible*.

Ned had bought the script after seeing it performed because, at the time, he identified strongly with the evidence-faced intellectual purity of the scientist, seeing in the modernity and justified certainty of Tomas something of his own position in relation to the fusty professorial time-servers of the UME History department. This identification may have been encouraged by the fact that Miller's Dr Stockmann was explicitly a self-portrait of the playwright's virtuous opposition to the McCarthyite witch hunt.

But, re-reading the text a quarter of a century later, Ned saw that the dramatic balance was more complicated. Tomas can be regarded as an unpleasant zealot obsessed with personal as much as scientific progress: declaring that the baths are poisoned, he can't resist adding that he has been proved right, having told the local politicians years before to put the health centre in a different place. And Ibsen, overlapping with Freud, suggests that Tomas and Peter are partly driven to disagree by sibling hostility; a dynamic familiar to Ned from his elder children.

His discovery about the water permits him to piss on his brother's parade. Was it possible that there had been a less brutal solution than the total closure of the baths? (Ned made a mental note to Google the history of chlorine and filters.) Certainly, Dr Tomas Stockmann now seemed to Ned less unequivocally a victim than had been the case before.

Our Lady of Sorrows

There was still a supermarket opposite the war memorial, although the blue facade of the Mac Fisheries (a now vanished franchise) of his childhood had been replaced by the green, as familiar a colour in comfortable England as well-trimmed grass, of Waitrose.

He found a metered parking bay on the road that sloped down from the church. Despite the chilly breath of the BMW's air-conditioning, he had been forced to blink and shake away sweat several times as the M25 – the slow lane, the only speed at which he now felt confident to drive – blurred before his eyes. And, since stopping, he had felt a thicker film of perspiration dampening his scalp. Even before his fall, Our Lady of Sorrows had always unnerved him. He officially linked this with memories of his father's funeral, but suspected that guilt at his fugitive (he was not yet ready to say lost) faith was another trigger.

Visiting his mother at the time of the divorce, Ned had come to understand that anyone prone to depression at the evidence of passing time is best advised to avoid – along with squash courts, TV re-run channels and old photograph albums – the high street of their childhood town. Though belonging to a profession that chronicled epochal progress, Ned felt no less dismay than non-historians at contradictions to his memory of the place he knew best.

Some changes were merely name-deep – Abbey National translating into Santander, Kentucky Fried Chicken becoming KFC – but most sites had converted their purpose, and generally in one direction. Two shoe shops, Universal Toys, Best Records, the Cork and Bottle wine bar and Art and Craft Supplies were all now coffee franchises, as was Goodread Books, where his mother had taken him after Holy Thursday mass and told him that he could choose any two paperbacks he wanted; a reward, he later realized, for still coming to church with her at seventeen during the Easter holidays, when so many of her friends' children had 'lapsed'.

His first selection had been Geoffrey Elton's *England Under the Tudors,* which, forty-three years later, was still on the shelves of his study, its margins bearing perky, Biro-ed notes about 'ecclesiastical corruption!' and 'Katherine Catholic!' He was about to re-read the second Christ-bribe, concertinaed from attention and spotted with holiday sun cream: Rattigan's *Plays 2,* which he had picked in memory of his father and because one of the plots he knew best had appealed to his vivid teenage sense of being obscurely persecuted, although not as strongly as it spoke to him now.

Martyred with hay fever all his life, Ned had never had a feel for flowers, depending, when courting women, on Interflora to deliver bouquets which, more than once, he had removed from the bedroom while their recipient was in the bathroom, in order to prevent his climax consisting of unstoppable sneezing. But he knew, from emergency birthday presents for his mother, that Waitrose sold single orchids in a ceramic vase. This floral ostrich neck seemed to him a paltry gift but Emma had assured him that they were a prize for the horticulturally literate, and this had seemed to be true in the past.

He used self check-out to avoid the risk of being identified, or having an awkward conversation with a clerk who turned out to be the child of a schoolfriend. Walking back up the hill towards the car, he was averting his eyes from Our Lady of Sorrows on the opposite side when a woman's voice, aged to a croaky alto but still mentally re-dressing him in shorts beneath a low desk, called: 'Is that who I think it is lurking under that baseball cap?'

Mrs Ricks. Children have no sense of age but, as she had been a Mrs not a Miss at Saint Barnabus, she was probably in her thirties then, so eighties now. He had a clearer memory of her than of other teachers because, as a friend of his mother through church, she had been at Mum's sixtieth, seventieth and eightieth, and his nephews' First Communions and Confirmations.

She blinked at the flower he was holding. 'Oh, Lord, have I missed your ma's birthday?'

'What? Oh, no. I try not to be one of those once-a-year sons. This is a non-particular visit.'

'Bless!'

But when she read it in the papers, she would guess.

She nodded a crash helmet of grey perm towards the spire. 'I'm lighting a candle for Desmond. It's his anniversary. It has to be locked these days because of – well, vandals and, er, satanists, I suppose – but the cleaners and counters have keys.'

He felt a nostalgic pang for the comfortingly clubbish rituals of religion. 'Yes. Mum said. I always wonder how many devil worshippers there actually are breaking into churches, especially in Kent.'

'You may say that, Edmund. But Monsignor has stories that would make your eyes water.' Her tightened mouth widened into a smile. 'I was watching you the other night,' she said, using the phrase common to stalkers, spies and TV viewers. Even now, when his deepest desire was to become invisible, there was egotistical pleasure in recognition.

'What was it?' his admirer asked herself. 'A repeat, I think.

Late. I couldn't sleep. No. I can't remember. Anyway, you were as good as ever.'

'Thank you.'

'Are you working on another "blockbuster"?'

'We're sort of between series at the moment.'

'I still get a "kick" out of it when I tell people I taught you – sometimes they're thrown at first because I'll always call you "Edmund" – but then they say . . .'

Oh my God, not the rapist?

'. . . *that* Ned Marriott,' she concluded. Her face was instantaneously pained and he wondered if she somehow knew or suspected, but the grimace was explained by her saying: 'Did your mother tell you about Patrick Rigby?'

Class 6, which was Year Whatever now. Ginger, freckled, once caused a storm by teaching ten-year-olds on the playground (including Ned) what turned out to be an IRA marching song.

'I'm not sure.'

'They buried him last month. Pancreatic cancer. Four children.'

He suddenly wanted – a general instinct intensified by their connection of half a century ago – to tell her what was happening and that she must not believe it.

Mrs Ricks was also remembering St Barnabus. 'It's the school's seventy-fifth anniversary next year. I'm sure Monsignor will be in touch about asking you to do the honours.'

'Is it? Wow. So it must have been the Silver Jubilee around the time when I was . . . I don't remember any celebrations . . .'

'Do you know, Edmund, I think you're right . . . ?'

'But I think people generally made less fuss about stuff then. Actually, you know, I think they might be better off with Father Tony.'

Anthony Glascock, presumably tormented by his cohort for his surname, now St Barney's other publicly-known alumnus, as 'Father Tony' (shrewdly Christian name only), a Jesuit priest and regular contributor to *Thought for the Day* and *Songs of Praise*.

'Ah,' his old teacher said. 'Of course, you'll be very busy.'

Mrs Ricks' eye-lids and lips pressed together in parallel, a never-forgotten expression that instinctively quickened Ned's heart-rate and loosened his sphincters, which were already less reliable than when he had disappointed her as a child.

'It's just that I've got a book to finish,' he told her, then tried a joke: 'You of all people wouldn't want me being late with my homework.'

The affectionate metaphor either escaped her, or was ignored.

'Well, it must be all go for someone like you,' she sighed, at the very edge of courtesy.

He glanced pointedly at the orchid as if it were a watch. 'Well, I don't want my mother's burnt beef on my conscience.'

'No, of course. Tell her I'll see her at counting.' A roster of parishioners totted up the cash and 'planned giving' envelopes after mass. 'Keep up the good work, Edmund.'

'Thank you, Mrs Ricks.'

'Oh, silly boy, I've told you: surely Harriet by now.'

But, after a career in education, she must know that calling former teachers by their first name remained forever an intimacy as forbidden as incest. Watching Mrs Ricks fumble-juggle with the keys at the side door of the church, he wondered if he should help her, but was distracted by a premonition of the humiliation to come.

Turning to look down the hill at the town, he thought: *once they know, I will never be able to come back here.* The Marriott Cup for Excellence in History would be discontinued from future St Barney's prize-givings, like Savile's messianic gravestone being levelled in Scarborough.

As he settled in the car, Ned felt the dampness of his clothes against the seat. He shakily located in his jacket pocket the wrap of Diazepam and swallowed another 5mg with a slug of his traffic-jam Evian, already tepid from the morning sun.

On the Common, a groundsman with a heavy roller was squeezing any remaining bounce from the batsman's paradise of a pitch on which the teenage Ned had once scored an undefeated 130 for the village team. As he turned onto Westside Road, his pulse, despite the drugs, started thudding. Going home had felt as portentous as this only once before, when he came to tell his mother that he was leaving Jenny; but divorce was within the rehearsed fears of a mother, even a devoutly Catholic one, for her children.

Most writers of profiles of Ned Marriott mentioned the coincidence (which they called an 'irony') that a historian who had written about Henry VIII had grown up in a Tudor priory, although no one had noted the actual historical irony of Catholics living in a building once seized from their church.

Delaying his entry, using the excuse of allowing the sedative more time to take effect, Ned looked up at the three black-and-white triangular eaves, which, in his childhood, he had imagined as the sharpened cowls of scowling nuns. Inside were the rooms he had mentally toured, on Tom's advice, as a sleep aid.

Unless abused or embarrassed by their family, most people are soothed by the sight of the home they grew up in: the memory of certain summers, birthdays, Christmases, meals, sleeps. Ned floated for a moment in the warm calm waters of his past. Then he was hit by the rip tide of the circumstances of his return. He lifted the vase from the passenger seat, the crackle of the cellophane sounding like stamped gravel in the sound-proofed cell of the vehicle.

His mother, having heard the engine, was already standing at the open door. He felt an ache at her smallness and frailty, deep into a parent's final journey of becoming her children's child. Ned stooped to kiss her cheek and then, taller than the sixteenth-century norm, ducked through into the hall.

'Was the traffic bad?' she asked, which he took as a rebuke for being later than he had said.

'It's never not now, is it? England is a building site. I got you this.'

He passed over his guilt gift.

'Oh. You don't have to, Jack, er, Ned.'

Though she had so far avoided diagnosable signs of dementia, his mother increasingly suffered from the geriatric tendency to alternate family names, calling her son after his stepfather or occasionally, more happily, his father (Val, short for Valentine, one of the two gentlemen of Verona). More and more, when she spoke, an unfound verb or noun was replaced with 'thing'.

I am bringing you a flower and also shame that will long outlive it, boomed the newly melodramatic inner voice that medication could apparently do nothing to suppress.

Beef in its final stages of roasting – his desert island smell – infused the reception room. Ned's stepfather was meticulously levelling out a glass of sherry that stood beside a generous whisky already poured.

'Ah, Edmund,' he said, without turning. 'Welcome.'

Jack Starling used a towelling slop-rag to dry a hand that he then abruptly stuck out in front of him. The Marriott-Starlings would never become one of those blended families, seen in American movies, in which everyone hugs each other regardless of blood. Ned returned a stiff stranger's handshake.

Like a game-show host with the last two prizes, Jack held up bottles of Diet Coke and elderflower cordial. 'I'd offer you a proper drink but you'll be driving.'

Ned pointed to the low-fat cola. He looked at the name on the side of the bottle and let out a sigh he had intended to be silent.

'Nick was the closest we could get,' the resident bartender explained. 'Your mother hasn't found a Daphne yet either. Of course, we Jacks are laughing. Damn pity I can't stand the stuff!'

His mother and stepfather sat on the sofa, with a bodily closeness that always made Ned – choosing what had always (did Jack know this?) been Dad's chair – feel like Hamlet.

They sipped or slugged, depending on beverage and temperament, their drinks.

'You're sure you don't want a glass and ice for that, Edmund?' Jack asked.

Ned raised the bottle to his mouth in reply, prompting Jack, in a rearguard action for social manners, to hand him a red linen napkin. When Ned had swallowed the acidic fizz, he said: 'Oh, Mum, when I stopped in town, I met Mrs Ricks . . .'

'Mrs . . . ? Oh, *Harry*.'

'*Harry*? Mum, I haven't got as far as Harriet yet, so that one's abridged too far for me.'

'What?' She laughed, always his best audience. 'Oh, very good. You should use that one.'

'I have.'

Highly trained, as an insurance broker and obsessive golfer, in artificially sustaining conversation, Jack contributed: 'One of my primary school teachers was named on the door as Miss U Pagett. All year, we scratched our little, nitty heads, wondering what on earth the initial could stand for, and eventually decided that it could only possibly be Umbrella! Of course, in retrospect, obviously Ursula.'

As his mother giggled, Ned busied himself with drinking. For a few minutes, their small-talk took its usual course, Jack arguing that Ed Miliband's adenoidal voice and Communist father made him untenable as a potential prime minister, while Ned riposted that David Cameron's Etonian tones and stock-broker daddy hadn't prevented him from being an amateurish plodder in office. Both men then joined in incredulity at Ned's mother's continuing tolerance of Nick Clegg.

They discussed what they had recently seen on television. Mum said she had been enjoying the honourable thing – *Honourable Woman*, Ned corrected her – but Jack said that he had given up infuriated, not knowing what side he was supposed to be on, the Jews and the other lot being as bad as each other in his humble opinion.

More drinking in silence, which Ned broke with: 'Er, Jack, if it's okay with you, there's something I really need to discuss with Mum alone? It's a bit . . .'

Imperfectly disguised fury on Jack's face, at being ordered out of his own living room; terror, not at all dissembled, in his mother's features, as she computed what her son might be willing to tell only to her.

'Darling?' Jack asked his wife to adjudicate.

'Oh, er.' Familiar with being cast as conciliator in their ad hoc clan, she pleaded with her eyes for Ned to withdraw the dilemma.

'I'm sure Mum wouldn't mind if there was stuff your girls wanted to discuss with you,' Ned said.

His mother redirected her optical semaphore towards Jack, who reluctantly stood up. 'There's an e-mail to the council about double-parking by the Common that I can be drafting. Grub up in, what?, twenty minutes?'

'Yes, love, I'll call you.'

The hospital consultant turns over the cover on a folder of notes, the job interviewer peers at an applicant's CV, the politician is asked on television a question that dare not be answered truthfully. Some pauses are as ominously loaded as storm-clouds.

'So,' his mother said. 'You've got me worried now, of course.'

'Mum. First of all, I'm really sorry to have landed you with this, and all I can say is I'm as shocked as you will be . . .'

'Edmund, just tell me,' she said, gently but tensely.

The pressure of wanting to impress and protect her was still too much and all he could say was: 'Look, I've got a serious problem.'

'Oh, dear,' she said, never a swearer. 'It's not . . . not . . . everyone you hear about seems to have . . . *cancer* . . .'

The word was spoken as vehemently as an expletive. And her guess was good enough; it was a code people used: *the doctors have found a problem.*

'No, not cancer,' he said, wanting to add, ruling out the second greatest societal terror: *and not paedophilia either.*

'But you don't look well, Jack, er, *Edmund*. You work too hard for your age.'

'Well, I *am* ill, sort of, but not . . . it's the *stress* of . . .'

'That's what I'm telling you. They didn't think about pressure then, but I've always been convinced it's what killed your dad . . .' A second possibility struck her. 'If it's you and Emma, I'd be sad, very sad for Toby, and you know my views, but you'd still be four short of Henry VIII . . .'

'Mum, there's no easy way of saying this: someone has made an accusation of . . . sexual assault . . .'

She gave a harsh rasping out-breath as if a bullet had just hit her lung. Her cheeks coloured as she sniffed and blinked. A memory flared of his mother turning away or leaving the room in the years after his father's death. But she was looking straight at him, although foggily, as she said: 'Someone where? At work? The university or the television?'

'No. Well, not now. In the '70s. What they call . . .'

'Historic,' she completed, fluent in the dark jargon of the days.

'Yes.'

'And not . . . not . . . Oh, *Edmund* . . .'

'Not children. Absolutely not,' he returned the service by completing her sentence. 'She was in her twenties. As was I. At the time.'

So, against all expectation, a conversation so far filled with good news for his mother: her son was neither dying nor a child-abuser. Ned now had to address the question of what he was. *Allegedly* was.

'Do you remember Betty Thomas?' his mother asked.

'I don't think so.'

'Yes, you do. Eliza Thomas, the year below you. There was a younger one, Imogen, as well. She . .'

'Which one is *she*? You just mentioned three different women?'

'Betty Thomas. She was left by her husband when the children were little and married again, to a teacher, who had children of his own and one of them, who's a deputy head in Lincolnshire, tried to take the iPhone off a boy who was using it in class. But, because he touched him, the parents cried thing. Instantly suspended. Now he's banned from teaching for life.'

If you want to reassure me, Ned thought, tell me stories of justice, not injustice.

'Yes, Mum. But that's not quite . . .'

'What I'm saying, though, is that, these days, if you touch someone on the arm, it's sexual assault. Girls of my generation, we used to get home from work with our backsides black-and-blue from all the pinching. And, at the Christmas party, you could have done with an . . . an . . . *armoured* bra . . .'

'Yes, well, that's more sexual harassment. That isn't what it is in my case . . .'

Another silence heavy with the threat of what was wanting to be said.

'Oh, Edmund . . .'

'What I've been accused of – and obviously I completely and utterly reject the allegations – is . . .'

He knew what the next word had to be but, like an actor whose tongue is suddenly stalled by fear, he could not say it. Nor could his mother; her lips made the shape without any sound coming out, in the way that women of her class and generation had found for taboo usages. Mum voiced the excremental expletive as 'S-H-1-T', so perhaps would eventually find an equivalent formula: 'R-8-P-E.'

'Yes,' he confirmed.

'Oh.' The speed of the blood-rush to her face made him think of an upended egg-timer. 'How. Are you . . . well, you can't be all right but . . . is Emma being supportive?'

A mother's first instinct, then, not to suspect her son but to question her daughter-in-law.

'She knows it's open season at the moment on . . .'

He stalled, unable to call himself a celebrity. But she understood and, clearly not having considered this explanation, seized on it: 'Yes. You're a sitting thing, someone like you. So, this is some *little madam* trying to get some money?'

Previously used for loud or show-off conduct on public transport, Mum's preferred phrase for a misbehaving female now effortlessly stretched to include the malicious invention of claims of sexual assault.

'I don't know what reason the person has.'

'But you know who it is?'

Ned had to wipe his brow with the napkin Jack had given him.

'Do I . . . ? The police give you a name.'

'And you knew her?'

Such situations exploded one question – *did you do it?* – which wife, lawyer, friend and now parent all carefully avoided asking, for reasons of personal or professional etiquette.

'Well, I . . .' His mental speech preview system deleted *came across her*. 'She was someone I . . . knew. I don't recognize at all the situation she describes.'

Although an accusation of murder would clearly have been worse, the denials – *I wasn't there, I didn't do it, what would my motive have been?* – were at least clearer-cut; the allegation he faced had shades of interpretation, especially with a mother, where even the matter of whether sex had taken place could not be raised.

'The fact is, Edmund, that a lot of these things come to nothing.'

'Yes. But some of them do. And there's no way of knowing which one you're in.'

'At least you're sure to have absolutely the best lawyers.'

He told her how events might develop from now on, and their possible length, at which she grimaced.

'And, Mum, I don't think Tim needs to know yet . . .'

'What? Well, with the time differences, we don't . . . and it's hardly the type of thing you'd say on Scope.'

This time, he did not correct her pronunciation to Skype. 'I mean, obviously, if it gets into the papers . . .'

The unhealthy blush again. She hadn't thought about the humiliation being public.

'And, if that happens, Mum, when it comes out, you might be rung up or even have papers outside. The price of democracy is that they can get your address from the electoral register. The closest to nothing – literally nothing – that you can say, the better.'

'Well, Jack would most likely answer the phone or the door.'

Disgraced Historian's Stepfather Urges Death Penalty.

But he was relieved by how well the conversation had mainly gone, even though most parents, he knew, assumed the best of their children. In documentaries, he had seen mothers holding candles outside Death Row as their serial-killing off-spring were strapped to the gurney inside. Some parents, though – in America, especially – never got the chance to disbelieve the charges, getting a text telling them to turn on the TV news, which was reporting that their kid had shot a few dozen fellow students as a prelude to suicide.

Mum said she had to go to check the potatoes, but she went first to the room at the back of the house that they called the Office, where Jack would be savouring the best phrases to denounce council road-flow policy. Ned heard whispered voices and after lunch, at which Jack began but then suddenly aborted a discussion just before he mentioned an arrested children's entertainer, his stepfather reached for his mother's hand, held and squeezed it, and said: 'Edmund. Whatever happens, we'll support you. You should know that.'

Home Truths

'Are you sure Ned's a good idea to take in with you?'

'He's my best friend, Hells.'

'Yes. But he's not exactly standing on the high moral ground, is he?'

'He's the Executive Dean's darling.'

'*Was*. But, anyway, I thought he isn't allowed to go into the university either, while *he*'s suspended.'

'Yeah, well, that's why the hearing takes place in some after-noon love motel.'

'Do they have those round here, sweetheart?'

'Trick question. Very funny. So I've heard.'

'The point is, love, that at least some of the rubbish about you is from women – and you say that HR are mainly female – and so is it really wise to have a rapist in your corner?'

'No way is Nod a rapist.'

'Tom, we *hope* he isn't; we don't know yet.'

A Silent Epidemic

As a woman who had acted for defendants in rape trials, Claire was either a credit to her profession or an enemy to her gender, depending on your perspective, and she knew people who held each opinion.

On the first occasion, she had panicked that conniving to make the CPS or the jury distrust a rape victim was treachery to feminism, and felt relieved not to be a barrister, required personally to subject the tearful account to scepticism. During long silent cross-examinations of herself, she had more or less come to accept that a claim was merely an allegation and that the strength of a legal system depended on rigorous examin-ation of all charges. A lawyer who worked on the defence of a serial killer was not suggesting that those who had died were lying but seeking to ensure that the evidence, examination and sentencing were scrupulous and fair.

Even many liberals, though, seemed to suspend their respect for *habeas corpus* when it came to rape. She had seen and heard it called 'the worst of all crimes', a description originally reserved for murder. As a woman, she could almost follow the logic of this view because the victim of rape remained alive with memories that may damage her possibility of love and family but, as a lawyer, she knew that all allegations had to be chal-lenged. The presumptions of a state were not always safe.

She had friends – and, in fact, a sister – who sincerely argued that the best way of increasing convictions – at a time of a 'silent epidemic' of sexual assault, with as many as 'three million unreported rapes annually' according to some accounts – would be simply to accept what women said had happened. But her legal training made her wonder how claims that were never made could be tallied so exactly and to baulk at the thought of assuming the total sincerity of any plaintiff.

Her profession had introduced her to people who hadn't murdered anyone but swore they had, from motives of deluded celebrity-seeking or protection of a loved one. She had been utterly convinced of the innocence of a Miss Marple-ish old lady, who was later shown in court to have redirected to herself, with an ingenuity a master fraudster would have envied, legacies her late husband had intended for the children of his first marriage.

If we always knew when someone was telling the truth, there would be no law or, probably, life.

And, in cases of rape, testimony was especially suspect. After hurt denunciations from female friends – and the many cases of famous Tweeters forced to 'apologize unreservedly' for advancing much the same case – Claire was now careful never to differentiate between the effects or severity of rape by a knife-wielding stranger on the towpath and the man who refuses to take no for an answer after drunken dinner in a flat.

But there was a distinction between such incidents in the possibility of reconstructing to the satisfaction of a jury – through forensic, narrative and character evidence – what had taken place.

And, while it was no longer worth risking the Twitter death threats and severed friendships that came from saying so, she continued to believe that there was a difference between being assaulted while out jogging and a date gone wrong. A man who jumps out from behind a tree and attacks an unknown woman cannot plausibly claim that his intentions were misunderstood, whereas relationship or recreational sex were

153

notoriously subject to disconnecting levels of desire, technique, pleasure and regret.

She suspected that even the most mutually devoted lovers, sent to separate rooms and asked to describe their most recent encounter, would differ significantly in the vocabulary and interpretation that each gave to phases and sensations they had both consentingly enjoyed. So how much more scope was there for warring reports if the encounter was casual, unhappy or, as seemed to be the case among so many of the young now, conducted while blind drunk?

The law was a bad forum for adjudicating what had happened in private between two people. A college boyfriend and her choice of career had combined to give Claire a silent joke. Q: What do the law courts and Danny the Fresher Chemist have in common? A: Neither of them are much use in the bedroom.

Although armoured by such rationales, she still felt unease about asking an intern to search newspaper databases and the web for references to Wilhelmina / Billy Hessendon-Castle under the various iterations of her name, seeking embarrassing or contradictory facts that could be used to scare the CPS into dropping the case or, if not, then to undermine the defendant in court. Ned Marriott had told her that political campaigns called such trawls 'opposition research' – she had her own term for them – and they had become a standard legal tactic now that even an upper-class woman approaching her sixtieth birthday maintained Facebook and Friends Reunited pages, a Twitter account and contributed to websites dedicated to her years at school (Cheltenham Ladies' High) and university (Durham, International Relations).

That Tuesday afternoon, Claire was working on the bundle for an unfair dismissal case. At a private school in Suffolk, a teacher had repeatedly asked a thirteen-year-old student to stop chewing gum in lessons. When the boy again denied that he was, she had asked him to open his mouth; when he refused, she had pulled his lips apart. Although this action resulted in his proving her right, by spitting sucked pulp onto the desk, the boy's parents had complained to the school and threatened to go to the police and claim assault unless the staff-member was removed. With writhing reluctance, the Head had opted to avoid the possibility of a prosecution and the loss of future fees from the gum-chewer and his two siblings in the junior feeder. The teacher, unless she cleared her name, would never work in education again. Claire was confident of the impact on the hearing of opposition research showing that the student had been posting defamatory remarks and violent threats against the teacher for two years before the incident.

The direct line on her desk-phone lit up.

'Ms Ellen?'

'Yep.'

'Richard Dent at the Met. I'm calling about Ned Marriott.'

She had an elated instinct that Dent was calling to say that 'no further action' would be taken on the Hessendon allegation.

'Look, we always hate to do this . . .' He was delaying the humiliating admission that the case was abandoned. 'But I have to tell you that we've received another complaint.'

Lessons From Royal Gynaecology

In the first days of waiting to be unmasked, Ned searched his name on the web each morning – and sometimes so far before dawn that it was technically still night – to check if anything had broken in the newspaper web editions.

If his respectability remained, the relieved release of adrenaline made sleep impossible and he stayed online. He started with the sites flagged as favourites: Gillingham FC (incurable infection from a Kent childhood) and Liverpool FC; Amazon to check his sales figures but not the reader comments (he was already insecure and depressed enough); UME History and Harvard History.

And then out into the badlands where the policing of taste and fact had no jurisdiction. For an historian, schooled in sources and cautious assertion, it was like being a celibate on a porn-film set.

Citizen historians asserted that President Obama was Kenyan, Muslim, white, gay, female, extra-terrestrial. Some of the claims about Tony Blair were argumentatively sustainable – war criminal, closet Tory – but others – paedophile, transsexual, Liberal Democrat – absurd. Plane crashes and disappearances that had mystified the aviation and investigative industries for years were solved by a sequence of letters in the tail-fin or a line in some movie the captain had apparently watched the night before the flight.

And one site – The Royal Baby Hoax – claimed that all births in the British Royal Family for at least sixty years had involved a network of secret surrogate mothers and sperm donors, created by Royal gynaecologists after their apprehension that the Hanoverian descent was fatally compromised by genes conferring haemophilia, porphyria and insanity, the incidence of which was likely to be increased by the fact that, if a European Royal said to you 'meet my wife and my cousin', they were often referring to one person. However, as recent British princes and princesses had sometimes pioneeringly wed a non-relative, the theory was adjusted to exclude more recent brides (starting with Princess Diana) from ordinary breeding on the grounds that their reproductive tracts had allegedly been ruined by cocaine use or sexual promiscuity, or that their husbands were impotent as a result of suppressed homosexuality.

The main evidence attested by the cyber-detectives was that Charles and Edward were visibly less macho than their 'father' the Duke of Edinburgh and that William and Harry, though 'brothers', looked different. Confining the Duchess of Cambridge to home or hospital during her 'pregnancy' with Prince George – due to a 'diagnosis' of hyperemesis gravidarum – was a clever stratagem to avoid her having to wear her prosthetic baby-bump too often at events and so risk exposure by beady-eyed keepers of websites; the citizen journalist warned the public to expect the same subterfuge to be used for the 'second baby' that the newspapers were expecting Kate soon to be expecting. The fact that Princesses Beatrice and Eugenie were more or less a morphed self-portrait of their parents was, like all contradictions faced by conspiracists, ignored.

Although Ned was a Republican – a fact that the BBC had warned him to keep quiet while promoting his monarchical documentaries (now there *was* a conspiracy theory) – he could see that, beyond the logistical complications of this plot, there would be a fundamental flaw in removing from a Royal family the one thing that gave it legitimacy: the bloodline.

But, amid these lunatic falsehoods, there was one invention so demented that Ned was tempted to appalled applause. The Surgeon-Gynaecologist to Queen Elizabeth II's Royal Household for the most recent births had been Alan Farthing. He, on assuming the post, had reportedly been informed of the secret IVF and surrogacy programme and, as a man of honour, had threatened to go public. So, fearing the downfall of the House of Mountbatten-Windsor, the security services had arranged for his girlfriend, the broadcaster Jill Dando, to be murdered on her doorstep in West London as a warning that he would be next. (The inconvenient truth that Farthing had joined Royal service nine years after Dando's killing went typically unmentioned.)

Then, during Kate's 'pregnancy' with Prince George, Buckingham Palace and MI5, alerted that some blokes with body odour sitting at their laptops in bedsits had spotted what was going on, paid Australian DJs to phone the hospital where the Duchess of Cambridge was being 'treated', pretending to be the Queen and Prince Charles, then murdered a nurse but made it look like suicide. The result was that anyone now typing 'Kate hoax' into a search-engine got so many stories about the hospital tragedy that the citizen journalist websites heroically publicizing the Royal gynaecological conspiracy were forced to the unread reaches of the queue.

In another crazy circuit of confirmation, the failure of the mainstream media to report any of these stories proved that they were true, as the owners of those newspapers and networks were required by either educational connections or sexual blackmail to protect the Royals and other establishment figures from exposure.

For someone who was soon to be pushed out into this incubator of speculation and graveyard of fact – where his entire character and career could be rewritten by any moron with a keyboard – these lunacies should have been reassuring proof that nobody should take seriously most of what was said.

But here Ned discovered another paradox of the Internet. Although he knew almost everything online to be false, he was sure that readers would assume everything written about him to be true.

Preparations for War

Phee had phoned, the day after the lunch at which they broke the news to the girls, to say that Emma and Ned might want to change the privacy settings on their Facebook accounts and check which friendship and gaming groups Toby might be in and what the security levels were. Phee argued that, if Things Got Difficult (a euphemism Emma gratefully stored for use in conversations with others), 'hacks' and 'trolls' might be able to access any family photos on the sites and even target Tobes. 'And what about paedophiles?' Emma had blurted, a mother's instinct, but her stepdaughter had replied: 'Oh, hacks and trolls are much worse.' The girls, in rare agreement, were protecting their settings on Facebook and leaving Twitter (at least for the moment) and she suggested that everyone in the family did the same. When Emma admitted that she wasn't certain she and Ned would know how to, Phee offered to come round and sort them out the following night.

'I still think of myself as young,' Emma told Ned. 'But, if things get difficult, I would lock the door and draw the curtains, without thinking that most people have a window permanently open now.'

'It would never have occurred to me either,' the historian agreed. 'It's a sort of modern equivalent of digging a moat before a war.'

Friday Suicide Call

Ned was now afraid, he had told Tom, to answer any call from an unknown number in case it was a reporter. But during the time that both men were waiting for the verdict on their pasts, Tom at least had the consolation that his disgrace remained local: his suspension had been briefly mentioned in both student newspapers, and then, suggesting that the next generation of journalists may require as much regulation as earlier ones, amended online to add the crucial information that Dr Pimm denied the charges. There had been nothing, though, in a national or even yet the *Higher Ed.*

So, when the screen vibrated with a stranger, Tom risked picking up and, when a voice of professional friendliness asked, 'Dr Pimm?', feared he had stumbled into a journalist, until the caller responded to his confirmation with: 'David Wellington, WH.'

The light baritone, trust-me tones of the catastrophe professions: airline pilot, surgeon, personnel.

'Are you happy for me to call you Tom?'

'In Dr Traill's dodgy dossier, many people call me much worse.'

'Good you've kept your sense of humour. There's a lot of evidence it helps. It'll be David and Tom, then. The University asked me to be available to you. I'll be checking in now and then if that's okay with you?'

'Well, I . . . what will we be saying to each other?'

'I'm here to be a non-judgemental pair of ears if you want to download anything.'

'Well, now you mention it, I've been stitched up in a way that makes a banana republic' – Tom momentarily panicked that the man might be black – 'er, look like the US Supreme Court.'

'Ha, well I'm not going to argue with a leading light in the Nussbaum School of American Politics' – this flattery told Tom that Wellington had been reading his file – 'on that one. But what I'd say is that you're going through a process and all outcomes of that process remain open.'

'Yes, well, that wasn't the impression that Sp, er, Dr Neades gave.'

'I'd be surprised if that were the case. But you were, quite understandably, under pressure during that meeting.'

Wellington's delivery seemed naggingly familiar and now it hit him that the soft, incantatory rhythm was an echo of the man on the Mindfulness tapes.

'Tom, my plan is to check in with you regularly. I thought Friday afternoons might be a good time.'

'Checking I haven't killed myself before you leave for the weekend? Don't want to have to come in from home on a Saturday or Sunday, do you?'

Although he felt better for saying it, the inner lawyer he had been forced to employ immediately regretted offering an example of temper.

'I fully understand the anger you must be feeling, Tom. But the process is designed to be fair to both the victims and the accused.'

'But even that sentence isn't fair: *accused* suggests two outcomes but *victims* implies the decision has already been made.'

'Wow, Tom. Maybe we should transfer you to the School of English.' Paranoid and happy-pilled, Tom was unable to judge whether this comment was a joke or a solution that had been floated. 'Look, I was talking loosely. All I can do is ask you to trust the process. Is there anything else you want to say to me at the moment?'

Yes, actually. 'Have you been appointed as Samaritan to my mate Professor Marriott as well?'

'Tom, I think you'd hope I wouldn't discuss you with anyone

else. And so it follows that I wouldn't discuss anyone else with you.'

The answer was pious but right and infuriatingly reassuring.

'Tom, are you happy for me to continue this process?'

'Which one? The witch hunt or ringing up once a week to check I haven't killed myself?'

'I think it's good that you feel able to express your anger to me, Tom. Will I call you again this time next week?'

'I suppose so.'

'And obviously feel free to get in touch with me at any time. As soon as we've finished speaking, I'll message you my contacts. And, should you feel you need them, we can also put you in touch with therapists and counsellors. Now, take care, won't you?'

In his page-to-a-day desk diary, Tom flicked through seven sides and wrote: *3.30pm – Friday Suicide Call.*

Digging a Moat in the 21st Century

'Tobes, can you come down, please?'

Ned had to repeat the line four times in ascending volume – until he sounded to Emma like the nanny in *The Turn of the Screw* – before the request eventually penetrated their son's headphones. There was then the standard further delay until he had reached an extractable position in the video game he was playing.

Toby arrived in the kitchen looking characteristically worried, biting his lip with the new meat teeth that were still a surprise in his smile.

'It's okay, you're not in any trouble,' Emma said. 'We just need to ask you something.'

But this encouragement seemed to trouble him even more. He ran both hands agitatedly through that wild burst of hair. Great, Emma thought, now he thinks we're getting divorced. She nodded at Ned to lead the questioning.

'Toby,' he said. 'We won't be upset if you are, but we just need to know. Are you on social media?'

'Huh?' His big exaggerated, American sitcom shrug.

'Facebook, Twitter, that kind of thing?' Emma translated.

'No.'

She and Ned confirmed with their eyes that they should wait.

'A bit,' he said.

'And is your page private or public?' asked Emma, confidently employing terms she had just learned from her stepdaughter.

Toby flexed his shoulders upwards and backwards again with the casual elasticity of young boys. Again, they waited.

'I play FIFA with people on line. We message each other. And a sort of Facebook thing at school. I don't do much.'

'Tobes,' Ned said. 'You know we told you about the bad people who are saying things about Daddy?'

'Yeah. Have the feds got them yet?'

'Er, not yet. No. But they might use, er, social media to pick on us. And so your sister Phee has suggested that we make everything private. She's very kindly popping in later to do it.'

'I'm on it!' Toby bellowed, pulling the laptop towards him, swiftly clicking and scrolling and then adding, from his thesaurus of motivational sporting phrases: 'Job done!'

Emma pushed the shopping-list pad, with its pencil on a loop of string, across the table. 'And, Cupcake, write your passwords for everything on here.'

'Oh, Mother!' His strop-word for her. She gave him her perfected glower of insistence.

When Emma saw the list he had written, she said: 'And which device they're for? I may be analogue but I'm not that dim.'

Toby complied with so many shrugs that some letters jumped out of the words.

Then, perky again, he asked: 'Now do you want me to change your settings as well?'

She looked at Ned, who gave a gesture of resignation as theatrical as their son's. After a few more expert taps and slides, Toby asked: 'Should I close your Twitter account as well?'

'I suppose, yeah,' said Emma.

'Tobes, you don't have one of those as well, do you?' Ned checked.

'No way! Only, like, really old people tweet.'

'Well, correction. I am and I don't,' Ned laughed. 'But I don't suppose you could do my Facebook? I don't just want to go private. Delete it.'

Through the anger at him that kept flaring for getting them into this mess, Emma felt a pang of sadness for the fantasy of anonymity that she sensed so often now in a man who had wanted to be famous.

Erasing his father's digital footprint seemed the most complicated of Toby's tasks so far, his tongue protruding through the last gap in his top row of teeth. But soon he announced, 'You're good to go,' the line of a child privileged to have been a regular at airport check-in desks.

And, with that, their child had adult-proofed the family technology. The moat was filled, the drawbridge raised.

A Vision of the Future

After waking at 2am, to the usual sleepless five hours, then the deep two-hour coda-coma induced by another zonker, Ned woke at 9.28am, a time he had never seen on the bedside clock on a weekday, to a vivid vision of what his future, his near-future, would be. He saw himself sitting on the sofa in a vest in the middle of the afternoon, drinking the cheapest supermarket red wine from a dusty bottle as he watched warring sisters-in-law being held apart from each other on re-runs of American problem shows. But he soon knew that this destiny was unlikely to become reality, as he could see, at that moment, no possibility of ever getting out of bed.

Warning

Horrified by the prospect of poverty, Ned, after decades of a serious black-cab habit, now waved at the enticing orange light only when he felt too exhausted to walk or frightened of being recognized. Putting into his expenses tin the receipt he had requested for a taxi ride to the flat from Claire's office – in his diminished circumstances, claiming travel against tax might make a difference – Ned, smoothing down the white rectangle of paper on the pile, noticed, printed at the bottom, the words: *WARNING See Over*. He flipped the slip and read:

WARNING
Every year in London, there are 100's of rapes
and sexual assaults and 1000's of robberies
committed by unlicensed minicab drivers.

He noticed first – then hated himself for doing so – the false apostrophes in the numbers. His next thought was that the allegation he faced grouped him with cabdrivers who attacked their customers. Until now, he would have argued that there could be no categories of (he forced himself to think it) rape but now he was desperate to separate himself from a man who parked his car, with a stranger in the back, in some unlit alley. He was coming to understand, though, that, in trying to prove the claim against him was fiction, he would be accused of suggesting that all claims were false. You were either a rapist or a rape-denier: the debate had squeezed out any space in between.

A Winslow Man

PA NEWS: 01–06–14: 23.38: In response to media inquiries, Buckinghamshire police have confirmed that a sixty-year-old male from Winslow has been arrested and questioned in connection with an historic claim of sexual assault, following a complaint passed to Operation Millpond. He was released on police bail until September 1st. Police refused to comment on speculation about the suspect's identity, citing the protection of a continuing investigation.

Mud and Smoke

The impact of accusation was measured in three substances: human, natural, man-made. The first was shit, which at the start poured torrentially at any memory of the arrest or thought about the trial, but later proved reluctant to emerge at all due to the inadvertent hunger strike caused by the shock and the stoppering that resulted (a recognized consequence, the leaflet advised) from the drugs designed to trick his mind into thinking that he was wrong to be frightened.

Mud and smoke affected Ned merely metaphorically, but devastatingly. The two most familiar cliches about the ruining of reputation – that mud sticks and smoke is never present without fire – sounded in his brain during sleepless nights and aimless days.

The adhesiveness of dirt, he knew, had only been increased in the swamp of digital memory, which created stains that could never be washed away. And, above the mud, the clouds of allegation and defamation swirled forever, regardless of how loudly the law declared that there had never been a blaze.

In a world of twenty-four-hour news and 24/7 views, all mud stuck and smoke thrived without fire.

Doorstep

Starting to reverse, Ned braked when he saw the green Polo in the rear-view mirror. The school run must have been quicker than usual; spending more time at home, he had become attuned to the rhythms of Emma's schedule. When he wound down the car window, she leaned in and kissed him on the lips so strongly that he received the electric flash of a romance's early days.

'We'll celebrate when you get home.'

'Yes. Well, Em, it may not be as clear-cut as . . .'

Ned had told her that he and Claire were going back to Paddington Green to give the detectives their detailed rebuttal of the Billy Hessendon allegation.

Emma made him promise to ring as soon as they had seen the police.

May Contain Flashing Images

A rough percussion of slammed car doors and raw chorus of excited voices rose from the road below. It was a sound more normal in the early hours of the morning – a party breaking-up – than at 11.30am on a weekday. Unsettled by a presentiment, Ned pulled the living room blind forward and looked round the edge. A firework burst of flashes confirmed his fear.

'They're here,' he said.

'Who are? What?' Claire asked, kissing her lipstick neat as she came back from the bathroom.

'Hacks and paps.'

He went to the window and was going to open the blind for her when Claire said quickly: 'No. Don't give them startled woman at the window.'

'They've already got terrified suspect.'

'Shit.' Calmer now, professional etiquette taking hold. 'Look, Ned, we've always known it was going to get out . . .'

'Yes.' But there was a difference between expecting and experiencing.

'Five minutes back, when I got here, there was no one outside. So it's not a stake-out. Someone's given them a time.'

'Someone! Reports say police are looking – into the fucking mirror . . .'

'Ned, they'll still have to be incredibly careful what they write.'

Their phones pinged simultaneously. Looking at his, Ned

expected the withheld number of a reporter, but it was a text: **Phee says it's all online. You okay? E xxxx**

He switched off his phone. Closing the cover of hers, his solicitor said: 'The taxi's here.'

Ned fussily double-locked the door, a rhetorical declaration of privacy rather than a precaution against burglary. Would he do the same on the day he left for jail? As they went down the final flight of stairs, he saw on the tiles of the entrance a half-moon of brightness cast by the morning sun through the fanlight, like a gilded memorial engraved on a cathedral floor. His eyes watered at the reminder of the first morning.

'You okay?' Claire asked.

'Yeah. Hay fever.'

'The air app said the count was high today.'

The noise was rising on the other side of the door. The pack was close enough to have heard people coming downstairs.

Claire spoke more quietly: 'Ned, I know it's tough but some rules for running the gauntlet. They want you to look an inch from the gallows – that's why they're here – so give the air of going off to a football match – played by a team that's bound to win. And, whatever you do, don't kick or punch them, even if they do it to you. Ready?'

'I guess you've done this a lot, have you?'

Her gravelly giggle. 'Honey, I'm disappointed if I'm ever *not* doorstepped coming out of a house.'

So often on television, Ned had watched people ducking and blinking through a photographic explosion, prefaced by the presenter's warning to epileptics that the pictures may contain flashing images. He had idly wondered what it might be like for the quarry but speculation was no preparation for the reality.

From his height, on the top step, he was staring into the sun but, looking down, he was blinded by another one, as the flashes fizzed, close enough to his face to feel the heat. He tried to smile, as Claire had told him, but the natural instinct of the dazzled was to squint and shy away. The classic shame-face you saw in snaps of the accused was people trying not to lose their sight as well as their names.

Forcing a route through was like trying to exit a Tube during rush hour, a disconcerting combination of violence and intimacy, your body suddenly pressed against the soft or solid outline of strangers. Yelled questions – 'Are you a rapist, Professor?', 'Are you a paedophile?', 'Is this the end of your career?', 'Did you know Jimmy Savile?' – peaked, faded from earshot and then were repeated more loudly as Ned and Claire forced their way across the pavement, dodging a long curl of sun-baked, fly-buzzed dog shit, and made the haven of the taxi. Stoop-stumbling in, Ned caught his head on the edge of the door.

Claire had given the address of a school in the road behind the police station, a probably pointless precaution now. And if it was an infant school, he would probably be locked up on sus. The driver was sure he knew Ned from somewhere, but they had almost reached their destination before he shouted: 'Got it! The Hitler Guy!'

Ned touched the sting on his scalp and checked his fingers. Blood.

The English Witch Hunts

Like a newsreader, DI Dent squared papers on his desk, checked a line, then met the eyes of his audience.

'This complaint relates to 2005,' he said.

Although Ned tried hard to show no reaction, Claire noted that he was visibly whiplashed by this date. The more distant an allegation, the easier it was for the accused to dismiss, with the additional reassurance that, if it came to it, juries were reluctant to follow cold trails. But nine years ago was recent history. Toby was how old? Ned must have been with Emma by then.

When they had left the police station after the Hessendon allegation, he had been shocked but convinced by her that the charges were a brief surreal interlude in his usual life. But the media rat-fuck outside his house had jolted him and the recency of the latest claim landed as a punch on a fresh bruise.

Claire saw a lot of clients in extremis. She had represented two people who had taken their lives while under police investigation: both teachers accused of sexual abuse of students. One of the suicides, she suspected, was guilty and sentenced himself to death to avoid a trial; the other, she feared, had been entirely innocent but unable to endure the public scrutiny. Two accusers might or might not, she reminded herself, make her client more likely to be guilty. The claims of the state must always be tested.

In a gesture of solidarity, she rested her hand on Ned's arm. His instant tensing interested her because it suggested a man suspicious of tactility from women. She wondered if this was a reaction against past mistakes.

'As this date is relatively distant, I am going to mention three events that happened in that year within the range of dates given by the victim.'

'Complainant,' said Claire. The detective carried on but at least she had put the objection on the tape again.

'Within the time-range of the complaint,' Dent went on, 'the Live 8 concerts took place at Wembley. London was awarded the 2012 Olympics and fifty-three people were killed in a series of terrorist suicide bombings on the London Transport system.'

Although her client was the historical expert, Claire's recollection was that those events had happened in close succession – she had a memory of the Mayor of London talking about the bombings from abroad, where the Olympic decision had been announced – which was worrying: it looked as if this woman had given a precise date.

Claire wondered if any of the allegations made to Yewtree or Millpond were supposed to have happened on November 22, 1963, or August 31, 1997, when the accused would be forced into the tricky position of insisting that they couldn't remember what they were doing on the days that President Kennedy and Princess Diana died.

'DS Walters,' said Dent, 'will read the victim's . . .'

'Complainant's?' Claire offered.

'*Victim*'s statement into the record.'

The detective sergeant played this role neutrally, with no apparent attempt at characterization: 'My name is Jess – short for Jessamy – Pothick – P-O-T-H-I-C-K . . .'

Claire glanced at her client and, on the basis of the face he made, pledged never to partner him in the world poker championships.

'In 2005,' Walters read on. 'I was twenty-four and employed by Ogglebox, a television production company, as a researcher on a four-part documentary series called *The English Witch Hunts*. The presenter was Professor Ned Marriott. I had never met him before working with him but had grown up watching his work on TV and knew some of his books from when I was a history student.'

The line about having seen Ned's shows as a child was potentially ruinous with a jury, seeding the idea of him as a predator and her as vulnerable. Its inclusion – perhaps even its extrusion through a question from the detectives – suggested that the police were trying to give the CPS dirt to work with. Claire subtracted a decade from Ned's age now: fifty versus twenty-four wasn't legally anywhere near child abuse – it was a common enough age-gap in showbiz marriages – but fell into the category that Claire thought of as Twitter Criminality: the sort of relationship that the more conventionally romantic, many of whom made up the pool of jurors, found creepy or, in some communities, even blasphemous.

'The word in the industry was that he could be very difficult but he was always pretty easy and funny with me. In July 2005, we were filming in Hertfordshire for the section dealing with Jane Wenham, who was tried for witchcraft in the early eighteenth century. We were on location for three days at Hertford Castle. The production team – including Professor Marriott – stayed for two nights at the County Hotel in Hertford. I can be fairly certain that the night in question was July 7th–8th, 2005, because I had become very upset during that day about the fact that London seemed to have had its "9/11 attack" and I was frightened at going back to London, where I lived, and travelling on public transport. At dinner in the hotel – and afterwards in the hotel bar – I became upset and Professor Marriott was kind to me, telling me that he had lived through the time of the IRA attacks on London and that Islamic terrorists' – another police rabbit punch, Claire noted, encouraging judges of the evidence to label Ned a racist rapist – 'were harder to deal with but that the campaign was unlikely to be as sustained. At that point, he put his arm around me and kissed the top of my head, saying that he had already had to reassure his teenage twins on the phone and was happy to do me for free.'

At that detail, Ned scowled and shook his head in either rebuttal or regret. *An incestuous racist rapist*, Claire thought, but what she wrote on her pad was: *his twins?* Notoriously phobic about the term, Ned was unlikely to have used it in the conversation quoted and so its appearance raised the possibility that either the complainant or the detectives had subsequently done some Google-gilding.

'At around midnight, there were four of us left in the bar: myself, Professor Marriott, the producer-director Dominic Ogg and a camera or sound guy whose name I can't remember but I think was possibly called Dave.'

Ned interrupted the testimony for the first time: 'That wouldn't narrow it down very much in broadcasting.' Claire laughed supportively and Dent gave a small smile but Walters glared before resuming: 'Dominic Ogg said that he was going to bed and that Professor Marriott should probably call it a night as well, as he didn't want him looking puffy-eyed on screen the next day. Professor Marriott said that he would switch to water but that he wanted to just run through his links – which meant his speeches to camera – for the next day with an audience. He was looking at me when he said that. The techie stayed as well. He had made it fairly clear throughout the shoot that he was interested in me and so I think he was trying to do that thing that guys do at university of trying to be in the last two still up.

As soon as Mr Ogg had gone, Professor Marriott ordered another bottle of red wine.' An *alcoholic* incestuous racist rapist. 'Professor Marriott poured a glass for each of us and then started practising his links about Jane Wenham's arrest by Sir Henry' – Walters hesitated over the pronunciation – 'Chauncy? – C-H-A-U-N-C-Y.'

Walters said H as *haitch*.

'I forget how it's pronounced,' Ned said. 'It's a long time ago.'

The level of detail in the statement would impress the CPS but, at any litigation stage, it would be easy to raise the suspicion that the complainant had constructed or bulked-up her memory with a viewing of the DVD: a known risk factor in cases involving the publicly visible.

'Professor Marriott spoke the links to me, ignoring the techie, who, after a few minutes, said that he had to listen to this stuff all day and he wasn't going to listen to it all night as well.' DI Dent began, then abandoned, a laugh. 'He left his glass of wine almost full. When he had gone, Professor Marriott tipped half into each of our glasses. While he was rehearsing one speech, I queried a date and the full name of the judge at Wenham's trial. I said I had the research file and copies of the books I'd used – he was always insistent about knowing where everything came from – in my room and that I would check and tell him in the morning. Professor Marriott said he wouldn't sleep from worrying that he'd memorized the wrong stuff and so why didn't we go and put our heads together now?'

Unable to obey her advice about maintaining a brave or at least straight face under accusation, Ned was bent forward, looking down at the table.

'I did worry about letting him come back but he was such an old guy and he had mentioned his daughters.' As Ned's head fell even lower, Claire sensed the heat on his cheeks. 'Before we left, he ordered two more bottles of red wine, specifying twist-able caps rather than corks because, he said, "There's nothing worse than being stuck in a hotel room without a screw." He said "screw" not "cork screw". I said I wouldn't want any more to drink but he said that it would "lubricate your hunt". I remember very clearly the phrase he used.'

Claire tried to follow her own rules of facial dissimulation – except when it suited you to ridicule police tactics – but she feared that her eyes had at least started a roll. She would re-assure Ned afterwards that you couldn't be prosecuted for schoolboy smut but, while this remained true of the statute books, you were increasingly at risk from jurors who followed online law, where giving offence to anyone at all over anything was a capital crime.

'I was worried about refusing him because of the effect he could have on my career.' *Unsustainable innuendo*, Claire scrib-bled. 'So I let him come back to my room. I can't remember the room number but I recollect it being on the first floor, up one flight of stairs. On the stairs I stumbled. I wasn't used to drink-ing that much.' *WT search?* Claire wrote, as illegibly as possible because she hated herself for even thinking about it. 'He took my arm to steady me and didn't let go.' Which might be enough these days, Claire thought, to constitute sexual touching. 'We got back to my room, which had a single bed: the firm had a reputation for being stingy with the junior staff. Professor Mar-riott looked at it and told me that he had a suite with a four-poster. I didn't say anything. I think I probably smiled nervously. The research files and the history books I had used were stacked on the bedside table. Professor Marriott sat on the bed, picked up a book and then lay back in the middle of it. I remember that the bed was so small that his legs stuck over the end. Professor Marriott said: "So what about our date?" I asked him what he meant. He said that we were going to look up a date. I asked him to pass me *English Witchcraft*, I think it was, and he told me to come over and get it. We had a bit of to-and-fro about that and eventually – because of who he was – I went over. As I reached for the book, he grabbed my arm – not sharply, but against my will – and guided – pulled really – me into a sitting position on the bed. He looked over my shoulder as I was flicking through the book and rested his head on my shoulder. He pulled himself up from the bed and sat beside me on the edge. He had placed the two bottles of wine on the floor beside the bed and he picked one up and wedged it between his thighs – suggestively, I thought – to open it, even though he wasn't using a corkscrew. Without asking, he went into my bathroom and came back with the only plastic toothbrush glass. He filled the glass, handed it to me and drank from the bottle himself. We checked a couple of other facts. I tried to avoid body contact with him but the bed was squishy and had a dip in the middle and I kept finding him with his thigh against mine, especially when I had to move to put the glass on the floor or pick it up. He tried to go over some of his PTCs – pieces to camera – but he kept forgetting lines and his speech was very slurred. I told him that he needed his beauty sleep before tomorrow, actually, today by then. He said: "Oh, you flatterer." I suppose he meant the word "beauty" but I had only intended it as an expression. The last thing I clearly remember of the time he was in my room' – though she showed nothing to the cops, Claire was calculating the advantage of the allegation being the reconstruction of a drunk – 'was that, when he was drinking the second bottle, he kept trying to refill the tooth glass, even though I asked him not to, while taking slugs from the bottle himself – he put the empty to his mouth and sucked the neck of it in a strange slurpy way.' Claire checked on her client, who was bent over the table, with his chin resting on paired fists. 'I woke up at 3am, with a terrible headache, a horrible taste in my mouth and feeling very sick. I was alone in the room. When I was able to stand, I went to the bathroom and vomited. While I was cleaning myself up, I noticed that my blouse buttons were open to below my breasts. I had not been wearing a bra as I found them uncomfortable in summer. There was a sticky substance on my breast, neck and clothing, which I am sure was semen.' Claire rehearsed in her mind the car-crash moment in court when defence counsel had to ask her if she had tasted it to check. 'Because I had vomited, I could not be sure if any had entered my mouth. However, it was my assumption that Professor Marriott had forced me to perform – or attempt to perform – a sex act against my will. I vomited twice more during that night. Subsequently, I wondered if Professor Marriott had drugged the wine.'

Claire sighed and double underlined her note about innuendo. In the days before the cops and prosecutors took the decision to accept everything they were told, a sneering DCI would have asked the complainant just how Professor Marriott would have ensured that only the wine poured for the complainant was spiked.

'When we were filming the next day at Hertford Castle, Professor Marriott was cold and distant with me' – yeah, and, if we locked up every guy who was like that after an unwise night, the jails would be even more bulging – 'and constantly found fault with my work: blaming me for the fact that he was having trouble remembering his links, telling the producer-director, Dominic Ogg, that it was because I had printed out the location copies in too small a font, although, in my view, it was more likely to have been because he had drunk so much. I recall that the PTCs also took a long time to shoot because it was difficult to frame the shot due to Professor Marriott having a large cut on his chin. I don't know how he got that.' Claire's writing of *how?* coincided with the spoken word. 'I completed my work on the series – Professor Marriott was distant and chilly, but never behaved inappropriately on another occasion – but I was subsequently never employed to work with Professor Marriott again, although I was a specialist historical researcher and later AP (Assistant Producer) and Producer on history series with presenters including Professor Simon Schama, Lucy Worsley, Dan Snow and Dr David Starkey. Subsequently, I was never offered another contract of employment by Ogglebox, until this year when I was hired to do research and development on possible new presenters for historical TV series. During a discussion on a shoot about historical abuse by broadcasters including Jimmy Savile and Stuart Hall, I mentioned the broad outline of my experience in 2005 to [Name redacted] and was advised that the police should be spoken to.'

A pause was broken by Dent saying: 'That is the end of the statement from Victim B. Mr Marriott, do you have any response to what you have heard?'

Ned turned to her: 'Could I speak to my solicitor alone, please?'

Dent informed the recorder that he was stopping it and then did so.

A Winslow Man (2)

PA NEWS: 04–06–14: 15:30. In response to media inquiries, Buckinghamshire police have confirmed that a sixty-year-old male from Winslow, previously arrested and questioned in connection with an historic claim of serious sexual assault, following a complaint passed to Operation Millpond, has been arrested and interviewed in connection with a second allegation of sexual assault arising from the same investigation. He was released on police bail until October 1st. Police refused to comment on speculation about the suspect's identity, citing the protection of a continuing investigation.

Present Tense Presentiment

Because her sister went through an adolescent spell of loving horror movies – another issue on which they differed – Phee was more familiar with the art form than she would have wished. And, because of this, lodged in her memory with the usual chunks of poetry from school and pop songs with special meaning, was a line of dialogue that seemed almost obligatory in the genre.

At the moment when the school janitor peeled back his face

to reveal an underlying set of features in green slime, or the mother placing a temperature strip on her eight-year-old's forehead noticed the burning numbers 666 etched into the skin above eyes of hellfire, someone – in the most extreme cases, the Pope, his own eyes suddenly glowing red – would announce, 'It is beginning,' or, occasionally: 'It begins.'

So, when Emma texted her to warn that there had been reporters outside the London flat when Daddy was leaving to give his defence to the police, Phee set up an alert for his name. Supposed to be reading a book for her thesis, she tried to take notes but would look away from a half-read, zero-comprehended sentence to the corner of her laptop, where new messages arrived. And, after thirty-five minutes, he broke on BBC News: *TV Star Arrested Over Sex Allegations.*

It was beginning. But the plural *allegations* was sloppily wrong; he must get that corrected quickly. The headline misled her into hoping that it would be one of those anonymous teaser pieces – *the man, who cannot be named for legal reasons* – but, in the opening line, she found *Professor Ned Marriott, 60,* and worked out that he wasn't identified in the banner in order to make surfers click to know who it was, possibly disappointed that it wasn't the actor or comedian they had imagined. And now here she was: *He has twenty-five-year-old twin daughters, Cordelia and Ophelia, by his first wife, college lecturer Jennifer Marriott, and a nine-year-old son, Toby, by his current partner, literary agent Emma Humpage, 41.*

She hated the way that, in the older media, women had children *by* men, making the mothers sound like brood-mares. Why didn't they go the whole race-horse way and put *out of*? Surely it should be *with*. It was unclear to her, anyway, why the names and ages of the relatives of those involved in scandals were so precisely listed. She assumed the details were intended to quicken the moralism of readers, helping them to picture the women and children whose lives might have been destroyed by the accused or, if they hadn't been, now might be by the reporting of the case.

Guided by alerts, now arriving almost by the minute, Phee worked through the news sites. Within an hour, there was a version everywhere, headed or divided by a picture of Daddy, eyes glistening with what she hoped was sweat, pushing aside a hedge of hands and cameras. All of the later reports specified *two historic sexual allegations*, though most quoted his lawyer's *absolute denial* of the claims.

Unknown Number showed on her trembling, muted phone. From a sudden instinct of the hunted, she let it ring to voicemail, where she heard: 'Ms Marriott? This is Graham Gardener from the *Telegraph*, at 2.45pm. I'm writing a piece about the rape charges against your father. I'm happy to talk to you on or off the record and you can reach me at.'

Charges? Cutting him off before the first digit, she wondered if there would be hacks outside the flat when she left for college.

It begins, she texted her sister. **Poor poor D. What can we do? x**

But, after two hours, there had been no reply. She told herself that Dee had switched off her phone because of calls from the press.

Charge Sheet

Dent had suggested that they spoke in the cell, where the custody sergeant, as a compromise, did not quite close the door. When Ned said nothing, Claire encouraged him: 'Lowish voice and we'll be fine.'

He was still silent. She prompted: 'So – Jessamy – *Jess* – Pothick?'

'Well . . . I mean, if you'd asked me yesterday who was the runner on the witches thing, I couldn't have told you. The thing is, there were just so many . . .'

Claire had an amused *are-you-sure?* look for moments when the client seemed about to say something dangerous.

'No, what I mean is that I've worked with so many people on things . . . obviously once I think back to English witches, I'm sure she's telling the truth . . .'

It was never good to repeat the warning dare so quickly.

'About having worked on it, I mean. It would be useful if they had a photograph . . .'

'You know what, it probably wouldn't . . .'

'Of her. Look, I know this isn't great but I often don't tend to remember – even at the time, never mind afterwards – the names of my crews . . .'

And the names of your screws? was the first line of dialogue her mind offered her, but she bowdlerized it down to: 'And what was your reaction to her account in general?'

'I . . . it's difficult . . . we definitely didn't have *sex*-sex . . .'

'Thank you, Mr President. Her statement didn't suggest that you did.'

'No. Look, I'm not proud of any of this but . . . look, this is my problem . . . I think I'd drunk too much for anything to have happened but – because I'd drunk so much – I can't remember if it didn't . . .'

So a jury would be left to decide between accounts retrieved from pickled synapses – a frequent feature of sex trials these days. The defence line would be that the participants were as bad as each other but the prosecution would argue that a fifty-year-old man with an employee half his age should have known better.

'Claire, how bad is this?'

Doctors, when asked this question, had scans and tests. Lawyers had to second guess the conclusion of a dozen people who had so little to do during the day that they didn't try to get out of jury service. Or, before it came to that, of a prosecution service that now seemed to want to delegate as many decisions as possible to the public.

'If they do charge it, then there's the question of the wording . . . the first one wouldn't have gone anywhere near rape at the time it allegedly happened, but might now. Or possibly serious sexual assault. It's the sort of thing Mr Assange is facing in Sweden. The second one – even as the code is written now – is probably closer to sexual assault by penetration . . .'

'Okay, but obviously, from my perspective, it's a bit like being told what kind of cancer you've got. When what you want to hear is that you're clear . . .'

'I understand what you're saying. But, actually, that's a good analogy. In both cases, there are some where you've got more chance of seeing your kids grow up. Juries are more likely to call the lesser charges as A said-B said and, if they don't, judges are going to be reluctant to fill up a cell.'

'I see all that. But those are legalistic distinctions. When it comes to media and social media . . .'

'Yeah. Not so much.'

'Claire, can I ask you something possibly touchy?'

'Sure. If you won't be touchy if I don't answer.'

'Is this tricky for you as a woman . . . ?'

'Ned, I hope you're not going to be sexist . . .'

'I'm serious. For you to be dealing with this stuff?'

Doctors are taught always to see their patients as bodies not buddies – *clinical distance* – and sensible lawyers soon learn a version – cases not mates – for themselves. But she liked it that Ned was even aware of the dilemma; some clients are so certain of their virtue that they act as if they are doing you a favour.

'Well, the law school answer is that, if you're asked to represent vegetarian terrorists who've blown up a burger bar, it's irrelevant whether you like roast beef or nut roast on Sundays. In practice, I'm wary of being used as table decoration.' She responded to Ned's go-on face. 'I mean, if I think someone's trying to convince detectives or the jury that they can't be a rapist or, indeed, a racist because I'm on their case, then I think at least twice. But I've acted for you before and so I know that's not your game.'

'I can assume, though, that you wouldn't have taken it if you thought I was the new Yorkshire Ripper or whatever?'

He had gone too far.

'That sets the bar low and, you know what, Ned, I never think these conversations are useful.'

Cuttings

BLAIR CHUM BBC HITLER MAN IN 'RAPE' CLAIM

One of the BBC's highest-paid TV presenters, who is also a close friend and former adviser to ex-premier Tony Blair, is being investigated over two historic allegations of serious sexual offences, it was revealed yesterday.

Professor Edmund 'Ned' Marriott, 60, has hosted a string of top-rating and award-winning documentaries for the BBC, Channel 4 and The History Channel, including *Hitler: A Study in Evil*, *The English Witch Hunts* and *Elizabeth 1 – Elizabeth 2*.

Known as 'Professor Perverse' for his outrageous dis-respect for historical fact – including a notorious attack on HM The Queen during her Diamond Jubilee as 'a pointless figurehead paid tens of millions to cut ribbons' – the con-troversial academic was appointed by the Blair government as 'History Tsar', advising on which aspects of the British past should be taught to schoolchildren.

Doubts were raised about the appointment because Marriott is a self-confessed 'half-Marxist'. In his work for Blair, the controversial don caused widespread outrage by downgrading national heroes such as Lord Nelson and Sir Winston Churchill in favour of contemporary non-English figures such as Martin Luther King, Fidel Castro and Nelson Mandela.

It emerged yesterday that the father of three had been arrested and interviewed under caution last month on one allegation of rape involving a young woman and was inter-viewed by detectives again yesterday in connection with a second claim of sexual assault.

An industry insider said last night that the arrest and questioning of a man who has been one of TV's most-respected figures represents 'another shattering blow for British broadcasting' after the thousands of sexual abuse and paedophilia allegations against the late BBC broadcaster Jimmy Savile, who died in October 2011 before any charges were brought, and another leading figure at the corporation, children's and sports presenter Stuart Hall, who is currently serving a six-year jail term for charges of sexual assault against girls aged between nine and seventeen.

No allegations have been made against Marriott involving children. But there were calls at Westminster last night for urgent inquiries into whether either the BBC or Blair might have been aware of the incidents involving him.

Marriott's solicitor, Claire Ellen, said as they left a West London police station: 'Professor Marriott completely denies these allegations and is co-operating with detectives in order to refute them. We are deeply disappointed that the media appear to have been given advance information about his movements this morning and will be raising further questions about this. He asks for the privacy of himself and his family to be respected at this time.'

Last night, there was no sign of occupancy at Marriott's £1million elegant detached Edwardian town house in Winslow, Buckinghamshire, where the divorced broadcaster lives with his girlfriend, literary agent Emma Humphries, who is two decades his junior, and their seven-year-old son Tobias. A neighbour at the TV star's £500,000 flat in West London's Kensington, a district popular with figures in the left-wing media, said that he had not been seen there since before his arrest yesterday morning. Contacted separately, his twenty-six-year-old identical twin daughters, Fi and Dee, refused to comment.

There was speculation online that the accused broadcaster and his current family may be staying at one of the numerous properties owned by Tony and Cherie Blair in London, Buckinghamshire and Bristol. A spokesman for the Blair Faith Foundation last night declined to comment 'on any aspect of this matter at this stage.'

A representative of Ogglebox, the production company that has made the majority of Marriott's series, said last night that they 'are not working on any projects with him at the moment' and that it would be 'inappropriate' to comment on possible future commissions.

Staff in the History Directorate at the University of Middle England, where Marriott has taught history for more than three decades, refused to speak to reporters but posted a statement online: 'Professor Edmund Marriott is currently serving a precautionary suspension on full pay as he answers charges that have no connection with his employment at the university. It would be inappropriate to comment further at this stage.'

Police declined to say anything beyond the statement: 'A sixty-year-old Winslow man has been questioned by detectives about two historic allegations of serious sexual assault. He has been released on police bail until October 1.'

The History Channel announced last night that it had decided to postpone three planned repeat screenings this month of Marriott's Nazi documentary, *Hitler: A Study in Evil* because of 'respect for the sensitivity of the situation.'

Take Care

He was aware that almost everyone he now met – or spoke to on the phone, or even e-mailed – ended the conversation with the same words: 'Take care, Ned.' Or, from some, 'Take care, won't you?' or 'Take care of yourself, okay?', the phrase delivered with a tenderly apprehensive parental inflection (even when not from his mother) and, in face to face meetings, a solemn inclination of the head to match the lowered tone.

It was true that, before the fall, he had sometimes been encouraged to take care of himself, but, then, it had merely been a platitude. Now, it was a fearful pleading, a worried instruction, a euphemism that meant: 'You're not going to kill yourself, are you?'

Cuttings (2)

'PERVERSE' TV PROF 'RAPE' RAPS

A BBC star, who advises politicians on what to teach kids, has become the latest celebrity questioned over sex allegations in the wake of the shaming of paedo hosts Jimmy Savile and Stuart Hall.

Known as 'Prof Perverse', due to his wacky opinions, 60-year-old Ned Marriott has made publicly funded TV films calling Sir Winston Churchill 'a war criminal', HM The Queen 'a pointless expense' and Adolf Hitler a 'genius.' And, during an appearance on Radio 4's *Desert Island Discs*, he proudly described himself as a 'half-Marxist'.

As an adviser to PM Tony Blair, he also outraged parents and teachers by urging that British kids should study black radical leaders instead of kings and queens of Great Britain.

The divorced dad of three has denied to detectives allegations of raping or sexually assaulting young women on two occasions in the past.

But, as the investigation continues, the perverse prof was last night 'suspended' from teaching at top university UME, while the BBC said that it had no plans to work with him again.

Legal Advice

'Surely I can fucking sue them, Claire? It's outrageous . . .'

'Okay. Simply, practically, it's hard to bring a case of defamation while you're facing allegations of . . .'

'But what I called Hitler – I've got the script here – is an "evil genius of malevolent divisive rhetoric". I didn't say he was a fucking *genius*. And all this *Professor Perverse* stuff, readers are supposed to read it or think it as pervert . . .'

'Yes. It's clever journalism.'

'Clever, Claire? It's fucking evil!'

'The two aren't mutually exclusive. I've met clever murderers. It doesn't imply approval. Being known to friends as "Foxy Knoxy" doesn't mean you murdered someone in a sex game gone wrong in Italy but the court of public opinion decided it did. Be careful with your monickers, I guess, is the moral.'

'Right. But with the Hitler and Savile bits, it's supposed to make me sound like a Nazi paedo. How is that not contempt of court?'

'Yes, it might be prejudicial to a jury and we'd address that if it came to it. But at the moment, this isn't anywhere near court.'

'Well, let's get it there so I can clear my name . . .'

'Ned, clients often think that. And I understand why. But a trial – especially a defamation one – is like paying two million quid for a hotel room that may have a sheer drop behind the door.'

'But it's so fucking sloppy, Claire! Half of it's vicious and the other half is vicious and wrong. Emma gets four different surnames, my children change age between papers and sometimes between paragraphs. Can't we even get those corrected?'

'Yeah, we could, but there's whether we should. Some of us reckon that the hacks do it on purpose, so that they can repeat the central allegation in denying it. "In our report 'TV Star Arrested For Rape', we inadvertently mis-stated the names of his much-younger girlfriend and the name and age of his illegitimate son." You get the idea?'

'I'm getting it. And now you'll tell me that it's all right for them to say . . . "rape" when that isn't actually the charge?'

'It's within the charging band, the worst they could throw at you. Again, the papers probably know what they're doing. How much good does it do us to have a correction that it might *only* turn out to be serious sexual assault? You sound as if you're plea-bargaining rather than innocent and every woman with a Twitter account complains that you're playing the not-really-*rape*-rape card. Look up how that one went for Oprah. And, for all we know, Dent may be briefing the press with the serious end to see if it flushes out other claims.'

'So you're saying I just have to take it?'

'That's basically all that's open to you at this stage. Ned, I fully realize how shit it feels now, but this stuff won't go beyond today. Even the chancers won't write much now until we know the outcome of the bail. You might turn up in lists of the accused. But that's . . . I'm not going to say *all*.'

'Good. Thanks.'

Cuttings (3)

THE MOLE

As Professor Edmund 'Ned' Marriott, BBC history presenter and close friend of Tony Blair, sweats it out on police bail over allegations of historic sex offences (which he denies), he still has the support of Emma Humpage, his partner of ten years.

The 40-year-old literary agent has a son, nine-year-old Toby, by the divorced dad of two who, ironically, celebrated his 60th birthday with a swanky £100,000 London party the night before his arrest by Operation Millpond detectives at his £500,000 *pied-à-terre* in a trendy West London square.

But 'Em', as she is known to friends and clients, may be rather nervously checking the Most Played list on the Prof's iPod. The Mole has been listening to an edition of *Desert Island Discs* from 2008, on which the telly don's choices included Tom Jones's 'Delilah' and the finale from Mozart's

Don Giovanni. It was during the same broadcast that the academic notoriously confessed to being a 'half-Marxist'.

As fans of the big-tonsilled Welshman will know, 'Delilah' is a lament by a man who has just stabbed his girlfriend to death because of her infidelity and who explains why he did what he did just before the police come and 'break down his door'. And, while readers of this publication are too cultured to need telling what the Spanish Don was famous for, they might run to their libretti for a refresh of the history don's particular choice from the opera – sung after the sex offender has gone down, the finale *Questo è il fin di chi fa mal, e de' perfidi la morte alla vita è sempre ugual* translates as: Such is the end of the evildoer: the death of a sinner always reflects his life!

Emma will surely be hoping that her prof has changed his tune!

Legal Advice (2)

To: nhmarriott@freeserve.co.uk
From: claire.ellen@frasers.com

Dear Ned. I appreciate that this will seem astonishing to you but it is difficult to see what action we can sensibly take at this time with regard to the item in 'The Mole' diary which references your selections on Desert Island Discs.

If court proceedings were under way, the newspaper would assuredly be in contempt of them. But it is a consequence of the rot-in-limbo tactics being used by the Met in such cases that there is an indefinite period before you would receive the protections of a defendant and, paradoxically, it is our hope that you will never have to.

The only other route available is to take action for defamation. But, as is often the case, the phrasing is sly. The piece does not suggest that you have killed a lover but that, from your musical tastes, your partner could be nervous that you might kill her in a crime of passion if she were guilty of infidelity. It is mightily hard to disprove a hypothetical. If the piece had suggested, for instance, Emma had reason to fear that Toby might be at physical risk from you, then the accusation is so specific and malicious that it could only be an attempt to damage your reputation. However, in this case, they would almost certainly attempt to defend the sentence as humorous and I would be reluctant for you to spend days being taken through the lyrics of 'Delilah' by the newspaper's QC.

The second suggestion – that you are a sinner who may end up in hell – is ultimately a point of contention for theology rather than law and would likely be defended by the newspaper as 'fair comment'. As the paper's duty lawyers doubtless told them, we would struggle to bring a libel case over something sung in Italian at Covent Garden. It is also probable that the publication would rebut any approach over these issues until your position in the other matter becomes clear.

Ned, I know how difficult this is and how disappointing my response will be. But clients such as you occupy this curious middle ground between innocence and potential guilt and, in this territory, can be kicked almost at will.

You have been very strong so far and, I'm afraid, must continue to be so.

Claire xx

Home Truths (2)

Age makes the mind stall and skid in reverse and Emma had a saving moment of confusing 2005 with 1995, which would have been before they met, until she placed not just the year but the month, four before Toby was born.

'When I was pregnant?'

His silence and refusal to meet her eye were enough confirmation. The story no amount of social equality could rewrite: a man who has to fuck someone else the minute the woman he's with can't or won't.

'Adultery as well as rape! Great!' she yelled.

He shushed her, lifting his eyes to Toby's room above, but one benefit of a generation that wore headphones at most times was that their parents could express fury with impunity.

'It wasn't – whatever you think of me – it wasn't . . . *rape*. And . . .'

It was the sort of pause that occurs not when someone finds nothing to say but when they abandon an intended sentence.

'Go on!'

'No. It wasn't . . .'

'Just say it. Ned, it couldn't be anything worse.'

He looked away. She wondered if he had been going to say that it wasn't strictly adultery because they weren't married. She had rejected the next question as a demeaning cliché but found herself compelled to ask it anyway: 'How many times with this . . . this . . . *Jess*?'

'Oh, look . . . once.' It was the damage-limitation answer: could she believe him? 'Not even that, really . . .'

'What? Then how . . .'

'Em, I know it doesn't make much difference but it wasn't even *actual sex as such*.'

'For crying out . . . Oh, eating ain't cheating. Is that from Tom Pimm's Clinton seminar?'

Did it make any difference? The mental image, she found, was no better.

'Okay. You on her or her on you?'

'Em, do we have to . . . ?'

'Yes.'

'Her on . . . I . . . *think*. I know it's no excuse but I was so hammered I don't really know what happened . . .'

She had warned him about his drinking on location, fearing that it sometimes showed on screen. Though she obviously watched him with more attention than average viewers, she could sometimes see red-wine tongue when the camera went in close on a link.

He was offering her a version in which what happened had not been very much. And, even though he might be lying to keep her on side, she could take consolation in that being his aim. The forgiving part of her heart argued that she would never have known about this Jess thing except for a sudden British madness of mass accusation; the suspicious side that she might be living with a serial cheat and / or rapist.

'Has there been anyone since her?'

'No. No. It was . . . at that time . . . too much drink and maybe not enough . . .' The unspoken word lay between them like a thrown grenade. 'Em, I'm not making excuses for it . . .'

She saw an image, as crisp as an advert, of the champagne chilling in the fridge for tonight's planned celebration of his being cleared of the charge, the first charge.

'They just sprung this one on you, did they?'

She was pleased with the question; relationships make everyone a detective.

'What?'

'Well, you told me that you and Claire were going there today to blow apart the charge . . . the *first* charge?'

As he worked out the best answer to give, she saw the cunning defendant he had become. 'So, yeah . . . they'd warned Claire they might have something else to ask but she didn't think it was going to come to anything.'

'And what does she think?'

'Look. She . . . obviously her criteria are different but she doesn't think there's anything criminal here . . .'

A month before, what Emma was hearing might have destroyed her. But, though she could only speak by gulping down breath and forcing back tears, shock, like alcohol, prepares the body for the absorption of more. She took the lawyer's narrow definition of Ned's guilt almost as an exoneration of him. Except that, with both drink and distress, there comes a tipping point.

'Ned, are there going to be more?'

'No. No. Well, I didn't think there were going to be *these*. But. Em, I know you must hate me . . .'

'I don't hate you,' she said, but in the manner of an actress testing a line to see if it rang true.

'But . . . look . . . these *allegations* . . . it's one thing I didn't even know had happened and one where something – not what she says but – something may have happened but I'm not proud of it and I, I . . . cleaned up my act afterwards. I swear I can't think of anything in the last ten years that anyone could . . . unless they just made it up . . . what I'm saying is, there has to be a . . . a . . .'

'Statute of limitations?'

'What? *No.* Because there wasn't anything legal, I mean *illegal* obviously . . . but there has to come a point when you judge people on how they are now not *then* . . .'

He tried to pull her to him but she shrugged him away. Not yet. When? Possibly never, but probably not. The atavistic instinct to keep her family together was less strong than it had been on the morning the police came – because this allegation affected her more directly – but she still felt an instinct to, as the newspapers always put it, 'stand by' him.

Why did the betrayed stay? The thought of starting again became more alarming the older you were, and with no guarantee of avoiding the same problem; she knew too many women who had taken refuge from one faithless fucker in the arms of another. And because the judgemental – a group that seemed to encompass whole countries these days – tended always to assume that the innocent party had somehow been at fault.

And because Ned's plea chimed with an instinct of her own. How far – and how far back – could the sins of the past be redeemed?

Whore Trawl

Because Wilhelmina Hessendon Castle was – the electoral register revealed – fifty-eight, opposition research was unlikely to throw up the defendant's holy grail of her fellating alternate Ibizan waiters while a clearly female head is scarcely covered by her micro-skirt. If such scenes had been as common in the past as they seemed to be now, the early participants had the protection of not being shown from phone to phone moments afterwards.

Usefully, the first accuser's unusual name made her a Googlewhack, meaning that Claire did not have to waste time reading about numerous irrelevant soundalikes around the world. The woman now lived in South-West London in what appeared to be a flat – there was a B beside the street number – with another occupant, in the 18–25 age category, called William Alexander Castle. A divorced or separated single mother, with – cf. her status as a friend on the Facebook page of Gemma Alexandra Castle, who seemed to be studying late-night drinking with a bit of light Psychology thrown in – a daughter at University.

Claire noted that WHC (her abbreviation in their case documentation) had become a mother relatively late. As a single woman of thirty-seven, this pleased her; as a lawyer, it raised the worry of the prosecution dramatizing a plaintiff who struggled to form relationships because of an early sexual trauma.

The alleged victim had been, either side of the Millennium, a director of two companies – Castle Technology Ltd and Castle Technical Solutions – in which the other director was Alexander Peter Castle. A 192.com for him revealed that he [60–65] lived in Holland Park with Sally Jane Castle [30–35] and Alexandra Jane Castle. *Who's Who* confirmed that his *m 1st, 1989 to* Wilhelmina Dawson (née Hessendon) had produced *1s, 1d* before, after (*marr. diss. 2008*), his *m 2nd, 2009 to* Sally (née Botting), with its resulting *1d*.

To Claire's surprise, the Facebook page for the first Mrs Castle still had a public profile, suggesting that her solicitor was either old-fashioned or naive about opposition tactics. The lines for relationship status and birth-date were both blank, the second omission possibly a response to the first. The *friends with* column lacked what would have been the jackpot – Jessamy Pothick – and contained no other overlaps that obviously spoke to motivation or collusion.

The photos were mainly of a boy, in poses graduating from tricycle to motorbike, and a girl whose journey took her from pony to polo pony to VW Polo. There were only three snaps of the page-holder herself, of which the most recent showed her smiling shyly, alone with a glass of white wine at a table with sparkling sea and Med-like light behind. Claire would have given a lot – and, in a crime novel, would have handed that amount over to a private detective – to know who took the photo.

Claire mentally transferred this person, minus the wine and sun glasses, to the witness box. On the English class-by-glance test, WHC looked like a doctor or magistrate and from her listed interests – theatre, gardening, reading – probably sounded like one as well. She was the sort of rape complainant whom the defence rather than the prosecution wanted to give evidence from behind a screen.

It would fall to an intern or work-experiencer to read through the Facebook conversations pages, in the small hope of finding a succession of postings praising the historical documentaries of her old friend Prof. Ned, but Claire's skim-inspection found nothing. The most frequent exchanges involved one friend who shared photos of rescue dogs and cats and another who seemed to spend much of her time as a volunteer taking the sick and disabled to Lourdes. Neither of these was what you were hoping for on a whore-trawl. And Google threw up only local newspaper reports of fruit and vegetable prizes at gardening fairs and some book reviews (Mantel, Waters, Barnes, Rendell, Kingsolver, Haddon) on the website of a Notting Hill reading group. Claire thought of the old-school QCs who would have seized on a liking for *Tipping the Velvet* to suggest to the jury that the witness was a closet lesbian, but such tactics were thankfully over.

After two hours, she had found nothing destructive. She was professionally disappointed, personally relieved.

The Literature of False Accusation (3)

Summary: In a 'certain city' in early 1974, twenty-seven-year-old Katharina Blum – who works as a housekeeper for an elderly couple and as an occasional freelance caterer – turns up at the doorstep of the Crime Commissioner, who is dressed as a sheik for a fancy-dress party, and confesses to having shot dead that day, in her apartment, Werner Totges, a reporter for the sensational local daily, the *News*.

Four days previously, Katharina, a young divorcee, attended a party where she seduced / was seduced by – asked by police if he 'fucked' her, she replies, ambiguously, 'I wouldn't call it that' – a young man called Ludwig Gotten, who, it turns out, is a political radical on the run from cops who consider him a suspect in murders and a bank robbery. Reporting the story of Gotten's liaison and escape, the *News* accuses Katharina of being red (politically), scarlet (sexually) and destined (theologically) for the white-hot flames of hell.

These Werner Totges exclusives draw on interviews with Katharina's elderly and unwell mother and her splenetic ex-husband to create a portrait of a Marxist – her late father, his pastor confides, was a notorious Communist – whore, who, apart from the one-night stand with a left-wing criminal, was also conducting an affair with Straubleder, a married man.

Reader Review: At 140 pages, *The Lost Honour of Katharina Blum* occupied Ned for only part of a sleepless night. Heinrich Böll was obviously influenced by Kafka – an alternative opening might easily have been: 'Somebody must have been telling lies about Katharina Blum' – but with the twist that this protagonist willingly offers herself for trial on an irrefutable charge of murder, although Böll clearly directs the reader to indict her only of manslaughter on the grounds of diminished reputation.

While some of the nuances of German politics of the period must elude an English reader – such as Böll's repeated ironic refrain about living 'in a free country' – there was an obvious suggestion that the tabloid press were the new Nazis or a West German Stasi. One incidental pleasure for Ned was the conviction that he had spotted the inspiration for a favourite film, the East German surveillance movie *The Lives of Others*, in the passage where the narrator wonders: 'What goes on in the "psyche" of the wiretapper? . . . Does he find himself in a state of moral or sexual excitement, or both? Does he become indignant, feel pity or even derive some weird pleasure?' But he was also startled by the novella's contemporary English relevance: phone-hacking is used by both the state and newspapers and one reason for suspicion of the young woman is that her apartment is considered improbably luxurious for someone of her means, a standard journalistic innuendo still.

What most impressed Ned, though, was the narrative arc. Most readers would suspect – and most writers decide – that the logic of the destruction of Katharina's reputation must be suicide, but Böll, perhaps aware that this outcome simply gives the journalists another front page, subjects Katharina's destroyer to homicide. Ned saw himself handcuffed outside the house of Billy Hessendon or Jess Pothick, holding out, like the guy who shot John Lennon, a battered paperback as explanation.

Whore Trawl (2)

There were four Jess Pothicks in the online world, one a junior minister in the New Zealand government, another a student in Hawaii and a third teaching high school in Idaho. So, from location alone, *Jess Pothick, 34, London*, was obviously the one and her professional status line – *freelance researcher-writer-*

producer, TV – confirmed it. Her dating data read *in a relation-ship with Jeremy Milligan*, whom search engines revealed to be a freelance director-producer with a list of credits including Ned's history of Britain and the Elizabeths film.

Emma made a note of his name with a query beside it. Ned had intermittently reported rows during shoots – usually over the director wanting him to wear, say or do something stupid – and, if Milligan felt wronged or his career blocked, then it was possible that a nerve had been touched when his girlfriend mentioned a connection with the presenter. The next thought – which she tried to ignore – was that Ned and this Jeremy had competed for women when they worked together and that the director was horrified by the retrospective discovery that they had both fucked his new beloved.

Ned had refused to tell her the surname of the second complainant but there was no password protection on the new cheap laptop in his workroom (the police refused to say how long their Macs would be held), which might be taken as confirmation of his claim to be faithful now. When he was out at an appointment with Dr Rafi, she had found the details she needed in a Strictly Private and Confidential e-mail from the solicitor.

Even allowing for the fact that a person's cover photo on Facebook will be carefully posed and chosen, Jess Pothick was dismayingly attractive: shoulder-length blonde (not obviously bottle) hair, tanned (not obviously spray) skin, wide, kind-eyed smile and, out of shot, that infuriatingly tight, childless vagina. And, when she had done it (whatever it was) with Ned, she had been a decade younger, unless this picture was from then (a minor perjury by online standards) but would that be better or worse? Emma stared at the picture and tried to see in it a twenty-four-year-old woman who had cunningly seduced a pissed fifty-year-old man.

Most of Jess Pothick's friends on Facebook were men and women of about her age, huddled over wine bottles lined up like skittles, pulling silly drunken faces made demonic by flash red-eye. A more unexpected find in the friend line was Dominic Ogg, who identified himself as an *award-winning TV producer* above a cover photo in which he beamed in a tuxedo while making an X with two BAFTA trophies. Emma added *Ogg?* to her notes.

The tweets from *@jesspolondon* (dropping the *thick* from her handle seemed a sensible precaution in this medium) were infrequent but cheery, posting a link to the website of a programme she had worked on or making some insider point-scoring comment about the photography or continuity in a series that was trending.

Sometimes, when a well-known person was 'found dead' or revealed a terminal illness, Emma would scroll back through their tweets looking for signs in the tone or topics that they had been depressive or going for tests. Reading through two years of *@jesspolondon*'s – 73 followers, following 148 – mundane professional and personal comments, she tried to identify the time when, during conversations with friends and detectives, she had identified herself as a victim. But the woman gave away no more than being a moderately self-obsessed user of the new communications.

Emma clicked back to the nights out in the Facebook time-line. It was clear, even to a non-lawyer, that there was ample material here for the favoured rape defence that the complainant was an alcoholic fantasist.

Although the concept of a Sisterhood had largely been a fiction during Emma's personal and working life, it depressed her that a sex case forces women to hate, blame and shame another. She wondered how the solicitor dealt with that, and would perhaps get to raise the question in the court canteen.

Emma had been asked by her mother and Helen Pimm (the only friend brave enough to do so) whether, if the worst happened, she would be making the daily hand-holding walk across the court concourse, striding by her husband to signal more importantly that she was Standing By him.

And, although the prospect terrified her, she thought she

would. She understood the possible impact on jurors of her refusal to do so and also knew that, if she didn't, then she was telling herself that she was living with a sex criminal. And, even in her bleakest sleepless moments, she could not believe that.

All trace of Jess Pothick had been cleared from her screen and desk when Ned got back from the doctor. They had stopped kissing each other in greeting but were keeping their conversations civil.

'How was it?'

'I'll live. Unfortunately.'

'Ned!'

'Joke. He wants to wean me off the zonkers at night but he's upped the dosage of the happies as a consolation.'

'Ned, did you ever work with a Jeremy Milligan?'

'Where? Teaching or TV?'

'TV. Director or producer, I think.'

'Not that I remember. But there were so many of them. Why?'

A lie was required and arrived with satisfying rapidity. 'Oh, he was in some discussion on Radio 4 about history documentaries.'

What if he wanted to search it on iPlayer? But her deception had worked. 'Yes, well, I don't want to know what he or they said while I'm having my breakdown.'

'You're not having a breakdown.'

Epistle

From: frtony@stignatius.rc.uk
To: nmarriott@historyman.com

Dear Ned (if I may), I have followed your career with some interest, as we are both alumni (though some years apart) of

St Barnabus School. In fact, as I have my own media profile, although much lower than yours, I was invited to be the speaker at Speech Day there last year, where my duties included presenting the Marriott Cup for History.

As I appreciate that privacy must be of some importance to you at the moment, I should tell you that I got this e-mail address from our former teacher in common, the redoubtable Mrs Ricks.

I have noted your recently publicised troubles. I am in possession of neither the facts nor the right to make any judgement. However, I can say that, whenever I have met anyone who knew you through either our school or through broadcasting, the comments on you have always been positive. I am also acutely aware, from the direction in which my own profession has taken me, of the impact that such stigmatization, in whatever circumstances, can have on someone.

Might you ever feel it useful to speak to me – whether as a priest or simply a sympathetic listener – I would be happy to arrange to meet.

I appreciate that the fact that someone has been raised and educated as a Catholic does not mean their faith has endured but I offer you my pastoral care at whatever level you may wish to receive it and I will (again, if I may) pray for you.

With best wishes, Father Anthony Glascock, SJ

There Goes the Neighbourhood

When he had to go out – to see Claire or Dr Rafi – Ned left the house as early as possible, hoping to meet no one. But, on the first Thursday of his disgrace, Olliphant, the heart surgeon, was coming out of Number 22. The two men were on nodding terms, which they continued, but the medic now extended to conversation.

'Er, one never knows whether to say anything. But are you all bearing up?'

Olliphant was looking away shyly but his voice sounded genuinely kind, perhaps from a career of telling people that they might be dying, or people's relatives that they just had.

'Well, you can probably imagine.' Olliphant nodded. 'I'm sorry about the scrum outside the house. Yes, I did say *scrum*.'

'Ha! My dear chap, we know you didn't invite them. And yours was nothing compared to what went on with our Secretary of State across the way or poor Mr Mercury down the road. Look, Ned, if I may call you . . . ?'

'Sure.'

'One has had many colleagues in malpractice cases. Almost to a man exonerated. Eventually. I'm sure we can't but if there were anything the Residents' Committee could do for you . . .'

'Just don't believe everything you read in the newspapers.'

'Well, indeed. I'd have thought these properties, even the flats, are worth far north of what the *Daily Mail* estimated, wouldn't you? Now take care, won't you, er, Ned?'

Friday Suicide Call (2)

'Tom?'

He knew at once the gentle recitativo but withheld the recognition. 'Yes?'

'David Wellington. So, how you are getting on?'

'I assume there must be a relief when I answer. So you have that relief.'

'I can see I'm going to have to be on my mettle for these. A lot of people who have these forced breaks of routine . . .'

'Well, that's one way of putting it.'

'A lot of people undergoing this, what they find most difficult is the loss of structure. So are you able to get some reading and writing and so on done at home?'

'I've been doing a lot of reading.'

'Well, that's one good thing, Tom. I always think, if I could have a long painless illness with a guaranteed recovery, I'd have a big stack of books by the bed.'

'Well, maybe you should arrange to be secretly investigated by Dr Traill.'

'Ha. I can understand why you'd say that. Tell me what you've been reading, Tom?'

'Actually, I've been enjoying a lot of Kafka. Especially *The Trial.*'

'Ah. I know *of* it. I've read the cockroach one. But . . .'

'This one is about a man who is told one day that he's on trial for unspecified crimes in a process that seems to have secret rules.'

Though attempting non-judgemental listening, Wellington judged that he should change the subject. 'Tell you what, Tom. One of my dreams in retirement is to read the whole of Shakespeare.'

'Oh, yes, I've been getting through a lot of old Shaky. Especially *Othello.*'

The gaps before Wellington's answers were becoming longer. 'Right. Well, unless I'm missing something, that one should take your mind off things.'

'Not really. "*I have lost my reputation. I have lost the immortal part of myself and what remains is bestial.*"'

'Tom, I think I missed some of that. There was a lot of noise in the corridor.'

Tom repeated the line with an even heavier stress on *lost* and *reputation*, briefly the actor he had dreamed until university of being.

'What I'm wondering, Tom, is whether you might require a greater level of professional support than I can give you.'

Born a Paduan aristocrat, he lived as a monk – probably the most celebrated and almost certainly the maddest apart from Rasputin – and died as a heretic, hanged and incinerated in Florence in May 1498, the burning of his corpse possibly a cruel allusion to the notorious Falò delle vanità – bonfire of the vanities – that he had carried out – no, stoked was better, Ned thought *– had stoked in the city the previous year. That great blaze contained paintings, writings and items (such as cosmetics) that Girolamo Savonarola considered religiously or politically incorrect.*

Ned reversed the adverbs, using *religiously* as a buffer between *politically* and *incorrect* to disguise slightly the contemporary rhetorical reference, the most consistent complaint of critics being his fondness for comparisons between history and news stories. Although, of all his projects, this was probably not the one for such objectors.

Whereas other religious preachers had been most concerned with cleansing the souls of the people, Savonarola wanted to sterilize their tongues, eyes and minds. He sought to bring thought and discourse in line with sensitivities that he personally identified and protected. Among his main targets were university teachers and the preachers, pamphleteers and prophets who were the entertainers and media of fifteenth-century Italy

The research had revealed the compelling detail, which he would carefully footnote to Professor Donald Weinstein, that Renaissance preachers would be dropped from a certain church or a period of the liturgical calendar (Easter, Christmas) if their congregations dwindled during a series of sermons. It was a metaphor too tempting for this historian.

university teachers, preachers and pamphleteers and the preachers, who, like television presenters today, could lose the best slots in the pulpit if their ratings with the congregation went down during a series of talks. And that is not the only contemporary resonance of the false prophet who ended up as cinders on Florentine cobbles. Girolamo Savonarola's mission was above all a war on what could be said and seen in a society. In this respect, though a figure from the Renaissance period, he can be considered a guiding spirit of our own times.

Ned saw himself delivering this speech – repeatedly because of different camera positions and revving scooters – on location on a hot day in Florence, an attractive young woman runner dabbing his scalp with perfumed wipes between takes. No, a male gay runner.

Home Truths (3)

'I don't want to sound flippant, but to be accused of rape once may be accounted etc. . .'

'That's unfair, Hells. It's self-perpetuating. After one allegation, there's more likely to be another. It's called clustering . . .'

'Maybe, sweet, but mightn't the women in HR – and they usually are women, from what I've seen – see it as a sort of v-sign? Like walking into your drink-driving trial on the arms of Jim Beam and Dom Perignon . . .'

'If someone tells a lie about you, it doesn't become the truth because someone else tells it as well.'

'Oooh, mmmm, well, pattern of behaviour?'

'No. Pattern of *allegation* is what it is . . .'

'And, anyway, Tom, in this case, it's not a lie being repeated, it would have to be two people making separate things up. I really think you should consider taking someone else . . .'

'Hells, do you believe *I'm* innocent?'

'Silly, you know I do.'

'Well, I think Nod is.'

'Tom, yours is some corporate brainstorm. Ned's is . . . is . . .'

'Okay, suppose I were accused of rape, would you believe in me?'

'Gosh, well . . . what a grim what-if . . . well, of course, I would . . . you're just not that kind of man.'

'And you think he is?'

'That's not what I'm saying, Tom.'

Stranger Danger

In the *Guardian*, Ned read about a survey in which people were asked what they would do if they saw a weeping child standing alone on a street. Three-quarters said that they would walk on because of the risk of being falsely accused of abuse.

It was a perfect illustration of the law of unintended consequence: children were more at risk from paedophiles because adults who weren't paedophiles were so afraid of being taken as child-abusers.

The Documentation Stage

Before they got out of the car, each of them swallowed an upper. 'Anti-snap!' said Tom. Almost every parking space was empty, although a flickering squiggle below the name sign boasted: NO VACANCIES. This type of motel, double-glazed against the rumble of traffic from a motorway junction, was aimed at sales reps, who would leave early and arrive late. As he had done many times since his fall, Ned played out in his mind a counter-life of being known to nobody except those close to him and in which a disaster would go largely unremarked.

A Golf and an Audi, each with child seats in the back, were parked alongside each other in the L-bend of tarmac that couldn't be seen from the road.

Tom nudged Ned and pointed towards the vehicles. 'Somewhere in the county, there's a husband and a wife wondering why their other halves aren't answering the mobile.'

Ned laughed but felt a malevolent desire for the couple to be caught, which shook him, although, for his friend's consumption, he said: 'At least if we happen to bump into them in the corridor, they're unlikely to tell their friends about it.'

'Yeah. And, if the paps snap us going in for the afternoon and draw the wrong conclusion, we can sue the buttocks off them and pay our legal fees.'

Mirror tiles on the walls of the lobby must originally have been intended to make the space look bigger but now maximized the shabby decoration. Beside the reception desk, a stand-up glossy billboard showing a family of four with lottery-win grins as they held knives and forks above plates of bacon and eggs, the yolks blindingly yellow. The receptionist, face kissingly close to a computer screen, didn't look up even when they scuffed their feet noisily on dark green carpet tiles deeply grooved by vacuuming. Tom shuffled a pile of leaflets for a performance by a Coldplay tribute band at the local theatre.

The employee completed his task and acknowledged them. 'Checking in? What names?'

He looked twentyish, residual spots on a face topped by a burst of ginger hair that resembled a cartoonist's drawing of a roaring fire. He might be a student at the university, Ned guessed, in which case the discreet location would be useless.

'No, er, I think Meeting Room 1 is booked for us,' Tom said.

'Got you. Your colleague's already there. Lift or stairs to the basement and end of the corridor.'

Prints of a hunting scene and a fishing trip – school, no kindergarten, of Constable – hung on the walls of a windowless room almost filled by a varnished table. A man with steel-rimmed spectacles and a neatly trimmed grey beard – profession-guessers on a train would have taken him for a science teacher – stood as Ned and Tom came in.

'Good afternoon. Stephen Cooper, Workplace Harmony. This – as I hope has been explained to you – is the documentation stage of your process.' From his crisp handshake onwards, Cooper radiated the incurious neutrality that Tom remembered from urinary-genital clinics. Their corporate warder gave no flicker of recognizing Ned from the news or campus gossip, although he surely did. 'You have two hours to examine the material and may make written notes but must not take any photographs or other visual record.'

As if in an examination room, a notepad, pencil and closed folder were placed in front of two chairs at the far end of the table. A student, though, would panic at the size of the test being set: the paperwork was as thick as the telephone directory of a major metropolis.

'Christ,' Tom whispered to Ned as they sat down. 'They had less on Adolf Eichmann.'

At the other end of the room, their carer was reading one of C. J. Sansom's Tudor thrillers. Was this coincidence or, if Tom were a lecturer in Spanish, would Cooper have filled the time with *Don Quixote*?

'Excuse me?' said Ned. 'We *can* talk to each other presumably?'

The referee of harmony in the workplace bookmarked the novel with his palm and looked up. 'Of course. And I'm not involved in your process so you don't have to worry about overhearing.'

Their anxiety and catastrophizing only partially controlled by medication, Tom and Ned tried to discuss with their eyes whether Cooper's promise was a double bluff.

Printed on the sky-blue cardboard covers were the words: Strictly Confidential – The Traill Report into the Conduct and Culture of the UME History Directorate, May 2014. Each of their copies had a numeral – Tom's 3, Ned's 4 – printed in the top right-hand corner, indicating a tight control of distribution that Tom knew would be of little use if it ever suited the university to leak the contents.

Flashed back with appalling clarity to his Finals, Tom watched a drop of sweat hit the cover and form a ragged island. He felt Ned's hand on his and turned to see his friend motioning that they should go together. Butch and Sundance, they synchronized their opening of the document.

Still aping an examinee, Tom flicked through the pages to

summarize the contents. More than two thirds of the material consisted of print-outs of e-mails sent or received by Tom through the college intranet system, from as long ago as September 1996 to as recently as the previous Easter. In common with most writers and academics, he had fantasized about his correspondence one day being published, but had imagined his exchanges with Ned appearing in a handsome hardback from the Harvard University Press rather than in a print-out with the subheadings *Personal Remarks About Staff* and *Abuse of The UME Intranet System*. After thirty years of teaching Nixon, he had become him.

At the edge of his vision, he saw Ned shaking his head as he read.

Apart from this anthology of his communications, the two most substantial sections of the report were headed *Victim Statements* and *Witness Statements*.

The complainants were disguised by the ciphers V1 to V7, making them resemble German war weapons, while witnesses were hidden behind the letter W and a number, giving these sections the feel of a map of West London.

In a technique he had used since student days for deciding quickly which research documents required more detailed study, Tom skimmed the statements for key phrases. V1: *I regard myself as a 'good team player' and tried to be a 'sounding board' for Dr Pimm, as with all my colleagues. However, I consistently found him to be distant and to appear eager to get away from me on the occasions when we would fall into conversation.* V2: *My GP has diagnosed me with a condition called 'nominal aphasia', which leads me sometimes to forget or to transpose names and words. I have never let this condition interfere with my teaching but I have been told by [W2] that Dr Pimm has on occasion 'entertained' other staff with cruel parodies of my lectures.* V3: *I was horrified to be told by [W2] that Dr Pimm would refer to me in conversation by the nickname 'Horny', which I assumed to be a reference to the fact that, since the death of my husband from a rare and aggressive form of cancer, I am a widow who has on occasion used newspaper or online dating sites. I found this description sexist, unpleasant and demeaning.*

Ned nudged him and, when Tom looked across, was pointing to those phrases.

'Christ,' he whispered. 'She's even more Horny than we thought.'

Laughing, Tom noticed Cooper staring at them disapprovingly. He returned to his savaging by anonymous quotation. V2: *Owing to a mishearing in a staff meeting, I was for a time labouring under the false impression that a lecture was being given by Professor AJP Taylor rather than, as it in fact turned out, in a room named in honour of someone who, it turned out, had been dead for some years. It was subsequently brought to my attention by [W3] that Dr Pimm had made mocking comments to colleagues about my mistake, and a story subsequently appeared in a student publication questioning my educational credentials.*

Speed-reading, in this case, also solved the problem of being unable to tolerate more than flashes of the contents. V4: *Although I am a long-established authority on Latin American history, Dr Pimm, in syllabus and examination meetings, would frequently challenge my arguments and opinions, even though his own specialty was the politics of the United States of America. This undermined my authority and caused me public humiliation among colleagues.*

The statements were a catalogue of petulant defamations, slyly redesigned anecdotes and evangelical self-righteousness. Moments in meetings up to two decades previously – when Tom had supposedly failed to support or acknowledge a colleague's argument – were recalled with a clarity of detail and analysis of motivation that had notoriously eluded the aggrieved in their teaching of history.

Tom thought of the former subjects of the GDR, discovering, in the Stasi files released after the fall of the Berlin Wall, that colleagues, friends and even relatives or lovers had been informing against them for decades; or elderly employees of Hollywood learning, from releases of declassified files, that there had been many more snitches than they had feared during the McCarthy period, and that the worst culprits often lay among the unsuspected. And even though Tom, unlike East Germans and movie-workers, had received some preparation for character assassination through the internet and social media, he was astonished by the monster depicted through a collage of misrepresentations and resentments.

The file alternated between allegations for which he could see no basis – such as V6's *Then Dr Pimm made a joke about paedophilia that shocked me so much that I had to check with [W14] that he had actually said it* – or V7's *I am a committed Christian who was brought up in a house where swearing was not allowed and so was horrified to hear Dr Pimm, in his lectures and seminars, frequently employing the most foul expletives* – and stories shorn of their context, such as V2's: *In departmental meetings, Dr Pimm would routinely adopt sceptical or sarcastic body-language. He would often sigh heavily when [W1] was presenting the agenda and, on other occasions, would seem to stifle a sigh when [W1] spoke*, which was clearly a reference to the period when Rafferty, at Special's bequest, was pushing through the particularly lunatic initiative in which students became customers and staff were warned to avoid at all costs being 'academic' in case the shoppers were put off. Sighed? He wished he had vomited.

Like Enigma-breakers at Bletchley Park, Tom spotted a hole in the code. From the supporting detail, W1 could only be Joanna Rafferty, Special's steadfast deputy, apparently considered either the first or most important witness against him. Numerous internal details suggested that W2 was Quatermass (who had never forgiven him for leaving the union), which meant that it was possible to have both a V and a W code without cross-referencing.

On the notepad, he wrote: V1 = Daggers, V2 = Savlon, V3 = Horny, V4 = Quatermass. He placed question marks beside V5, V6 and V7. The last two sounded like students, although, as he didn't recognize the incidents, it was impossible to be sure who they were.

The *Witness Statements* section contained the full W testimonies. Certain verbal tics and ferocious certainties confirmed that W1 was Rafferty and W2 Quatermass, while also exposing the equations: W4 = V1, W5 = V2 and W8 = V3.

In his freshers' week lecture on sourcing, Tom warned the students about the risk of false circuits of confirmation. If B quoted the view of A, then you had one rather than two sources for the claim and, even if C and D then went into print with either the A origination or B's endorsement of it, there still remained a single witness rather than – as, he liked to say, 'poor historians and almost all modern journalists believe' – four. So a 'fact' about the Black Death or the Suez Crisis that produced a Google-crop running into tons might have been grown from a single and possibly blighted seed.

Dr Traill, though, had either not taken precautions against, or chosen systematically to ignore, the problem of 'Chinese Whispers', although that term itself was probably now at risk of offending Orientals.

Special, Savlon, Horny, Daggers and Quatermass were routinely cited as 'supporting witnesses' to a claim made by one of the others, although, in most cases, all this meant was that they had swapped complaints or even, in an extreme case, that W8 had been told by W2 that W5 had been told what had happened to V1. So, on occasion, Traill would claim to have multiple witnesses to an incident for which the only source was the person who told the original story.

Scattergun attacks on Tom's character had also been encouraged and the most effective under-cutter of his reputation was the ninth of the anonymous witnesses, who gained credibility from not documenting personal suffering but commenting with an air of historical authority.

I think a lot of his problems, W9 argued, *come from the way he talks. Almost everything he says is a pun, a joke, a nickname: he has private names for most of the department. Yes, apparently he does have one for me. It's [redacted]. Yes, I think what he does is to identify somebody's weakness. He's a world-class sarcastic. But, even if he just says 'hello' to you, it's likely to be in a foreign language or accent. He says the word 'so' in Anglo-Saxon. Instead of 'no way', he started saying 'Norway' which then became 'Denmark' – it's a sort of private language. Trying to find a time everyone can make for a meeting first thing the next day, he'll ask: 'Anyone for tennish?'*

Tom found funny again a joke of which he had been very proud at the time – several years ago – and tried to remember what the meeting had been and who might have been there. Whereas most of the other depositions were vividly marked by the sensibility, rhythm or catch-phrases of a character in the departmental drama, W9 spoke more neutrally – and sometimes even approvingly – although with intermittent stings: *Why does he talk to people like that? I suspect he finds most people rather boring. I think it's twisted.*

On his list of suspects, he wrote a question mark beside W9 and then tripled and underlined it.

Maida Vale

The woman checked her reflection in the mirrored wall, patting down the collar of her blouse and then trying her fringe and nape for dryness. In the days before the idea of sex became treacherous, Ned had always found the sight of a woman just dressed from the shower deeply sensual.

Looking up from his screen, the presumed student asked: 'Are you checking out, Madam?'

So, parsimony getting the better of discretion, they must have negotiated an afternoon rate rather than paying for a whole night in advance and then leaving early, as Ned would have done in the days when he did.

Skin already pinked from hot water and almost certainly earlier exertion, the woman blushed instantly, a response that took at least two decades off her age and made her a pupil rebuked by a teacher.

'Or, er, my, my . . . partner's just on the way down. I'm, er, just taking something to my . . . *the* car.'

Although the item must be contained in the compact hand-bag that was her only luggage. Lowering her head so that the damp strands fell across her eyes, she hurried out.

'So I wasn't the only person who just spent two hours in this hotel getting totally fucked,' muttered Tom.

'Don't,' Ned said.

They were sitting on a padded bench opposite the lifts between two towering but insect-nibbled pot plants. The man from WH had left, after stuffing the two copies of the Traill Report with his Tudor thriller in a rucksack.

'Hwæt,' Tom said, opening his notebook, prompting Ned to do the same, but then the lift pinged and a man stepped out, flush-faced, no suitcase.

'Romeo,' muttered Tom, and it seemed an irrefutable guess. While the woman had left the hotel trying to look as if she had been attending a boring meeting, the man wore like an advertising board an air of giddy victory that omitted only whistling. He was paunchy and balding, another beneficiary of women's commendable but counter-Darwinian generosity towards male decay.

Ned visualized the lingering last kiss against the door or wall of the rented room, but was surprised not to feel the usual reflex of envious resentment at lovers. His only thought was to hope that the two of them would never come to believe different histories of what had happened between them.

At the desk, the man was settling the bill with twenty-pound notes, although this precaution was being recorded on the CCTV angled in the corner of the ceiling and wall.

'Hwæt,' Tom asked. 'Give it to me bare-backed. How bad was it?'

'Honestly?'

'Oh, Nod. That word always guarantees that someone isn't going to be.'

'Tom, you know me better than that. I mean, I understand that reading that stuff must be like being stuck in a cupboard at the AGM of your enemies. But there have always been two factions in that department – the high standards and the high-handed – and this is the latest battle between them. Nothing sexual, physical or financial. Not even anything that most people would think of as, I'm going to have to say it, bullying . . .'

'*Bensoning*. Yes, well, did you read their definition of that? You could get a quadriplegic with it if someone took offence at them for not shaking hands . . .'

'Or, indeed, if someone felt offended by that metaphor.'

'Oh, Christ, they've got the microchip into your head now, have they?'

'No, they haven't. But, if you look at it, they're mainly trying to get you over the way you speak.'

'Look, I talk how I talk.'

'And people hear how they hear. Especially now.'

'One thing, Nod: I think my prat-nav has matched most of them. But Maida Vale escapes me.'

'What? You've lost me.'

'And I can't find *it*. Maida Vale – W9.'

'Oh.'

'Who the fuck is that?'

'Asbo?' Ned wondered.

'No. Asbo is W14. Definitely. I recognize his account – or rather half his account – of the meeting about no-platforming.'

'Well, I don't know who it is then,' Ned said. 'But all you need is for the appeal to show some sense. What do we know about the guy from Creative Writing?'

People of the Enemy

Henry Gibson was UME's Professor of Creative Writing. This subject, until the Millennium a distrusted and even despised minor module of the English course, had become, in the new century, a surprising academic powerhouse, as an epidemic of self-expression spread through Britain, encouraged by the industrialization of diary-keeping in online blogs and the huge sales of autobiographies by victims of poor or abusive childhoods.

At most universities, including UME, CW was now a separate faculty, with thousands of annual applicants, apparently convinced that writing had become a vocational profession, like medicine, ignoring the brutal truth that there existed no National Literature Service and that readerships would always be more fickle and elusive than disease.

The monetization of literary pipe-dreams had obvious benefits to colleges but also to established authors who were the most plausible tutors for this sought-after craft.

At a time publishers' advances and sales of fiction were diminishing, authors suddenly had the compensation of a new source of income – dropping monthly into bank accounts, with paid holidays and even pension contributions – from encouraging others to join their devalued profession. It was as if miners made redundant in the 1980s had been retrained to teach at an Academy of Coal-Extraction.

The Executive Dean of Humanities was also quick to see that these late-career lecturers and professors often had publication histories – including op-ed pieces for mass-circulation newspapers, or a Jubilee-pegged biography of The Queen – that amassed impact points far beyond the capabilities of traditional staff with their books and articles aimed at a narrow elite of peers.

Henry Gibson had been the department's star catch: an English novelist who, his fame having declined at a far slower rate than his sales, was still known to those who would read fiction if only they could find the time, continued to receive prominent solus reviews on the shrinking fiction pages of broadsheet book sections and was commissioned by editorial pages to write articles on subjects such as immigration, sex education and (he was a quarter-Glaswegian) Scottish independence, making these already contentious topics even more so with his reliably counter-populist positions.

As a novelist, he had made his name in two senses. Early in his career, Gibson had become irritated that, perhaps due to the slovenly enunciation of radio presenters and increasing ignorance of classical literature, a dismaying number of those he met were under the impression that he was a nineteenth-century Norwegian dramatist. An anecdote much-quoted in profiles had the novelist yelling at a late-night local radio broadcaster: 'I did *not* fucking write *The Wild Duck!*' Pre-Twitter, this outburst had not ended his career, as it might now.

Subsequently, he used the name 'Harry Gibson' on the cover of his third novel *Independent States*, cross-epochally intercutting narratives featuring Earl Mountbatten of Burma dividing India, the death-bed of Mother Teresa of Calcutta, an Asian student racially murdered in 1980s London and a trans-gender Pakistani astronaut on an international space mission to Mars in 2162.

When the book was shortlisted for what was then the Booker Prize, and won the John Llewellyn Rhys, the earlier novels were reattributed to Harry Gibson, under which identity there appeared a hefty novel approximately every five years; including *Watt, Watt*, in which the eponymous protagonist of a Beckett novel and the Scottish engineer who gave his name to the international measurement of electricity somehow met during a power-cut in a lighthouse on the west Irish coast. Marking a change of direction, his most recent novels had been Kafkaesque fables, in which nameless protagonists in unspecified countries with impossible topography and dystopian governments suffered threats of disgrace or violence from male strangers, punctuated by graphic seductions from mysterious women. *The Strange Day of Ignatius P* had won the novel section of the Costa Prize.

For reasons of educational bureaucracy, however, the Professor of Creative Writing was listed on all campus documentation under his birth-certificate name, with the result that he was again mistaken for Henrik Ibsen by some students. Gibson was unconsoled by colleagues who told him that the ability to make the error revealed a level of literary-historical knowledge rare in those currently studying English Literature.

But under Gibson's direction, CW, like a chain of coffee houses, had franchised out into other faculties. Tom's and Ned's students were now offered options on 'Writing Popular History' and 'Writing Historical Fiction'.

Ray

Emma felt like a detective, except that she was hoping not to find anything. In the messages she checked, Toby and his main mates – Seb, Jordan and Oscar, plus Bobby and Aidan, two names she didn't remember from birthday parties – traded misspelt, syntax-free digital grunts about 'sick' goals and cheats on PS4. The other communications were largely pooled attempts to establish what homework had been given, when it was due and whether one of the others might share the answers.

She couldn't decide how suspicious to be. The fact that the group included only boys was probably normal for his pre-hormonal age and conversations during a football simulation game. But might it mean that girls (encouraged by their mothers) were ignoring Toby?

She speed-read, as if with a manuscript she had already decided not to accept, what seemed to be several metres of inane exchanges. It struck her that a lowered IQ was a likely consequence of being a digitally responsible parent.

There was a lot she didn't understand but it was in areas – gaming, American TV shows, football, the lunches at Abbey Grove – that represented no concern. Then she noticed something and checked the other messages from the same sender; it was something that had only recently begun. Was she being over-sensitive? No. The question that her historian partner had taught her to ask: what benign explanation fitted the facts?

'Tobes?' she asked. 'Why has Seb Landrose started calling you "Ray"?'

'I don't know.'

'You *do* know.' A jolting echo of her mother's voice from childhood. 'When did this start?'

'Mummy . . .' He wasn't looking at her. 'It's just, like, a joke about one of the Man City players.'

The maternal instinct, arriving almost with a child's first words, for a lie being told. 'Oh, which one?'

'Huh? Like you'd so know any of them, anyway.'

Avoid being so interfering that your child is encouraged to deceive you, a *Guardian* article had warned.

'Okay. But you will tell me if anyone gives you any grief over . . . ?'

Toby nodded.

The Bonfire of the Sanities

'The title's great.'

'Well, a bit obvious, I suppose.'

While a lunch at the Ivy had been a ritual of every previous commission – symbolic of both editorial budgets and confidence in the project – Ned currently detested restaurants. Public recognition, once validating, now led him to imagine prosecution and sentencing from those who glanced at him and then looked away. Opting for a sandwich in the office of his editor also brought the benefit, he reckoned, of not having to explain why he was off alcohol.

But as he walked in, Jack Beane was already filling two glasses from a bottle padded with a silver freeze-sleeve.

'Prof, I think you need this, what you're going through,' said Beane, one of those men who maintained into late middle-age their waistline and hairline, the whitening of the latter the one concession to seniority.

'I'm driving,' he said, the only explanation for sobriety that he found at least some hosts accepted. 'But thanks.'

The dust jackets of some of their seven books together were butterflied behind glass. Ned wondered if display was a qualitative judgement or based only on sales.

'It goes without saying,' Beane said, 'that nobody here thinks you're anything but a thousand per cent innocent. In fact, HR insisted that we asked around before you came in if anyone had ever had any problems with you and it was totally fine.'

Even though this secret trial had cleared him, Ned felt despair at the revelation that such shadowy assizes were judged necessary before he could enter a building. And, if an objection had been raised, would Beane have mysteriously pressed the case of some nearby diner where the waiters were all elderly men?

Beane lined up both wine glasses on his side of the desk and passed across a substitute tumbler of water. The publisher waved at a plastic platter of snacks from a sandwich franchise, a reduced version of the catering at book launches. Appetite still absent, and unable to digest without cascading sweat, Ned took a small slice of vegetable wrap and, with minimal actual nibbles, stage-ate.

His host, anyway, was looking down at a print-out of the proposal for *The Bonfire of the Sanities*.

'Wow! I like this. You'll be arguing that Savonarola was right?'

'What?' Ned wondered if the publisher was actually reading the treatment for the first time. 'No, of course I won't. He was a mad fucker working out a political and psycho-sexual pathology.'

'But you're Professor Perversity – you always go against the grain.'

Ned felt the irritation of finding that someone who seemed to have missed the point had actually seen it. 'Oh, yeah, well, I suppose, in a way, in this case too, yes. I'll be arguing that our academic, judicial and media institutions seem to have taken the mad monk as their inspiration.'

'Wow! Sales and Marketing will love the coverage potential!' As publishing struggled to come to terms with the twin tenets of the digital revolution – that anyone could write a book but nobody should have to pay for one – Ned had suffered the sensation, in recent meetings with Beane, that his editor was being dubbed into another language; when they first worked together, the publisher had just completed a Ph.D. on Martin Luther and considered Ned a reckless populist. 'Prof, do you think this is something we could position for the Christmas market?'

'I suppose so. Just the thing for the family member who has been witch-hunted.'

'It's great you can laugh about this. I'm sure it will help. Do have more sandwiches. Otherwise, they just go to the food bank.'

'I had a late breakfast. I stayed up writing last night.'

'Good, good. That you're writing, I mean. Ned, I've told them you won't want to but I've been asked to ask if you would totally rule out a memoir of what you're going through? Assuming, of course, that it all turns out . . .'

'I am making that assumption, yes. And, if it doesn't, I can always sell *The Prison Diaries* to Penguin instead.'

'I'll take that as a joke.'

'But, yes, you're right: it remains my ambition to remain the only person to have been on television who hasn't published an autobiography.'

'But you might sort of be there somewhere behind Savonarola?'

'In the folds of his habit. Yes, possibly.'

'Ned, you're sweating up – should I open a window?'

The deal done, Beane, by convention, should now tell Ned that the company was thrilled to have the book and would publish the fuck out of it and then they would drink a toast (though, on this occasion, half non-alcoholic) to the project. But the publisher went off-script: 'There's talk here about a poppy Shakespeare biog for the death quatercentenary in 2016. Editorial are talking about the usual dames and sirs, of course, but I'd like to float you for that, all being well?'

'Well, hang on, let's get this one sorted first. You'll talk to Emma about the contract as usual?'

'Look, Ned, this stuff is decided way above my head. My advice is to get reading, even writing, but the word from Legal and HR is we can't sign off on anything until you're in the clear. They stress that this position is not in any way presumptive or judgemental.'

Dialogue With A Daughter

'All the evidence shows that almost no women make it up!'

'Does it? Then why are so many men acquitted? Just recently, Will . . .'

'Oh, for fuck's sake! If you lose a trial, it doesn't mean you're lying . . .'

'Oh, no? Just that the jury didn't believe you . . .'

'Yeah. And why's that? Because the culture propagates the myth that women who've been raped are deceitful and / or money-grabbing sluts.'

'No, no, no. Because jurors know that in the – look, I promise you, I wouldn't ever have wanted to talk to you about this stuff – in the bedroom, sometimes, there are . . . are . . . misunderstandings . . .'

'Blurred lines? Right. I hope they play Robin Thicke for you on prison radio.'

'Look, sweetheart . . .'

'Ew! Did you call *her* that *before* . . . ?'

'Oh, come on. This isn't fair. Whatever she *thinks* happened it isn't as if I . . .'

'Jumped out from behind a tree in a ski mask?'

'You know what I . . . ?'

'Haven't you got it yet, guys of your age? Rape in an under-pass with a knife or in a living room with a bottle of Chablis and Barry White on your iPod, it's still all rape. There isn't nice-rape and date-rape and posh-rape. It's all *rape*!'

'I actually agree with that.'

'Do you? How? Doesn't sound like it . . .'

'And – which is the point, what I am saying – is that there are also claims of, er, rape, that are false . . .'

'Statistically, the facts . . .'

'Look, seriously, I know you're angry with me for dragging us into all this, though obviously I didn't do it deliberately, but you must know that there are reasons – regret, anger, whatever – why a woman might sometimes convince herself that . . .'

'Professor Marriott . . .'

'Why are you calling me . . . ?'

'There was a survey recently into so-called malicious allegations . . .'

'I'm not saying it's always malice. I'm saying people have a . . . a . . .*fucked-up fuck* . . .'

'Ew!'

'And later one of them – to explain it to herself or to a part-ner . . .'

'Her? So false accusation is just a girl thing?'

'Oh, Cordelia, *Cordy*, please . . .'

'Do you know – in this survey – do you know how many rape prosecutions there were in the period under survey . . . ?'

'No, of course I don't, not exactly . . .'

'Five thousand six hundred and fifty-one . . .'

'You actually know the exact . . . ?'

'Yeah. Women and their memories. Annoying, eh?'

'Oh, please don't do this . . .'

'And do you – in all that time – do you know how many women were prosecuted for making a false allegation of rape?'

'Not very many, I'd guess. But . . .'

'Thirty-five. *Thirty-five*! And, like all our family, our *first* family, I'm crap at maths but isn't that, like, less than one per cent of prosecutions? So, if this woman has invented it all, she's in pretty select company . . .'

'No, no, no. That's a false statistic . . .'

'*What?* False claims, false statistics. Never trust a fucking girlie, eh?'

'Please, Dee. Listen to me. You're confusing two things . . .'

'Really? Blurring the lines, am I?'

'Yes. *LISTEN!*' Almost a decade away from the normal father–daughter wars of adolescence, it was a long time since she had heard him shout and she resisted a vestigial trigger to storm out, slamming the door. 'The fact that only a few women have ever actually been hauled to court for lying is meaningless . . .'

'Oh, right, really?'

'Yes. Because the standard of proof for perjury is very high. It doesn't mean that every single one of the others is automatically one hundred per cent right about what happened.'

'It means the police didn't think they were lying.'

'Mmm. Yeah. *Ish.*'

'Oh, is that what you are? A rap-*ish.*'

'Oh, please, this isn't really you . . .'

'Right. And who are you, really?'

'Darling . . .'

'Don't call me that!'

'It's not as simple as lying or not lying. Look, every single day, doctors see loads of people who are absolutely convinced they're fatally ill, although, in fact, they're not. But those patients aren't lying about dying.' The rhyme and rhythm made it sound even more like his TV voice. 'They've misread the signals or they're working out some other problem or someone else has convinced them it's a terminal condition. That's all I'm saying.'

'All! It's quite a lot to say.'

'It isn't. It's saying that when there are two people in bed – and, yes, I am going to say that's different from running up behind a woman with a knife – there are often two stories. Espe-

222

cially now there's this thing that young people seem to do now of letting people sleep in their bed who they aren't actually sleeping with – or, at least, in their mind they aren't – or who are just – that awful term – *fuck-buddies* – and so the potential for crossed wires becomes higher. And so the decision has to be in which cases a jury should get to decide between those versions. Look, in America, there are degrees of sexual offence . . .'

'Well, maybe you should go and try your luck there, then ...'

'Oh, *please*! But the point is that you actually get more convictions that way.'

'Okay. Well, to what degree are *you* guilty?'

'What? Well, not at all, obviously.'

'Right. So there we have the problem.'

'Dee, you're obviously very very upset about this. So I have to ask. Is it that you've been – please tell me – that you've been yourself . . .'

'Oh, Jesus, brilliant, now we've got the full Monty. *Daddy*' – it was the first time she had brought herself to say the word but spun it like an insult – 'I'm not saying this stuff because I've been raped. You don't need to have been killed to be against murder!'

A Theory of Domestic Economics

When the girls were something like seven, Ned, driving them back from some treat, stopped on a double yellow to use a cashpoint. Alert to the threat from traffic wardens and kidnappers, he remained half-turned at all times, watching the car.

When he returned, there was no ticket or ransom note attached to the windscreen But, safely back in traffic, Phee, always the worrier, piped from behind him: 'Daddy, why do the banks give you money?'

'Well, muffin, they don't really give it to me. I have money in the bank and that machine – what people call a "hole in the wall" – is one of the ways of getting it . . .'

'But where do *you* get the money from?'

'Well, Daddy is a teacher, like Miss Sharp, but to much older girls and boys. And the university – which is a sort of very big school – pays him for that. And Daddy also talks on television and radio and other people give him money for doing it.'

But, put like that, the economic system sounded ridiculous and flimsy and clearly unsustainable. Ned suddenly felt like a banker watching a frenzy of selling on the screen.

'So,' said Dee with her soft solemn voice. 'When you say you don't have enough money to buy us a horse, you could just talk more?'

Dialogue with a Daughter (2)

'Look, Cupcake, you may not want to talk about it at all – which is fine, these aren't conversations anyone really wants to have – but if there is anything you need to . . .'

'What is there to say? I don't believe them. I do believe you.'

'Well, that's really . . . oh, fuck, can you, there's a box of tissues under the . . . thanks . . . I promised I wouldn't . . .'

'I think I've probably done enough blubbing over the years in front of you, Daddy.'

'Yeah, well, that's the normal . . . oh, Jesus, I'm sorry . . . I . . . the only thing I really hold against my mother is that for some reason I never learned to blow my nose properly . . .'

'Should I get you some water?'

'No. I'm fine . . . I . . . I think I've got some kind of summer cold which makes it worse . . . all I'm saying is: don't listen to your sister . . . I don't mean it like that – everyone has to get through this in their own way . . . but it was like being accused of . . . of . . . *infidelity* . . . which I suppose, in a way, is how she sees it . . .'

'I know what you mean. But she took the . . . the divorce worse as well . . .'

'Oh, don't remind me . . . I haven't exactly been a good

advertisement for masculinity . . . it's a wonder that you're not both . . . oh, God, all this stuff, I suppose it would be too weird if I asked you to teach me to blow my nose . . . ?'

'Lesbians?'

'What?'

'A wonder that we're not both lesbians?'

'Oh, God, no, don't tweet I said that. Look, I don't care what your sister . . . that came out wrong . . . of course I care . . . what I'm saying is that I'd understand it if you're angry with me but talk to me instead of letting Dee . . .'

'Look, I don't need much encouragement to disagree with her. Although that isn't why I'm doing it.'

'I can't really complain. She's got the argumentative gene.'

'Oh, right. And I got the pushover one?'

'No, of course you didn't. The peacemaker one. Like your mother. Who, incidentally, has been great over . . .'

'We talked about it. As Mummy says, if every man's sex life was put on trial, there'd be a Wormwood Scrubs on every street corner . . .'

'Yes, well, I know that Jen, that Mum means well but my lawyer and I, we're sort of going for the line that I'm innocent rather than that all men are guilty. But I want to be clear that, though these women are mistaken, I'm not blaming . . .'

'Well, I am. I think they're silly self-indulgent canutes.'

'Can . . . ? Oh, Phee, I forget you even have your own swearing . . . Oh, God, I'm going to need you to pass me that box again . . .'

'It's fine, Daddy. As Granny always says, better out than in.'

'Take this as a warning. This is what it will be like when I get Alzheimer's.'

'Well, if it is, it is. That's fine.'

'Take this as a warning. This is what it will be like when I get Alzheimer's.'

'What? You just . . . oh, stop it, Daddy! If they try to lock you up for your jokes, don't come to me.'

The Literature of False Accusation (4)

Summary: In 1996, Professor Coleman Silk, a Jewish-American sixty-nine-year-old (or possibly sixty-eight-year-old, fiction generally being more precise on years of birth than days) teacher of Greek and Latin classics at Athena College, a humanities institution in New England, is urgently summoned by Professor Delphine Roux, ambitious Dean of the new Language and Literature department that has recently absorbed Classics. He is told that two students, who are African American, have brought an allegation of racism against him.

The complaint relates to the sixth week of the semester when Professor Silk, noting that two students in the register have not turned up all term, asked the class aloud: 'Does anyone know these people? Do they exist or are they *spooks?*' Though now most associated with ghosts and spies, the word is also an antiquated racial insult against black people. Silk points out that the phrase makes no grammatical sense as bigotry – 'Do they exist or are they African American?' – but he is placed under formal investigation.

This academic crisis, though, is a flashback from the main narrative, which takes place in 1998, during the summer when President Bill Clinton is facing disgrace and dismissal over his sexual relationship (fellatio and mutual masturbation but no penile penetration, according to the Starr Report) with White House intern, Monica Lewinsky.

At seventy-one (this age specified), his academic career over, the widowed Silk – blaming the death of his wife, Iris, on the stress caused by the ruin of his reputation – has spent two years writing a memoir of his fall, called *Spooks*, and is involved in an intensely sexual affair with Faunia Farley, a thirty-four-year-old uneducated woman who works as a cleaner at Athena College and the local post office. She is estranged from her husband, Les, a psychotic Vietnam veteran who is taken to Asian restaurants under supervision as part of therapy for his hatred of people who remind him of the region in which he fought.

Yet neither the academic scandal nor the sexual folly are Silk's biggest humbling. His life coming to resemble one of the Greek tragedies he taught – the final section, the fifth act, begins with the tolling words 'Two funerals' – it is revealed that the professor ruined by an accusation of racism was himself born black but, being light-skinned, was among those who, in the pre-Civil Rights era, were able to *pass* as white.

Reader Review: *The Human Stain* was not quite Tom's favourite among the novels of Philip Roth, the American writer he most admired – that was *The Counterlife,* with its unnerving reversals of perspective – and its status had been further lowered by the poor movie version in which the casting of Sir Anthony Hopkins as Silk turned it into the story of a Welsh academic who had pretended to be Jewish in order to prevent anyone knowing that he had once been a young black actor who looked nothing like him. He had always, though, considered it Roth's cleverest title, the stain referring both to the pigmentation of skin and the mess left on Monica Lewinsky's dress by the President.

But re-reading the novel during the summer of his own suspension from teaching was a lesson to Tom in how experience changes perspective. When he had read this hardback copy in 1998 – mainly on a beach in Sicily, he thought, a suspicion confirmed by a trickle of sand when he opened the pages – he had seen it as a story about race relations.

Now he was struck by the extent to which Roth details the departmental infighting. Because of old career grievances – his appointment to a job others wanted or his position on the opposing side of a departmental debate – faculty colleagues refuse to support Silk over the allegations. And, in a logic that Tom now entirely recognized from the Traill report, one of the complainants, challenged over his failure to attend any of Silk's classes, explains that he was too frightened of the possibility of suffering racism from the professor to turn up. Though it reduced the resale value of a still fairly pristine English first edition, Tom scored three exclamation marks in the margin.

Tom had always been dismissive of members of Helen's and Emma's book-group who judged fiction purely by the extent to which the central characters matched – or did not – their own experience and values. But now he had no doubt that, although Tom had personally never pretended to be anything except white, Coleman Silk was, otherwise, him.

What most surprised him was that his clear memory was of Silk being sacked by the obtuse campus yes-woman Dean Roux. In fact, he resigns, wrong-footing many colleagues who had merely been using the 'incident' as an excuse publicly to adopt liberal positions but had not been seeking his expulsion. Although he would almost certainly have won his case, Silk could no longer tolerate a place that could question his integrity with such malevolence and incompetence.

Tom came to a decision. Once he had been cleared, he would leave and find a job elsewhere. If his life subsequently continued to mirror Coleman Silk's, there would at least be the consolation of a torrid affair with an illiterate erotomaniac half his age. But then, admittedly, the drawback of violent death and the revelation that his entire life had been a lie.

The Upside of Ruin

While comparing symptoms of trauma and stress or medical treatments for them, Ned and Tom also swapped anecdotes of kindly interventions. A revered broadcaster, whom Ned had met only occasionally at the BAFTAs or in BBC 'talent' boxes at Wimbledon and the Proms, sent a handwritten note offering to 'help out' with legal costs needed to resist this 'persecution', leading Ned to wonder, from the malicious questioning that had become his mental default, if the man himself was concerned about, or had even already suffered, the Millpond knock.

Then, so soon after many of the same people had bought

lavish birthday presents for him, there were the gifts delivered almost daily, by van or hand, to a front door that Ned no longer dared open himself: bouquets (most, because of his allergies, immediately redirected to a nearby hospice), wicker baskets of mini muffins, ribboned presentation boxes from chocolatiers, several half-crates of his preferred Riojas, and, most imaginatively or perhaps egotistically, Amazon gift-wrapped box sets of little-known shows about deputy mayors of Seattle that well-wishers had enjoyed themselves. But, although the wine and the DVDs were the most practical and pleasurable offerings, they also alarmed Ned because they defined him as a man with no work: free to spend hours watching TV, with a hangover if necessary.

Tom, who moved in less high-earning circles, received a bounty more modest in content but not volume. Ciara Harrison, Professor of Irish History, possibly influenced by her troublesome subject to become a source of conciliation and kindness in the warring department, sent a box of wine from a website, followed by regular e-mails enquiring about his well-being, often attaching amusing photographs of her dog, Tess. A pile of recommended reading was sent by the other three – apart from Ned, who had no need for a formal gesture of support – of the Modern History Friday five-a-side football team, with Ben Loxley, who boycotted Amazon, driving over to deliver his gift by hand. All of his Ph.D. students sent messages of bewilderment at the claims. The colleagues who did not contact him – Daggers, Horny, Savlon, Quatermass – he took as proving that they were among Traill's complainants.

If the conflagration of their reputations showed the cruelties of which human communities were capable, a contrasting kindness had been demonstrated by the belief and concern of so many who knew them.

'As JFK didn't quite say,' Tom proposed a soft-drink toast to Ned. 'In order that the many might do good, it is necessary for the few to do evil.'

Reaching across to pour Ned another glass of the Elderflower Cordial he had brought – because of their chemically-coshed sobriety – instead of his usual bottle of Spanish red, Tom noticed on his friend's desk a stack of paperbacks. Having poured the drinks, he examined the titles sideways.

'Kafka, Ibsen . . . and the one with the B, how do you . . . ?'

'I say it to rhyme with troll. I've never known how to pronounce the dots above the . . . never did German.'

'Despite being the Hitler guy. Weird.'

'Fuck off.'

'Bit of a pronunciation crash course. That South African bloke – how do you?'

'Like a lady's knees meeting the Queen, I've always said it. But I've heard *cots-ay-ah* on the radio.'

'*Disgrace, The Lost Honour Of* . . . oh, and *The Crucible*. Nice bit of escapism, Nod.'

'Well, that's sort of the idea. Hair of the dog.'

'I've just re-read the Roth. Mainly, I use this guy with a voice like velvet who whispers in my ear that I mustn't worry if my mind starts to wander. But the thing it keeps wandering to is whether he actually fucking talks like that the whole time. *When I ask you to pass the marmalade, is it possible that what I'm actually saying is . . .*'

'Is it doing any good?'

'This is the thing. As I say to Dr Rafi, we don't know what we'd be like without it. Well, we could come off it all and find out, but Rafi doesn't want to do that, presumably in case we top ourselves.'

'Have you thought about that?'

The hardest question. Tom gave the answer he always gave to Rafi and Helen. 'No.' Then: 'You?'

Ned broke eye contact. 'As I think I said in the sad cafe, I've thought about thinking about it.' Looking back again. 'But I have whole moments now when I'm convinced I'm going to be cleared.'

Whatever *cleared* means, Tom thought. He waited with an expectant expression and, when nothing came, said: 'In the etiquette between defendants, I think this is where you say you're sure I'll get off as well.'

As if in apology, Ned refilled Tom's glass. 'Well, that goes without saying. I mean yours is just Special getting his truss in a twist. Once he tells the Executive Dean he's got all the children playing nicely, he can get back to looking at supersize trouser sites.'

An effect of the Sertraline, Tom had found, was a generalized feeling of benevolence so the rising of his temper felt as surprising as an erection in church. 'Jesus! I suppose it must be like this in jail – as you may be about to find out . . .'

The entry of enmity into friendship produced a physical whiplash reaction from Ned. 'Tom, why have you suddenly gone all Daggers on me . . . ?'

'This fucking convicts' oneupmanship: *I'm in more trouble than you are.* From here, it really doesn't feel . . .'

'Mate, I'm not diminishing the shit you're in but I'd rather have yours than mine.'

Tom tried to remember the bit from the Mindfulness CD about forcing out your bad feelings through your left big toe, or whatever it was that you were supposed to do, but, without the purring commentary in his ear, the mechanics eluded him. He tried the old-fashioned talk-down strategy of three breaths. 'Sorry, Nod. I think it's the lack of booze talking. I do know what you mean. Legally, it's better for me: no cops, no court, whatever the outcome. But, at the moment, it doesn't feel much different. We may neither of us work again or dare put our names into a search engine; we're both on pills to trick our minds that it isn't as bad as we think. And at least your nemeses have got names. I'm being ruined by people hiding behind trunk roads and postal districts.'

'Exactly. Which is one of the reasons I find it hard to take the whole thing seriously. At some point, someone's going to step in and send Special back to drawing the squares for the timetable.'

'I don't know. I feel like someone with a very rare disease. Because it's so unlikely, it feels as if it must have been meant to get me. Even the things that seem mad in what they call their "process" make sense from a certain angle. The documentation stage is crazy because how could someone ever work again with those people? But perhaps it doesn't matter because the aim is to make him unable to work with them?'

'I can see why you think that. But . . .'

After briefly wondering if this was going too far, Tom interrupted: 'In fact, to be honest, Nod, the reason it feels personal is that, if it were more general, then surely you'd be in the dock yourself.'

'Well, steady on. I never did anything.'

'Excuse me. Neither did I.'

'Er, no, no, I know. But – this isn't a criticism – you have always had a rather more abrasive relationship with – I'm not denying they're tricky – but with members of the department . . .'

'Well, maybe I paid the price for standing up for standards when some other people were playing Billy All-Mates. And at least I've never traded grades for gash.'

Was Ned flinching at the language or the allegation? His workroom was converted from a cellar – he believed that he wrote more in a windowless room – with a thickly bricked ceiling to which he gestured and said: 'Sshhh! Anyway, the Eighties was the Eighties but since then . . .'

'Yeah? *Professor Marriott is in error on his dates*' – the posh snotty voice in which they parodied *THES* reviews – 'if we believe the departmental rumours.'

'Yes, well, I thought we *weren't* believing them, Tom.'

They sipped their soft drink as attentively as if it were a thirty-year-old wine. Tom considered it a credit to his personality that Ned's celebrity and wealth had never fractured their friendship. But now, an equal experience had caused a gulf.

Eventually, Ned said: 'We're letting the stress get to us. We've each got enough enemies without making one of each other. I'm sorry about today and I'm totally behind you.'

Tom let him wait as long as he dared before saying: 'Same. Same.' Then he asked: 'Do you mind if I . . . ?' He angled his phone and took a picture of the spines of Ned's pile of books.

The Saint File

Of the two main reasons that Ned now left the house, he at first looked forward more to meetings with Claire than those with Dr Rafi. But it soon became apparent that medicine and law had significant similarities for clients. With his solicitor, as with his GP, there was a risk that each meeting would contain the revelation that something newly ominous had been found or was being sought. And, once he had been convinced that the symptoms of shock and stress were unlikely to kill him, he felt more at risk of a terminal diagnosis at the legal practice, terrified of what shadow or recurrence of an old problem might be found.

His lawyer, however, was reliably smiling and optimistic and, in the middle of one of their meetings, when Ned was despondently totting up what the half hour so far had cost, said: 'I think it might be an idea to build a saint file.' In response to his mouth-twist of doubt, she explained: 'A set of character statements about how you're rarely seen out without a halo. The idea is to make the police and the CPS think about them being read out in court if it got there. And, if it did get there, then we'd put as many of your attending angels as possible on the stand.'

'Okay. But to take an example from my own area: the fact that Henry VIII didn't kill all of his wives doesn't mean he didn't kill any.'

'Absolutely. The other side will always try to argue that the experiences of C to Z don't negate what A and B say happened. But, in stuff like this, with only narrative evidence and no forensics, it comes down to whether you're the sort of guy who might have. The aim is to make the pattern of good behaviour bigger than the pattern of alleged bad behaviour. I know this sounds yucky but the golden ticket in this sort of thing is people you've slept with saying that you always folded your socks and said please and thank-you.'

'And then they're online forever for Emma and my children to read or to be told about?'

'No. Because, if they work, the only readers will be the people who decide that it's too big a risk to go to court. I hesitate to ask but your divorce didn't happen to be one of those no-fault jobbies, did it?'

'I'm afraid not. Certainly not at first. But we're on talking terms now.'

'And so she might not want you thrown in jail?'

At any mention of this prospect – even in connection with a tactic to avoid it – Ned saw imprisonment as a sequence of vivid scenes: none involving showering, so common a stereotype that he hoped any such danger would by now have been removed, but rather images of being confined to the hospital wing due to physical collapse and threats from other prisoners; eating putrid food; waiting at a visitors' table once a week to find out how many of his friends and family remained loyal.

Unsure how to interpret his pause, Claire asked: 'Could you ask her or ask one of your daughters to raise it?'

'I could ask one of them, yes.'

Ex Certificate

Nervous of being late, which might be reported negatively back to Dee, Ned had allowed half an hour for the fifteen-minute walk. Jenny, visibly miffed at arriving second, tilted her cheek while he inclined his head, casual movements that could be passed off as everyday twitches if the other person ducked the kiss.

The sexless embrace had been perfected by his children and their friends – who seemed easily to exchange full-length hugs with casual acquaintances of both genders – but older generations were still experimenting with manners between former lovers. Ned's dread about his daughters marrying – except, now, the expense – was the awkward moment when the photographer (they were presumably tipped off about blended families) would position him and Jenny at opposite ends of the smile line alongside their new partners, with a buffer of aunts and uncles between them. He had been to too many weddings where the divorced loomed as a warning, like a corpse in the corner of a hospital ward.

Reluctant to name The Best Cafe in an e-mail – in case Jenny Googled it and panicked that he was reduced to ruin – Ned had arranged to meet her by the Pilates gym on the opposite corner.

'I assumed it was a landmark rather than an invitation,' she said. 'I haven't brought my kit.'

The laugh he gave was louder than the joke deserved. But Ned, who had always taken pride in being something near to himself on TV, was conscious, since coming under suspicion, of behaving in public in a way that exaggerated the better aspects of his personality. He felt himself to be always playing a man who was warm, generous and, above all, unthreatening.

'No. There's a coffee shop nearby that I write in.'

Jenny nodded across the road, to where the dots of stick-on steam cloud above the bright green cup of tea were curling off like abandoned Christmas decorations.

'I hope it's not that one.'

'You know, it actually is.'

'Ned, are you okay?'

'Yes, of course I am. History should be written among the people.'

Without ever declaring it a formal policy even to himself,

Ned now made sure he was never left alone with any woman except those he totally trusted: Emma, Claire, Phee. He would have extended the same confidence to his other daughter, but the opportunity was unlikely to arise.

Thrown by Jenny's order for herbal tea, which wasn't among the dozens of possibilities on the white boards, the stern server eventually found a faded sachet of Moroccan Peppermint in the back of a cupboard. At the corner table he now regarded as his, Ned brushed can against tea cup, a substitute for their aborted earlier kiss.

'Cheers,' she said. A sip of the tea, recoil from its heat and then: 'So are you shagging your solicitor?'

'Jennifer!'

The conversation faltered at this reminder of the marital disputes in which he would use her full name punitively.

'All I'm saying is she sounded your type on the phone.'

'Look, I know I was a crap husband to you but I promise you I'm improving.'

'Oh, great. So I'm like the schmuck who sold the land before they struck oil on it.'

Jenny looked down, busied herself with stirring and drinking. He sensed old hurts returning. His own flashbacks were not to rows, lies and silences but to winter walks, her nose pink under that Cossack hat he bought her, and waking up slowly on Sunday mornings. He had a stabbing understanding of why Facebook and Friends Reunited reignited so many old flames.

With her hair cut shorter than before and more expertly dyed, she looked healthy and high-spirited. A partner who has willingly left feels the opposite of a lover's jealousy, actively wanting the other to be seduced to diminish their guilt of betrayal. He hoped that her current bloke – David, reported by Phee to be a Maths professor with four kids from two marriages – would be enough to tear the final pages of hatred from the Book of Ned.

She gave him the look of a mother to a sick child. 'I'm not stupid enough to ask how you are. But . . .'

'I don't want to end up like Dreyfus, with people saying: "Enough already about the persecution." But . . . I suppose everyone imagines the knock on the door, don't they?'

'Do they?'

'I think so. If you grew up with the Birmingham Five, the Guildford Four, I think you always fear one day it might be . . .'

'The Winslow One?'

Fierce teasing had always been her way. When they were married, he could have told her to fuck off, but he restricted himself to an exasperated face. 'I'm serious. It's a sort of apocalyptic version of finding out you were adopted – everything you've ever believed about your past and your self is . . . is . . . overthrown. Everyone assumes that it could never happen to them but . . .'

'Not if . . . not if they haven't . . .'

'Done anything? No, well, this is the point: some of us haven't . . .'

Raising his voice, he sensed the elderly couple behind them – drinking tea and reading the courtesy tabloids scattered on the tables – and compromised with a sort of whisper-shout. He continued more levelly: 'At least, in the golden age of injustice, they planted evidence on people and classy stuff like that. But now someone says something about you and next day you're off work and wondering whether to buy one of those things to remind you when to take your drugs.'

'It can seem very unfair,' Jenny said.

She had hit a placatory note and he echoed it: 'Thank you for thinking about helping me.'

'Nobody wants to see someone they've . . .' She left the past participle blank. ' . . . going through something like this.'

Phee had passed on Claire's request to Jenny, who had agreed in principle, but with the condition that she wanted first to meet Ned, who was eventually persuaded by his solicitor that this was not a police trick. He regretted his concession when Jenny asked: 'So did you rape those women?'

'Jennifer!'

'Remember I've been lied to by you, so I've got something to measure the needle against.'

Once past the shock of the question and the lie detector metaphor, he felt that this was very Jenny. She probably would come through as a witness for him but was protecting herself by some detective work first, a conversation that also permitted some delayed revenge. He gambled on the deafness of the pensioners at the next table.

'No. Absolutely not. I've already had the argument with Dee about ski masks and strangers but these – both cases – were . . . relationships . . .'

'When did they happen?'

A memory of the stack of detective fiction always on her side of the bed.

'Er, 1976 . . . and . . . and more recently . . .'

A note of hope behind the incredulity: '*Emma*?'

'No, of course not.'

'But recently means . . . what . . . ten? . . . twenty? . . .'

'After you, if that's what you're asking.'

'Poor Emma.'

A tangible relaxation in Jenny. If Ned had been a rapist, it had been before and after her, which probably shouldn't matter but seemed to, with the bonus that he had cheated on the woman he had betrayed her with.

'And, if you didn't do it, then why do they say that you did?'

Another detective-level question. Perhaps they should close Hendon Police College and just give the candidates a hundred cop novels to read.

'That's . . . obviously that's crucial. What I think is that, if the news is full of swine flu or Ebola or whatever, everyone starts to think they've got it . . .'

'Well, you certainly would.'

'And so if something is suddenly everywhere, then . . . I never thought I'd been bullied at school or at work – it was just stuff that goes on in classrooms and offices – but then, when they start publishing codes and putting names on it, you start to wonder if you were. And with . . . with . . . *this one*, when every headline is saying that there was this undetected epidemic, I suppose people start to think, well, maybe that night . . .'

He wondered about saying the next bit, thinking that it was the sort of thing that led to people on Twitter being forced into hiding. But this was a private conversation in a cafe on the edge of an industrial estate. 'And . . . and . . . I suspect that sometimes people get to a point in their lives when other stuff has gone against them and they start to think . . .'

'Oh, for crying out loud!'

The swish of a raincoat draped over a chair as one of the tea-drinkers turned to target the argument.

'Ssshhh! If I get barred from The Best Cafe, it's sitting on the kerb drinking takeaway next.'

'But I mean, it's bitter vengeful women, is it? Well, bloody lucky you haven't had a charge from me, then.'

'I'm not saying it's a women thing . . . there've been teachers – male and female – accused by old pupils: boys and girls. In custody battles, mothers are branded sluts or drug addicts by their ex-husbands. If you want to get someone, allegations are the best ammunition and sex is Semtex . . .'

'Oh, Lord, are you going to start a campaign group? I don't want to switch on the news and see you bungy-jumping from Big Ben in a Spiderman suit.'

'This isn't about me, Jen . . .'

'You'll appreciate my scepticism on that.'

'This could happen to absolutely anyone, except people who Tweet, apparently. There are genuine victims of paedophiles and . . . and . . .' – more mouthing than speaking – 'rapists out there. But, if you test for something in a whole population, you'll get false results. Especially if you assume in advance that every result is positive.'

In the over-loud voices of those with weakened hearing, the couple behind were discussing the parts of the argument they had gleaned. Ned heard the words: *poor woman*. He laughed.

'What's set you off?'

'I was just thinking that Darby and Joan over my shoulder will be thinking we're heading for divorce.'

Jenny smiled. 'Phee's solidly in your corner, which is good.'

'That's tactfully put. I don't know what to do about Dee.'

'Look, when have those two ever been on the same side over anything?'

'That's what . . .' He stopped.

'What Emma said. It's okay. You can say her name. In a minute, I'll tell you how amazing David is in bed.'

Although it was a joke, and offence was one of the reflexes subdued by his medication, Ned still felt a competitive twinge, but forced a grin.

'Look, Jen, I can see how tough it is for the girls. The last thing children want to think about is their parents' sex lives . . .'

'Yeah. Despite – or is it because of – being evidence of it. Do you worry about them?'

'What? Of course. All the time, in the background, on and off. But, if you let it get too specific, you'd never sleep . . .'

'I just hope they're okay. You read these stories about women – this almost never happens to men – whose lives are ruined simply because they got involved with the wrong bloke.'

'Are you talking about us?'

'What? *No.* Ned, you, you may remember me making this point at times before – not everything that everyone says is always about you. No, I mean those girls, women, you read about who marry someone, live with them, even just go back to their house once for a drink and they get murdered or, or . . .'

'Raped?'

'*No.* No. I'm just saying that I think that people, the girls' generation particularly, they've made it all so casual. This, this' – Jenny had always been a nervous swearer and whispered the expression – '*fuck-buddies* thing they have apparently, I mean, how can that really work? Who you . . . hook up with, and how, can have such terrible consequences for your life. Our daughters' lot are trying to make *sex* the simplest thing in the world at the exact moment that people are being locked up in cells over a, a *shag* they had forty years ago. I just hope the girls are being careful . . .'

'Dee just seems so moralistic about it.'

'I've told you. And, if Phee was, then she wouldn't be.'

'Sure, sure. They're the world's least similar identical twins. But when the point of dispute is whether Dad is . . . a . . . a . . .'

He couldn't say it.

'Well, Dad isn't.'

Though opaquely phrased, it was the endorsement he sought. 'So does that mean . . . ?'

'Look, show me a woman who hasn't sometimes had sex when she didn't want to . . .'

'Yes, well, that might not be a helpful line to take in court.'

'Ned, you're an arrogant, faithless, philandering bastard, but you're not a rapist.'

'Thank you,' he said, sincerely.

When they said goodbye at the corner, he kissed her cheek, awkwardly but warmly.

The Literature of False Accusation (5)

Summary: A twelve-year-old cadet, Ronnie Winslow, is sent down from the Royal Naval Academy at Osborne, having been found guilty by a secret internal investigation, at which he was not represented, of stealing a five-shilling postal order from a classmate and then cashing it. The boy insists to his wealthy businessman father, Arthur Winslow, that he is innocent and the family tries to retain Sir Robert Morton, a leading KC, to sue the Admiralty to withdraw a charge that will result in the family being shunned by society and the boy becoming unemployable.

Morton, in a mock cross-examination, reduces Ronnie to tears and incoherence by accusing him of lying. The Winslows are appalled by this brutality and the truth that the interrogation apparently reveals. But, in one of the great reversals of audience expectation, Sir Robert drawls: 'The boy is plainly

241

innocent. I accept the brief.' He subsequently explains that, during his interrogation, Ronnie volunteered several potentially incriminating details and refused a loophole offered (that he had briefly stolen the postal order as a practical joke) which could have reduced the charge to a lesser one.

After public and government pressure to drop the case, Sir Robert demolishes the eye-witness evidence of a postmistress and wins the case.

Reader Review: The Winslow Boy had been the favourite play of Ned's father. A family outing to a London production – probably, from the dates, for his dad's last birthday – was one of his final memories of him. The play held special meaning for this reason and also because that theatre trip was the only time he had seen his father cry, Val Marriott producing a large handkerchief and thunderously blowing his nose at the moment of the cadet's acquittal. Subsequently, Ned had wondered if his father had ever been the subject of a calumny.

With some guilt, Ned, in his TV series about the 1950s, had used the plays of Sir Terence Rattigan as an example of the stultified culture blown away by youthful revolution although, in that documentary and many others, he had knowingly attempted versions of Sir Robert's stunning misdirection: building up facts to lead viewer-jurors to a certain conclusion before proving it untrue. He went to see the play whenever it was on – most recently, a couple of years previously, at the Old Vic – and, during intermittent culls of the DVDs stacked in the TV room, the 1999 movie version, improbably directed by the combative American dramatist David Mamet, had always remained in the survivors' pile. The play had no influence on his decision to live in Winslow but, once he did, the connection pleased him.

Sent down from the Academy himself, he filled one of the suddenly empty hours by reading the text again. It was only the awareness of how strongly he was identifying with Ronnie that made him see the extent to which he had previously empathized with Morton. The KC was no longer the brilliant barrister Ned had once dreamed of becoming but a template for the QC he might himself need. But, in any test questioning, the only loop-hole he could be offered was that the sex had been consensual, whereas the Winslow boy had never touched the postal order.

He had occasionally seen it as a weakness that the audience is sure of Ronnie's innocence so soon. But Rattigan's subject was the ordeal of false accusation, during the 'two years' it takes to clear Ronnie's name. Writing in 1946, Rattigan could not have been expected to represent the prejudicial pressure of social media. It turned out, though, that the dramatist weirdly almost had. Morton complains about the guilt implied in a popular song, 'How, Still, We See Thee Lie, or the Naughty Cadet', which includes a refrain rebuking Ronnie: 'How dare you sully Nelson's Name, Who for this Land Did Die?'

Equally timeless was the instinctive assumption of many citizens that it would be impossible for the authorities to have got it so wrong. 'Their ways of doing things may seem to an outsider brutal – but at least they're always fair,' says Ronnie's sister's boyfriend. 'There must have been a full inquiry before they'd take a step of this sort.' (Ned scanned these lines and e-mailed them to Tom.)

An Almost Optimistic Dream

Surprisingly, despite having no history or experience as a For-mula 1 driver, Ned won the Belgian Grand Prix. But, as he was spritzed with fizz on the podium, Lewis Hamilton sulking on the second step, it was announced that stewards had upheld a complaint from Fernando Massa and that the entire race would be restaged. 'You beat him once. You'll beat him twice,' Tom Pimm in red mechanics overalls bullishly encouraged him. But, as he was led back to the starting grid, Ned wondered how to tell the engineers that he had never before driven above speeds of 100mph and was worried that he was too fat to fit into the car. Waking with the tainted-water after-taste of Diazepam and

Sertraline, he checked the bottom of his oversized UME sleep T-shirt to check that the champagne-spraying had not been a nocturnal displacement of peeing or a wet-dream. What did all that mean? That there would be no trial or a trial that he won and then lost on appeal?

A Positive Response

Instead of the usual single manila wallet on Claire's desk, there were two this time, the top one bulging. A rivulet of sweat stung Ned's eye before he was able to fish a tissue from his pocket. He always feared new paperwork would be fresh charges or amplifications of the existing ones.

But his solicitor tapped the highest stack and said: 'This is very good.'

'Is it?'

'Yes. It's the Saint File.'

'I don't know how religious you are . . .'

'My ancestors were animists.'

'But you do know that saints are only created after death and most of them were persecuted and martyred?'

'Okay, well, actually yours is more a Not A Saint But file. We've got thirty-six people willing to say that you could be a bit up yourself but you didn't deserve this . . .'

'Thanks!'

'No, it's good. Look, you want a bit of grit in these testimonies. It makes them more credible. People know people are flawed – except for themselves of course. It's a basic human truth. This is a very positive response.'

She passed him the cover sheet that listed the three dozen witnesses to his general decency. As with many aspects of his ordeal, there was something posthumous about it: reading the book of condolence. With fondest memories from . . . Tom Pimm, Jenny Marriott, Ciara Harrison, Jack Beane plus another editor, the MD and two publicists at his publisher, numerous producers and technicians who had worked with him in television and the makings of an impressive top-table placement at a British History Society annual dinner.

The alphabetic arrangement of the names, though, made it easy to detect absentees.

'No Tony?' he asked, adding, when Claire looked inquiringly, 'Blair. No Helen Pimm?'

'Look, you never get a total take-up on these things. He's busy trying to stop wars. Counterintuitively, some would say. And maybe Mrs P. reckoned Tom could speak for both of them.'

Ray (2)

'Ned, it's me.'

'Oh, hi, darling, hi.'

'Look, odd question. But do Manchester City have a famous player called Ray?'

'That is an odd question. Why?'

'It's boring. Do they?'

'Let me . . . not that I know of . . . but ask Tobes. He's Statto . . .'

'Yes. I . . . what was that?'

'Dr Rafi just called my name on the tannoy. Talk later. Love you.'

'See you.'

The Literature of False Accusation (6)

Summary: Betty, the ten-year-old daughter of an American religious minister suffers a mysterious illness, which local women attribute to witchcraft; the priest's young niece, Abigail, was seen dancing in the woods the previous night with a black servant, Tituba. An expert in necromancy comes to the town and, during his investigations, Tituba and Abigail report up to a hundred local women for having consorted with the devil, including Elizabeth Proctor, the wife of a local farmer, John, with whom Abigail had an affair seven months before. During a trial that is interrupted when a complainant claims to have seen Satan in the form of a yellow bird on a roof beam, Elizabeth's attempt to save John by denying his adultery, which he has already confessed to the investigators, inadvertently puts him at risk of hanging, which he can only avoid by confirming that his wife is a witch. Proctor and another local man, Giles Corey, decide to die rather than lie.

Reader Review: Always cast in authority parts because of his height, Ned had played Judge Hawthorne, state instrument of injustice, in a school production. The play had also been one of Dee and Phee's A-level set-texts and his copy of *Miller: Plays One*, a black-jacketed Methuen paperback with an abstract painting by the author's daughter, Rebecca, on the cover, had white striations on its spine from frequently being cracked and held open – *The Crucible* was in the middle of the volume – while impatiently helping them to write essays on whether or not John Proctor was a hero, a process complicated by the fact that the girls were constitutionally required to come to opposite conclusions. He had seen all the major stage revivals – most recently, in the final weeks of his previous life, a version by a South African director at the Old Vic – and the movie adaptation with Daniel Day-Lewis, who married Rebecca Miller as a result, playing Proctor.

Among the texts about reputational destruction, this was the one that Ned knew best; and so he assumed that he had understood it. But only now, re-reading it while on police bail and academic suspension, did he truly comprehend the moment when Proctor refuses to sign the false confession that he has seen the women with the devil: 'Because it is my name! Because I cannot have another in my life! . . . How may I live without my name? I have given you my soul; leave me my name.'

A hand raised from the book was not quick enough to stop

a teardrop joining the blotches of coffee and ketchup (whatever home tuition he did on access nights was during supper time) on the pages of the play. And, if bile did not rise from deeper in the body than tears, then that liquid might have stained the paper as well when Proctor, appalled by the court's apparent willingness to believe anything said by the women, asks the court: 'Is the accuser always holy now?'

He was struck again that part of the power of the play comes from John Proctor being – like the whistle-blowing Dr Stockmann in Ibsen's *An Enemy of the People*, Miller's inspiration – an imperfect representative of rightness. He has not committed the crimes of witchcraft for which the court tries to force an admission but he is guilty of something: adultery with a teenage servant girl.

Miller makes it clear that Proctor shouldn't die for that, although admits in an afterword to having raised the age of the accusatory ex-mistress Abigail to seventeen, when her historical model was much younger. The dramatist may have helped his prospects with posterity by disguising Proctor's paedophilia, or the play could now be banned in twenty-first-century Britain and America.

And, even so, there might be theatre-goers these days who concluded that the farmer deserved to go to the stake for seducing an employee half his age, regardless of whether he had been trafficking with witches.

In other circumstances and places, there grew up new Salems.

TBOTS – Ch 3, Dr 1

Savonarola's rise was helped by a revolution in communication: the introduction of the printing press in the 1460s allowed prophets and moralizers to reach a mass audience for the first time. A Florentine convent began to print pamphlets of apocalyptic predictions and hell-fire condemnations that were sold on the street to the literate and told in the market squares to the illiterate by itinerant actors. And, while some of Savonarola's disciples in the contemporary community of historians seek to outlaw contemporary parallels with past events, it is striking that our current festival of moral condemnation – the bonfire of the sanities – was enabled and exacerbated by the biggest change in the dissemination of ideas since the ability to print – digital interaction.

A Better Person

After the scandal began, people would frequently express to Ned variations of the sentiment: 'Nobody would want to go through this but you'll find you come out of it a better person.' Or, more egotistically: 'I know you'll come through this a better person.' (A version of the personal guarantee he had heard people give to victims of cancer: 'I know you'll beat this thing,' a curious formula in which dying would rank as damaging the credibility of a friend.)

Until it was put to him in this way, it had never occurred to Ned that professional ruin and public disgrace might be a route to self-improvement. In one way, the thought was supportive, as it worked on the assumption that he was innocent and would be cleared; surely even the most constitutionally optimistic or Christian of his acquaintances could not think that his personality would be enhanced by a jail term for rape.

As it became an increasingly regular suggestion that being suspended and becoming a defendant might somehow make him nicer, Ned even began to expect, and to examine himself for, signs of his soul's progress.

The more he reflected on the question, however, it became clear to him that he had not become a better person, but a far worse one. The clearest evidence of this was that, for the first time in his life, he found himself regularly fantasizing about the sudden – and, ideally, painless, although, if there had to be pain, so be it – deaths of the people who were doing this to him.

The Theatre of False Accusation

Officially a tourist in Edinburgh, he kept a notebook in his rain-coat pocket in case of ever being required to write about the final summer of the United Kingdom. Ned had at first turned down the trip, until Tom cannily persuaded him that an historian of British politics had a duty to see Scotland in the run-up to the independence referendum.

Ned had been to the city three times, never happily. As a student in 1973, he had directed a cut-down version of *Macbird*, Barbara Garson's satirical conflation of Macbeth and Lyndon Johnson, in a double bill with *MacHeath*, his own translation of *The Threepenny Opera* to the administration of Edward Heath. The script, though, deteriorated after the prom-ising spot of the similarity in the names of the highwayman Macheath and the prime minister and, regardless of the order in which they performed the plays, most of the audience failed to come back for the second. On many nights, they passed the Festival test of whether a show should go ahead – more people in the auditorium than on stage – only through clumps of sup-portive friends or relatives of the company.

Steered from theatre towards academia by this failure, Ned had next taken the north-east train – with its breathtaking coastal coda when the carriages seem at risk of toppling into the sea – to be interviewed for a lecturer post at the University. On the return journey, he chose a seat on the left of the aisle to watch the splash and dazzle of the waves again. But, after suf-fering a second rejection by Edinburgh – though in kinder terms than the *Scotsman* review of his productions – he had stayed away, even irritating his publishers by declining invitations from the literary festival, until 2005, when Dee, who had inevitably proved to be the more theatrical of his daughters, appeared with the Leeds University Drama Society in a version of Brecht's *The Caucasian Chalk Circle* which Ned had feared was unlikely to be an original choice and proved to be one of seven stagings in the Fringe programme. Four of them unfortunately were performed by companies starting with a letter higher in the alphabet than L, putting Dee and her friends at a further disadvantage with browsers.

So, when Tom called during the July of their joint infamy, and said, 'Up for a cultural weekend in Edinburgh, Nod?' he replied: 'No.'

'Oh, why?'

'Never been a lucky city for me. Gave me the bum's rush as a theatre director and a teacher. It just doesn't feel like the summer to go to unlucky places.'

'Becca's taking a play up.'

'Really? Which one?'

'*The Crucible.*'

'Christ!'

'Yeah, I know. It's like Daggers going to see *One Flew Over the Cuckoo's Nest*, or Savlon *Dumb and Dumber*.'

Ned feared that this Miller play might be as over-represented in the schedule as Dee's Brecht but the difference was that you could probably never have too many productions of *The Crucible*. Even that didn't budge his refusal. But, when he mentioned the turned-down excursion to Emma, she forcefully pointed out that they were having no holiday that year; it was a condition of Ned's bail that he could not leave the country and he was terrified of being recognized in Cornwall. And Becca, she added, was his goddaughter, which duties he ignored almost completely apart from birthday presents bought and sent by Emma, who was not even the godmother.

So Toby was dispatched to his mother's parents for four days. The lure of his beloved train journey was overcome for Ned by horror at the prospect of sitting for almost five hours in proximity with people who might know who he was. So they drove north in Emma's Land-Rover, with the Pimms added to the insurance for four days. The always organized and organizing Helen WhatsApp-ed a roster, dividing the driving into quarters, but Emma took both Marriott-Humpage turns because the newest of Ned's neuroses was an inability to understand how it was possible to be at the wheel of a car without killing everyone in it and possibly all those on the road.

Phobic as well about being known in hotels, Ned had last-minute.com-ed a self-catering apartment in Palmerston Place, close to the Sir Arthur Conan Doyle Museum. Throughout their stay, days and nights of movie-force storms lashed the city, until the street bands on the Royal Mile tired of the irony of striking up 'Singing in the Rain' for the tourists in their wind-rattled rainwear. But a bright blue cagoule, the hood tied tight to show only an oval of face, proved more reliably obscuring than the usual baseball cap.

Waterproofed like a North Sea trawlerman, Ned passed as just an anonymous member of a tribe terrified by rain, as he stood with Emma, Tom and Helen outside an Episcopalian church in the Old Town. The city's numerous religious denominations compensated for declining contributions to the collection plate by renting out their premises for August to theatre groups; a deal that suited both parties except when certain content – Judas, say, betraying Jesus due to a gay triangle involving Simon Peter – was declared blasphemous by a local councillor or columnist.

As they waited in a queue of respectable length for the previous show – *Savile: The Musical!* – to end, they could hear, from some of the huddles of rainwear, American accents. These tourists, bewildered by choice, had presumably reduced the risk by choosing something they had seen or studied.

Inside the church hall, unsteady wooden chairs had been arranged in several lines of ten. Almost two-thirds were occupied, although mainly by couples of around the right age to be parents of cast-members. Ned remembered from four decades before the company's elation at occasionally playing to a ticket-buyer who was not related to an actor. Because of the extra legroom, Ned took an aisle seat with, their usual formation in theatres and on planes, Helen beside him, then Emma and Tom.

The cast all wore blue jeans, topped by bright white blouses for the women, contrasting with the men's black polo necks.

The only variations to these costumes were an English judicial wig of ridged wool for Judge Hawthorne, plain wooden crucifixes hanging round the necks of Reverend Parris and Reverend Hale, and an American cop's gun holster in the belt of the Marshal. Between scenes, the music from the descent into hell from *Don Giovanni* played with heavy reverb from speakers. This setting invoked less seventeenth-century Massachusetts than late-twentieth-century Royal Shakespeare Company. During the climactic scene of hysteria, the scheming, screaming girls pulled mobiles from their pockets and began to tweet and text.

As the play's situation already had depressingly endless relevance, this attempt at universality seemed unnecessary, especially for Ned and Tom, for whom the action was biographical rather than historical. But even so, and though trimmed to seventy-five minutes because slots in every venue were compressed to maximize revenue, the play retained its power.

Becky Pimm was Abigail Williams, who leads the charge of witchcraft. She and the others cast as accusers had the advantage of portraying an age close to their own, while the students playing the Proctors had to double their years and the actor cast as Giles Corey to multiply by four.

Despite choosing neutral dress and setting, the director curiously seemed to have demanded period regional accents and, to Ned's godpaternal pride, Becky's was among the best approximations of the nasal honk. She was also chillingly convincing in the scene where Abigail claims to be seeing Satan as a yellow bird in the eaves of the courtroom.

The phrases that had most affected Ned on the page were even more devastating in performance. When Proctor, a stocky Asian man with a beginner's beard, began the speech, *If she is innocent? Why do you never wonder if Parris be innocent, or Abigail?*, Ned knew what was coming next, but the line still stung like a knife slicing the cheek, and, on the word *holy*, he sensed Emma turning to look at him and Helen twisting in her husband's direction.

Towards the end, when Deputy Governor Danforth, his vigorous pacing releasing a cloud of the talcum powder used to blanch the student performer's hair, asked Proctor why he refused to sign the confession, Ned, although pledging not to cry, had failed before the reply arrived and, when it came, had to cough and sneeze in the hope of passing off his emotion as allergies. 'Are you okay?' Helen whispered. He noticed that she did not touch his arm or squeeze his hand. Ned braced himself for the calamitous impact when Corey's last words of defiance were reported but the lines had been cut, either simply for running time or because the director was too young to understand heroic sacrifice.

After a last roar of Mozart's condemnatory score over a tableau of Proctor being led to the gallows, the snap blackout was followed by the over-emphatic applause of friends and relatives, punctuated by youthful whoops and whistles that Ned attributed to lovers and siblings of the cast. Touchingly, Becky blushed as she took her bow, then did a double-take at some booing from the audience.

'I hope they were jeering the lying bitch' – those words shushed by Helen – 'not Becks,' Tom said as they were leaving.

'I've seen it happen to Iago,' Ned told them. 'Some people treat every play like a pantomime now.'

During the shuffling exit from the room, rainwater spilling on the floor as coats were shrugged on, Ned kept his head ducked but was convinced that at least three people spotted him and then looked away. After Ned and Emma had carefully complimented Tom and Helen on their daughter's performance, they discussed the play.

'I'm afraid I see all things through the prism of my predicament now,' said Tom. 'An inquiry into W & S, or witchcraft and supernaturalism, with Abigail as the main complainant and Danforth the Director of History.'

Outside, the weather continued to permit Ned hooded anonymity. When Becky came out, her face streaked orange and white from cold cream smeared over make-up, they exchanged hugs and her mother's worry that the actress would get cold without a coat.

'Just what we needed – a bit of escapism,' Tom said.

'Oh, Dads.'

'Wow, Ned,' added Becky. 'You look like you've been blubbing?'

'What? Oh, no. Scottish pollen. No immunity. I've hardly ever been here.'

Becky deflected their enthusiastic capsule reviews: 'I only got it because I'm a midget and look about fourteen. If they'd cast me as Lizzie Proctor, we'd probably have had a visit from Operation . . .'

A paedophilia joke from the rehearsal room, Ned supposed. One aspect of notoriety was things said by enemies, but another was the sentences that friends desperately cut off.

A Sex Act

Even with the assistance of pills, Ned woke most nights, his thoughts pin-balling, three or so hours after going to sleep. Which, on the Saturday night in Edinburgh, was 4am. They had taken Becky, Judge Hawthorne (who seemed to be her boyfriend), Elizabeth Proctor and Deputy Governor Danforth to an upmarket burger joint on George Street.

Terrified of the judgemental suspicion of strangers, Ned had tried to avoid the outing, citing flu-like symptoms, which Emma, suddenly a citizen physician, possibly punishing his earlier explanation for wet eyes, attributed to allergies and directed him to the anti-histamine in his shoulder bag.

In fact, Becky's friends appeared to be unaware of either Ned's fame or infamy. The incuriosity of students about the news, infuriating to him as an educator, was welcome as a defendant. When he proved familiar with the play – more so than Mrs Proctor, who was apparently under the impression that it had been written at the time of the events in Salem –

Danforth asked him, possibly opportunistically, if he were a theatre director, responding to Ned's confession of teaching by asking what he taught and, when the answer was history, grimacing. The students, he concluded, had agreed to tolerate oldster conversation with people who were not even their parents in exchange for food better than they would otherwise get.

He had become used to lying awake beside the sleeping Emma but, this time, to his surprise, she was awake, reading by the long summer light American galleys of a crime novel she was trying to sell in Britain. From what she said when she started it in bed that morning, *Your Love Always* was one of those techno-domestic suspense stories: two days after burying his wife, a man starts getting texts that seem to be from her.

'You . . .' He gargled away some night and wine gunge. 'You okay?'

'The rain on the window. It's like Toby's bloody drum kit. You were fine tonight.'

'Yes. But I couldn't have known that in advance. I could equally have turned up to find all of them wearing No Means No fleeces. I was a beneficiary of their solipsism. Genghis Khan could have eaten a cheese burger in peace among that lot.'

'Anyway, I don't think people are as obsessed as . . .'

'*Obsessed*?'

'Not obsessed. As *aware* as you are.'

He was startled by footsteps outside the door, then remembered where they were. A toilet flush was followed by fast feet on carpet. Tom, he guessed, from the heavier tread.

'So is she alive?' he asked.

'Who?'

'The wife.'

'Oh. It seems like it. We've just discovered that the fire in which she died' – with a hand lifted from the page she put inverted commas around the verb – 'left the body unidentifiable.'

They were keeping their voices low to avoid disturbing the Pimms in the next room.

'So why go to the trouble of faking your death and then start texting hubby?'

'I know. There's another hundred pages to go. But it seems that Harper had a psychopathic ex-lover. So either she's escaping from him to start a secret new life with Scott. Or Gabriel has already killed Harper and now he's pretending to be her to lure Scott.'

'Mmm,' Ned said. 'Or it was Gabriel in the blaze. And the texts really are from Harper. Having done in her lover, she's now luring her husband for a twofer because she's secretly got someone else.'

Emma laughed. It felt easier between them than it had been since. Since. 'That would be pretty far-fetched wouldn't it?'

'Yes. But that sort of book is about fetching far. The solutions aren't about human motivation or plausibility. They're about the outcome the reader is least likely to guess.'

'I'll let you know if you're right.'

'Why are you reading it?'

'Because this woman is going to make someone a lot of money. And we might . . .'

Need it were the words she cut off. As apology, she did not move her legs away when his touched them.

They need not have worried, it turned out, about disturbing the others. The sub-division of the house into apartments had used thin interior materials and, from the other bedroom, leaked a low murmur of gossip and giggling and then a soundtrack unmistakeable, although still impressive in a long marriage: the rhythmic creak of bed springs, then breathlessness and a climactic grunt. Ned guessed that the Pimms were celebrating their daughter in the most appropriate way.

Nostalgia and competition began to arouse him.

'Some people are having fun,' he whispered.

'What?'

'The Pimms are . . . coupling.'

'What? Really? I hadn't noticed.'

256

Ned moved closer, so that she would feel the thickening pressure against her leg.

'Oh,' Emma said.

The disgrace or the drugs – or doubt about her reaction – had damaged his desire. Even if she wanted to, he probably wouldn't be able to. In crises of desire, it had usually been enough to touch her inside. He tried. Unusually, she was wearing knickers.

'Oh,' he asked, 'are you bleeding?'

It struck him that this excuse – even if a lie – might be a relief all round. But she said: 'No.'

'Oh.'

'Sweetheart, I don't think I can. It's not the . . . it's the . . .'

The omitted words were as stinging as if she had spoken them. The terrible eloquence of the unsaid. His third Edinburgh rejection.

Turning from her, he reached for his paperback. She adjusted the wide, bound pages on her raised knees. They read in silence.

The Literature of False Accusation (7)

Summary: Twice-divorced David Lurie, fifty-two, a professor of Communications (previously known as English Literature) at the Technical University of Cape Town, screws a twenty-year-old student, Melanie Isaacs, a promising actress, on the floor of his house. Subsequently, they have sex again at her shared flat and then once more at Lurie's house, into which she briefly moves, apparently after a row with her boyfriend.

The professor is visited in his office – and has a lecture and a theatre trip disrupted by – the woman's boyfriend, who knows about their relationship. After Melanie withdraws from his seminar on the romantic poets, she brings a charge of sexual harassment under Article 3.1 of the university's Code of Conduct, to which the college adds an allegation of falsifying records to disguise Ms Isaacs' absence from lessons and a test.

When Lurie appears before a panel, chaired by the Professor of Religious Studies and comprising senior staff and a student representative, he is reassured that this is not a trial but a hearing, which will come to no decisions but merely make a recommendation to the college authorities, and that his identity will not be revealed. Lurie admits both charges but, ordered also to make a full confession and apology and to undergo sensitivity retraining, refuses and chooses to leave.

With the aim of turning his forced hiatus to advantage, Lurie stays with his daughter, Lucy, at her farm in the Cape, where he intends to write a long-contemplated opera about Byron. During the visit, he serves as a junior assistant to Lucy and her black farm manager, driving with them at dawn to sell the land-grown produce at a local market. The spoiled academic also helps out at a local veterinary practice.

This interlude is ruined when the farm is raided by burglars who brutalize Lurie and gang-rape Lucy. The ex-professor wants to pursue her attackers through the law and an Afrikaans neighbour suggests going after them with a gun but the young woman refuses both options, arguing – a Portia of post-feminism and post-colonialism – that mercy must be shown to the men because what they have done to her is a punishment from her black countrymen for their long suffering under white South Africans.

Reader review: There are three sexual relationships in the book: Lurie and Melanie (consensual but in breach of teacher–student rules), with the second of their three encounters categorized in his mind as 'not rape, not quite that'; Lurie and a female vet (consensual but adulterous on her side); and the violation of Lucy by the intruding youths. But, while the professor is treated as if he had raped his student, his daughter, who undoubtedly was a victim of this crime, refuses to involve the authorities.

As in *The Human Stain*, the professor resigns rather than being sacked and Coetzee also coincides with the Roth in the way that the academic scandal proves to be a prelude to a greater destruction and disgrace. Lurie's volunteering as a farm-hand can be seen as a self-imposed form of ostracism but brings him no expiation.

Never giving interviews and avoiding publicity tours, Coetzee was the most Google-proof of novelists but was known to be a university teacher and so the reader was inevitably encouraged to prurient speculation about the extent to which the fiction was personal history. Had the writer witnessed – even suffered – something like this in further education? Did he perhaps have a daughter and – if so – what was her work and where?

But, if the first way of reading fiction these days was to assume that it was telling the writer's story, the second was to measure it against the reader's CV. Ned often rebuked Emma for judging manuscripts – and books she read for pleasure – by the extent to which the heroine resembled herself, but he now found that he was interested only in books about the ruin of reputation, measuring himself against the protagonists.

When Michael Haneke's film *Amour* was released, awarded five stars in the *Guardian* and called 'deeply moving' on the artsy broadcasts, a number of friends had refused to go, saying that they felt unable to watch a film about Alzheimer's 'because of mummy' or some other personal connection. And, though Ned could see that cultural obstacle coming to him one day, it had never occurred to him that he would develop a similar problem with novels about sexual violence, especially when, as in Edinburgh, he was reading one with an impenetrable lover in bed beside him.

Early in his spell of disrepute, Ned had recognized the risk of interpreting everything through the perspective of his alleged offence. He once had to abandon a newspaper article because his eye caught a peripheral reference to the painting *The Rape of the Sabine Women*, although he knew that in that case, rape did not mean *rape*. (Linguistically, as it had the antique meaning of siege, rather than criminally or morally, he hastened to add, even in his mind.) So, reading the sequence in which Lucy decides not to go to the police, he fought not to take it personally, but failed.

Was it possible that his generation of men had to accept accusation – even jailing – over sex as a payback for what women had suffered over centuries?

The Comedy of False Accusation

'Bloody Hell! Hogwarts!'

Tom was pointing at the Edinburgh skyline, which for the first time during their visit was not obscured by rain or fog.

'What?' Ned said.

'Just, when you suddenly see it like that, all those Gothic turrets and battlements, you see where JK got it from. The wizard academy isn't fantastical, it's Scottish realism. Like one of the English guys at the Uni-perversity once told me, Narnia is basically Belfast: you put one map on top of the other and the hills pretty much overlap. C. S. Lewis taught at Queen's.'

Ned tried to concentrate on his friend's architectural-cultural lecture but was distracted by checking the passing crowds for accusatory faces. Out in the city for the first time without veils of rain-splashed plastic, he felt conspicuous and vulnerable. In the clear evening – a rainbow crowning the glistening castle – there was no meteorological need even for the baseball cap Ned wore as a last line of defence.

They were walking along Princes Street towards Edinburgh's upper tier; their comedy gig was on the Mound at nine. When told which comedian the men were going to see, Emma and Helen had pulled faces and selected instead a piece of Canadian music-theatre about children with Asperger's syndrome, followed by supper at an Italian restaurant that offered the most acceptable compromise between edibility and quick service.

On the road that wound round Waverley station, young men and women with imploring expressions – the showbiz equivalent of beggars in the developing world – pressed flyers at Ned and Tom. The aspiring theatricals were already skilled in sliding the glossy paper into hands held out flatly in refusal. Watching people hungry for fame and to be on television, Ned felt like a syphilitic who finds himself in a restaurant on Valentine's Day.

People arriving on the Mound were divided by yellow-jacketed stewards into lines for the Military Tattoo, Michael McIntyre and Jim Davidson. Police stood at intervals between the first two queues.

'Presumably the cops are here because of the Tattoo?' Ned suggested.

'Really?'

'The British Army marching under floodlights without their guns. Prime target for The Evil Ones, wouldn't it be?'

'Oh, I guess so.'

Ned felt the rare glow of having thought something that Tom hadn't, although his friend soon regained the conversational advantage: 'Although I suppose they could be here to arrest Davidson again. There's no . . .'

Ned's flinching look made him stop. 'Oh, God, sorry, Nod. I didn't mean . . .'

'I just hope that sentence wasn't going to include the words *smoke* or *fire*.'

Looking away, Tom gestured at the soot-stained stone of the university building they were waiting to enter. 'See what I mean? You could teach Ron how to use a broomstick in there.'

'I never knew you were quite such a Potter scholar,' Ned teased.

As he spoke, a woman in front turned round.

'No choice. Becky was in the exact catchment zone.'

'Oh, yeah. Tell that to the Traill Inquiry, you . . .'

The safety-catch in his brain saved him from saying *paedophile* here. When he made eye contact with the customer in front, she looked away. Sixtyish and wealthily dressed, she was part of his core television audience and clientele at book signings. Recognition would generally have led to a shy, polite acknowledgement of loving his documentaries. So he hoped that her failure to speak now was from kindness, but feared it might result from embarrassment, pity or disappointment.

One of the stewards walked along the line and said in the slow, capital letter tone of a primary teacher: 'Just checking everyone in this queue is expecting to see *No Further Action?*'

'Oh, Lord, no!' exclaimed the tourist who had spotted Ned. She and her companion were redirected to Michael McIntyre. As they headed towards the much longer queue, she glanced back, perhaps to check if the television professor and his friend had made a similar mistake and were following. His choice of stand-up comedy would doubtless become part of her anecdote about his general decline in her estimation.

'You're sure you wouldn't rather watch soldiers in kilts pulling cannons about?' Tom asked. 'Or even routines about how hard supermarket packaging is to open?'

'No. I have to see this,' Ned told him. 'For, as it were, historic reasons.'

A few minutes before the advertised start-time, they were invited up the clanging stone steps and into the intricately chiselled lobby. 'Hogwarts and all!' exclaimed Tom, looking round.

Beside the staircase that led up to the theatre was a bar where the comedian they had come to see was standing. In a three-piece businessman's suit, he was orange-skinned from vacation or cosmetics, and holding a glass of what looked like water as he told three other men a story that involved facial expressions and exaggerated voices. The actors Ned knew liked to be alone in their dressing room before a performance but a comic possibly needed to warm up by hearing people laugh.

The venue was a converted lecture hall, with steeply tiered seating. As the lights went down, a spotlight swung a moonrise across the stage, then steadied for Davidson to bound into it. At a certain point in the career of comedians or musicians, when the audience consists entirely of admirers, shows begin with an ovation. The one that Davidson received provoked him to claim that he had thought of leaving Edinburgh that morning, so appalled was he by the reviews in two liberal newspapers.

In honour of the comic's debut at the Edinburgh Fringe, there was some tailored stuff featuring memories and impersonations of his late Scottish father. But the early material was a swearier version of what Ned remembered from television in the '70s. Davidson recalled once meeting a really fat and ugly bird with two young children in a stroller. When he asked her how old the 'twins' were, she corrected him that they were brother and sister single births. 'Sorry, madam,' he apologizes. 'I just couldn't think of anyone who would fuck you twice!' Cataloguing various sexual encounters, he riffed on pubic manicures: ginger women should not have a Brazilian because it made 'their fannies look like a fish finger'. A gag about the Paralympics involved a mime of deaf runners failing to hear the starting gun.

The audience responded with loud laughter, in which Tom joined, but Ned, fearing that his reaction might be noticed and socially mediated, didn't.

In the middle section of the set, no one laughed at all. Davidson related his arrest by detectives from Operation Yewtree over historic sexual allegations involving first two women and then, as publicity brought new claims, several more. Ned was conscious of Tom watching his reactions, in the way that Emma did during plays or films about young boys suffering their father's death, which meant that he was trained in appearing neutrally engaged while under scrutiny. From a defendant's perspective, he was intrigued that Davidson had applied, to different cases, all three of the available exonerations: with some of the women he had consensual sex, others he had known but never sexually, while a third group he had never met at all.

Apart from using disguises for the complainants such as 'Scouser' and 'Penguin' – required, even in a stand-up act, to respect their legal right to lifelong anonymity – the comic's account was angrily factual, except for humorous incredulity at the proof of his intimacy with one accuser – with whom he claimed not to have had an intimate relationship – being her memory of his 'ginger pubes' which, as he pointed out, was a reasonable guess from his head.

The audience, though, greeted that detail with the same attentive but uncomfortable silence that they gave to the entire Yewtree routine. Ned felt that it was a creative mistake for Davidson to change his tone so severely for this part of the show; a Lenny Bruce would have made a savage comic monologue from such arrest and accusation.

Even as a deliberately serious interlude in a comedy show, there was a problem with the shaping of the tale because the outcome – a letter from the cops advising that 'no further action' would be taken – was anti-climactic and even non-comic narratives required a punchline.

Davidson returned to knob and fanny gags – and an anecdote about a wacky comedian who did a shit inside the guitar of a musician who was on the same bill – and the audience happily relaxed. Ned heard only the bare details of each story. Davidson was an ideal candidate for the opposite of *schadenfreude*. And yet his was not a clean case of false accusation; perhaps none was. The comedian's defence was that he was a casual shagger and serial adulterer but not a rapist. This confession might be effective legally but how did it work morally and domestically? The act contained the information that Michelle, his fourth wife, was standing by him.

Ned felt even more relieved that Emma had decided to skip this show.

Friday Suicide Call (3)

At the established time on the usual day, the words Suicide Call flickered on the display. Tom, with his nickname habit, appreciated the dumb gullibility of his phone in never querying an identity entered.

He let it ring. Keeping mock office hours in his spare-bedroom study, he was reading a Kindle import of a new book on Dallas '63, which suggested that Bobby had plotted with Lyndon Johnson to have JFK shot.

Tom watched the call being diverted to voicemail, switched the phone to silent vibrate mode, then went back to the text. The book's hypothesis required the writer to ignore the strong evidence of hostility between LBJ and RFK (he had the advantage to be working on a period in which the fashion for triplicate initials offered an alternative to the biographical problem of the repetition of the subject's name), which had led many earlier authors to argue that Johnson, convinced that Bobby was plotting to remove him from the ticket as Jack's running mate in '64, had conspired to make the president unavailable for re-election.

A trembling on his desk alerted him to a *901* recorded call. He ignored it. One of Tom's distinctions among scholars of American history was his resistance to conspiracy theories. The explanation for the ballistic discrepancies in the Warren Commission's conclusions on the Dallas shooting that most convinced him was that the President had accidentally been finished off by a bodyguard returning fire (the argument of a volume published on one of the decadal anniversaries), which the US government, from understandable embarrassment, had subsequently covered up.

Fifteen minutes later – exactly so, heightened awareness of time being a consequence of house arrest – the phone shook mutely with another Suicide Call. Tom watched it divert to the answer service and then repeatedly alert him to the message.

He scrolled to *Chapter 9: Oh, Jackie!*, in which the Albuquerque academic argued that LBJ had coerced the president's brother into the murder scheme by threatening to expose his affair with Jacqueline Kennedy.

One disadvantage of electronic readers over traditional books was that, while throwing the former to the floor in exasperation might be just as therapeutic as jettisoning a hardback, it was more economically prohibitive.

While Tom had always been dismissive of the old theories about LBJ being a conspirator, at least that speculation had some evidential basis. The vice-president had been at risk of being dropped from the re-election bid and was without doubt the main American beneficiary of the death, which is a factor often considered by investigations of killings, even though such connections are not necessarily decisive: the fact that A is run down by a bus and B receives the insurance pay-off does not automatically mean that B fixed the brakes of the vehicle.

A further Suicide Call, followed by another *901* diversion.

This LBJ–RFK hypothesis, in contrast, seemed based on nothing except the desire to find a new route across over-trodden ground. The proposed co-conspirators would have had to overcome the obstacle of scarcely being on speaking terms. And, while a sexual relationship between Bobby and Jackie had been suggested by some, any such affair was assumed to have begun as desperate mutual comfort after the President's death, which made psychological sense, rather than as a long-standing secret that had to be hidden by homicide.

After the third of the voicemail prompts, Tom, from curiosity rather than duty, went to the queue.

3:30: *Hi, Tom. David Wellington. You're probably on another call. Give me a bell or I'll try you in a tick? Ciao for now.*

3:45: *Tom? David Wellington again. Didn't get an answer from you just now. I'm sure it's nothing. You're probably just tied up somewhere.*

Yeah, hanging from a beam in a barn, David.

4:00: *Tom, it's David. Look, I'm getting a bit concerned that you haven't made our usual rendezvous. Listen, if I haven't heard from you by 4.15, I'm going to have to enact protocols. Take care.*

It is a common fantasy of the wronged to imagine the reaction of their persecutors on receiving news of the suicide and Tom was now given a glimpse of this satisfaction without the biggest drawback. He wondered if Special had been phoned or e-mailed to be told: *He's not answering his phone.*

During the next fifteen minutes, he tried to focus on the tenth chapter – 'The Wink: We Done It, Son' – which argued that LBJ's closing of one eye after being sworn in as President on the jet that carried his predecessor's corpse was not, as previous intriguers had suggested, a shared moment of satisfaction with his wife and co-conspirator Lady Bird Johnson but a signal to Bobby back in the Attorney-General's office, watching the footage on TV.

Why, the Texan historian argued, would Johnson have risked such a public gesture when he could have whispered quietly to his wife within moments in the presidential cabin that was now theirs? The only explanation was that he needed to get a message to someone who was not at the ceremony. As was common with bad history, a small truth spawned a hugely unsafe conclusion. The new commander-in-chief's certainly inappropriate and therefore possibly mysterious eye movement might more likely have been directed at a distant observer but that didn't mean the target was – as with B receiving the death payout from bus victim A – in any way inevitably Bobby.

Tom was also not sure where exactly RKF had been at the time of the assassination and, as the sport of historians is identifying inaccuracies in the work of their peers, got up to look for, on shelves that had once been alphabetically arranged, Manchester's *The Death of a President*. Pausing between the M and the K sections, while trying to remember if his Kennedy library was arranged by author or overall subject, he began to wonder what the *protocols* mentioned by Wellington might mean. The arrival of a Workplace Harmony rapid response team at his door? A call or e-mail from Special?

He had just found the book he needed, under D for Dallas, when his phone tolled an entry in his in-box.

To: tkpimm@chatter.co.uk
From: c.harrison@ume.ac.uk

Subject: U Okay?

Tom, just checking in again. You bearing up? Do let me know if you need to talk again or there's anything at all I can do? C XX

His own laugh had been a rare sound recently and, with the village quiet because most people were at work, it startled him. So the *protocol* involved asking his kindest colleague to be a corporate equivalent of neighbours peering through the net curtains. Had Wellington asked around in panic that afternoon or was Ciara's name stored as a precaution, like the next-of-kin box on a medical form? He resented the university for taking advantage of her nature but what she had done was merely an extension of the kindness she had already shown him. So he replied:

> I'm surviving. A little writing, mainly reading: relieved to find that I can still tell good history from bad. T XX

After the experience of seeing years of his e-mails printed at the back of the Traill Report, Tom almost omitted the kisses but even Salem Academy could surely not claim that message sign-offs had any significance. He got back a Good and another two virtual smooches, imagining the news being passed to Royal and then to Special and corporate relief all round that they would not yet be called to a coroner's court.

In the Manchester book, he discovered that the Kennedy author, as well as being implausible in his broader claims, was also wrong about where Bobby had been when hearing of his brother's death: the Attorney-General was eating a tuna sandwich in the swimming pool of his Virginia mansion.

The errant academic – as most now did in a culture where teachers were judged by public impact – printed his office contacts at the bottom of his Author's Note. Tom had a tone for shame-mails (he might also post something on one of the K sites later) and it flowed easily: *While you are entitled to your fantasies, however absurd, in interpreting the Kennedy assassination, certain basic facts are incontrovertible. At the time of his brother's death, Robert F Kennedy (see Manchester, p 195) was . . .*

He stopped. For the first time on one of these corrective missions, he pictured the recipient: hot, hurt, their work interrupted, cursing the nit-picking English prick. Tom deleted the message.

Are you sure? his laptop queried. He was certain. His wounds had made him unwilling to spill the blood of others.

Pistory

Professor Ned Marriott may or may not be a sex criminal – he denies allegations that are currently under investigation by the Metropolitan Police's Operation Millpond – but the under-a-cloud don and TV face now confronts another struggle to clear his name – over accusations of plagiarism.

The historiat may recall that the telly Prof already has form in this area. In 2000, the BBC and the production company Ogglebox apologized and paid damages to the publishers Pan Macmillan after admitting that multiple phrases from the educational set-text *A Little History of Tudor England* had been included without attribution in the scripts and tie-in BBC Books hardback for *The Six Lives of Henry VIII*, Marriott's 1999 project charting the changes in King Harry's reputation.

At the time, the wholesale theft of several sentences was blamed on a 'misunderstanding at the research and scripting stage.' But, with the prof-on-the-box's career already under threat from the allegations that he sexually assaulted two young women, TV bosses will be alarmed to hear that a detailed study by *Pistory* of the alleged rapist's broadcast and published output has uncovered evidence that the under-a-shadow academic has continued to dip his fingers into the word-till when he hopes that no one is looking – which, with the declining ratings for his recent TV work, may have seemed a safe bet!

Until, that is, *Pistory* came along. We have uncovered multiple examples of suspicious overlaps with pre-existing texts.

In 2005, to mark the thirtieth anniversary of the fall of Saigon, Marriott wrote and presented a BBC2 documentary, made by Ogglebox, called *Why Weren't We In Vietnam?*, which looked at how, in the mid-to-late 1960s, the then British Prime Minister, Harold Wilson, resisted requests from the American

President, Lyndon Baines Johnson, to give UK military support to the American war in Vietnam.

The script included these lines:

> Marriott (VO): Campaigning for President in 1964, Johnson had opposed sending US combat troops to Vietnam and was said, in private conversation, to have called it 'a raggedy-ass fourth-rate country', over which no American blood should be spilled. But, by 1965, President Johnson was commander-in-chief of 184,000 American soldiers in Vietnam.

Although lightly paraphrasing in places, this script largely reproduces, in content and order of facts, a paragraph in *America: A Narrative History* by George Brown Tindall and David E Shi (Norton, 4th ed, 1996):

> During the Presidential campaign of 1964 Johnson had opposed the use of American combat troops and had privately described Vietnam as a 'raggedy-ass fourth-rate country' not worthy of American blood and money. Nevertheless, by the end of 1965, there were 184,000 American troops in Vietnam. (p. 1425)

Note the word 'nevertheless', which is about the only thing the sticky-fingered professor hasn't filched. Nevertheless, this isn't a one-off. Marriott's Channel 4 TV series and related book *The Fabulous Fifties* (1990) both contain these lines:

> The Labour Foreign Secretary, Ernest Bevin, was obsessed with bread: the economic significance of its price but also its taste. This was partly because he had hated the austerity 'British Loaf', introduced during rationing. He claimed it gave him flatulence!

And, in Professor Peter Hennessy's *Never Again: Britain 1945–1951* (Penguin) we find this:

> Bevin was obsessed with food, bread especially . . . he didn't like the austerity 'British Loaf'. It made him belch. (p. 375)

It's not just Bevin who suffers from regurgitation, Prof Marriott! But, to be fair, the scandal-hit academic does also sometimes find his *own* words coming back on him. A passage describing the Coronation of Queen Elizabeth II that featured in *The Fabulous Fifties* is partially reproduced, with minimal revision, in both *Elizabeth I – Elizabeth II: Who Wins?* and *The British People*. Marriott's description of the politics of sixteenth-century England in the Elizabethan book and series is also repeated more or less verbatim on page and screen in *The English Witch Hunts* (2005).

Whatever else the notorious historian may be guilty of, he certainly seems bang to rights on literary pillaging!

Nuance

'Ned, it's Claire. I've had a look at that blog you sent me.'

'Good. And?'

'I understand how galling this sort of stuff can be but I tend to advocate a sticks and stones approach.'

'What? Throwing some at the smug, sanctimonious teaching assistant fucker?'

'Er, no. More along the lines of blogs will never hurt you.'

'But it's clearly damaging.'

'Potentially, yes. With those already determined to think the worst of you. Whether it's actually defamatory, though . . . some of the passages he quotes are quite close.'

'But the details of the Vietnam War or the Attlee administration remain the same. What historians do most of the time is put it in their own words. Tom Pimm calls us paraphrase-medics.'

'I can see that. But it's one of those things that a prosecutor can – I'm not saying it is – make sound lazy. Bevin's belch is the sort of thing a decent QC . . .'

'Okay, Claire. So, with that, you notice that the arsehole hasn't put a date on Hennessey's *Never Again*? That's because his book came out in 1992, two years after mine.'

'Wow! This is. You're saying he stole it from you?'

'No. *No*. It's complicated.'

'Oh, dear. Then, as a general rule, don't take it near the law.'

'The point is, I got it from an article Peter wrote – in the '80s, I think.'

'Oh, well, again, when said with an eyebrow raised under a wig . . .'

'But it's properly credited to him at the back of my book. The guy's just done some quote-check without reading the footnotes. And the others – I mean, is *self*-plagiarism even plagiarism?'

'Well, in strict legal terms, I'd think obviously not. Any more than self-abuse is abuse. But again – in an adversarial context – it can be made to seem – again, I'm not saying it is – dodgy . . .'

'But he hasn't really got anything on me. In every case, it's a matter of nuance.'

'Ah. So – to your average juror, Nuance is the name of some reality TV star's latest baby.'

'But how can he just get away with it? That phrase about being caught with my fingers in the word-till . . .'

'Yes. I tend to advise being wary of suing over metaphors. Judges and juries allow quite a bit wriggle-room in interpretation.'

'No, the point I'm making is that he's nicked it from Martin Amis. *The Moronic Inferno*, I'm pretty sure. He's plagiarized a phrase about plagiarism!'

'That's very funny. But it's more a point for Twitter than the courts.'

'I don't twit.'

'I know. But I can easily find someone here to get that up if you want it. Fight fire with fire; fight posts with posts.'

'Claire, it's like going to the doctor and being told to try a glass of water.'

'Well, sometimes that might be the best thing for it.'

'Okay. But, even you – the bit about *literary pillaging*!'

'As I've said, metaphors . . . and what happened with the Tudor thing is on the record.'

'Well, we know what happened there.'

'Yes, we do. But it's in cold print.'

'Yeah, yeah. But pillage is a half of a well-known phrase. The Vikings, they pillaged and they . . .'

'Oh, I see. Yes.'

'So what this shabby hack is trying to say is he's guilty of pillaging and so he's nudge nudge guilty of . . . of . . .'

'Well, he *may* be.'

'Jesus fucking Christ, whose side are you on?'

'Oh, Ned, you know better than that. All I'm ever doing is imagining how it will play. Legally, you are under a suspicion. We are in the process of demonstrating it to be false. But we can't go after some blogger who's probably only read by his mother for being suspicious of you. I can force him to specify what the allegations are and that you deny them. But my advice is that would make things worse.'

'Yes. I . . . I'm sorry.'

'Okay, Professor. From now on, I won't tell you whether Churchill deliberately let Coventry be bombed and you won't tell me who to sue.'

Shaving Luxury

Eager to economize – because of the loss of the fees from TV and the potentially bankrupting legal costs to come – Ned downloaded onto his cheapo phone an add-up app, which compared expenditure on a range of items (under the headings Groceries, Leisure, Fuel, Sundries) week to week, month by month, year on year.

Finding – pleasingly – that his writer's mind still functioned through the fug of uplift pills, he was struck that the names given to the categories were not the words that most people would choose. Food, entertainment, petrol, miscellaneous were surely the more universal terms. But in Australian cricket, extras were referred to as 'sundries', and so perhaps Bank-Balancer had originated in Oz, although, 'groceries', he reckoned, must have been chosen because weekly shopping covered not just food but other stuff.

Which included, in this case, an escalating indulgence exposed by analysis of Ned's cash flow. His purchases of shaving foam, it turned out, had risen by almost half a month in the period since his fall. At first, he wondered if the speedier beard-growth was somehow a result of the antidepressants.

But then he understood. A reluctant and painfully inaccurate shaver, he had been, throughout his adult life, a weekend scruff, letting stubble grow unchallenged from Friday morning until he stumbled into the bathroom early on Monday. The roughness of his chin was a symbol of not being under pressure or on show.

His father and stepfather, born between the wars, had shaved every day, shaped by the Depression prejudice that a man whose face was neither clean nor officer-bearded was unemployed and careless of the figure he cut. And this prejudice may have been true because Ned's weekend hairiness was designed to advertise that he was not, though through his own choice, working.

Now, with his profession threatened, he instinctively adopted the wisdom of his family ancients that to be unshaven was code for the dole. Since the humiliation, even with the trembling hands of the first few weeks, he had forced the SuperSmooth Fusion 4 across his jaw each Saturday and Sunday morning. Ned was determined that no observer – or, worse, photographer or reporter – would be able to say: 'I saw him looking wild-eyed and unshaven in the street.' He entrusted the eyes to the drugs and took care of the bristles himself.

As a result, he was shaving seven times a week instead of five, an increase of 40%. The further 8% of shaving foam purchased to make the alarm-triggering 48% was presumably explained by the fact that he was grooming himself more carefully than before, desperate to appear respectable.

Recovered Memory Syndrome

She was watching a discussion on *Newsnight* about the future of the Liberal Democrats. One of the guests turned out to have a stammer. Poor man, she thought, watching him panic and start constructing his answers to avoid consonants that might block him.

And then – which must be how this worked – it was as if her mind cut away from BBC2 to a picture of two people on a grotty sofa. And. And. Of course.

When her solicitor answered the phone, she said: 'It's Billy Hessendon Castle. Do you know what? I think I may have narrowed it down a bit.'

The Opposite of Schadenfreude

Until now, when some unfortunate person became the latest quarry of the mob – the politician who made a 'gaffe', the footballer whose nightclub lover kissed and told, the bureaucrat with whom the buck stopped for tragedy or corruption – Ned would follow and enjoy their suffering as much as everyone else. The only possible mitigation was that his participation in the gleeful momentum that called for the miscreant's resignation, sacking or exile took place at dinner parties rather than on Twitter, a bonfire of inanities that he had always refused to feed for fear of its flames being turned on him.

He had touched on this cruel human instinct in his last, latest, TV documentary – a compendium of political scandals to mark the fiftieth anniversary of the Profumo affair – although the link had been rewritten because Dominic Ogg said that C2 and DE viewers wouldn't understand the word *schadenfreude*. Beyond the usual dismay at editorial infantilism, Ned's fury was increased by the lack of any satisfying equivalent single word in English. All of the alternatives were phrases. The Australians spoke of 'tall poppy syndrome', the desire to scythe down the asymmetrical stalk, and the Japanese of the highest nail being hammered back into place, while Ned had picked up an evocative expression from upper-middle-class English. 'He's fallen off his mighty perch,' Emma's mother would say with relish of the newly disreputed.

Since his fall, however, Ned felt the opposite impulse when watching the parade of the disgraced: the cabinet minister accused of calling Downing Street coppers 'plebs', pop stars who contrive to pay less tax than fans who spend their PAYE-deducted salaries on gigs and records, the unknown who become globally notorious within minutes by posting a tasteless comment or photo, the doctors or social workers who missed the warning symptoms so glaringly obvious to phone-in callers and columnists, the forgotten disc jockeys, comedians and presenters arrested by Yewtree and Millpond.

Now, Ned wanted them all to be innocent victims of conspiracy or misunderstanding or, if not, forgiven, retaining their careers and character. Immediately imagining conversations they were having with their families and the state of their bank balances, gastro-intestinal tracts and sleep patterns, he needed them to get through it as proof that it was possible to do so.

Did the Germans have a word for that?

Nup

Claire had been to some bleak weddings, including the expensive ceremony of a client who she knew was gay and whose divorce she was retained to negotiate within eighteen months, and another where she herself had slept with the groom for the last time (or what, to be legally precise, they intended to be the last time) forty-eight hours before the ceremony. She was convinced she had blushed at the question about just cause and impediment. That marriage had endured, although so, intermittently, had the affair.

But those services were ecstatic and sacramental in comparison with the union of Professor Edmund Horatio Marriott and Emma Jane Humpage, held at Aylesbury Register Office at 11am on an unseasonably wet August morning, witnessed by Ms Claire Ellen, Mr Tom Pimm and Mrs Helen Pimm.

Tom, the sort of man who seemed to see everything as a set-up for a joke, kept referring to Claire as 'Cupid' and it was true that the marriage was happening because of her. When she had advised Ned to transfer the house into Emma's name as a precaution against civil actions from the complainants, she had mentioned that there would be advantages for him in being married, although, anti-romantically, these would apply mainly if the couple ever split up. She assumed that Ned's proposal had not actually stated that it was better to get married in case they ever divorced or he went to jail, but the offer had been accepted. Due, though, to the bureaucratic motives of this matrimony, they had excluded all relatives, including Toby, who had been sent to stay with Ned's mother. Claire had also advised her client that it might be better to tell as few people as possible. 'Oh, fuck,' Ned had said. 'You're saying there'll be women chained to railings, holding up placards saying "Don't Marry A . . . "?' Claire had replied: 'I'm not saying that.'

The Registrar – a large woman, who looked Nigerian to Claire – wore spectacles with bright red frames, suggesting an habitual jolliness, but, behind her novelty eye-wear, looked wary. Claire guessed that the official had picked up on the strained mood of the group – she was used to couples who were, however briefly, in love – but could find no visual evidence to suggest the likeliest explanations of an arranged or passport-chasing marriage. When, just before the ceremony, Ned discreetly swallowed a small yellow pill (presumably a tranquillizer), she visibly relaxed, perhaps intuiting the third reason for an overshadowed marriage: that one of the couple was terminally ill.

Ned and Emma had written their own vows, which was a relief to Claire, as she could only imagine what Tom's eyebrows might have done during the traditional bits about *for richer or for poorer*.

Reversing the church order, Emma had chosen to speak first: 'I, Emma Jane Humpage, ask you, Edmund Horatio Marriott, to be my husband. Do you promise me that, on every day we are together, we will trust and support each other regardless of what troubles may come?'

'I do,' Ned replied. 'Do you, Emma Jane Humpage, accept my promise that I will never again do anything to hurt you?' As a human, Claire was moved by the honesty of these words; as a lawyer, alarmed. 'And that I will always prove myself worthy of your love and loyalty?'

'I do,' Emma said.

'I'd get it in writing,' Tom called. The witnesses stood in a curve behind the couple, like antiquated bridesmaids.

'Congratulations,' the Registrar said. 'You can kiss now if you want to.'

It was a cousin's pucker, Emma angling her cheek for her new husband to peck. When no-one took photographs during the signing of the register, the Registrar looked panicked again, possibly now suspecting that they were suicide bombers.

The wedding breakfast consisted of coffee and dunked Italian biscuits in a nearby branch of Nero, with Tom joking about the honeymoon being in Winslow. Though it was absolutely none of her business, Claire found it hard to imagine this union being consummated.

Millpond

Since the day he came under suspicion, Ned had avoided answering *unknown number* calls, assuming them to be a journalist calling from a newsroom. He also ignored numbers that failed to match to a name in his contacts and so might be the mobile of a more canny reporter. So, when the same strange 07801-number had shown several times, Ned, true to his precautions, let it ring out, the failure to leave a voicemail seemingly confirming his concerns. But when an e-mail from Ciara told him that Terry

Basham had contacted the department trying to get hold of Ned, the number she gave was the one he'd been avoiding.

He clicked the blue numerals in the message. A male snarl, warning callers they had better have good cause: 'Yeah.'

'Oh, er, Terry, it's Ned Marriott.'

'Teach! When are you gonna start calling me Bash?'

Whereas Tom's nicknames were at least inventive, Ned had always struggled with the baptismal wit, imported from professional sport, that simply cut someone's name in half or stuck the letter y on the end. Probably because Marriotty would have sounded distractingly Italian, Ned had blessedly been allotted something more resourced.

'Teach, how you doing?'

'Well, you can probably imagine.'

'Sure. But you're not gonna top yourself?'

Did anyone ever answer yes? 'No.'

Terry Basham, retired CID, had been Ned's 'investigating officer' on a documentary called *The Princes in the Tower – Case Re-Opened*. Ogg and his producer had clearly hoped the co-presentation would bring class war – encouraging 'Bash' to keep apologizing for failing History O-level and Ned to bring up two unsolved London murders on the detective's file – but they had quickly bonded through the usual masculine glue of drinking and football, although these had not been enough to sustain a friendship after filming.

'How much do you know?' Ned asked.

'Enough to know that a lot of the people *twattering* about it know fuck-all. This is Millpond?'

'Er, yes. Richard Dent and Heather, I think, Walters.'

'Don't know her. Denty's classic fast-track bastard. Not a bad lad, though. Spare me the ins and outs but have they got anything except old verbals?'

Simultaneously translating as *historical* and *anecdotal*, Ned answered: 'No.'

'And your defence is two consenting adults?'

'Well, yes, and that one of them wasn't really even sex . . .'

'Good luck with that one. It didn't go a bundle for Old Billy Clinton. And how many women? I'm assuming it is *women*?'

'Oh, er, two, but at least one is . . .'

'Two,' Basham cut across him. 'And how close are the dates of the claims?'

The maths was part of the stuff he had tried to deny and so he struggled with the sum: 'Er, twenty-nine years apart.'

'Can they claim a pattern of behaviour?'

Ned forced himself to replay the mental tapes again. 'I . . . don't think so . . . they were very different situations . . .'

'And the complainants are more or less from your neck of the century?'

Basham asked all the questions you didn't want to answer; his two uncaught murderers must have celebrated when he retired.

'The first one is. The second . . .' Twenty-five years. 'There are a couple of decades in it . . .'

'And I'm guessing she wasn't older than you? Location thing? Missy clipboard?'

'Something like that. It happens, as you know.'

The weighted pause of two men who have stuff on each other.

'Can you be reasonably confident no more'll come forward?'

'Well, I never expected these.'

'Okay. The threshold for a cluster prosecution is ideally nine, seven minimum. I think, if nothing else drops, you're looking at the difference between being a criminal and being a sleazebag . . .'

Though now a defendant, Ned retained the self-righteousness of the innocent: 'Well, thank you very much.'

'You know me, Teach. I call it how I see it. And the line I've drawn keeps you out of court. What's your brief reckon?'

'She's getting together a stack of character references and some inconsistencies in the complainants' statements.'

'Yeah. Well, that's not going to make any difference.'

'Really? I sort of hold to the idea that, at some stage, I'm going to be allowed a defence.'

'Mate, I've warned you about reading the *Guardian*. Denty's straight. But Millpond are acting on orders from the top. They're playing Yewtree Rules. Automatically accept what the *victims'* – sceptical tremor in the word – 'tell you. Believe it even more if they're bawling when they say it. Because they didn't fix Jim, the Met and the CPS are under pressure to get convictions and they want it to be *faces*.'

A memory of slang from gangster movies. 'You mean criminals?'

'Wha? Nah. *Famous* faces. I feel for you, mate, which is why I got in contact, but this is how the force works. Do bugger-all about something for forty years, then bugger everything for twelve months.'

'Yes. Well, it may not be the only place that happens.'

'Look, I have channels to Denty and I'll find out what I can. But I fear it's a waiting game now.'

The question that haunts medicine and law: 'How long do you think it will be?'

And the same answer: 'It's impossible to say. You've clocked up the air-miles a bit, have you, over the years? The documentaries, posh holidays.'

'I suppose so. Why?'

'I'm afraid, in my experience, coppers will never willingly give up a case that involves the possibility of foreign travel. If they get a tip-off from the Maldives, or anywhere else with a decent beach, you could be looking at three years on bail.'

Ray (3)

There had always been a sort of war between the boarders and the dayers. They talked in different ways about different things: home and sisters and dogs and being able to watch football matches on Sky Go in their bedrooms, or dorm and who did the most inhuman farts and who definitely couldn't be Jewish and playing midnight games of cricket with a rolled-up sock and a folded *Four Four Two*.

But at least you knew which side you were on. The boarders talked about who had the biggest willy, the dayers about whose family had the biggest car. That was what you got to know, depending on whether you were among the ones who went through the dark brown double doors after Prep or Activities, or the ones who went out onto the gravel where the nannies or mummies were waiting. There was almost never a daddy, except for Stirling's, whose was so old the boys thought it must be his grandpa until he told them although, once he had, people kept forgetting and asking him again. Now Toby's own daddy – who wasn't as old as Stirling's, but still older than most of the others – picked him up a lot of evenings. Toby wished he didn't because it only made things worse.

It was one of the reasons he hadn't minded at first when Mummy suggested that he flexi-boarded once a week. Ellis said it was because his folks wanted him out of the way while they made him a little brother or sister, which was, like, *ew*, but, anyway, everyone knew Ellis was a bully. Now it was two nights some weeks because Mummy said it was all stops out on a big book that was going to make them all a lot of money. Ellis said that probably meant his rents were getting divorced.

But now it was like Uncle Tom said sometimes happened if a footballer went from one of the big London or Manchester or Merseyside teams to their deadly rivals. The boarders didn't think he was a boarder and the dayers didn't think he was a dayer. In break-time games, he'd always played for what was known as the go-home team against the home team but now the dayers sent him over to the boarders, who didn't pick him either.

The dorm, though, was the total nightmare. He got put in with boys from his year and Oscar Thomas, who had always been one of his mates, was a boarder now, so it should have been okay. But Oscar, it turned out, now thought of himself as, like being Manchester United till he died, and Toby of being, well, Man City. Sometimes it was fine, if Seb Landrose was flexing as well, but, if he wasn't, Oscar ganged up on him with Langton and Sweetman, led by Ellis.

'Give me an R!' he chanted, then, when he got it, the same for A and Y. 'What have we got? Ray!'

The others joined him in the chorus: 'Ray! Ray! Ray! Ray!'

Alice in Custody

No *Peter Pan* or *Alice in Wonderland* in the library, or adaptations of either at the theatre, where *Entertaining Mr Sloane* can also no longer be seen; opera listings lacking *Billy Budd* and *Death in Venice,* and a space on the wall where *The Swing* should have hung in the Wallace Collection and Caravaggio's *John the Baptist* would have shown in the Pinacoteca Capitolina in Rome.

During one of his three-hour stretches between drugged sleeps, Ned compiled a mental list of the cultural figures who could be judged lucky to have lived before the internet and the post-Savile investigations.

Art historical gossip, hardened into history, was that the Caravaggio painting of Christ's herald was based on a boy the artist was fucking. Such research methods in the twenty-first century would have brought a knock on the studio door and possibly imprisonment, so could the statute be back-dated to the seventeenth century? It is obvious from the diaries and biographies of Joe Orton that he made prodigious use of rent-boys, in Leicester, London and Tangiers, and that this experience informed characters such as the cock-artist Sloane. So should the play now be banned in case the royalties from it constitute immoral earnings? And the comedian and anecdotalist Kenneth Williams accompanied Orton on some of his African holidays, so should repeats of *Just a Minute* be censored, just in case?

Lewis Carroll and J. M. Barrie clearly had – to put it as

neutrally as possible – a fascination with children as fictional subjects and social companions. Taking advantage of the visual mementoes available to him at the time, Carroll was a keen photographer of children (some attribute to him a nude picture of a pre-pubescent girl), so what possibilities might later technology have given him? Can you imagine the hard-drives of Carroll or J. M. Barrie? Or what might have happened if they had appeared on *Jim'll Fix It* to fulfil the dreams of some young fan of Peter or Alice? And which websites might now feed the fascination with what lay beneath a young girl's skirt that is hinted at in Jean-Honoré Fragonard's *The Swing?*

Benjamin Britten commissioned operatic libretti on subjects featuring a sodomized young man (*Billy Budd*) and an old man obsessed with a beautiful adolescent (*Death in Venice*). He invited certain boy sopranos to private lessons and solo auditions and admitted to attending evensong to enjoy the aesthetic beauty of choirboys. No associate has ever gone on the record with allegations of sexual assault but even the best biographer is less assiduous with their inquiries than the Sex Crimes detectives and investigative journalists who would be on his case now.

The best defence of these cultural suspects was being dead but so, at the time of his exposure, was Jimmy Savile. The others had been dead much longer than him, which might invoke a posthumous statute of limitations on sexual suspicion, though not according to some journalists. A TV documentary had asked whether Carroll was a 'Victorian Jimmy Savile' and, though never answering the question, had left it hanging. Britten had been described by a distinguished music critic as 'a paedophile at least in his mind'.

Ned imagined a news helicopter hovering above Snape Maltings, with forensics officers glimpsed through windows shaking open Britten's scores in case incriminating notes or photos should fall out. And demands for the Royal Shakespeare Company to lose its middle name would be swift if an academic identified the topic of a sonnet as an underage male.

The pursuit of historic allegations, as Ned severely felt, raised doubts about the possibility of establishing guilt from distant and conflicting memories. What hope, then, for supposed offences even deeper in history?

It was an excellent subject for a documentary. When his name was cleared, he would suggest it to Ogg.

Upminster

Sitting side by side with the man in the afternoon in the lobby of a Buckinghamshire motel – a scenario until recently inconceivable – now felt almost routine. Hunting scenes and screen-printed still lives of pies and chips hung on the wall behind a youthful check-in desker – blue-tinted spectacles and an artful tangle of blonde hair – who, Ned was certain this time, was a student and possibly even one of theirs. He wondered if any academic adulterers had been rumbled by this flaw in the venue's promise of discretion.

Although the nature of Ned's role was undefined – somewhere between best man and death-row chaplain – he felt it fell to him to take the lead. When he gave their names, the receptionist issued directions to the meeting room where the others were already waiting and then said: 'We all hope you, like, sort this shit out and you're back soon, Dr Pimm.'

The kindness of the comment did not prevent a terrified look in Tom's eyes. Ned guessed that it was the first time during his controversy that he had been identified. But after a moment of Germanic pleasure that Tom was suffering a fraction of his own ordeal, he became distressed that either the history student had only identified one of her lecturers or did not believe in the innocence of the other. On reflection, he blamed the efficacy of his baseball cap.

Decor in the basement room was hotel-regular: carpet of Neapolitan ice-cream vomit, Turner-wannabes framed behind glass sun-spotted by angled ceiling lights. On a sideboard stood bottles of still and fizzy water and silver pots with black press-tops, labelled Coffee and Hot Water. A pair of chairs had been arranged on either side of the meeting table: a job interview scenario or, as Ned guiltily thought, in this case no-job inter-view. He wondered why there were three laptops but only two interviewers.

The witch-finders were fussily fixing their hot drinks. Turn-ing at the footsteps, the woman from HR put down her cup, exclaimed 'Dr Pimm, Professor Marriott!', then held out her hand and said: 'Jani Goswani, Workplace Harmony.'

'Yes. We've met before,' Tom said coldly, but the comment went unacknowledged. Ned wondered if she had genuinely for-gotten the encounter or this was bureaucratic hygiene, each stage of the process supposedly discrete. Then he understood that the blankness was to avoid the revelation that she had also met Ned when he gave evidence.

Next to her was a slight and wiry fiftyish man, grey mop and goatee combining with his almost albino-pale face to make him resemble a photographic negative. Scruffy jacket, jeans and dust-encrusted Nikes advertised that he had come to Academia via Bohemia.

Professor Henry Gibson had puddled water and milk on the table during his attempt at refreshment and dried his hands with a napkin before exchanging skin-stinging shakes. It seemed to Ned that he made a condolence face to both men. Tom's best hope, Ned had told him, was that the Gibson might have been vaccinated against becoming a full UME management Moonie by artistic humanity and the brevity of his tenure.

Place-cards had been set on the table and, once they matched the bodies, Gibson said: 'Although it may sound like writer's wank' – Goswani flinched and didn't commit this sentence to her laptop – 'while this is called a formal hearing, I'd like it to be as *informal* as possible. I'm supposed to confiscate your phones and the like but I'm not going to.' His colleague recoiled at this defiance of guidelines. 'Just show me they're off or show me you're turning them off and then you can put them back in your pockets.'

This flight-mode moment over, he explained that he would lead the questioning, with Ms Goswani supplementing and taking notes. Professor Marriott, he explained, was essentially present as a supporter and observer but could intervene if he had any concerns or 'useful elucidations', a phrasing that Gibson seemed to relish as he said it. He sought and received permission to use first names in the conversation, then asked if they had any questions.

'Yes,' said Tom. 'In the Traill Report, witnesses and alleged victims are V2 this and W5 that. But presumably I can speak of the people behind the armaments and post-codes?'

As this was mere procedure, the chair facially deferred the question to his right.

'Well, no,' said Goswani. 'The process is anonymized to protect victims . . .'

'*Alleged* victims,' Ned interrupted, echoing his solicitor at his own interrogations.

'To protect victims and witnesses. So you can't use their "real" names because you don't know them.'

'But I do,' said Tom, jettisoning early on Ned's coaching note about being less stubborn. 'V1 is Professor Desmond Craig-Jones, V2 is, er, Dr Henrietta Langham . . .' Ned could see Tom struggling to use passport names in place of his own caustic cast-list. 'V3 is Dr Alexandra Shaw . . .' Goswani had both palms held out like someone frightened of walking into a wall in the dark but Tom ignored her. 'V4 is Professor Daniel Kempson.'

'For the purposes of this process,' Goswani said, 'all speakers will remain codified. You may *think* you have identified individuals but you do not *know* who they are.'

'Look, I'm not trying to be difficult' – Goswani's look refused Tom's excuse – 'but part of what we do in our day jobs, when not suspended from them, is working out whether anonymous or pseudonymous statement B might also have been made by known protagonist A, which we do partly from patterns of language. And, actually, most people, after knowing someone for twenty years or so, could easily tell which was their Christmas card, even with the names redacted, as I believe you guys say.'

Gibson was nodding, which encouraged Ned's first intervention. 'As perhaps Professor Gibson, *Henry*, above all, understands' – Claire had advised Ned to flatter the arbiter where possible – 'people have a sort of spoken or written fingerprint. Catch-phrases don't just happen in sit-coms. I was with Dr Pimm at the documentation stage and it was reasonably clear who most of the speakers were.'

Goswani openly showed irritation that the rules were being debated rather than applied. But Gibson played sceptical cop to her dogmatic one: 'Tom, I appreciate that this process may seem Kafkaesque to you.'

'No, actually it doesn't.'

'Oh. I'm pleased to hear that,' Goswani said.

'No. Josef K knew that he was on trial; he just didn't know what for. I didn't even know I was on trial.'

Gibson smiled and nodded, in the way that batsmen of the gentlemanly generation sometimes did when they received a particularly good ball. 'However,' the novelist said, 'for good or ill, the decision has been made to give very heavy protection to those making the complaints. All I can say is that I am aware of their advantage and will weigh it in my considerations.'

If ending up as a defendant is a standard human nightmare, a common fantasy is becoming a judge and Gibson was relishing the role, although also showing hopeful signs that he accepted the responsibilities. Ned made a mental note to check if a legal sub-plot figured in Gibson's next book, alongside the campus narrative already rumoured to be included.

'I am pleased to tell you, Dr Pimm,' Goswani said, 'that no claims of sexual misconduct were sustained.'

'Although,' Tom objected, 'the formula you use implies that some were made.'

Goswani ignored him. Gibson coughed the court to order.

'So,' he declared, vocally donning wig and robes, 'Dr Pimm, are you a bully?'

Ned felt the tactician's vindication of having coached his man for just this opening, fashioned to trap him into an angry dismissal that would serve as confirmation. He was pleased to note that Tom took the agreed breath and five-count before replying: 'Well, on the given definition, everyone from Mother Theresa of Calcutta to Zebedee in *The Magic Roundabout* might be. Not to mention almost all of the UME History department. I wonder if either you, Professor Gibson, or even your colleague here would survive if everyone you've ever worked with were given the opportunity to say anything they wanted about you without their name being attached to it.'

The answer, though combative, fell within the spectrum of Tom being Tom, which might be fine, unless Tom being Tom were the matter under challenge. But the *even* beside Goswani's name was unnecessarily provocative and had its effect. Completing her catch-up typing, she sighed. 'We are here to discuss the outcome of the process, not the process itself. And, in my experience, that process generally works better with just yes and no answers.'

'Well,' Gibson queried. 'I teach my students that detail is key.'

'Okay,' said Tom. 'In that case, No. No, I am not what you say I am. Although the witches of Salem gave the same answer to little end.'

Gibson nodded again. 'I acknowledge that historical metaphors may be a habit. But maybe if we stay in contemporary Middle England where possible? Do you accept that some of your behaviour may have made some of your colleagues or customers unhappy?'

'When it comes to what I persist in calling students, it's like, I imagine, a doctor with patients: they can't all be given the outcomes they want. Or at least they couldn't; I've missed some departmentals while suspended. And so some of them will be unhappy with you. When it comes to colleagues, I'm sure there were times some of them wanted to kill me and I can tell you as fact that there were times I wanted to kill some of them. Which makes it an ordinary workplace.'

Goswani grimaced as if chewing a boiling coal. 'But – to be clear – you are not suggesting that you ever employed or threatened violent behaviour against a colleague or customer?'

Tom's expression told her that there was now a hit list of at least one name. Gibson smiled. 'I think I understood the homicidal reference to be a figure of speech. Tom, you were asked about the existence of – and possible causes – for unhappiness in History? I realize that sounds like an impossibly general essay question but . . .'

Tom smiled: another piece of prior advice that he had so far failed to take. 'I think probably all offices are the same. Every time a job is given to someone, those who didn't get it are left angry, bitter, jealous, plotting. And, especially these days, we spend more time in meetings than teaching. A lot of this rubbish about me, as I understand it, involves meetings. And, by their nature, it's hard to imagine a meeting that everyone leaves happy.'

Goswani's shaking head. 'If the meeting is well run, then they should.'

'Well, I disagree with you in theory and, more importantly, in practice in our department. If Sir Richard Agate, Kevan Neades and Joanna Rafferty had presided over the first council of the Pilgrims on Burial Hill, I doubt that anyone would even have heard of America now.'

'Are you sure it's wise to personalize this?' Goswani asked.

'Well, their decision to sack me feels fairly personal,' Tom replied.

Ned was uncertain how to read this meeting. From the perspective of an employment lawyer, it was almost certainly going badly; but Sir Thomas More or Giles in *The Crucible* would surely admire Tom's refusal to accommodate authority. *More weight.*

Gibson bent over typed foolscap, reflecting. Goswani's tone

and folded arms suggested that she was showing the Creative Writing guy how it was done. 'Dr Pimm, do you accept that you could be intellectually intimidating?'

'Wouldn't that be an extraordinary accusation in a university?'

'You haven't answered my question.'

'*You* haven't answered mine. I hope I *was* intellectually intimidating.'

'Really?'

'Yes. Otherwise, there truly would be grounds for my sacking.'

'I find that an extraordinary answer.'

'I found it an extraordinary question.'

'Would you describe yourself as a trouble-maker?'

'No. But then who would? Except possibly a wrestler or darts player, who might have it emblazoned on their jacket? Tom "The Trouble" Pimm.'

'Okay. Do you think other people would describe you as a trouble-maker?'

'Possibly. *Probably*, if that other person were Kevan Neades.'

Goswani typed lengthily, ending with a wriggle of the wrists, like a pianist completing a cadenza. She turned to Gibson, in a gesture that felt more despair than teamwork.

The novelist said: 'Okay, I want now to go through some specific allegations. One complaint is that you used obscene language while teaching.'

'I find that highly unlikely.'

The purpose of the third laptop was now revealed. Goswani spun it round to show a frozen image of Tom in mid-shot at the front of the Tuchman lecture theatre, the heads of the first rows bent low over their keyboards or notebooks. When she hit a key, the pause symbol dissolved and Tom said: 'one fucking thing after another.'

The pop-up box apparently containing only those five words, the screen faded to black. The filming of lectures had officially been introduced to increase the value of the 'teaching offer' by giving 'customers' the chance to catch up or revise on the department website, but had soon been used to provide online courses for remote students. The unions had pushed unsuccessfully for extra payments, but no fears had been raised of the footage being used as evidence.

'Presumably you're not going to deny that this is a clip of you lecturing to first-year students?' the woman asked.

'No, but it's a quote from Alan Bennett's play – and, indeed, film – *The History Boys*, in which a student complains that history is *just one fucking thing after another*.' The HR woman shuddered at the curse-term. 'I've used it in my freshers' lecture for a few years.'

A Sherlock Holmes moment for Goswani. 'And you consider that appropriate language in front of vulnerable young people?'

Ned laughed aloud. 'I don't know whether you've done much teaching. But it's considered a triumph these days if you get through a class without one of the students dropping the f-bomb on *you*.'

'Wouldn't one *damn* thing after another have been equally effective?' Goswani asked.

'No. Because that isn't what Bennett wrote. And the rhythm and impact of the joke are simply less without *fucking*.'

Goswani flinched at the word again. Ned was struck by the improbability that, five decades after the *Lady Chatterley's Lover* trial, the dynamic was being repeated in this hearing: a puritanical judicial establishment and an academic elite speaking different languages.

Recklessly pedagogic, Tom expanded his case: 'And, in fact, the irony – and, against fashion, I am using the word correctly – is that the joke does partly depend on the incongruity of a student using that word in class. I gambled that our intake here was sufficiently mature and robust to enjoy that fact.'

'Well, it seems that V7 disagreed with you. Do you not consider the possibility that some of your students may come from sheltered and protective environments?'

'It's – historically – a strong statistical possibility. But surely they come to university to be exposed to a wider range of influences. I now fully expect that incomplete quotation – *they come to university to be exposed to* – to be lopped off and circulated out of context as evidence of my record of indecent exposure.'

Ignoring this, Goswani dealt a new piece of paper to the top of the deck and said crisply: 'V6.' Ned waited for a copy to be shunted across the table but the HR director said: 'I think I will read this one aloud.'

Like an actress at a poetry reading about to deliver an extract from a children's classic, she seemed physically to shrink and, when she spoke, her voice was a parody of a young woman in a documentary about child abuse: 'In my second year as a student in the History Department, I took the option of Dr Thomas Pimm's course on the American Presidency. We were set an essay asking us to compare and contrast the "New Deal" and the "Great Society". Subsequently, I received an e-mail from Dr Pimm asking me to attend a thirty-minute appointment during his office hours.'

The vocabulary and tone – amplified in Goswani's rendition – were those now familiar from television documentaries as the preface to a sexual allegation. A tactical ambiguity that Ned had introduced into his own evidence now seemed on the verge of being proved true. But then Goswani, role-playing late-teenage distress, said: 'He made an elaborate show of leaving the door open, which I found suspicious and which unnerved me.'

'Objection!' Ned heard himself shouting. Gibson and Tom laughed in ragged overlap. 'Sorry. Too many episodes of *The Good Wife*. But, seriously, is the ducking of witches the model here? If Dr Pimm had *closed* the door, it would doubtless have proved his malign intentions; but it turns out that so does doing the opposite. Can we set on the record that the teaching guidelines for staff advise leaving the door open during individual tutorials?'

'Objection noted,' said Gibson. 'I won't call you "Counselor", though. Ms Goswani?'

Like a theatre Cleopatra interrupted by a mobile phone or

a fatality in the audience, she re-accessed her character with fussy breaths and flutters. 'He reached down and aggressively pulled out . . . my essay. He sarcastically told me that it was too poor to be given a grade and that I stood very little chance of completing the module successfully. He suggested that I might find another course that suited me better. As I am a hard-working customer, whose family made great financial sacrifices to send me to UME, this was deeply upsetting and demotivating for me. I fled from his room in tears.'

'Another advantage of leaving the door open, I suppose,' Tom said.

'Is that your only comment on this charge?' Goswani asked.

'No. I have others. For example, did the student actually describe herself as a *customer* or do you lot Newspeak it later?'

'I hardly think that's important.'

'But it's interesting textual evidence – sorry, this is what I used to do for a living – of whether the statements are genuinely verbatim or she was rewritten later.'

'With respect, you don't know the gender of the victim as the evidence is anonymized.'

'With rapidly decreasing respect, I do know because I remember this student. Her essay was unforgettable. She attributed the New Deal to Theodore Roosevelt rather than FDR and, as for LBJ, was under the impression that he had entered the White House following the assassination in Dallas of President *Nigel* Kennedy. And don't get me started on the historical consequences of Martin Luther having been shot on a hotel balcony in 1968 rather than dying of natural causes in the Holy Roman Empire in I think – forgive me, my medications sometimes make me muzzy – 1546.'

Goswani, who had not bothered to type any of this, said: 'Do you accept that you made her cry?'

'No.'

'So you are saying the customer lied?'

'No. You are saying the *student* may have *cried*. But that doesn't mean I *made* her cry. One of the things we try to teach the students is the difference between consecutive and consequential. Roosevelt – the one called Franklin – died two months after the Yalta peace conference. But that doesn't mean he died because of it. However, the outcome of the conference may have been affected by his infirmity during the negotiations.'

'Well, I don't think we need to get bogged down in history.'

'I fear it may be too late for me. Look, I'm sorry for inflicting this lavatorial detail on you but I was physically sick – from tension, incidentally, not guilt – twice this morning before this meeting. But would it be fair, Ms Goswani, to say that you *made* me vomit?'

'I fail to see how I could have done as the meeting hadn't yet happened.'

'Okay, if I have another chunder afterwards, will that be your fault?'

'These exchanges are possibly becoming a little emetic,' said Gibson. 'Should we leave that one there?'

Prompted by his recent research into the possible motives of accusers, Ned cut in: 'Do we happen to know what grades Dr Pimm ultimately gave to V6?'

'I fail to see what relevance the victim's academic performance would have.'

The two History teachers exchanged a sceptical look, in which they then tried to include Gibson, but his head was down as he prepared the next question.

Goswani turned the third MacBook towards her, did a quick double-tap and angled it towards the defence bench again. A stilled video showed Tom in lecture pose, mouth open.

'On a number of occasions,' the lead prosecutor said, 'you mocked the religious or spiritual affiliations of your customers.'

'Now there's a cross to which I never expected to be nailed,' Tom said, ignored by Goswani as she clicked the pictures into motion.

On film, Tom, closing up his laptop as the students in the foreground could be seen ducking and shuffling for coats and bags, said: 'Ladies and gentlemen, thank you. I'll see you next

Wednesday at 9am then, Inshallah.' The clip folded and scrolled into him performing the same actions, although in different clothes, and beginning this time in mid-sentence: ' . . . see you next Wednesday at 9am then, Deo Volente.' The clip, it became clear, was a sort of Vine, with similar clips edited with escalating tightness, so that Tom paid off in quick succession: 'day at 9am then, Buddha allowing . . . 9am then Darwin willing . . . then by the grace of Dawkins . . . if L Ron Hubbard permits.'

All four people in the room looked away from the black screen as Goswani asked: 'How would you attempt to defend those comments, Dr Pimm?'

'Er, I'm not clear of what I am being accused?'

'Please. I think you know.'

'Ah. When, at the start, I said "ladies and gentlemen", should it have been "ladies, gentlemen and trans-gender customers"?'

Gibson did a big, slow blink, removed his spectacles and polished them with the paper napkin that had mopped up his slopped coffee. His colleague was no longer attempting to hide her anger: 'As you clearly must see, you are charged with giving offence to a person or people of faith.'

'Yes, I thought that might be the area we were in. Could you tell me if it was a person or people? And whether he, she or they represented Islam, Judaism, Catholicism, Buddhism, creationism, atheism, Scientology, or Anglicanism?'

'As you will understand, within the limits of anonymity, I can only tell you that a person of one faith raised concern on behalf of those within their own belief system, others and none. Come on, Dr Pimm, surely you can see why those comments offended people?'

'I thought you just said it was one person?'

'Representing others.'

'By petition or by self-election?'

'Can I take it that you are not entering a defence to this charge?'

'Well, clearly I never expected to be reviewing a showreel of my own lecture theatre sign-offs. But now that I am, the clips in question would seem to me to show either someone furiously but confusedly seeking a meaning in life, veering on a weekly basis between different theisms or atheisms. Or – alternately – a teacher attempting to employ what I believe – if I dare use that word – is described in your guidelines as inclusive language.'

Ned, watching, felt like a soldier's mother in the Second World War, intellectually accepting that the battles had to be fought but horrified by the prospect of the bloodshed reaching so close to home.

'But, Dr Pimm, what has caused offence is that you were clearly "sending up" these faith systems.'

'Was I? Would you have been happy if I had ended each lecture with the word *goodbye*?'

'I don't think I can see any objection to that.'

'But the word is a secular conflation of the Christian valediction *God be with you*. I suppose, if anything, I was riffing on different faith-related ways of saying farewell. Although I can't claim to have thought about it that deeply.'

'Indeed. Dr Pimm, what so offended V7 was the suggestion of equivalence – as if Allah and L. Ron Hubbard might have the same weight.'

Tom released the noisy out-breath – 'Ha!' – which, Ned knew, was a sign that the other speaker had lobbed up an argument that asked to be smashed into the empty court. 'But, Ms Goswani, as I understand the university's non-discriminatory policies, I must treat a Muslim and a Scientologist entirely equally?'

Gibson wiped his mouth with his hand, but not quickly enough to cover a smile.

'I notice,' Tom went on, 'that you omitted from my anthology of see you next Wednesdays the week when I ended *May the Force Be With You*. I don't have the precise current figures but, last time I checked, around 2 per cent of the student population self-identified as Jedi Knights.'

Goswani finally spoke: 'I advise you not to try to be clever, Dr Pimm.'

'If restored to the academic staff, I will bear that in mind.'

'The point is that disrespecting all religions equally, Dr Pimm, is not the same as respect. It seems to me that crucial to this is the question of where, as it were, you were coming from. What are your own religious beliefs, if any?'

'Oh, now . . .' Gibson began to interrupt but Tom in turn cut in on him: 'I decline to answer on the grounds of privacy and conscience.'

'But it is a matter of public record, Dr Pimm, that you have been prominent in opposing gestures of support for Palestinian intellectual freedom.'

'Well, I saw it more as supporting the right of academics from Israel to teach or speak here. Oh, I see why you're heading into this disputed territory. I took the stance I did because – call me old-fashioned – I believe that universities should be places of free debate. I'm not, in fact, Jewish, as I could prove to you with a simple visual gesture, although one that might easily, in the present climate, be misunderstood.'

Goswani's mouth fell open but Gibson raised a hand to advise that no words should emerge from it.

'I think we should perhaps move on,' the novelist said. 'It is also alleged,' – he spoke in a colourless tone that could be taken as either neutrality or contempt – 'that' – speech now entirely bleached of meaning – 'while lecturing you told a joke about Jimmy Savile.'

'You wouldn't happen to have a year or a subject to help me narrow it down?' asked Tom.

'Individual allegations are not dated,' Goswani explained. 'But it is my understanding that the investigation covered a period of around thirty years.'

Instinctively developing juridical instincts that he hoped were a final performance rather than a rehearsal, Ned shook his head with arthritic deliberation and eye-flashed incredulity.

Sensing the reaction, Tom turned the mime into a duet, which he broke to say:

'Even within such a wide range of dates, it's hard to imagine the circumstances in which such a quip would have arisen.'

Blank-faced, Gibson skimmed another witness sheet, headed V8. Tom speed-read it, sniffed explosive derision. 'Okay. In a lecture on US–UK relations in the middle 1970s, the fact that the prime minister at the time was James Callaghan and the president was Jimmy Carter led me to remark that, as it turned out, neither country benefited from a *Jim'll Fix It* effect. I apologize.'

The first smile from the personnel expert. 'That's good to hear, Tom.' The virgin use also of his first-name. 'To V8 only or to all the victims?'

'No, for the pun. Obviously, it's embarrassing to be confronted with a lecturer's lame attempts to keep the attention of a few more freshers. But, in my defence, I never expected to be put on trial for my wordplay up to two decades later.'

Gibson reached out and recovered the witness statement, wriggled bifocals around his nose as he checked some sentences low down. 'Ah, yes. On the occasion cited, the gag does perhaps extend a little further.' Expressionless recitative again. '*In fact, Dr Pimm went on to say, it can be argued that both Jims did to their countries what the other one is alleged to have done to so many unfortunate young people.* So, Tom, that seems to make it more recent?'

'Okay. Kill him for his bad jokes! But why would that be … be … an example of what I am accused of?'

Goswani apparently suffered sudden gastroenteritis. 'I wonder if you would explain the humour in your comment to me, Dr Pimm?'

'I think, with jokes, you either get them or don't?' Tom said. His questioner, luckily, didn't seem to catch that one either.

'You were suggesting, were you, that the politicians in question had – what? – had abused the countries, had interfered with them?'

'You know what I was saying.'

'I am not sure that I do.'

She was goading Tom to make a comment at which she would then express horror.

'Well, if you want me to say it, that they had fucked them, fucked them up.'

'And is that appropriate language to use in front of students who may be eighteen years old?'

'But I *didn't* use it! The whole point is that I *avoided* using it!'

Ned touched a hand to Tom's back, as if to find a dial there to turn down.

'Would it ever occur to you that V8 might have been a victim of child abuse?'

'What?' The agreement in coaching that Tom must not lose his temper was now broken. 'For fuck's sake, what are you suggesting?'

Ned placed a firm hand on his friend's arm. 'Tom, I don't think there was any suggestion that the student was abused by you . . .'

'No, indeed,' Goswani confirmed.

'Just that HR, er, WH thought he or she might have been offended by the comment because . . .'

'Of him or her being a Survivor. Yes, indeed,' the interrogator agreed.

Tom did now take some calming breaths, but there was heat in his cheeks when he spoke again. 'When you mention the Great Fire of London, you can't worry about whether one of the people hunched over a ring binder once lost a significant other to arson. Does an historian of the High Middle Ages not mention the Crusades in case a Muslim student is offended?'

'Such a policy should surely at least be considered,' Goswani argued. 'No business sets out to give offence to its customers.'

'Well, we can argue about *business* and *customers* another time. But, on the broader point, I don't believe we can treat everyone we meet as if they're an intolerance-bomb waiting to go off.'

Having recorded those thoughts on her laptop, the Harmonic representative said: 'Why, Dr Pimm, did you refer, in your joke, to the crimes of Jimmy Savile merely being "alleged"?'

Tom opened his mouth, as if to speak, but released only a wheeze. Ned, although he had agreed that he would not give the first answer to any question, felt compelled to address this one. 'Because, being dead, he is unable to answer to his crimes or be tried for them. So they remain allegations. It is a fundamental principle that people are innocent until proved guilty.'

'Thank you, Professor Marriott,' she said, and, for a moment, there were two defendants in the room. Ned assumed that there had been meetings at the university before his own suspension. A picture of Special and Goswani competing to carry out most unthinkingly the bidding of those above them.

'A final question from me, for the moment, Dr Pimm. Would it be fair to infer from what we have just witnessed that you have a tendency to lose your temper?'

A laugh so loud that even the studiedly unruffled Gibson started slightly. A sardonic undertow remained in Tom's voice as he said: 'There's always a risk of generalizing from a small piece of evidence. If you see me running in the street, am I an athlete? If you see me at a roadside motel with Professor Marriott in the afternoon, are we having a homosexual' – correct Grecian pronunciation, *hommo*-sexual – 'affair?'

This was what Tom was like in argument: fluent, infuriating, inventive in language and fact. But for him to speak in such a way in this place, Ned feared, was equivalent to a murder suspect answering the door with a red, wet knife. Goswani bang-typed enthusiastically at length and then deferred to the meeting's leader.

Gibson waved several stapled sheets of paper. 'As the given designation suggests, the largest number of complaints comes from V1 . . .'

'Yes, well, this is Professor Desmond Craig-Jones,' Tom interrupted.

'You don't know that,' Goswani said.

Ned looked past her to the novelist. 'Professor Gibson, it does seem to me that there's a procedural problem here. If Tom is accused of behaving in a certain way to certain people, then how can he give his side of the story without being allowed to identify the person?'

Goswani, quickly: 'If he did it, he did it. It's irrelevant who he did it to.'

Gibson, after thought: 'I inherited, rather than invented, this process. I imagine a parable. A is telephoned at home and asked if he thinks it possible that he may have walked past someone without noticing them.' The present-tense, parabolic, Kafkaesque voice of Gibson's later fiction. 'A replies: "I was deep in thought on Friedrichstrasse this morning. Might it have happened there?" But the investigator responds: "I can not tell you where it might have been. And did I say it was this morning? I am simply asking you if you have *ever* walked past someone without noticing them." I can see you have something of A's difficulty, Tom.'

Goswani appeared to be considering if the process allowed for the tribunal chair to be put on a charge. 'This is a *robust* process, based on best practice in equivalent businesses. The process *is* fit for purpose.'

Ned tried to play peacemaker: 'Could we set on record both Tom's contention that he knows V1 to be Professor Craig-Jones and Ms Goswani's insistence that he doesn't?'

'I will include this point of dispute in my report,' agreed Gibson.

'Thank you,' said Tom. 'Then, if V1 is who I think he is, his complaints focus on my alleged refusal to take his advice and alleged reluctance to spend time with him. If so, then the latter was because, though I make no claims to be a qualified psychiatrist, he was someone who had a disturbing – and, in my view, disturbed – personal manner. If I failed to use him as a "sounding board", in the way that he desired, then that might be because he was, in my experience, not only batty but inaccurate and incompetent.'

Goswani reacted as if he had used another swear word. 'Can I suggest we park incompetency for the moment? This isn't about incompetency.'

'Isn't it?' Tom challenged her. 'If he'd done his job properly, we wouldn't have clashed as often.'

'So you admit you clashed?'

'Yes. Over his supernaturally low standards and increasingly bizarre contributions to departmentals.'

'That may be your view. But while the university has no policy on competency, it does have one on bullying. That is the point.'

Tom showed astonishment; Ned spoke it. 'You have no policy on incompetency?'

'There is no formal code – no.'

'That's fascinating,' said Tom. 'If V2, as I believe, is Dr Henrietta Langham . . .'

Goswani leaned forward to object, but Gibson said: 'Let him.'

'Then,' Tom went on, 'I am surprised because I have had very little contact with her. Her complaint, as far as I can tell, is that people said to her that I said something to people about her teaching. Leaving aside reliance on hearsay . . .'

'*Mocked* her, in fact,' Goswani cut in.

'Well, *teased*, I'd say, at most. And not to her face.'

'And does that make it better?'

'Well, I think it pretty obviously does, doesn't it? I mean, a certain amount of gossip and bitching between colleagues is inevitable . . .'

'Not in a well-run workplace, no,' claimed Goswani, whose CV, Ned suspected, must have contained a long sabbatical on other planets before her hiring by UME.

Tom had taken on a conversational determination familiar from the college meetings that were a large part of the reason he was being interrogated in this motel basement. 'Although I am no more a medical practitioner than I am a psychiatrist, it is my belief, from the dementia of my father-in-law, that

V2 suffers from a condition known as "nominal aphasia", in which the names of people, places and items are forgotten, transposed or misplaced. While potentially problematic in many professions, it is especially so in the teaching of History. The confusion between Thomas Cromwell and Oliver Cromwell, usually removed from history students in the early stages of secondary school, remains a common misunderstanding among students at UME because V2 will often speak for several minutes or even whole lectures about one when she means the other. And markers of Renaissance History papers have become used to reading of the fierce moral scourges of a monk called Savlon-arola, the fault not of their historical illiteracy or pharmaceutical confusion but of the unknowing inarticulacy of their teacher.'

'Ah. Which is why,' asked Gibson, 'you would apparently refer to her behind her back as Savlon?'

'Yes, I admit I have a tendency to come up with names for people. But, as I say, any of you, if everything you said was tape-recorded for even twenty-four hours, there'd be . . .'

'So. This might be a good time' – Goswani rattled transcripts to locate the required page – 'to focus on your prejudicial terms for colleagues . . .'

'Well, I'd say *prejudicial* is itself prejudicial.'

The inquisitor's finger on the line she wanted. 'Let's take "Special". That was your cruel term for the Director of History?'

'A jokey name, I suppose, yes.'

'The joke being "Special Neades"? So a piece of humour about vulnerable young people with learning difficulties?'

'What? *No*,' Tom said. 'The target was Neades' surname and possibly his monumental self-importance, not slow students.'

Goswani's grimace, closely followed by Ned's, previewed her reaction: '*Slow*?'

'I do apologize for that, I'm sorry. It's quite high pressure, this . . . this . . . inquisition. Sometimes one doesn't use quite the word one wants to. In trying to avoid an out-dated term, I inadvertently used another.'

'So your head is full of offensive expressions that need to be deleted?'

'Not *full*. I have adjusted some of my vocabulary. As most people of my generation have had to.'

Ned was unsure whether Gibson's extended absences from the interrogations were judicial aloofness or a surrender to his superior in disciplinary procedures. But, as Tom's observer and supporter, he felt he had to intervene. 'Professor Gibson, although you have asked us not to make comparisons with certain seventeenth-century events in Massachusetts, it will be increasingly difficult now that your colleague seems to be pursuing the defendant over things that he might have thought about saying and then decided not to.'

This speech made Ned feel as if he were in *To Kill a Mockingbird* and Gibson responded in similar timbre: 'I rather agree.' To Goswani: 'Jani, can we concentrate on what is actually supposed to have been said?'

A thought of arguing back before: 'It is the belief of V3 that you called her "Horny" as a sexist joke about her use, as a bereaved woman, of dating sites?'

Ned tried but failed to stifle a laugh, prompting Goswani to ask: 'I see it amuses you even now, Professor Marriott.'

'No, no,' Tom joined in. 'He's laughing because it had nothing to do with that. Until we read her Stasi statement, I don't think it occurred to either of us that she was looking for dates.' Ned spotted another potential offence, but Tom was already defusing it. 'I mean, there's no reason why she shouldn't but it just never crossed our minds.'

A smile from Gibson meant that amusement had spread to three of the four people present. 'Would it have been something along the same line – as it were – as V1 being known to you as Daggers?'

Relieved not to have been a target of the phone-hacking scandals, Ned realized that he and Tom had suffered a different and perhaps more systematic surveillance of their conversations.

'As I've already said' – Tom was addressing Gibson directly

– 'I don't think anyone would have a very happy afternoon defending their gags and gossip over a period of more than a quarter of a century.'

'Indeed,' said the novelist, who was fumbling in an inside pocket of his jacket. When he removed and opened his wallet, Ned's first thought was that they had some sort of compromising photograph of Tom. But he waved what at first looked like a credit card but turned out to be a similarly-sized reproduction of the London Underground map on shiny plastic.

Grinning, Gibson said: 'Am I right in thinking that Daggers is short for Dagenham? Whereas Horny stands for Hornchurch, another destination on the District Line?'

Tom rubbed his hand across his mouth, as if signalling or attempting to induce speechlessness. Ruefulness was the mood Ned was trying to project.

Gibson consulted his route map while saying: 'So the joke is that Professor V1 has gone either three or four stages beyond Barking, depending on whether "Daggers" stands for Dagenham Heathway or Dagenham East? Whereas Dr V3 – "Horny" – is six beyond Barking.'

'Well, it's hard to answer,' said Tom. 'Because we don't, of course, know who V1 and V3 are.'

Gibson moved his head up and down, Goswani hers from side to side. 'Even so, to call anyone these terms was rude and cruel.'

'As I said earlier, it was said *about* them not *to* them.'

'So behind their back is better?'

'As I also said before, Ms Goswani, yes, I think it is. I fear that – through a combination of political piety and social media – we're coming dangerously close to a culture in which everyone is expected to speak at all times as if they're a politician wearing a live lapel mic. I think once you start trying to prosecute chat between chums . . .'

Gibson again seeming to favour the defence: 'Well, it's certainly ruder than calling a bear Paddington. But the wider point is well made.'

Imagining, perhaps, the private gibes that might be revealed by the future publication of *The Letters and E-Mails of Henry Gibson*. But his fellow arbiter was not to be persuaded. 'You'd see these kinds of remarks as *banter*, would you?' she asked, her delivery suggesting reference to an extreme sexual perversion.

'The word I'd prefer is persiflage.'

Gibson nodded, Goswani looked confused. Ned translated for her: 'It's an Old Etonian word for banter. Well, not merely OE: public school, generally.'

She frowned and turned to Tom: 'Are you comfortable, Dr Pimm, with that reference to your educational background?'

Ned's laugh overlapped with Tom's. 'There's really no cause to give Professor Marriott a V-code. He frequently takes a pop at me over my elitist education and I respond in kind in relation to his studies at a superior Catholic state school. And, before you call in reinforcements of the thought police, he doesn't mind my ragging him for being one of the Pope's battalions either.'

Goswani's fingers on the keyboard seemed to be playing one of the more complex stretches of Rachmaninov.

'We've become stuck on the District Line,' said Gibson. 'London residents insert your own jokes here.' A final look at his map card before putting it away. 'I dread to think which of your colleagues was Upminster or have you – or, indeed, they – not gone that far yet?'

A judge's jokes are always laughed at, but, in this case, there was no perjury in the men's response, which Goswani overrode: 'Did you, by any chance, have a jolly little nickname for Professor Padraig Allison?'

Professor Prick Anything. 'No,' Tom was saying. '*No*.'

'I think we should address,' Goswani said, 'the complaints made by V4 . . .'

'Professor Daniel Kempson,' Tom said.

'By *V4*, which, I should inform you, include a charge under the code of Insubordination.'

As Gibson found the right page in his pile and shunted it

across the surface, Goswani was already reading it aloud. In contrast to her colleague's detached delivery, she spoke the testimony like an actress auditioning for a Greek tragedy: 'I was tasked by the Director of History, Dr Kevan Neades, with leading the steering group to formulate a "Tariff of Expectations" – or agreed teaching and research requirements – for each departmental member. Despite my misgivings, based on his reputation and prior attitude towards me, Dr Tom Pimm finished sufficiently high in a ballot of teaching staff to be invited to serve on this steering group. In meetings, he was consistently negative and aggressive towards my approach and proposals. Although the Tariff of Expectations had already been set as working practice going forward by Director Neades – and the role of the steering committee was merely to devise and implement it – Dr Pimm consistently questioned and even attempted to overturn the Tariff. As well as verbally challenging my authority and judgement, he also frequently sighed – or, on other occasions, seemed to be stifling a sigh – as I set out my suggestions and decisions. The acceptance of authority and seniority is fundamental to decision-making in any organization and it is my belief, after discussion with Director Neades, that Dr Pimm was not only himself guilty of Insubordination but also encouraged Insubordination in others, delaying the successful roll out of the Tariff of Expectations".'

Goswani stopped, removed and re-sheathed her reading glasses in a green pouch. 'What is your reaction to that, Dr Pimm?'

A noisy out-breath from Tom, followed by a pause and then the beginning of a similar sound, abruptly swallowed. Gibson seemed to fight a smile. Ned admired his friend's insolence – yet more weight – but feared for its consequences. It was unclear whether Goswani had translated the charade but she sounded to be dampening exasperation as she said: 'Dr Pimm, do you accept that you have given wide offence to colleagues?'

'No.'

'Do you accept that offence has widely been taken?'

'I would have no control over that. Any more than several of my colleagues presumably intended to provoke the fury, bemusement and exhausting extra workload in which they have frequently resulted for me.'

'Even so, as it is clear that offence has been taken, would you be prepared to apologize unreservedly to anyone who has taken offence?'

Gibson noticeably frowned at this proposal, which was promising because Ned knew that it was a solution Tom would never accept. 'Without invoking any particular historical parallels, I do not see how I can be expected to sign a confession for something I do not accept that I have done.'

'The point I'm making, Dr Pimm, is that, if someone felt you were being insensitive, then, to all intents and purposes, you were.'

From Tom, the longest sigh yet. Ned provided lyrics to the tune: 'Can that really be so? I hope you never become a divorce lawyer or a car insurance company, as, in either case, it seems unworkable to have a system in which, if someone thinks it's your fault, then it is.'

'You understand,' Goswani asked, 'that your refusal to make an apology and accept censure may count against you?'

'Fully. Can I ask you something?'

'If it relates to the process, I can see no reason why not.'

'Have *you* got on with every colleague you've ever had? Have *you* really never worked with anyone you thought was incompetent, or malevolent, or untrustworthy?'

'Though entirely understandable in this situation,' Goswani interrupted, 'emotion can complicate the process.'

But Tom carried on: 'And, when you read the testimony in Traill, does something not strike you as odd? That *every single one* of these employees is a paragon of equable temperament, a model of impeccable professional judgement, punctuality and understanding. None of *them* apparently has ever made an error, a sarcastic remark or an enemy of a colleague, or even to have sighed or rolled their eyes. I *will* admit to one mistake, which is to have found myself employed in a workplace staffed entirely with saints, against whose impeccable personal and professional standards I could only ever, in comparison, have been found wanting.'

Gibson nodded. Goswani shuffled her papers. 'Might I repeat an earlier question, Dr Pimm? Is it fair to say that you can be short-tempered?'

Outing

To: kateandtom@archers.com, julia@waitrose.co.uk, drpennythomas@ac.ucl.org
From: nmarriott@historyman.com
Subject: Outing?

Hello, fellow parents. Through a source, I have managed to secure five tickets for the home game against Chelsea at the Etihad on Saturday September 11. Jordan, Seb and Oscar have previously been included in our match-day squads and Toby has selected them again. As before, I'd imagine we'd get a ten-something am Virgin from MK to Piccadilly and then a six-something pm one home, so the boys should be back in Bucks by nine-ish. Lunch at a high end Mancunian burger joint will be included and Virgin snacks on the return journey. The only caveat is that, as our party will be in the home seats, they must only publicly celebrate City goals, regardless of affiliation, at risk of ejection from the ground. Please let me know – within, say, a week – if your son can come. Ned (Toby's daddy)

To: nmarriott@historyman.com
From: julia@waitrose.co.uk

Gosh, that would have been nice. Sadly, Sebastian is otherwise occupied that day. Their diaries! Soz. Julia Landrose

To: nmarriott@historyman.com
From: kateandtom@archers.com

Dear Professor Marriott. We're finding that Jordan is quite bushed on Saturdays now as they seem to drive them increasingly hard at Abbey Grove. At least that means good value for the fees, unlike some preppers we could mention! But the current policy of the parental committee is that our little chap should take things easy at weekends. Thank you very much for thinking of him, though. Best wishes, Kate and Tom A

PS – we do perhaps wonder if 'jokes' about Virgins are 'appropriate' in the 'circumstances'

To: ehumpage@thepageturner.org
From: drpennythomas@ac.ucl.org

Hi, Emma. This is a tricky one, so, as is my way, I'm going to be quite straight with you. I've seen plenty of people go through this kind of thing in universities and so I am absolutely making no judgement until the process is over. However, without using terms such as 'duty of care', I also have to think as the (single) mother of Oscar. Is your partner taking the boys alone or might you (as I hope) be going along for a spot of shopping / yart in Manc? I hate to ask this but, unfortunately, history shows that you just can't be too careful. Penny xx

To: drpennythomas@ac.ucl.org
From: ehumpage@thepageturner.org
Subject: Fuck Off

My husband (actually) has been accused of trumped-up 'historic' sexual offences against adult women, which he absolutely denies and is in the process of disproving. The suggestion that this means he might be any kind of risk to nine-year-old boys is astonishing, illogical and grossly defamatory. I will say nothing about this to Toby, so that his friendship with Oscar can continue if they wish it to. I wouldn't hold your breath, though, about ours. Emma Marriott.

To: tkpimm@chatter.co.uk
From: nmarriott@historyman.com
Subject: Ya Ya?

Hi T. Through an old mate at BBC Sport, I have three tickets for Man City v Chelsea on September 11. Fancy coming with me and Tobes? N x

To: nmarriott@historyman.com
From: tkpimm@chatter.co.uk
Subject: Ya!

Love to, Nod. And love to Emma. In which regard, H is keen to see the Damish Dane at the Exchange (see link) and wonders if E wants to be Rosencrantz to her Guildenstern, or vice versa? T x

The Lady Doth Protest

Helen was nervous of being alone with Emma but keen to see Hamlet played by a woman and so agreed to the trip. She had suggested making a weekend of it, perhaps in the Pennines, but Tom's desk was stacked with spreadsheets projecting the impact of forced early retirement, so he was reluctant even to pay for Weekend First upgrades on the train, as was Ned, although, when Emma won that argument, it would have been rude for the Pimms not to join them.

Toby was wearing a replica Man City shirt and scarf, although the previous extent of his territorial connection had been another football trip to the city. He was so pale – not from worrying or being bullied, she hoped – that even the light blue of the favours made a contrast. Helen worried that Tom might tease his godson about not supporting the team of his birth-place, although personally it seemed entirely sensible to her to choose a big club over Wycombe Dons or whatever, according to Tom's puritanical rules, it should be. But, since the shock, her husband seemed warier of teasing people, aiming his humour more broadly towards, for instance, as the train drew into Crewe, a riff about other roles apart from Hamlet that actresses might colonize: 'Long Jean Silver? Henrietta the Eighth and her six husbands? Tammy the Tank Engine?'

The presence of a nine-year-old, sitting next to his mother at the table for four, with Ned on the other side of the aisle, gave a welcome excuse not to discuss the situations; a restraint continuing when they had lunch together in a pleasant enough Japanese restaurant with prices that seemed strikingly cheap to southerners. When the boys caught a tram to the match, Helen and Emma walked to the Exchange, talking about, on the way, the education of the younger children and the love lives of the older ones, and, when they arrived, discussed the unusual design of the new theatre, with the stage in a central pod, supported on stairway legs that resembled a lunar module. In the interval, they agreed that the cross-gender casting was interesting but confusing: Maxine Peake, as Hamlet, was supposed to be a man, although clearly remained keenly female to adolescent boys in the audience who nearly expired with scandalous arousal when Hamlet kissed Ophelia. Yet the actress playing Polonius was portraying a female version of the courtier, given in the credits as Polonia.

So it was only over tea at the Midland Hotel, where they had arranged to wait for the footballing contingent, that there was no subject obviously available to displace the one that hung over them like a doctor's printout.

'How do you think Ned's doing?' Helen asked.

Emma gave micro-surgical attention to a peppermint tea-bag. 'Fine.'

'You know I'd be surprised if that word really covered it?'

'Yeah.' The word emerged as a sigh. 'You're sort of always prepared somewhere – aren't you – for them to lose their jobs or get a terminal illness? And this is a bit like those – as if someone's taken a hammer to their personality – but also not quite because they're moping around at home but go on getting paid and they still might get the all clear. Does that make sense?'

'Yes. And, if they were sacked or sick, you wouldn't blame them.'

'*Blame?* You think Tom and Ned are responsible for what happened?'

'Well, not Tom. But . . .'

Appreciating her mistake immediately, Helen had it confirmed by Emma's snapped comeback: 'You're saying that my par—, my *husband*' – the term spoken in italics, like a foreign word – 'is a rapist?'

The expression about elephants in rooms concerned the impossibility of ignoring a topic but this elephant was not only a distraction. It had charged across the carpet.

'No,' Helen said with an intonation of contrition. 'Of course not. It's just that from what I hear . . .'

'Whatever he might have told Tom would have been in confidence.'

'Yes, yes. It was only very . . . general. But I guess sometimes people put themselves in situations where . . .'

An actor who dries on stage is desperate to speak but doesn't know the words; someone abandoning a conversation knows the line but dare not speak it.

'Look, Ned's never going to run for Pope. But then nor, probably, is Tom.' Despite decades of feminism, there survived a primal instinct to defend her man against another woman, which Helen resisted. 'There's stuff I'm fucking furious with Ned about. Like a lot of guys, he could have done with a padlock on his cock sometimes. But he doesn't deserve this. Because Jimmy Savile ducked the bullet, they're shooting people at random now. Do *you* think Tom's innocent?'

'Er, yes.'

'Well, there you go.'

'Look, what I, *we*, think is, it's complicated. Tom probably is guilty in the way that they define the crime. But we question the definition. It's like the water test for witches – you were a witch if you sank but also if you floated. Tom has been accused of saying things to people but also *not* saying things to people. And, get this, if the victims say he's guilty, then he is.'

'I know. Ned said.'

Her brain knew not to say it but was over-ruled by her mouth. 'Although whatever Tom said to him would have been in confidence.'

Emma's rapid flush and blink reminded her of besting people at school or in editorial conferences. The consequences were also similar. 'When you said that Ned brought it on himself . . .'

'I don't think I quite . . .'

'I mean, we all love Tom but there's a side of him that could be seen as a sarcastic bastard . . .'

However civilized they claimed to be, humans always divided into tribes or sides. 'Jesus, Emma!'

'I'm just saying – if you were an eighteen-year-old and away from home . . .'

'Eighteen? Some of these people are nearer eighty!'

'Really. Ned said it was students . . .'

'Did he? I can't imagine why. Well, there might be someone who wanted a first and got a third. But, no, these are faculty. Write your own gags about the ones they may have lost.'

From Emma's silence, Helen sensed victory, but was proved wrong. 'I need to ask you something, Helen. I wasn't going to but, as it seems to be dirty linen day . . . Ned has this Claire woman . . . oh, don't fucking smirk . . .'

'I'm not!'

'His solicitor.'

'Yes, I know. She's helping Tom now.'

'She's putting together these character references for Ned.' The match must be long over. Where were the boys? 'Ned said that you refused to give . . .'

The hesitation, Helen guessed, resulted from pulling out of, abandoning, the expression *give him one*. Why did almost every English expression carry sexual innuendo?

'So. Em, all I thought is that there wasn't much point in having two Pimms on a list. Anyone looking at it is just going to think: oh, she agrees with her husband, surprise, surprise.'

Scepticism or contempt – or a combination – twisted Emma's face. 'It was only writing a paragraph that he doesn't strike you as a fucking . . . as a rapist. You don't think you might be over-thinking this?'

A small but raucous chorus from behind interrupted them. A football chant in which she first picked out the clear tenor voice of her husband and the shy soprano of Toby and then made out the words: 'Who ate all the scones? Who ate all the scones? Who ate all the who ate all the who ate all the scones?'

'Oh, hello, darling,' she said to Tom, who kissed the top of her head. Emma pulled Toby into a hug, leaving Ned alone as the recipient of no affection.

'Did they win?' Emma asked.

'One–one. But, Mummy, we're boy . . . boy . . .'

'Boycotting,' Tom prompted.

'Yes, we're that word SpecSavers. Because they were spon . . . spon . . .'

'Sponsoring,' Tom said.

'The ref!'

There was dutiful laughter, more for the performer than the joke-writer, then a silence in which Tom made his Sherlock Holmes face. 'Oh, dear! I get the impression there've been some crunching tackles and red cards here.'

Date

When Claire said, 'I've just had a call from Dent at Millpond,' Ned could tell from her voice that the charges hadn't been dropped and that, worse, he was probably being summoned to hear another accusation.

'Bit of an odd one,' his lawyer said. 'They've come back with a date from the first complainant. And it's very precise. Between 10.15pm and midnight on Monday September 20th, 1976. Can you have a think and let me know if it sets off an alert in your mind or your diaries?'

A Letter to My Family and Friends

If you have had to open this envelope, then it will only be in circumstances that I could never – until this year – have imagined subjecting you to.

You will rightly be angry that I came to see this as the only option and will consider it selfish. You will say – as I have said of others in similar situations – that there must have been some alternative, that many people have come through worse and restored their lives to something like they were before; or, failing that, had a duty to avoid adding more damaged lives to their own.

All I can say is that it came to feel as if there were no alternative. In the past months, it has seemed to me as if a completely demonized, fictionalized version of myself had stolen and overcome my identity.

This false alter ego – which I had done nothing consciously to create but could also do nothing to destroy – overshadowed every conversation and every action. It felt that even people sympathetic or helpful to me were offering congratulations on not being like 'him' – or having ceased to be like 'him' – when it was my contention – and, I hope, of those who knew me best – that this monster had never existed. In public, I felt like a ghost – someone who was not expected to appear and who terrified and unsettled people by doing so – but a

317

ghost who was required to go on living and to make a living.

Was. To have your name and reputation ruined in this way is like receiving an incurable diagnosis. Shame and disgrace – even if unfairly imposed – are almost always a fatal disease, except to a few who are inoculated against the effects by levels of wealth or self-belief that I have never – and can now never – attain. One way or another, the shock and ignominy would have killed me anyway and so I have chosen a sort of Switzerland.

I can see that a butcher, for example, might recover from such charges because the accusations contain no implications for their cutting of meat. But my work involves the assertion of facts and the assessment of reputations and therefore rests on credibility and integrity. Anyone who puts my name into a search engine forever will find words that will corrupt their judgement of me. In the world we have made, even the innocent or exonerated cannot completely clear their name.

I beg my wife, children, friends, doctor and lawyer not to torment themselves with the thought that there is anything they could have done to prevent this happening. None of you have let me down. I, however inadvertently and unknowingly, have let you and myself down in somehow provoking this persecution.

Please understand that you could not have shown me more love. But love is no protection against the impulse to destructive judgement that seems to have seized the world.

I have left with my solicitor under separate cover a list of those who must under no circumstances be admitted to my funeral or to any memorial service that might follow, even if, from guilt or dull institutional duty, they should attempt to. However, having experienced the damage to wellbeing and reputation that can come from our culture of naming, blaming and shaming, it is also my wish that no other person involved in these events should be held responsible, either privately or publicly, for this outcome. Nobody else should be hounded to what I have done. By which – to avoid confusion – I mean only what I have done to cause this envelope to be opened.

I feel sorry to some degree to those who, for whatever reason, came to – or chose to – see me as the reason for reverses in their lives and careers. But I feel most sorry to those I loved – and whom I hope loved me – that I have been forced to a conclusion that was previously unthinkable. But, once your name has been taken, there is nothing left.

Confession

Even many Catholics didn't understand that confession doesn't have to take place in a dark box with the priest wearing a stole round his neck and a grille between him and the penitent.

Tony had once given the Sacrament of Reconciliation (as it was then called) to a commuter who had collapsed on a railway platform. He had gone to the man's aid as a citizen trained in first aid, rather than as a priest, but, as he loosened the starched collar and fat tie-knot, the dulled eyes had seen the line of white at his helper's neck and checked in a wheezing whisper if he was a Catholic cleric. The condition of discretion was difficult to fulfil in these circumstances but, kneeling between the paramedics as they worked, Tony had held his ear close to the patient's mouth, aiding both hearing and privacy, and heard the gasped transgressions of a life (infidelities, neglects, small cruelties). He granted absolution as the man went into cardiac arrest. When he read in the local paper that the traveller had died in hospital two days later, it bothered him that his ministrations might have slowed or obstructed the medical efforts and he suffered a very Graham Greene-ish period of dubiety, but the help he had given had been wanted and therefore, he had to believe, beneficial.

Confessions in extremity were rarer now, as was all individual penitence since the spread of general absolution, a system, prone to theological abuse in his view, which permitted sinners to mark their own sin scripts privately in their heads, with the priest wafting God's forgiveness communally across the congregation. Just once in recent years had he dispensed the Sacrament of Reconciliation and Penance (as it was now called) outside of the expected drawn-curtained suburban bedrooms, hospital side-rooms, hospices and rest homes. The recipient – an elderly Irishman – had been taken ill on a transatlantic flight and the PA plea for a medically trained professional on board had been followed by a request for any Roman Catholic priest in the cabins to come forward which, being rarer, won a whoop from the passengers. The apparently dying flyer recovered to the extent that he later sent a flight attendant to bring the confessor through to business class again, where he sought assurance that the details he had revealed would go no further in this life. When Tony returned to his seat, travellers nearby had asked him excited questions, as was often the case in such situations, about whether he had conducted any exorcisms. He had used this story, with details disguised, as the basis for a *Thought for the Day*.

Ned Marriott was not, he assumed and prayed, at specific risk of death but Tony suspected that he might be in need of some pastoral attention, whether or not confession. Having received no reply to his first e-mail, he sent a second version. *Dear Ned (if I may, again)* . . .

Everyone is Guilty

During the night before he answered bail, Ned re-read *The Lost Honour of Katharina Blum*.

The first of his second thoughts was that, although Böll gives the title character's age as twenty-seven, she is actually, according to the birth date and day of arrest specified by the writer, twenty-six: a version of the confusion caused online when the year but not the month of someone's birth is known, leading scrupulous Wikipedists to enter something like 48/49 in the age line. And yet 'twenty-seven' comes from a newspaper report and so it is possible that the novelist was being satirical rather than slapdash, inserting a sly comment on journalism's tendency to error. He also noticed on the re-reading, even allowing for his own exaggerated frame of reference, the extent to which Böll is a Catholic novelist, although without the doctrinal plotting of Graham Greene. The book was about the definitions of sin, guilt and redemption.

Ned's final re-reflection was that almost every protagonist in the literature of false accusation is in some way guilty: not of the charges used to destroy them, but of something else.

Only Ronnie Winslow is completely innocent. Thomas Stockmann is probably the best of the rest, but clearly an arsehole. John Proctor is an adulterer and, by modern standards, possibly a child-abuser as well. Professor Lurie breaks campus rules by seducing a student in an encounter that some readers might view as rape. Professor Silk has been, by any reasonable standards, 'living a lie' in the favoured tabloid phrase, and, although he intends no racial slur against the absent students, may not have used the word 'spooks' completely innocently; he certainly once knew the other meaning of the word, which could have lodged in his subconscious as an insult from his time as a negro. John, the professor in *Oleanna*, is provoked and traduced by a student of dubious intentions but his handling of a difficult teaching situation would have been unwise even before these inquisitorial times.

Josef K, who kisses his landlady on an impulse and has impulsive sex with at least two colleagues, would, these days, be vulnerable to charges of sexual assault and work-place harassment, while his raging denunciation of court officials clearly contradicts the University of Middle England's 'Workplace Harmony' code. So K is guilty of B and H.

Katharina Blum – although the book invites, even commands, readers to be appalled at her destruction by the media, trolling before its time – is a murderer, or at the very best manslaughterer, even if Böll strongly encourages the reader to see her actions as justifiable homicide because her reputation has been destroyed by society's tendency to demonize female sexuality and left-wing politics. The equivalent provocations in his own culture, Ned reflected, were male sexuality and celebrity.

The literary explanation for the ambiguity of these characters was that complex sinners make more satisfying fiction than simple saints. But an alternative interpretation was that everyone is guilty of something which, should they be indicted, will complicate their plea of innocence.

And so – in the humid, clock-ticking, too-bright night – Ned finally and properly contemplated the two questions that torment all of the accused: am I guilty? / will I be found guilty?

PART THREE

FACTS

Proposition / Preposition

She rolls the napkin into a point, and dabs at his chin, where she must have spotted some *bolognese* splash. He dislikes it when a girlfriend does this, the gesture of a mother not a lover. He pulls away.

'Hold still. You look like you've cut yourself shaving and bled orange.'

'I don't care.'

'I just want you to look your best,' she says in a pouty big-sorry voice.

'It's fine.' He waves at the plate. 'Would you like some more?'

'No, thanks. That was smashing but I'm full up.'

'I hope you've got some spaces somewhere.'

She either doesn't get it or pretends not to. He is already beginning a stiffie at the thought of the next stage of the evening. Their relationship is at a stage where, unless she is 'off games' or has food poisoning, agreeing to stay over means sex.

On the plastic portable TV set, with its bare wire aerial like an angel's halo in a school nativity play, *News at Ten* continues with the sound down. The small sandy-haired Carter and the tall, bald Ford standing at podiums in the presidential debate. A march of black people with banners in what might have been South Africa but, when they cut to Ian Smith chairing a cabinet meeting, is obviously Rhodesia.

Pointing to the screen, she says: 'Should we watch it?'

'No, no.' If she insists on seeing it to the end, they'll be lucky to be in bed by quarter to eleven. 'News makes historians nervous. We're not interested until it's over. It's like expecting lumberjacks to get worked up over acorns.'

'Oh, Edmund, you do talk bollocks sometimes. But I like you.'

He smooths some stray strands of black hair away from her brow. 'Why don't we just go to bed?'

'In a bit,' she says. 'Can I let my spaghetti digest? I want to talk a bit more about the play.'

He tops up her glass of Bulgarian red, but she says: 'That's masses.'

'*Play?* It's a series – goes on for about another seven weeks,' he corrects her, his irritability, he knows as he speaks, a payback for her delaying their move to the bed.

'You know what I mean. Is it historically accurate?'

'Wow, that's a big one. As the movie star said to the arch-bishop.'

She rolls her eyes. 'You've got a one-track mind. I'm serious. Was he really like that? It's not often you get to watch historical drama with a historian.'

'Ph.D. student. By *he* you mean Claudius?'

A shampoo-ad bounce of her hair on the shoulders as she nods.

'It's not my period.' He censors an innuendo about hoping it isn't hers either. 'But I think Robert Graves, who wrote the . . .'

'Yes, I *know.*'

'Was a proper classicist. The stammer and the limp are in Plutarch and/or Suetonius, I think. So that's accurate. And there seems be a widespread consensus that, if you had lunch with Caligula, then you'd be on the menu.'

During their brief relationship to date, he has learned that she likes to feel she has earned the sex first: with a film, play or serious conversation. So his energy in this impromptu lecture was entirely driven by the possibility of History being an aphrodisiac.

The payphone in the hall is ringing.

'Should you go and . . . ?'

'No. It will only be my mother. I'll call her . . .'

Billy checks her watch. 'Wow. Mummy would never ring *me* that late.'

A banging on the door, followed by the growly smoker's shout of Consuela, the Spanish teacher in 3, with a message in three staccato parts: 'Ned! Phone! For You!'

Seeing his guest about to speak, he puts his right hand across her mouth and a finger of the other hand to his lips. He waits until irritated feet clomp away and down the stairs.

'She'll take a message. I'd rather be here with you.'

He nudges her into a hug, which she does not resist. After a summer of record temperatures, September is also unseasonably warm. The greedy division of the house into as many bedsits as possible has left his with a single rickety window, which is open. Billy is wearing a summer dress, the cardigan she wore for work draped over the back of the sofa.

As they lie kissing side by side on the narrow cushions, he touches her outside and then inside her knickers.

'Neddles,' she says, a name he hates. 'Let's lie down.'

With the aim of keeping some division between his activities, he has placed the futon in the opposite corner from the desk. The small square of linoleum that forms the kitchen and a pull-across curtain that hides the patch of bathroom (loo, basin and shower so close that ablutions demanded dexterity) form the other corners of the rectangle.

'Let me clean my teeth, Sweetheart.'

'I like the way you taste, Wilhelmina.' Red wine and cigarettes: the tang of adulthood.

During a stumbling embrace, she raises her arms for the dress to be pulled up and over, then reaches to release the clasp of her bra, while he stoops to complete her nakedness. As usual, to his continuing regret, she leaves him to undress himself, apparently unaware of the erotic power of a shirt unbuttoned and belt pulled loose by a woman's fingers.

All through the months when the mercury burned in thermometers, she has slipped quickly under the duvet and he thinks it is modesty rather than coldness that leads her to do so again. As he lifts up the edge to join her, she says: 'Light.' He walks to the switch by the door, proud of the heft of his erection. Now, as she lies on the mattress, the bedding pulled up past her chin, he can see her only in stripes of streetlight that leaks around the roller blind.

He is still astonished at the regular availability of what seemed, until only four years ago, an unattainable pleasure. It is still more exciting that, on this occasion, she has not asked him in advance if he brought 'the gubbins'. Just before they met, she stopped taking the pill because of side-effects and is waiting to be prescribed an alternative brand.

As a lover, she is enthusiastic if traditional: never going down on him, although he does on her, and pleading a dodgy back if encouraged to go on top. But she is strong and responsive and scratches at his back as she comes.

'Oh, Ned,' he thinks she says. She is doing the sort of quasi-Scandinavian drawl-talking that leaves it an open question whether women saw a lot of motel porn movies or the makers of motel porn movies saw a lot of women.

'Oh, you,' he responds. 'You.'

To call her 'Billy' at these moments feels too gay to him.

Sensing the almost unbearable bursting tenderness, he gasps: 'What are we doing?'

Whatever she says is lost in breathlessness.

'What?' he checks, unromantically.

'Ah I'm . . .' – a runner's panting – 'ah on the pill,' he hears her say.

Relaxation of the mind overlapping with concentration of the body.

'Oh, God, I'm going to . . .'

Her position shifts suddenly under him. 'Oh! Oh!' Bucking him again. 'Come *in* me!'

He does, feeling the thrill of his warm wetness thickening hers. 'God. That was the best ever,' he tells her.

Ned senses her tension, even anger, immediately.

'What?' he asks.

She doesn't answer. He guesses that she is objecting to the implication of comparison. Are even women these days sensitive about that? 'I mean the best with you. I'm not . . .'

The strength of her body surprises him; she seems to be trying to throw him off.

'What?' he asks, pulling out of her. 'Was it finished too quickly?'

A Tariff of Expectations

During the now almost daily staff meetings that seem to have become the main purpose of the university, they have never seen Neades looking or sounding like this before.

He usually wears shapeless grey suits, like Babygros for grown-ups. But today he is encased in something smart, dark, creaseless and almost certainly expensive, as a man of his dimensions is unlikely to be able to shop off the peg.

His stature, though, is somehow reduced, and not just in the way that dark garments thin silhouettes. His physical presence cannot possibly have halved since the previous departmental, but that is the impression somehow given. Sir Richard Agate, though far shorter in height, seems to loom over his host, who introduces him not in the usual Belfast boom but a simpering whisper.

'I am pleased,' Neades begins, 'to introduce the new Vice Chancellor as he attends a meeting of the Directorate of History for the first time.'

Neades illustrates his delight by contriving a wide smile which, it strikes Ciara, is the first she had ever seen from him.

'And although Sir Richard will bring his exceptional wisdom and experience to bear on each and every directorate at UME, he should bring a particular insight to History because he is himself a historical figure.'

Desmond Craig-Jones and Alex Shaw respond to this comment with the sort of unrestrained laughter generally won only by the most accomplished stand-up comics and members of the Royal Family when speaking in public.

'Sir Richard,' the Director continues, 'spent the earlier part of his illustrious career as the highest of flyers in the Civil Service, ultimately becoming Cabinet Secretary, a position that has been described as "the real prime minister".'

This punchline draws another paroxysm from the Director's chortling Amen Corner, conducted, as normal, by his steadfast lieutenant, Joanna Rafferty. Tom Pimm gives a gale-force sigh and throws a roll-eyed glance towards Ned Marriott, thereby also taking in Ciara, sitting between them at the back of the Barbara Tuchman Lecture Theatre.

'Upon leaving Whitehall, he assumed a portfolio of powerful positions, serving as chairman of a leading defence manufacturer, deputy chairman of the BBC Trust, a board member of the Arts Council and a non-executive director of two international banks. It was this university's luck that most of these terms of office ended at the same time.'

Tom has a notebook open in front of him and writes in it: FUMO.

'Meaning,' says Neades, 'that when the recruitment process began for a new Vice Chancellor of UME to take charge from September 2012, the perfect candidate was available. And, to the luck of all of us here, he agreed to apply to the academic world the qualities from which so many previous fields have benefited. And, since starting last month, his impact has already been considerable.'

Neades, whose standard public manner is studiedly blank, visibly shakes as he speaks. They are witnessing a bureaucratic truth: their terrifying boss is terrified of his boss.

To whom he now turns and extends a trembling hand. 'Vice Chancellor, welcome to History!'

Agate gives a small nod to his introducer and then a deeper forward movement, almost an actor's bow, towards the teachers.

'Thank you, Kevan.' The stress, wrongly, on the first syllable. Although they would already have been together in innumerable meetings, Neades has clearly been too fearful of the consequences to correct him.

'When one's CV is recited like that,' Agate goes on, 'there is always a slight feeling of: follow that! But one will, believe one, one will.'

Tom uses the cover of Dr Shaw's delighted whoop – now counterpointed by Rafferty's deep laugh – to mutter sideways: 'Three ones don't make a right.'

Black pinstripe, blindingly white shirt, tie with the horizontal stripes of some educator or employer of posh men, deep RP tones that sound vaguely disappointed not to be reciting Kipling. Agate is a classic representative of the Establishment that the university hopes to join by getting his name on the letterhead. With the practised self-pocket-picking of a regular public speaker, Agate slides several sheets of folded paper from the breast of his jacket and, still without looking, unfurls them.

Now he reads: 'In my brief time at UME, I have heard great things about this department. Your customers have access to some of the country's most eminent historians, including Professor Ned Marriott, who, through his exemplary out-reach interventions in the media and publishing industries, has taught me history without my ever enrolling here.'

Tom smilingly makes a wanker sign in the direction of Ned, who is looking down as if carefully reading his notebook, although it is opened at an empty sheet. At the singling-out of Ned, Professor Kempson goes brightly red and clicks intently at the laptop to which he always attended throughout meetings. Desmond Craig-Jones, Henrietta Langham and Alex Shaw swaps looks and tiny head-shakes, their level of dissent restricted by sitting, as usual, together at the front.

'My working life has coincided,' Agate is saying, 'with a period in which most established institutions are re-imagining their contract with their customers and stake-holders in order to ensure that, going forward, they have enabled the skill-sets and solutions demanded by a twenty-first-century public service environment.'

It is Tom's habit to recoil physically when managers use corporate jargon or scrambled grammar. As Agate speaks, he seems to be being knocked about by an invisible heavyweight boxer.

'In Whitehall and in broadcasting, in the sectors of banking and military hardware and in the cultural community, I have been part of dynamic reform management. Change is nothing new to me. Everywhere I have worked has been in constant flux.'

'Chicken or egg?' mutters Tom Pimm.

'And you above all, as historians, will know that we cannot go on living in the past!'

Neades laughs loudly. But even the teacher's-pet-teachers at the front of the room seems unnerved by this assertion, having chosen this subject of study at least in part because it permitted retreat from the present.

'Through the excellent work so many of you do, we already provide a very good service to our customers. But it is my conviction that – with a few wee tweaks to our offer – we can provide a better one. Over the past few weeks, I have been working with Kevan on drawing up new targets and contracts for academic staff. Which I would like now to ask the Director to outline for you.'

Clever, Ciara thinks: if the changes are unpopular – as reform always is in this faculty – they will be associated with Neades, even though he is just a ventriloquist's dummy for the man above him.

'Vice Chancellor,' the Director says. 'Thank you for giving us such inspirational words and nutritious food for thought.'

Clumsily, and crumpling one side of his jacket, Neades eventually finds the printed sheets of his own speech. Explosively clearing his throat, he then seems to swallow whatever has been dislodged.

'As academic staff will be aware, in the most recent Research Assessment Exercise, UME was ranked in the top ten per cent of universities for research in England.'

Ciara thinks back to the year before the RAE cut-off: the struggle to get books finished or published in time for inclusion in the trawl, the generous sabbaticals rapidly available for those deadlines to be met, the envy and resentment of department stars who, as 'impact' was measured by audience reached, could count a broadcast programme or newspaper article as worth dozens of University of Yale Press monographs.

'And the History directorate was placed within the top two per cent of research departments within its subject.'

Craig-Jones and Langham begin a round of applause, which almost everyone in the room picks up, except for Professor Kempson, crouched over his keyboard, and the naughty back row of Ciara, Tom and Ned.

Agate looks puzzled and lasers a stare at Neades, who raises a hand to stop the clapping.

'But,' he says. '*But*. Now that our customers are paying their own money – or taking out loans – to come here, can we imagine them thinking: "I should take my custom and my money there because the staff are always away writing books and articles and appearing on TV and radio?" '

Those in the room who have not published or been heard from in public for years, who get through the research assessment exercise with reprinted books or essays in anthologies edited by friends, wobbles their heads in agreement.

'Our customers are paying to be taught. And so we will teach them. All practitioner contracts will be renegotiated' – Kempson, the union rep, briefly looks up, then types with heavy pressure on the keys – 'to agree new teaching duties and hours – at undergraduate and postgraduate levels. Each individual will be given a Tariff of Expectations, setting out a series of targets for teaching and other commitments. These will be assessed biannually.'

Biannually or biennially? muttered Tom. *It matters.*

Langham raises her right arm and waves it, probably in much the pushy perky way that she did at school three decades before.

'Could I finish myself before I attend to you?' Neades asks.

Please God none of us ever hears him say that in another context, Tom whispers.

'Absolutely, Director,' his reliable disciple agrees.

'This renegotiation of workloads,' Neades resumed, 'will be combined with a root and branch review' – a right hook to Tom from the phantom boxer – 'of whether the Directorate is fit for purpose' – jerked the other way by a blow from the left – 'at this moment in time.'

As Tom mimes taking a knockout blow, Neades' voice takes on a perorational quality: 'I will myself be chairing a special' – Tom recovers to give an air-tick to this word – 'sub-group of the academic staffing committee to examine whether our resources are currently being employed in the areas where they give best value to our customers.' Kempson threatens to break his keyboard. 'We will attempt to identify where efficiency savings and synergies suggest themselves. A survey conducted at the end of last term also showed that a number of our customers and their parents and guardians have raised concern about the robustness of the University's duty of care in the light of the incidents in which Professor Padraig Allison regrettably so betrayed the trust placed in him by the management of the directorate. As a result, I have tasked Dr Andrea Traill, from the directorate of Geography, with conducting a survey into the conduct and culture of History. I will cascade details in due course. Now Sir Richard and I are happy to take questions.'

To the hand already raised again: 'Yes.' For the visitor: 'Dr Henrietta Langham, early modern Europe.'

Tom writes in his notebook *Savlon*, followed by a colon, as if for a character in a playscript, then scribbles down, in bespoke shorthand, her intervention: 'It's not really a question. More an observation. As the song has it, birds got to swim, fish got to fly' – Tom improvises, quiely, *Darwin is surprised and so am I* – 'and teachers got to teach. So thank you, Director, for re-enabling our vocation.'

Neades, nodding thanks to his apostle, accepts a question

from her nearest neighbour, identifying her as 'Dr Alexandra Shaw, early modern Britain', while Tom writes *Horny:* and transcribes the gist of her inquiry: 'While agreeing entirely, Director, with everything that you and Dr Langham have said, that the provision of tuition must be paramount, will there be an appreciation that some members of faculty may have health and domestic circumstances that might make the body less willing, as it were, than the mind. Will the, er, Tariff of Expectation take that into account?'

Neades inclines an impassive face towards Agate, who says: 'All employment requirements will be agreed with – and supervised by – the WH directorate.'

The Director tries not to call on Kempson, who ducks the snub by simply shouting out: 'You talk of re-allocation of resources to maximize value. Translated, that means restructuring and job cuts?'

'Potential efficiency savings may be identified,' Neades concedes. Then adds, in an obsequious tone he reserves for Kempson: 'Subject, of course, to full consultation and agreement with the trades unions.'

Agate scowls: 'Well, okay. On that one I'd want to add that a course with very few students is a course that has failed to monetize the available funding potential. No successful company would go on selling products that customers clearly don't want. An educational corporation can – and should – be no different.'

Kempson, who teaches the increasingly niche specialism of early Chinese history, could rent out his cheeks as an alternative heat source. As twentieth-century British, Irish and American history are increasingly popular with students distrustful of the far past, Ciara, Tom and Ned have little to worry about from any arses-per-classes count. But Tom is an instinctive arguer – Ned, though the department star, almost never speaks in meetings – and responds characteristically when Neades, lacking any other options, is forced to acknowledge him.

'The new Vice Chancellor said that he is skilled at flux.' Sir

Richard nods acceptance of Tom's compliment. 'And so we can expect him to flux-up the university.'

Agate's blankness is so calculated that it counts as a reaction. Neades' great frame shakes like a building about to collapse.

Tom continues: 'Only a few months ago, before the RAE, I remember Dr Neades saying in one of our many meetings on the subject: "A former prime minister once famously said: 'Education, Education, Education.' I am saying: 'Research, Research, Research.'" Can we assume that promise has gone Blair-shaped?'

'Vice Chancellor, we encourage robust discussion here,' says Neades severely, then to Tom: 'No, I think I'm still saying Research, Research, Research. But now I'm saying Teaching Teaching Teaching as well.'

'Okay?' Tom said. 'Because Research Research Teaching I could understand or even Research Teaching Teaching. But – if it's Research Research Research Teaching Teaching Teaching – then you seem to be asking us to do twice as much as we're doing now, while, if I've got this right, also proposing to reduce the teaching staff?'

'Well, I am minded to think there will be a range of views . . .' begins Neades.

'Please sir! Please sir! Please sir!' pleads Professor Craig-Jones, laughing loudly but alone at his impersonation of a pupil some sixty years his junior.

'Oh God, no, not Daggers,' Tom mutters.

'Yes, Desmond,' Neades gasps gratefully, glossing him to their guest: 'Ancient Britain.'

'Steady on, Stanley!' screeches the elderly professor, in one of his repertoire of actual or invented radio comedy catch-phrases. 'I'm not that old! Oh, pardon me, I thought you said Ancient *Brit-on*!'

The VC, the only person present who has never heard this joke before, and with luck might never again, smiles nervously. Neades is breathing heavily.

'Oh, my Lord, now I've completely forgotten what I was going to say,' Craig-Jones complains. 'Oh, yes. What you were saying about research and teaching and so on puts me in mind of New York New York New York. So good they named it thrice!'

His personal amusement, though prolonged and loud, provokes no communal response.

'Well, I think we'll leave it there,' says Neades.

As the gathering disbands, Langham and Shaw immediately engulfs the VC, jabbering at him. Kempson is already talking fast and low on a mobile, presumably to a union deputy.

The trio of sceptics wait at the back, keen to avoid leaving with Neades and the VC.

'What does *Fumo* mean?' Ciara asks.

'What?'

'When Neades was doing the John the Baptist for the new VC, that's what you wrote on your pad?'

'Oh, just one of my jolly monickers.'

'So I guessed. But meaning what?'

'Not here. You never know who might be listening.'

A Few Words

Certain years lay under history like land-mines. In letters, diaries, documents, some dates – 1776, 1789, 1851, 1860, 1914, 1939, 1963 – bleeped at a researching historian like a metal detector. Those weighted days were always in the past but there had been a few, during his adulthood, that lay ahead, waiting to be stepped on. 1984, when he was thirty, because of Orwell, although, for tutors and students of British politics, the numerals soon flashed behind them as designating the miners' strike.

And then the present year which, if not quite Orwellian, vibrated from the title of that sci-fi series – *Space 1999* – that he had watched in the flat in Murray Road when he should have been revising for finals. The producers had picked it as impossibly distant, almost a quarter of a century hence, but now it has been and is almost gone. The world is two weeks away from another encumbered sequence of numbers – 2000, the second Millennium, would anyone this time gather on hills and await Christ's return? – and then, twelve months later, 2001, red-ringed because of Kubrick's *A Space Odyssey*.

Early for the meeting, Ned dawdles in Waterstones, drawn there partly because of his disappointment at not seeing *The Six Lives of Henry VIII* in the window display of Christmas offers. He goes, though, to the children's section first, books always his main contribution to his daughters' stockings, prone to buying them even more since the separation. But they are at a publishing cusp age – exactly between the sections 8–11 and 11–16 – and, though his habit is to flatter their intelligence by buying two years ahead, the books in the later range, especially the American ones, seem to be lightly novelized textbooks on sex and contraception. He has been startled by the hard-line moralist that being the father of near-teenage girls has made him.

He moves to adult Fiction and Non-Fiction, quietly enjoying discreet and polite recognition from his viewers: the eyes widening in surprise, smiling, then looking quickly away to avoid the vulgarity of a fan. Unable to find his Tudor book on the Bestseller table, he struggles not to show his fury. Leaning sideways, he finds the Ns – several Nicholsons, Norris – inconveniently close to the floor and moves his eyes to the left: Murray, Monroe.

'Professor Marriott, isn't it?'

A gangly man: early forties, with a parody academic's spectacles, beard and waistcoat, on which is pinned a plastic badge: MANAGER.

'Er, yes.'

'Were you looking for your own book?'

'No. No.' He can feel the blood-rush in his cheeks. 'Well, I was looking for presents, actually. But the eye tends to wander alphabetically.'

'Don't worry. That's nothing. A lot of them – and not just Jeffrey Archer – come and shuffle theirs to the front of the table.

To be honest, we're a bit un-chuffed ourselves. We were running out, ordered more asap but there aren't any at the warehouse, apparently. It's a twin bish because I could have got you to sign some. If you wanted to fire a rocket . . . ?'

'I'll see what I can do.'

Walking down Notting Hill Gate, he reflects that, if the automobile industry were run like publishing, the roads would contain horse-drawn carts rather than cars. He sends Jack Beane a text of contained rage about the lack of his books at a core London store.

The offices of Ogglebox are in a pre-fab on an industrial estate behind Olympia, although its owner is boasting of moving soon to architect-designed premises in Paddington: 'There's no shelf-space here for any more Baftas and Emmys.'

Tinsel draped around the framed stills from old shows, including Ned's, the receptionist in a jingling Santa hat – the giddiness of an office just before the long holiday. Ned, though, is apprehensive. To be called to see Ogg alone at short notice just days after the Christmas party might possibly be good – 'Listen, mate, Controller woke up this morning with a hard-on for yours truly on Stalin by fucking February' – but might also, for a freelance, be disastrous: 'Look, Prof, the network has decided to rest some formats, refresh the schedule.' Broadcasting is the only area of life in which the words *rest* and *refresh* are terminal.

A text from Beane – call me soonest – arrives as Cynth, Ogg's PA, dressed from curling green slippers to matching floppy hat as an elf, arrives to get him. Her kiss is on the lips and tastes of sugary cocktails; he wishes this was an office night out.

In the open-plan office, voices into phones are too loud, explained by the champagne bottles, ragged gold foil around necks, that rise beside each partition. 'Look, I want to do this deal but I'm not Father Christmas!' a large man shouts into the mouthpiece, to raucous laughter from his colleagues because he is sitting there dressed in a red and white tunic and cotton-wool beard.

Ogg, typically, is neither costumed nor intoxicated; it is more his way to file away for future use the bad behaviour of those who are.

'Prof!' he greets Ned, standing and aiming an air embrace.

They compare holiday plans and views on the seasonal TV schedules, the astonishing durability of *Morecambe & Wise*, even though Ernie was now dead as well as Eric. Then Ogg says, in a bad American accent supposed to invoke conspiracy thrillers: 'Professor, we have a situation.'

Ned's heart shakes in anticipation of the sacking that is never far away in this profession. Ogg shuffles papers on the table in front of him and, expecting to be handed some kind of arse-covering letter or press release from the network, Ned is surprised to see the producer holding up, like a prize-winning author at a photo-op, a hardback copy of the *Six Lives* tie-in.

Adrenaline is flooded out by endorphins. He must have been shortlisted for something. Aren't the Whitbreads out around now? And what about this Samuel Johnson thing?

Ned laughs: 'Well, you've done well to get one. I've just discovered they literally can't get enough in Waterstones. I've put a bomb under Beane.'

But the banter bounces off the look on Ogg's face. 'So they haven't told you?'

Five words you never want to hear in a hospital or office. 'Told me what?'

'I'm afraid the book has had to be withdrawn. The DVDs too. I'm afraid there's been a bit of an allegation of . . . *plagiarism*.'

Ogg gives the word an Italianate intonation, as if to take the sting off it.

It is the accusation academics most dread, except for *moral turpitude*, and perhaps the harder to survive professionally, as most reasonable people can understand the temptation to sleep with a nineteen-year-old, while stealing other people's words is now definitively criminal. Making notes for a new book, Ned uses three different coloured types for public domain material, original finds or insights by previous writers, and his own research or interpretation.

'Really?' he says, bullishly. 'Well, it's become the mud that people throw. I'd be surprised if it sticks.'

Ogg passes across the volume. It's from one of the early print runs, with the *As Read On BBC Radio 4* sticker on the cover. Pages are book-marked, early and late in the text, by the Post-its that Ogg uses for script notes.

'I've yellowed the sentences in question,' the executive says. 'The words are pretty much the same in your scripts as well.'

Ned forces himself to look at the highlighted lines, three paragraphs on the first marked page, two on the second. He wrote the book quicker than he would have liked – mainly in the early mornings during that month at the Mortimers' place in Tuscany – to hit the Christmas market, but is hoping the alleged overlaps will be arguable: quotes from documents that another author may have uncovered but can't claim to own, shared phrases drawing on the same small hoard of words for king, marriage, divorce.

And, when he sees the sections specified, he breathes out in relief. Writers remember which words are theirs, and even where they were written, seeing at once, in newspaper articles or on proofs, where editors have meddled. 'But I didn't write any of this stuff!'

'Whoah! Whoah!' says Ogg. 'That is indeed the position of Methuen Educational. But I think the Legal guys were hoping our defence might be a little bit more nuanced.'

Ned laughs, which Ogg tries to scowl down as inappropriate. But Ned is remembering the arguments during the shoot at Hampton Court: Ogg tapping emphatically at the sheets printed in the hotel business centre. *The audience may include lower socio-economic cohorts who don't have a History degree.* And: *It isn't dumbing down – it's respecting the spectrum of viewer intelligence*. Or: *TV is watched in lounges, not class-rooms*. It is a scene he plans to include in his memoirs.

'But, Dom, those are the speeches you forced me to put in. You said the viewer needed more *sign-posting*. I kept it for the book because I . . .' – was writing ten thousand words a day to get it done – 'because I couldn't face another row over it.'

Ned flicks to the final page of print, finds, just above the apology to Cordy and Philly for interrupting their holiday, a line that he points to: 'I thank you in the Afterword for your input to the scripts and the book.'

'Look, I think, at this stage, it's kind of irrelevant who wrote what.'

At first, Ned thinks that the boss is simply avoiding personal blame, a key element in his success in the industry, but then is struck by the possibility that there is multiplied discomfort: on location, Ogg had claimed authorship of the speeches, but per-haps he had been appropriating a staffer's work, making the words in two senses not his own.

'Well, I didn't write it,' Ned says. 'So *I* can't be guilty of plagiarism. You say it's an educational publisher?' Ogg nods. 'So someone here has copied it out of the *Ladybird Book of Fat Harry* or whatever.'

The parodic title is not entirely random but inspired by the words he has read vertically downwards – *The Little Book of Tudor England* – in a small line of books propped on the window ledge between mugs with jokey slogans.

'It's a cunt, I know,' Ogg says, in a brutal tone that seems designed to bind them together as men of business. 'But, at this point, we're not going to get the genie back in the bottle. I don't think this is anything that anyone did intentionally.'

'Well, only the person who wrote it can answer that – and it wasn't me,' Ned persists. He feels he is winning but Ogg dem-onstrates the cunning that has made him an employer rather than an employee.

'Okay, let's look down that road for a moment, should we? Suppose we come out and say: don't blame the Prof for this – he didn't write it. Well, fine. But then doesn't the Marriott Fan Club think: so he's just a puppet reading other people's stuff, like the guy on *Broadcast News*? We can do it, Ned, but I've always got the impression that the whole "written and presented by" was a redline for you.'

'It is. But so is not being called a *plagiarist*.'

'And nor would you be. We'll find a form of words. "Source notes inadvertently became merged with the final text" blah blah. Legal reckon the plaintiffs will settle for a "should have acknowledged the use of material" sticker until the next edition. Obviously, we'll pay the costs. I do think this is the best way through this. Team game, team blame.'

Cuttings (4)

TOP TV PRESENTER IN 'PLAGIARISM' STORM

An award-winning TV presenter has been forced to apologize and print a correction in his latest bestselling book after admitting to passing off sections of a children's history book as his own work.

Professor Edmund Marriott, 45, was accused of incorporating sections from *The Little Book of Tudor England*, a volume with a recommended reading age of 8–11, in the scripts for his BBC1 series *The Six Lives of Henry VIII* and a linked book that had reached number three in the *Sunday Times* non-fiction bestseller list when it was withdrawn from sale last December, following a complaint from an educational publisher. Marriott's book has since been reissued in a corrected edition.

The TV series was made by the independent production company Ogglebox. Managing director, Dominic Ogg, 49, who produced and directed the series, said yesterday, after the out-of-court settlement was announced: 'All factual TV needs to be scrupulous about facts and attributions – but history shows especially so. The audience rightly expects more from a high-profile documentary series and book. Professor Marriott is well aware that he has let viewers and readers down and has been reminded of his responsibilities.'

Bodily Fluids

Woken by a stinging spasm from the guts, Ned becomes aware of a field of pain searing from his scalp to shoulders. Powerless to stop the shudder rising in his throat, he manages to turn his head to one side, fighting the agonizing resistance of tendons in his neck, and vomit on the coverlet. It is the vinegary sick of regurgitated red wine.

Even allowing for the sensitivity of his eyes, the brightness of the room suggests that it is well after sunrise. He is lying flat across the king bed, fully clothed, in a posture suggestive, to a self-pathologist, of having blacked out backwards immediately after reaching the edge of the mattress.

The bereaved, loved ones reborn in their minds at night, want their dreams to be real; the guilty, waking to goading moments of recall, wish the reality to be a dream.

Trying to effect movement without employing any protesting muscles, he succeeds in raising himself slightly on his right elbow and twitching a pillow underneath his shoulder. The flat-screen TV is showing a news programme with the sound down. With eyes hurting and blurry from having slept with his contact lenses in, he can make out replays from the day before of dusty, bloodied victims being carried and helped from Underground stations. The public events of yesterday come back to him, dragging reluctant private memories behind them.

He looks away from the screen and downwards. His zip is split open, making physical a detail from so many nightmares of presenting and lecturing. As he tries to shift on the bed, a new flash of pain is added to those in his stomach and skull by a ripping soreness from the groin. A memory blinked away but then accepted. With gingerly skills learned from sticking plasters, he eases the stuck hair free from the cotton of his boxer shorts.

The worst kind of drunkenness, able to remember some of it. Jolting moments flash back. The spongy bed in the researcher's cheap room. Wine poured, spilled. Unwanted fragments of chat: *lubricate your, isn't it pronounced beaver?* The attempted kiss, minimally reciprocated. She opened his flies. He opened his flies. She sucked his. He pushed his. *Oh fuck, I'm sorry.* The big plastic key fob knocking against the door. Just lie down for.

A flashing red light. His phone, on the floor. Reminder your car is 8.30. JP booked with you. Cheers and ciao. Dom. 08.10 by the throbbing bright red of the radio alarm.

Finding himself somehow upright is as miraculous as levitation. Folding the coverlet over the sick patch. Hiding it from whom? Himself.

The unpeeling of the contact lenses another Elastoplast rip. Imagine the bathroom mirror as a camera. *Although she didn't know this, Jane Wenham was already as good as dead. To be called a witch was to be christened a corpse.*

Speaking feels as if a fist is lodged in his gullet. Watching himself back in edits, there is sometimes a whiny, sinusy note produced by tiredness or strain and today that is the only voice he has. Sounding like this, he would have to pick up the PTCs on AVR later, which never sounds or looks right, and, anyway, the lines he's just rehearsed are the only bits of any links that he can remember.

Without the contacts, his vision is soft focus but he can see that his eyes look puffy, unwell, terrified. Splashed cold water stings and narrows them, worsening the red-rimmed squint. He will look more presentable (no fucking pun intended) after a shower and shave but even the American morning telly shiny-eye stuff that Corinne keeps in her kit (sourced online after a sales ban caused by reports of users being blinded) would do nothing to fix this drunk, hungover haze of a gaze.

He steps away from the unforgiving mirror to undress. Sick

drips onto the bathroom floor from his shirt which he shrugs off and, dragging his foot across it, uses as a mop. The dropped boxers spread like a white water lily, speckled with shit, sperm, vomit, wine. He showers and shaves with a scouring intensity that feels less like washing than cosmetic surgery. He breathes in the hot steam to soothe his throat.

As he tackles a stubborn snag of beard, the blade shears deep into his skin. Blood pours across the floating foam in the sink, raspberry sauce on ice-cream. The cut fools him for a moment that it won't hurt, then does. He has washed off the drink, spunk and shit but now there is more bleeding. Bodies have so many ways of betraying us.

Nothing he tries – pressing with a towel, building a dam of Savlon, attaching a pad of folded tissue – will staunch the flow. Eventually, he puts his screen clothes in a suit bag, goes down to the car holding a towel across the wound like a boxer in the moments just before his seconds concede the bout.

Amazingly only ten minutes late, he apologizes to the driver who says: 'Another one anyway, innit?' He waits until 8.50 for Jess, then texts Ogg. His eyes not feeling ready yet even for soft dailies, he peers blearily at the reply, scanning in a panic for the words *suspension* or *police*. But the message is: **Crossed wires. She here. Ready to shoot when we see ya. D x** Has she forgiven, forgotten or is waiting her moment?

It is rush hour and the drive to Hertford Castle is slow. After fifteen minutes or so, he dares to pull at the towel, which sticks encouragingly, reducing his fears of haemorrhage or haemophilia. But, even in the smeary reflection in the car window, the cut looks big and is tenderly wet to the touch. If he manages to remember any of the words, he will have to deliver them in profile, like some Richard III.

Static in a tailback, he chastises himself silently, a combination of his mother and father at their most disappointed. *You're fifty-one. This has to stop. The drinking, the thinking that every woman wants to. You're not actually an -ic or an -ist. But this has to be a new beginning.*

A fresh splash of blood on the towel. He presses it to his chin again.

Dear John

Afterwards, he says, 'That was extremely satisfactory,' in the flat-voiced impersonation of John Major that everyone is copying from *Spitting Image*.

'Ditto,' she replies, smoothing down his chest hair, her hand sliding in the sweat, their sweat.

In the first paper she worked for, there had been a man and a woman who, on certain days, would both turn up with a packed roll-bag or hold-all, although neither of them had a business trip planned. At lunchtime, they would leave, five minutes apart, with their luggage, returning unencumbered, with the same time delay, at around 4pm, then making a staggered entrance next morning with their bags again. A colleague who had been abroad on assignment met them one morning on the tube from Heathrow and worked out that they were using an airport hotel, for a mid-day shag and then a night together, the packing an alibi against partners and suspicious staff. She and Ned don't bring cover luggage to the Marlow Motor Inn, although he always books the room for the whole night, which makes it less squalid. She wonders how many of the rooms are being used for this purpose this afternoon.

He kisses her, their most intimate tastes combined in each mouth.

'Can I ask you something personal?' she says.

'That's a strange question when I've just had my face in your . . .'

'Yes, all right,' she cuts him off before he can make her blush. 'It's about your daughters.'

'Yes?'

Wariness in his voice, the acknowledgement of the other life always a fraught calculation between secret lovers.

'Their names? Are they okay about them?'

'Oh, that. Bit of a strop when they were learning to write. We called them Cordy and Philly at home but their teacher made them write it out in full. So the length was a bit of an issue, the envy of those Janes and so on. But, look, I wasn't a nutter about it. I wouldn't have called them Othello or Autolycus. On the other hand, with Henry or John, people wouldn't even know you'd done it. I once met an American guy called Lear, but he might have been named after an aeroplane, or it was his mother's maiden name. If I ever had a boy . . .'

A pang of panic. 'Oh, are you and Jenny . . . ?'

'Hypothetically. Other lives, other times. If there ever was one, I'd like to call him Toby, which just sounds middle-class. The thing about Shakespeare is that the girls' names have lasted better than the boys' ones. Lots of Juliets, Helenas, Rosalinds. Hermione, I guess, is the one you almost never hear these days. Jenny took a bit of persuading over our two but, in the end, there are lots of diminutives they can use.'

They are facing each other. He pulls her closer. 'Would you like the other half of that, Mrs Pimm?'

She slaps his shoulder. 'I told you not to call me that. No, I'm expected at work. I'm "meeting a potential writer".'

'Well, maybe you are.'

'I can't see you having a column in *Perfect Kitchen*, Professor.'

'I could see myself having a column in you.'

He presses himself against her, ready to go again. She closes her legs tight.

'No. Quick cuddle and then you have first shower. You're slower than me.'

She gives him a hug that he tries to turn into more, until he is pushing against the slippery edges.

'No.'

She pushes him away.

'Was it not satisfactory for you?' he asks, impersonating the prime minister again.

'Of course it was.' Laughing, she adds: 'Well, I think we can be pretty sure that Major has never said that after an afternoon with his . . .' – *mistress* was a word she didn't like – 'his lover.'

'I am considerably certain that he has not,' Ned drone-tones.

Finished in the bathroom, she looks with the usual regret at the complimentary shampoos and lotions she can't filch because they would be evidence.

Ned is sitting on the corner of the bed, dressing. The peculiar allure of an unbuttoned shirt.

'Next week is a bit useless, I'm afraid,' she says. 'Tom's mum is staying and I get the full Torquemada about what I've done that day. I'm fine as long as I don't actually have to lie.'

'Helen,' he says. 'There's something you should know.'

If weeing – even, with effort, sneezing – can be controlled, then why not tears? Turning her head, she tries to blink away the instinctive response. That stuff about if he ever had a son. His wife is pregnant. This will have to stop.

She feels vulnerable, uneasy about removing the bath towel to put on her clothes.

'Look, Jenny and I are . . . splitting up.'

The horror that they are finished replaced at once by the terror that he wants them to be together permanently.

'What? *Oh.* And does she . . . does she . . . ?'

'Know about us? No. No. But . . . I think this should stop.'

She tries to make the buckling of her knees look like a decision to sit down. As if with a child or a stranger, she adjusts the towel for decency.

'Why? Can't we just see how . . .'

'Look, this worked because it was double jeopardy. Neither of us was going to leave. But now I am and you won't leave Tom.'

'Are you asking me to?'

His silence and blankness make her think of a politician on television asked the killer question.

'No,' he says. 'No, I'm not.'

The clarity of shock. 'There's someone else, isn't there? I mean, another someone else.'

Another pause. 'I don't think you should think that.'

'Christ! It's amazing you get any fucking work done.'

'Oh, Helen, please don't cry. Hells, this has been fantastic but I don't think either of us ever thought it had a future, did we?'

Preposition / Proposition

Even though he says, 'It'll just be Mummy,' she knows at once that the phone call is another woman, probably calling to see if he is free and she can drop round. In a moment of devilment brought on by too much wine – she always thinks it proper to bring a bottle and there was already one open when she arrived – she briefly considers announcing that it is about time she is introduced to his mother and going down to take the call.

Through the thin door of the cheap conversion – the thought of the other tenants hearing them doing it – they listen to the tinny rattle of the receiver shaking the cradle. Then it stops. She is wondering whether she is too blotto to brave the Northern Line and make it to her own comfy bed, rather than his Scandinavian pallet thing, when there are footsteps and an angry sort-of-Argentinian woman banging on the door. He is probably bonking her as well.

When he puts his hand across her mouth to shush her, she can smell the onion he chopped for the spag bol. A chap who cooks for you is showing willing, even if it could have done with a few herbs.

Once the Hispanic messenger has gone, he rests his head on her boob and nuzzles her cheek. She shifts so their mouths touch, the meaty, winey taste as their tongues brush. Far more than Unspeakable Peter (let's see if this is a woman who *isn't comfortable with her body*), Ned knows how to use his tongue, funnelling into her here and there.

When he puts his hand *on* and then *in* her pants, she knows she will be missing the last Tube. Ned is obviously a player but he doesn't seem to agree with Unspeak Pete's view of her prowess in bed and, unlike some people she could mention, he has obviously read *The Joy of Sex*, sometimes spending so long down there that she has to pull him up like a diver, worried he will suffocate. And, after the blood clot scare, he hadn't made a song and dance about it being up to him, always wearing a thingy or pulling out if she told him. This time, there is no need to check he has his kit. She has decided that she is going to, as it were, bite the bullet and get it over with. She is getting sick of him wagging it hopefully in front of her face.

As he pulls her towards the door-on-the-floor, she tells him she needs to clean her teeth. Call her a poor little rich girl, but she isn't big on bedsits. The bathroom bit is next to the bedroom bit, separated only by a sort of shower curtain, so, if one of you gets up to do a wee or worse, the other has to hear it all. If St Valentine had lived here, Feb 14 would just be a normal day.

She hopes that he might take the hint and have a go with the Colgate as well but he doesn't. When she comes back into the main room, shucking off the dress over her head, a move that always puts her in the mood, he is naked, standing sideways, with that always slightly terrifying right-angle. There is a fortune waiting for whoever can invent socks that didn't leave a tartan garter on men's calves. She tells him to turn off the light – she will need a total eclipse to have a go at what Izzy calls a Cornetto – and gets into bed. The bottom sheet – yuk – feels crinkled and stiff.

They do the business, his mouth busy above and below. She worries that her bucking will snap off his tongue.

'What are we . . . ?' he asks.

Having a sudden fear that he might think she has got sorted out at the GP, she warns: 'I'm not on the pill.'

But she feels his telltale swelling. Her cue to. She tries to push him off.

'No! No!' she tells him.

But he thrusts harder. There was only one way out now. 'Come *on* me,' she urges him.

With dismay, she feels him tighten than slacken, the brief streak of heat inside her immediately followed by a sudden clammy coldness on her scalp.

When he speaks, he sounds, unbelievably, pleased. 'That was the best ever!'

She desperately tries to visualize her pocket diary, counting the days since the X. Too many but not enough. How has this happened?

The Psychology of Prosecution

Academics rarely match their photographs. The smooth-skinned, dark-haired hopeful smiling shyly beside a lecture title in the symposium brochure frequently stands at the lectern with chin tripled and fringe silvered or gone. There is a professor in Cambridge whose appearance so contradicts the jpeg image still sent to conference organizers that he is known as 'Dorian Gray'.

Yet, even by such standards of vanity, the Director of History challenges photographic accuracy. The mug-shot featured in the management tree on the UME website – the only image of Neades that web-stalking exposed – shows a lean, tanned figure who could be the grandson of the gross, pallid man who, as she knock-pushes the glass door of his office, glances up as if irritated by her arrival.

'Oh, Dr Traill,' he says. 'Will you come in?'

Although it cannot be regarded as serious racism, she feels her usual guilt at finding the Ulster accent ugly; she has a similar difficulty with South Africans.

'It's good of you to help us with this,' Neades goes on, though on a note more of remonstration than gratitude. 'You received the terms of reference?'

'I did. What strikes me is that *conduct* and *culture* are quite broad concepts?'

'Those are the words used to describe the process to staff, Dr Traill. But, in practice, you are seeking to establish breaches of the codes relating to B & H and Insubordination.'

'Is this known to be a problem in the department?'

'Sir Richard has made it a red-flag issue across the business.'

'But I think, to some extent, in this kind of thing, it's about where you draw the line? I think most of us know these days what sexual harassment might entail – where someone might put their hands, what they might put in their e-mails. But bullying and insubordination – isn't there an issue of definition?'

'There may be a range of views – yes.'

'But do I judge people against all of them or one of them?'

'Say more about that?'

'What to one person is hurtful sarcasm is to another robust argument. Belittling / Rigorous, Aggressive / Forensic, Humiliating / Educative, Insubordination / Debate. Can these ever be objective oppositions?'

'As I say, there is a range of views.'

'So you keep saying. But what is *your* view?'

His long stolid stare is momentarily broken by a glimmer of irritation at being challenged. He seems to be waiting for her to speak again but she wills him to fill the silence.

Eventually, Neades says: 'My view is that those are academic distinctions.'

'Occupational hazard!' she jokes.

No reaction from the Director. There is another war of pauses, which, this time, she loses. 'Surely I need to be clear what I am investigating people for?'

'I'm not running this process. It's your investigation,' Neades says, raising his arms in an acting-out of neutrality that exposes matching oval sweat patches. 'But, I'd say, for me, the line is drawn where it becomes personal.'

'Well, okay. But there's no scientific instrument for measuring that. Who decides if it's personal?'

The Director sighed. 'A *person* does. A person who was *hurt*.

I suspect there's a risk in over-thinking this sort of thing. Let us proceed on the basis that you will report the cases to me and then we will decide the next steps, going forward.'

The building they are in trains minds to identify flaws in argument, although it is unlikely that Neades would welcome a demonstration of the method. 'When you say *the* cases, you mean *any* cases?'

His expression suggests that his own interpretation of Insubordination might be any disagreement at all. 'For the integrity of the process, it must be seen to have been thorough. It must not matter who a staff-member is, or how long he has been here.'

'He or she?'

His glimmer of a glower may reflect a defence of sexist grammar, or something else unspoken. Teaching, she thinks, is about clarity of meaning; management the opposite.

'Dr Traill, there is a risk that further discussion between us might compromise the independence of the process.'

Although he has used a full-stop end-of-monologue intonation, her mind is wired for dialogue. 'A trial that ends in acquittal can still be a proper application of the law, can't it?'

'No one is pretending that this is a court of law.' A pause that seems to freeze his whole body. 'Dr Traill, I should mention that there may be some tension.' The accidental rhyme makes him falter momentarily. 'It is known that we are looking to close posts across the business. As a separate matter, of course. But these efficiency savings may be playing on the minds of those participating in the process.'

The automatic insecurity of an employee suddenly summoned before a superior makes her fear that the Director might be attempting a form of subliminal suggestion, planting in her mind the idea that the process may be followed, one way or another, by dismissals. Could her own survival be dependent on successfully intuiting what she is being asked to do? It is impossible in these situations to know how suspicious to be.

This opaque conversation has given her an abrupt sense of

how institutions operate. She is unsure of the meaning of this meeting, or even if it has one. There seems no way of knowing if selection for this duty is reward or warning, prize or punishment.

Leaving

She spends six hours sleepless beside him, listening to his stentorian snores, unable to nudge him because that would require touching. Afterwards, her first thought was to call a minicab but, in such a state of agitation, it felt ridiculous to entrust herself to another stranger. She has read in the *Standard* about rapes by drivers.

The *Wash / Don't Wash* argument in her head. The need to be clean wins. Straddling the sink behind the plastic drape, sluicing herself as best she can, she feels more like a woman in 1876. Awake, she pictures the diary pages again, repeatedly doing the sum, unable ever to come to a number smaller than between twelve and sixteen.

Two or three cars start up outside. The traffic is building on the Finchley Road. Her watch is curled like a dog turd on the thinning carpet. Quarter past six.

Sneaking out of dormitory at Madingley Hall has left her skilled at dressing quietly. Yesterday's dress and emergency pants, although they don't have the fresh feeling she expects. She scrunches the soiled pair to the bottom of her handbag. No need to wee or clean her teeth until home. The cardigan lifted from the sofa as if it is a jewel in an alarm-protected case.

At the click of the door latch, he stirs.

Morning tongue-stuck speech: 'You going?' She doesn't answer. 'That was great. See you.'

Her heels ludicrously loud on the stairs. A scowling Latina might open a door at any moment. A sudden memory from movies that you are supposed to carry your shoes until the street.

On the noticeboard, a note in big capitals: NED. LUCIA

RING. PLEASE CALL HER. She imagines him insisting that his mother is called Lucia.

Although everyone is still pretending it's summer, the cold on the street makes her shiver and wish her woollen top was thicker as she buttons it tightly up.

On the platform, a workman in a donkey jacket slowly inspects her: heels, boobs, hair. He winks. 'Dirty stop out, eh? Lucky him.'

The awareness that she must look unbrushed, unshowered and and and and *fucked*.

Do tube trains always stink like this? Choosing a carriage as far as possible from the winker, she takes from her handbag the little book with the fake red leather cover and 1976 stamped in gold. She sees it as a birthdate. 1976–.

Her blue biro X is against the 7th. So. So. So. Thirteen.

Duty of Care

The reception area is decorated with frozen seconds of television: a hostage scene from an award-winning cop drama that is in her stack of unwatched box sets, an image from *The Big Jigsaw Challenge*. The latter looks as if it was taken just before the moment that has become known as 'heelgate', involving the allegation that the winner, in the speed completion round, knocked a rival's piece off the table and secreted it away on a cunningly chewing-gummed shoe. There are two gaps in the line of picture frames, looking too erratic to be a pattern. She wonders if the spaces once held photographs of presenters now exposed as paedophiles.

Double doors in the corner split open, admitting a tall guy with a sandy flat top, wearing ripped jeans and a T-shirt printed with the legend: Clever Clothing Slogans Are So Yesterday.

'Jess?' he checks. 'Dom's out of his LA call. Do you want to come with me?'

On an L-shaped sofa placed below two windows looking onto the canal, Ogg is flicking through a thick script, its edge rainbowed with replacement pages in multiple colours. Ignoring their entrance, he goes on reading. It looks like cover footage of a judge on the day of the publication of the report from an official inquiry. Ogg appears different, younger than she remembers. But TV, she has observed, is a rare area of life in which older men tend to have more hair and better teeth than when you last saw them.

Suddenly looking up, Ogg says: 'Oh. Hey, Jess. Come in. Come in. Thanks, Percy.'

The PA faces Jess and, forming a tea pot from one hand, performs a charade of pouring into a cup made from the other, while pulling a question-mark face. The gesture is borderline obscene and she wonders if it might not have been easier for him to speak, which she does: 'No. No, thanks, I'm fine.'

When he's gone, Jess says: 'Percy? That's not a . . .'

'It's his surname. Not a public school thing, by the way. His choice. People can be called what they want here. Except God. That one's taken. Arf Arf.'

Her intended real laugh was less convincing than his fake one.

'You're still happy with "Jess", Jessamy?'

'Sure.'

'So,' Ogg announces the start of the proceedings proper. 'Long time since we worked together. Thanks for mailing that CV. You've done some fun stuff.'

There is work around but it pays the same or less than it would have done ten years before, which is why she is so pleased and intrigued by the unexpected summons to Ogglebox.

The boss opens her CV on his iPad and reads it, making lip-shapes of approval.

'Herstory have kept you busy,' he says. 'You know Alice started here? I don't mind telling you: she's the one I dread pitching against for things.'

'Yes, she's great.' The freelance's dilemma of how to flatter this possible employer without criticizing the other in a way that might get back. 'They're very much into concept doc, I suppose. You're lucky if the presenter isn't in costume.'

'Lol,' Ogg says. 'Look, I'm certainly keen on finding something for you here.'

General rather than specific interest – the freelance's disaster.

'But, Jess, there's something else I wanted to try out on you . . .'

A warning blip on the radar that women in the workplace develop. The joke in the industry is that the only person at risk of sexual harassment from Ogg is himself. But has he somehow managed to operate under the level of gossip? The dinner to discuss the state of TV, the theatre trip on which a friend has just let him down. With lightning mistrustful calculation, she works out that Alice had just dumped him and she will be the get-back shag.

But what Ogg says is: 'Tell me as a matter of interest – back in the day, how did you get on with Ned Marriott?'

The scenario she had imagined and rehearsed as soon as she got the e-mail: an offer of work but with *him*. But this topic – her researcher's mind works out – was introduced as *something else* apart from possible employment.

'Fine,' she lies. 'I was very junior.'

'Indeedy. Indeedy. Look, Jess, I'm not going to beat . . . I'm not going to blow smoke up . . . Jess, I'm going to completely be frank with you. A colleague here tells me that you may have had a bit of a to-do with the professor once. A – let me clarify, we're not judgemental here – an *unwanted* to-do.'

A sudden thought of people, diagnosed with tumours, who are told: *it might have been growing for years*. And a sense of jeopardy, knowing that two paths are being offered but unsure of the destinations at the end of them. Professional good sense is to give the answer that Ogg wants. But what would that be?

'Can I ask why this has suddenly come up now?'

'You mean because it was a long time ago?'

'Well, nine, ten . . .'

She stops herself but he has got her. Ogg's colossal vanity and corporate vocabulary make it tempting to dismiss him but the caricature version of him could not have achieved such a career; the question that has trapped her gives a feel of his deal-maker's skills.

He does a lap of honour for the admission he has won: 'So, during *The English Witch Hunts*? Yes, that was the information I had.' A drop in his voice as marked as if he is obeying the stage direction *sotto voce*. 'Jess, can you tell me as much as you feel able to about what happened?'

The moment of invitation to identify herself as a victim. If she has not done so before, it is because she is unsure that there was damage or, if there has been, how lasting it is. 'Look, if anything happened, it was a . . . a location grope. Stuff – you must know this – stuff goes on on shoots. Less so now but . . . then . . .'

'I see. Are there other charges – or charges against others – you might want to bring?'

The shift in tone and language is disorientating, a doctor becoming a cop.

'Well, hang on. I haven't brought any charges against anyone.'

'Jess, my information is that Professor Marriott sexually assaulted you.' A memory of confiding in Alice once during filming. 'As Ogglebox had – and has – a duty of care towards you, we have passed this allegation to Operation Millpond, which is . . .'

'Yes, I know. But can you? . . . I'm not sure I . . .'

'My decision – on advice – was that to do this was consistent with our duty of care towards you.'

Her historian's training is to ask, when analysing an action, *who most benefits from this?*

'Look, if you . . . I have no complaint about the way the production company . . .'

'That would not have been a factor in our decision.'

She smiles.

'Why are you smiling? Jess, it is my understanding that officers from Millpond will contact you. This company will give you any support you need and, as I say, we are keen to work with you again. I can also tell you, confidentially, that you are not the first complainant.'

What she has taken for a pencil sharpener on Ogg's desk is, he proudly demonstrates before she leaves, a fold-up pair of roller-skates.

She must look shaken because Percy, escorting her out, offers a look of hyperbolic kindness, suspecting an applicant turned down for a job.

Leaving, Jess stares at the gaps in the wall of photographs as if they are complicated paintings.

W9

It is obvious that the ninth witness is used to being interviewed; after half an hour, they have received only cagey condemnations of the college management and admissions of *differences* with certain colleagues. This is a conciliator, a survivor.

Andrea glances at Jani and sees approval for the escalation they agreed in advance if necessary.

'In your view, are sexual relationships ever acceptable in an educational environment?'

A flutter under the calm charm he has shown so far. 'What an extraordinary question.'

During the ten days of taking evidence, Andrea has learned, as all interviewers and interrogators presumably do, that a pause is a trap into which one of two talkers will fall and it should never be you.

'Well,' W9 finally says. 'I think there's general acceptance now that such liaisons are not generally wise between teaching staff and students. Certainly, I accept it.'

Hasty training as an investigator has made her alert to the present-tense denial that may confess to past demeanours; the politician's 'there *is* no sexual relationship with this woman'. When they review testimony, her HR colleague is brutal about this verbal casuistry but Andrea is happier to concentrate on what is happening now – how many people could survive a review of their entire life or career? Jani, though, keeps repeating that the *scope* is *historic*.

In line with which view, she now gives the witness a clipped precis of his previous answer: 'There *is* acceptance now. So there have been times when there was not acceptance in History?' After a week and a half of confusion over this word, Jani adds: 'In the History department?'

The tense silence of a TV contestant facing the top money question. 'Are you making a specific accusation?'

Jani looks scandalized at this misunderstanding: 'No. Not at all. I am speaking generally.'

'And is this really within the remit of a study of the *conduct* and *culture* of the department?'

Renewed incredulity from Jani. 'Well, the university has rules on sexual conduct. Very much so. And it seems to me that this is well within the remit of the Traill Inquiry.'

The only pleasure for Andrea of this nasty task from Ncades has been to watch sharp, fast minds at work – in a percentage of staff at least – calculating whether to answer and then what.

'Let me say then, Ms Goswani,' W9 says, 'that it would be surprising if, in any place of further education, there has been no element of sexual indiscretion over the last two decades. And I doubt that UME would surprise us in this way.'

'Let me ask you very directly, Professor. Have you yourself ever broken the university's Customer Boundary Code?'

Andrea leans across, inviting a whispered conference with her colleague – she has not seen them being genital detectives – but Jani's look is fixed on the witness. He waits so long that Andrea wonders if he has decided on silence. But then he says: 'Can I ask when this code you invoke was introduced?'

A small smirk from Jani at another attempt to separate past and present. 'The code became a de facto appendix to all long-term and temporary contracts from the start of the academic year 2006.'

'Then – while setting on the record my concern at this line of questioning – I am confident that I have never crossed a boundary with a student.'

He is, she feels, being careful but candid, appealing to the god of second chances, and Andrea is about to take over the questioning when Jani goes on: 'And have you ever – at any time – had an inappropriate relationship with a teaching colleague?'

Startled by this line of attack, Andrea rests fingers firmly on Jani's arm to get her attention, but the intervention is shrugged away as if itself an example of improper contact. And, for the first time, W9's charm and calm cracks: 'Jesus Christ, did I miss the memo that Sharia law had been introduced?'

Jani types energetically. When she has finished, Andrea squeezes her co-questioner's arm firmly until she turns to look.

'Aren't we going off-map here?' Andrea whispers.

From behind a cupped covering hand comes the reply: 'Claims have been made against him.'

Whereas Goswani seems to have a prosecutor's purity, though of a terrifyingly zealous kind, Traill feels uneasily that she is here to achieve the result Neades has already ordained, like a theatre mind-reader reproducing the doodle that a volunteer has sealed in an envelope behind a screen. And she doubts that it involves the removal of the department's biggest star.

'I see him more as a witness than a suspect,' she murmurs to the woman from People. Then, audibly, to the witness: 'Professor, I want to ask you about your experience with some colleagues. Dr Tom Pimm?'

'Well, I certainly haven't had sex with him.'

Andrea's smile is partly powered by the memory that Pimm had made the same joke in reverse. Several of the witnesses have commented on the friendship of the men and she is starting to suspect that loyalty will make the interrogation pointless when, finally, they get something they can use: 'I have to admit that sometimes – as a friend – I have raised concerns with Tom about the way he carries on.'

'You mean his sexual conduct?' Goswani cuts in.

It strikes Andrea that, during a process that sometimes seems to have gone on longer than the Middle East peace negotiations, they have spent accumulated hours watching people deciding whether, or how much, to lie. The latest witness has come to a decision: 'I think I'll just leave it as having warned him about the nature of some of his relationships.'

'Are you . . . ?' her colleague starts, but the speaker continues: 'I think a lot of his problems come from the way he talks. Almost everything he says is a pun, a joke, a nickname.'

'That sounds quite cruel?' Traill prompts.

'Yes, I suppose if you're the one on the end of it.'

'He identifies a person's weakness?' Goswani asks.

'I suppose you could say that. I'd say more that he's a world-class sarcastic. But, to be fair to him, I think a lot of it comes from terror of being a boring talker. Even if he just says "hello" to you, it's likely to be in a foreign language or funny accent. He says the word "so" in Anglo-Saxon. Even just trying to find a time everyone can make for a meeting first thing the next day, he'll ask: "Anyone for tennish?" '

By the end, he's restored to the friendly, confident figure who started the session.

'My outburst earlier,' he says. 'I apologize if my tone was inappropriate. I just felt that it was all getting a bit . . .'

Andrea remembers the name he says but can only guess a spelling – Sovanarola? – which ignites the jagged red-line of the spellcheck, but she can sort it out later.

Goswani asks: 'As a matter of interest, does he have a nickname for you?'

'Actually, he does. Pretty kind by his standards, though. Because of something people noticed when I was first on TV. It's Nod.'

'Thank you, Professor Marriott,' says Andrea. 'Just a reminder that your evidence today will be treated as anonymous and should not be discussed with anyone.'

PART FOUR

FALL-OUTS

Your Love Always

'I want a hug.'

'Okay.'

Folding down a corner of the page, she balanced the manuscript on the bedside table and took off her reading glasses, a move incorporated into foreplay by this age. She turned to embrace him, her arms around his shoulders but hips and pelvis curved away, a move she had perfected with an early boyfriend before she was on the pill and he would try to get away without a condom.

She put her head against his and they rubbed them together. She thought of zoo animals. The feel of his scalp disturbed her. Although she shared Ned's concerns about money, she had tried to persuade him to keep going to the weave place. What was happening to him was odder than watching a bloke going bald; the unravelling of the strands was a reminder that the looks she had found attractive were an act.

He moved to try to kiss her lips but she shifted to offer a cheek. A loose long strand from his new hairdo tickled her eye. She understood that he was trying to become unnoticeable but, the way it was going, he was ironically at risk of being mistaken for that landlord who was wrongly accused of killing the poor young architect.

Ned tried to push closer, but she held the distance. Impressive lower-body strength. Pilates. As they cuddle-tussled, a half-erection brushed her thigh.

'Please, Em.'

'I still can't quite.'

'I've said sorry in every way I . . .'

'I'll get there.' A quick compromise kiss on his lips. Feeling the thrust of his tongue, she pulled away. 'Trust me.'

'Look, we don't have to actually . . . will you just let me . . . ?'

It was almost tempting, him, unseen, devoted only to her pleasure.

'I'd feel too mean.' She shrugged his hands away from her shoulders. 'It's not that I don't love you. But . . . anyway, I really need to finish *Your Love Always . . .*'

'What?' Not at first noticing the title, he had heard a rebuttal harsher than she meant. 'Oh, right. I . . .'

Her mouth felt dry. She drank some of her night water, was tempted to empty the glass. Replacing her reading glasses, she found the abandoned paragraph.

Voice grumped by bruised refusal, he asked: 'That's the texts from the dead thing?' She nodded. 'Well, that's a really lousy knock back. You've read it already.'

'And I need to read it again. I've got a call booked with the author tomorrow. I think it's between two of us now.'

He stroked her hair; she tried not to flinch. 'Well, let me relax you before your big conversation.'

'Ned, to convince her I'm the best representation she could have, I need to be able to recite the book line by line if necessary.'

'Well, from what you told me in Edinburgh, there isn't much to know. We only have Scott's word for it that his wife even died. He's an unreliable narrator – bet you any money.'

The verbal equivalent of knowing in slow motion that a collision is coming but being unable to brake: 'But you haven't got any money! Which is why I really need to sign this book.'

He made a liquid sniff that she hoped was not tears. 'I'm sorry, Ned. I'm sorry.'

He Showed No Emotion

In court reporting, which had recently replaced the sports pages as Ned's favourite form of journalism, it was almost always noted that the convicted had 'shown no emotion' at the moment of sentencing. This seemed to apply regardless of whether the charge was serial murder of children or false accounting.

The reports meant the observation as a judgement, indicating a lack of shame or moral perception. But, during his six months under suspicion, Ned had come to the conclusion that the insouciance might be pharmaceutical. His own experience of happy pills and knock-out drops was that, while efficiently removing negative thoughts, they also obliterated positive emotions. Complete loss of libido might be attributed in his case to the nature of the allegations against him, but appetite, enthusiasm, pleasure and energy were also reduced. His general mood was of dim benignity, as if he were watching things happen to someone else.

At the top end of the spectrum of offence, killers and paedophiles would almost certainly have been prescribed some kind of suppressants or anti-psychotics, and on the lower levels of criminality – the corrupt politicians, perjurious newspapermen and fiddling accountants – the accused were likely to be taking antidepressants or sleeping pills, and probably at higher doses than career criminals, who would usually have had more reason to expect investigation and incarceration. So those who showed nothing in the dock, he suspected, were not displaying signs of shamelessness but of sedation.

#nosmokewithoutfire

At first every morning – and then several times a day – Phee typed her father's name into a search box, followed by the word *rapist*. To how many other daughters could this appalling task have fallen? It started after Daddy told her that he could no longer bear to check what was being said about him. So as soon as she woke up and before she tried to sleep – and at other times, some in the night, becoming overwhelmed by what might be out there without her knowing – Phee turned into a curse-nurse, taking the temperature of Ned Marriott's notoriety.

For days and even weeks after each of the arrests, she found nothing new for twenty-four, forty-eight, seventy-two hours, which at least marked a ceasefire in the crisis, although the repeated details were always freshly distressing. In old movies, suave lawyers or tender lovers would reassure the ruined that 'tomorrow all this stuff will be wrapping fish and chips', but now cod suppers were rolled in bespoke waxed paper and bad news could be Googled until doomsday.

Even worse was the headline tagged *9 minutes ago* or seeing *Ned Marriott* between the plane crashes, controversies over offensive comments and *One Direction* split-up rumours trending on Twitter. Usually, the trigger would be the arrest or trial of someone who had played records, read the news or forecast the weather in the '70s. Finding the thread or hashtag, Phee scan-read the messages at speed, assessing their levels of malice and inaccuracy from certain words.

Her previous experience of debates, formal and informal, had involved the satisfaction of finding allies, her sense of identity strengthened by being in one pack against another: in Phee's case, liberals against conservatives. Amid these word-limited opinion-formers, though, she was as uncomfortable among her backers – men who considered the concept of rape a female conspiracy, ex-husbands who went off on tangents about the general duplicity of women – as her detractors.

A report of a pre-trial hearing for a regional TV meteorologist accused of sex offences against schoolboys had led @ *shepthedog*, a commenter mainly on broadcasting topics, whom Phee started following when he led reckless speculation about her dad on the day the story broke, to reflect on other overshadowed screen talent.

Shep The Dog (@shepthedog) 12m @louisgatt14 U say perv presenters 70s problem but #nedmarriottarrested still on box right until nicked

History Girl (@drhlangham) @louisgatt14 I completely concur

Comedy Northerner (@davepike41) Fook me @drhlangham *completely concur* #poshtwat

Phee hoped that the contribution from the class warrior would divert the conversation but the intervention in the name of the former *Blue Peter* dog had already been retweeted several times and so, like a nightclub bouncer deciding the line has been crossed between fun and a fight, she went in. She had used false names at times but the responses seemed equally brutal regardless of who she was thought to be and so she no longer tried to hide the bloodline.

Ophelia (@pheemarriott) @shepthedog vital to note #nedmarriottarrested not *nicked*, not even charged and denies charges #innocenttilguilty

Shep The Dog @pheemarriott yeah yeah #nosmokewithoutfire.

Jeremy Milligan (@jsjmilligan) Worked with #nedmarriottarrested and he was a total cunt especially to women.

Ophelia (@pheemarriott) some feminist u if u use c word

Comedy Northerner @pheemarriott Ophelia!!!! Get her. #poshtwat

Ophelia @shepthedog #nosmokewithoutfire Yes smoke no fire #nedmarriottarrested is innocent and will prove it

History Girl @davepike41 Get her? #toanunnery

Shep The Dog @pheemarriott #nedmarriottarrested *raped* 2 girls

Comedy Northerner @drhlangham Eh? Eh? #toanunnery *scratches head*

Ophelia @shepthedog #nedmarriottarrested did not *rape* anyone #innocenttilguilty

Cleopatra Bones (@cjones872) @pheemarriott but how u no? R 2 girls lieing?

Emily Spankhurst (@stopsexism) (@cjones872) she no bcos she @pheemarriott #daddysgirl

Ophelia @shepthedog @cjones872 @stopsexism point is this could happen to your father, husband, brother, son #innocenttilguilty

Comedy Northerner @pheemarriott It wont u silly cunt cos they not rapists

When that last remark had been retweeted 384 times, Phee left the conversation.

The Verdict Stage

Trying to concentrate on the *Guardian*, Tom was distracted from distraction by a blur of gold in the corner of the kitchen. Looking up, he saw Helen taking a bottle of champagne out of an Aldi bag.

'Oh, fuck, I'm sorry.'

'For what? Or alternatively what for?'

Her speech patterns reflected living with a pedant.

'It's these drugs I'm on.' He scanned the squares of September on the wall calendar. They'd just done their anniversary, and the kids were all March or April birthdays, in the middle-class way, from summer holiday sex, and Hells was a Taurus. 'What have I missed?'

'What? Oh, no, this is to celebrate tonight.'

'Aaaargghh!' A not-entirely mock scream. 'All this time, I thought I was the victim of a witch hunt and I was living with a fucking witch. Don't hex me, Goodie Pimm.'

Though such a committed rationalist that he considered Richard Dawkins a little mystical, Tom was superstitious enough to panic at Helen's anticipation of his acquittal, even though he was equally confident of the outcome. At the appeal hearing, Henry Gibson had seemed so wryly on-side that Tom subsequently ate and slept with intermittent normality and, for the last week, had been slicing the little white antidepressants down the middle, risking half a dose to deliver equilibrium.

They compromised by leaving the bottle on the work-top wine-rack, with an agreement that he would text her after his meeting with Special to tell her if – *when* – to put it in the fridge.

Tom could forgive Helen's optimism because she had given him a tip that seemed to confirm a positive result. At her office, she had told him, employees always knew that they would be given bad news – redundancy, suspension, re-assignment – if they were invited to bring a supporter or union rep to a meeting or if, on arrival, they found an HR representative present. So, receiving an e-mail summoning him to the Director's office to learn the 'outcome of his hearing', Tom had inquired by return if he should bring someone along with him and whether anyone else would be present in the room. Special's PA responded that *the Director envisages it being just the two of you.* In a follow-up which, if he did not boycott emoticons, would have finished with a winking face, Tom mentioned that he was currently barred from entering university premises and was told that the restriction had been lifted for this encounter.

Since his collapse, Tom always allowed extra time to reach anywhere, in line with the Mindfulness guidance on identifying and avoiding pressure situations. Turning onto the roundabout by the main campus road seventy-five minutes before his appointment, he spent three quarters of an hour in an Aylesbury coffee shop with his laptop, substituting and then removing mountingly exotic verbs and adjectives in a single sentence of his Kennedy–Bush–Clinton book.

Finishing his decaf Americano, Tom resolved that when Special told him the ordeal was over, he would be gracious, with no gloating; it had clearly been necessary for the allegations to be investigated.

At the main security door in reception, he brushed his swipe card against the plastic pad with a flourish. The failure of the glass to part was the physical equivalent of a credit card being rejected in a shop.

Turning away while forcing a casual air, he looked back to the Caribbean woman desk-guard, whom he recognized and so might be able to identify him in return.

'Oh, I think I need to get it renewed. Can I have a guest one for today?' he asked.

'Okay, honey. Dr Pimm, yeah?'

The now familiar moment of wondering how much someone knew.

'Heretosee?' The phrase employed so often that it had slurred into a single word.

'Spe . . . Dr Kevan Neades.'

She filled out the visitor slip, slid it into the safety-pinned plastic holder. She had written his surname with one m.

Waiting outside the glass office, he convinced himself that the chilling indifference of Elaine was professional rather than personal, her robotic 'you can go in now' no clue to the result of the meeting.

Special was hunched over the desk, lips moving while rehearsing typed lines, shattering Tom's optimism because exoneration could be ad-libbed but dismissal would be given in legally agreed words.

When the Director looked up, Tom held out his hand but the only response from Neades was a flick of the finger to tell him to sit down.

Reading upside down *speak slowly* at the top of the foolscap, Tom knew what to expect before the words ponderously began.

'Thank you for attending this meeting today, Dr Pimm. I have received the report of your hearing with Professor Gibson. It has been concluded that offence was taken and hurt caused by some of your behaviours. Accordingly, the decision has been reached that your contract will be terminated forthwith on the grounds of professional misconduct. Due to the circumstances of dismissal, you will not be eligible for any severance payment but the contractual terms of your pension continue to apply and a representative of Workplace Harmony can advise you of the position in that regard.'

Heart threatening to break his rib cage, throat scorched by bile, salt water stinging his eyes, Tom arrested the retch but let the tears drop. The only reasons to suppress this response would have been pride – which he had lost – and the discomfort of his executioner. Well, let the morbidly obese Northern Irelander appreciate the consequences of his corporately self-serving actions.

'Do you have any questions, Dr Pimm?'

Neades had squeezed a large white handkerchief from his trouser pocket and, for a moment, Tom feared that the Director would maternally proffer it. But, instead, he cacophonously blew his nose.

Struggling to speak over the tachycardial backbeat banging in his chest and temple, Tom did have a question. He was unable to match this conclusion with the wry, wise, kind presence of Henry Gibson at his appeal against defenestration. An historian describing this sequence of events would suspect an undiscovered document or a meeting in-between.

'Is this what Professor Gibson recommended?'

Neades' habitual swallowed fury at being challenged. A long period in which he considered whether he could get away with silence. Then: 'The ultimate decision would not have been his.'

'So it was yours?'

'There would have been a range of views. Unless you have any specific questions, Dr Pimm, I think we will leave it there. A business card skimmed across the table. 'David Wellington of WH is keeping all lines clear for your call, if you should feel in need of practical or emotional support.'

Driven not by politeness but the desire to prove Neades rude, Tom challenged Special to a final handshake, which was refused.

Because (2)

'What do you always say about becauses?' Ned asked Tom. 'I was sacrificed as one of society's apologies for not stopping that yellow-haired weirdo paedo in a Bacofoil shell suit. And you're being ruined because the University let Professor Prick Anything get away with it for so long. Without Savile, without Allison, neither of these things would have happened.'

Report

In the taxi to Paddington Green, Ned was struck by the peculiarity of English using the word *report* to mean both turning up somewhere and the spreading of news. But, thankfully, today reporters seemed not to have been alerted that he was reporting to answer bail.

Claire had outlined the possibilities from their visit: 'Bail extended – questioning on "other matters" – re-arrested and formally charged – or NFA.'

'No fucking . . . ?' he guessed. 'No fucking what?'

'Ha. Action. No *further* action, actually.'

Sweat settled on his scalp and neck. 'My students always said – *say* – multiple-choice papers are easier. They reckon there are always only two it could really be. Let's hope they're right. Any reason you put the best one last?'

'No. It was random. Dictionary – not youthful – sense. Look, I'm not counting our chicken nuggets. But, on previous form, if it's bad, they would have had hacks at the flat.' His hopes rose, though only briefly. 'Unless they'll be at the station.'

But only two or three shivering smokers, with no cameras or shorthand pads in evidence, stood on the dirtied stone approach. With a swig of bottled water, tingling his teeth in the December chill, Ned swallowed a Diazepam.

The custody sergeant was light and smiley during the security sign-in but might either be sharing vindication with the innocent, extending sympathy to the doomed, or been a keen viewer of Hitler documentaries who was under the impression that his hero by association had come in as a victim of crime. Ned and Tom (poor Tom) had agreed that there was no point trying to guess the outcome from people's expressions.

Despite these intentions, he found himself trying to translate the faces and handshakes of Dent and Walters and detected nothing except polite neutrality.

And then Dent said, 'So.' The age's universal punctuation, preface to everything from marriage proposals to terminal news from surgeons. 'So, how have you been, Professor Marriott?'

Ned sensed irritation from Claire. Was it dismay at the further delay or did experience lead her to infer something from these pleasant preliminaries?

'I'm alive,' Ned said.

His favoured formula was again effective. Dent's expression wanted to be nothing but had discomfort bubbling underneath. The detective scratched the back of his head so noisily that the sound must have registered on the recorder he had just activated.

'I'm glad to hear that.'

The taping worried Ned. If it were just a sorry-and-goodbye, would they still Nixon it? Police stations, like surgeries and hospitals, should have cheery leaflets in which brightly shaded cartoon characters receive simple explanations of what will be happening to them.

A sidelong glance at Claire to see if she had reacted, but she was auditioning to play Special in a film.

'So,' Dent said again, then stopped. The terrible influence on conversation of the results moment in TV talent shows.

'Professor Edmund Marriott, you have attended today to answer bail on allegations of sexual offences against Wilhelmina Hessendon Castle and Jessamy Pothick.'

Ned fought to quieten his breathing. The tape of this meeting would sound as if a gale were blowing through an open window.

'Following a detailed investigation of these allegations, a file was sent to the Crown Prosecution Service for consideration.'

Ned had often fantasized about the penalty in a World Cup final, championship point at Wimbledon, the putt on the 72nd hole at an Open. This must be a version of how it felt – a life of either ecstasy or regret proceeding from this moment.

'After consultation with the CPS, I can inform you this morning that no further action will be taken.'

Distantly, as if it were happening to someone else, he felt his hand squeezed by Claire. Ned had pictured this moment so often, endlessly played on a loop of the two alternative scenes but, now that it had happened, his reaction was neither of those he had imagined.

He showed no emotion.

It was either the tranquillizers or the understanding that, from this position, there could be no such thing as victory.

Dent nodded at Walters, who said: 'Regardless of the outcome, the complainants have the right of anonymity in perpetuity, until their death and, in certain circumstances, afterwards. You must not name them – or otherwise risk their identification – in speech or in writing, in public or in private. Nor should you contact or approach a complainant – yourself or through others – in any way.'

To have been exonerated yet still receive threats felt disconcerting. 'And what about me? Do I get a public apology?'

A twitch of irritability from Dent. 'We have a duty to take all accusations seriously. Charging someone and not charging someone are both doing our job.'

Claire's fingers brushing his knuckles. 'We can go through your options later.'

Of course he had never wanted it to come to court. But at least a trial was shaped to have a climactic moment of catastrophe or catharsis. This long ordeal ended – in a small room that smelled of fear sweat and coffee breath and cheap disinfectant – with an announcement that nothing would happen.

'I sort of feel someone should say, "You can go now," ' Ned said.

Dent slightly smiled. Walters was closing her folder as if it were a fiendish puzzle.

'We can go now,' Claire said.

The four-way handshakes felt like stumps in a drawn cricket match between two teams that hated each other.

The Present

In the spare room ('I do love you, Tom, but I need to get my sleep on work nights'), he managed pill-assisted oblivion from 10pm until five to midnight. Turning over the soaked side of the pillow, he tried, 04:18 the last numbers he saw on the clock, to put himself under again by reading (a notoriously soporific historian of US foreign policy), masturbating (flaccidly) and the virtual journey through the rooms of his childhood house (which had sometimes worked for him).

Each of these strategies seemed to fail but Tom was somehow deep in a dream – half replay, half terror, Director Neades opening a folder of medical test results – when Special's ringing telephone turned out in the conscious world to be Helen's extra-loud alarm clock across the landing. A bleary stare at the clock: 07:00.

Tom knew he should get up to see Hells off to work, do the dogs or make her tea and toast (he was desultorily attempting the duties of a house-husband) but his mind and body were screaming for more sleep.

He fumbled for the foil strip of Diazepam hidden under the paper tissues – after Dr Rafi ended the prescription to prevent addiction, he had bought some packets online – and, after swallowing one, tested his mental sedatives again: 'Caught between the proverbial rock and a hard place, the State Department bethought . . .' the long hair of a college girlfriend tickling his thighs as she bent over him, through the boot room and past the muddy wellington boots and the washing machine.

The dogs were barking at something in the garden. 10:45. His tongue was furred and throat sore but he felt closer than for a long time to the feeling of waking refreshed. Even so, he had to force himself not to try to sleep again. He understood why the depressed, redundant or bereaved could be driven to the deepest, dream-free drop-off in their hope of finding a place of not knowing.

As usual in their new schedules, Helen had piled the post beside his place at the breakfast table. Two envelopes with the UME crest he slid aside unopened, knowing that they must contain details of severance, pensions, the clearance of his office. And, although sure that the sentiments would be sympathetic, he felt no more able to cope emotionally with the rectangular hand-addressed mail that would contain the latest greetings cards from those colleagues – Ciara, the department five-a-siders – who were shocked at what had been done to him or fearful that it might happen next to them. He dropped in the bin unopened three offers of new credit cards; he could not decide if it would be more worrying if the lenders' algorithms had or had not spotted his impending insolvency.

That left the familiar cardboard rectangle of a book bought online. Economizing since the shock of unemployment, he did not recall ordering anything. With a smeared butter-knife, Tom slit the end and shook out a paperback. *Silas Marner* by George Eliot in an edition called New Classics. He had never read it but had once watched part of a TV version, failing again in his promise to Hells to sit through a period drama with her.

The sender had taken advantage of the discretion offered to gift-buyers and left blank the box on the invoice for payment details. Tom flicked through the opening pages to see if there was any kind of card.

He found nothing, although there was perhaps a sort of message. On the title page, a line said: *Introduction by Henry Gibson.*

Cuttings (5)

BBC GIVES 100 REASONS
NOT TO BECOME HISTORY

As the BBC prepares for what are expected to be tricky discussions over a new Royal Charter and licence-fee settlement from 2017, the broadcaster has announced plans for 'the most ambitious factual series in its history'.

In an apparent bid to underline the Corporation's public service credentials, senior managers attending 'Does British TV Have a Future?', an industry conference in Cambridge, indicated that executives are currently developing Who Was Who, a series of 100 one-hour documentaries about key figures in British history since the end of the First World War, which will run in five twenty-episode tranches across five years.

Those speaking about the show refused to discuss possible presenters or subjects, saying that the project remained in the early stages of development. But sources suggest that Who Was Who is likely to be a co-production between BBC Worldwide and Ogglebox, an independent company with a strong track record in historical documentaries.

TV insiders, however, are already predicting fierce debate about which historical figures will be included in the series. A leading programme-maker said: 'The problem with this sort of exercise is that there are a few you have to include – Churchill, Elizabeth II – about whom there's nothing new to say. And then the rest depend on your criteria: Agatha Christie or Harold Pinter? Margaret Thatcher and/or Tony Blair? Bobby Moore or David Beckham? And all of those people are white, which is another issue.'

Weaving (2)

Introduction by Henry Gibson

If there were Oscars for ostracism, the hero of George Eliot's 1861 novel would be prominent on the shortlist. Philoctetes, in the play by Sophocles, knew that he had been exiled to an island because of the suppurating wound on his foot. However, when Eliot's gentle 'weaver of Raveloe' is told to go anywhere but there, the instruction seems to come from nowhere, triggered only by a trumped-up charge involving a missing knife.

The book itself also, in a sense, came from left field. *Silas Marner* was a literary gift or accident, of the sort that will often invade as compensation a writer's brain when it is struggling to progress some other, complex project. In the late spring of 1860, when Eliot was travelling through Italy with the critic and philosopher George Henry Lewes, the male George was reading a book about Savonarola, the furiously censorious fifteenth-century Dominican monk in Florence. Lewes suggested to his female first-namesake that the mad monk might make good material for an historical novel.

Eliot eventually took up the suggestion – as *Romola* (1862–3) – but, as the novelist noted in her journal in November 1860, her work on that book was interrupted when 'a new story thrust itself between me and the other book I was meditating'. Something, though, of Fra Savonarola's moral condemnations and vicious theological division of sheep and goats pervades the story of the weaver who is quixotically kicked out of his village.

After 150 years, *Silas Marner* remains a fable for today. Kafka's *The Trial*, with which it has obvious thematic similarities, is perhaps too easily dismissible by Western European readers because the travesty of justice occurs in an Eastern European setting that has become associated with the milieu of Soviet Communism. In *Silas Marner*, the bewilderingly illogical unfairness and judgementalism occur in the heart of the English countryside – a setting as smugly lovely to us as, say, Wiltshire or Buckinghamshire. As a result, what happens to the weaver cannot be spun as something that would only happen somewhere else.

And, if Kafka dramatizes the fundamental fear of modern citizens that bureaucracy or authority may turn against them irrationally and unanswerably, Eliot touches on the equally elemental human insecurity that the community in which we live and work may reject and exile us without reason or appeal. (Such unexplained banishments have remained a trope in novelistic fiction, occurring as recently as Haruki Murakami's *Colorless Tsukuru Tazaki and His Years of Pilgrimage* (Harvill Secker, 2014).)

Contemplating Silas, falsely fingered as a knife-thief, today's reader inevitably thinks of all those in our society for whom the knives have been unjustly out – the long-bailed but never-charged suspects of operations Yewtree and Millpond and – perhaps above all – the employees, in a variety of institutions shamefully including places of higher learning, who have been found guilty and banished through processes as questionable to the humane as they are apparently unquestioned by the mob.

Irony

When Tom, failing to apply to his writing the energy that his two-hour post-lunch sleep should theoretically have given him, saw Ciara's e-mail address in the window, he didn't open it immediately, assuming it to be one of her regular check-ups on his liveliness, which it was but also, when he eventually read it, more specifically sympathetic.

To: tkpimm@chatter.co.uk
From: c.harrison@ume.ac.uk
Subject: Irony?

Hi, Tom. I know how strict you are about the mis-use of the concept of 'irony'. I think, however (have I put 'however' in the right place?), that the data I have attached can only be described as ironic.

As you will see, in the Customer Teaching Feedback Survey for the 2013–14 academic year, you finished in first place in History for Content of Teaching, Enjoyability of Teaching and Attitude to Customers. Admittedly, you finished in what I believe is known as the 'lowest percentile' for Fairness of Marking but most of us agree that asking students to grade their own work is like asking people to tell you how much they weigh. (Yes, Dr Pedant, I know that self-grading encourages over-statement and self-weighing under-statement but you know what I mean?)

The quotes from so many of those formerly known as students – about what they learned from you and how much you helped them – almost made me cry, so you should read them with care. You should, though, read them.

If it is any more consolation, there continues to be, as I am sure you will have heard, widespread horror here at what has been done to you. But, cowardly as it may seem, none of us dare say or do much because the overlords are so scary to deal with. I think that probably qualifies as another irony as well?

Take care.

With love, C xx

She did not mention Ned, either from tact over the divergence in the verdicts or possibly, Tom wondered, from unease over the nature of the charges against the professor. It was most likely, though, that she had considered Ned innocent until proven guilty and now proven innocent. If so, this attitude would make her as antique a relic of the English past as real tennis.

Home Truths (4)

'Do you know about this?'

'What?'

Emma origamied a page of the *Guardian* and held it up across the kitchen table. 'This big new history series.'

Ned glanced at the headline. 'I saw. It's the sort of thing you might hope your agent would tip you off about.'

'Fuck off! You'd have to be in the frame, wouldn't you?'

'Ogg has summoned me next week. Maybe that's what it's about.'

The Literature of False Accusation (8)

Summary: John, a college teacher of a subject that is never specified but seems to be educational theory, is seen in one tutorial and two subsequent meetings with Carol, a somewhat passive student. In the first scene, the teacher is cocky at the prospect of professorial tenure and the purchase of a new bigger house for a family just expanded by a son. John complains about the poor quality of an essay from Carol, in which she has struggled to understand a set-text book written by the professor. When she expresses intellectual insecurity, he puts a consoling arm around her shoulder.

During their next encounter, he is trying to persuade her to withdraw a complaint to the Tenure Committee, alleging that he inappropriately touched her and used sexist and racist language during their tutorial.

By the time of their final meeting, he has lost his job, house and (living alone in an hotel to 'think') possibly his wife. Arrest may soon be added to these problems, as Carol has upgraded her complaint to attempted rape. Just before the final blackout, the sacked academic punches and kicks his former student to the floor and calls her a 'cunt'.

Reader Review: Among the stories of seven denigrated men and one woman (Katharina Blum) on Nod's study list, *Oleanna* was the one that Tom had most resisted. He had seen it in (the play text reminded him) 1992, with Hells, Nod and the First Mrs Marriott, and, recalling that the teacher's downfall was caused by sanctimoniously accusatory pupils, feared that it would prove too close to his own situation.

As a ruined tutor, he now hoped for therapeutic elucidation from David Mamet. It was one of three texts on Reputation 101 (along with Roth and Coetzee) that were set in universities, and as all came out within a decade – *Oleanna* (1992), *Disgrace* (1999) and *The Human Stain* (2000) – the beginnings of the modern madness of amateur arraignment might be dated to campuses at that time.

Tom's memory was that, although his party had been impressed by the savage dialectic of the play, he and Ned had argued that such educational intolerance was specific to America and likely to be isolated even there.

But, re-read in his disgrace of today, the collisions of Carol and John seemed not just globally prophetic of colleges but of culture generally. The student objects to being exposed to facts and opinions in class that make her feel uncomfortable or confused, and demands the removal of certain texts from the syllabus. John's response – 'My job is to provoke you' – would be Tom's creed for teaching even now. And, when the academic refers to the 'accusations' of his student, she insists that: 'They are proven. They are fact.'

Here, decades before Millpond and Traill, were the statutes of the new inquisition. John even uses a legal metaphor to explain the difference between equality and necessity: everyone has the right to a fair trial but it does not follow that a life without becoming a defendant is somehow lacking. (Although now, it might be argued, an appearance in some dock or other was nearly obligatory.)

What surprised Tom was that, having initially seen John as the sympathetic protagonist and Carol as an almost satanic antagonist, he now found himself having more sympathy towards the young woman.

As she railed against male power, he appreciated that John may indeed have assumed a superiority to Carol that was possibly patriarchal. But can teacher and pupil ever be equal? Surely, for education to have any effect, the views of the instructor must be worth more than those of the learner. Imagine a driving lesson conducted on equal terms. And yet, as often on this forced reading course, he now saw that the male hero (and by implication victim) was less agreeable than he first seemed. Was this shift in perspective the result of Tom's contrition or his prescription? Certainly, the dramatist generally seemed to weight the scales in John's favour; it was surely not coincidental that, seven years later, Mamet would make a film of *The Winslow Boy*.

And Tom finally understood the title. This play was from a period – also including *Speed-the-Plow* and *Wag the Dog* – when Mamet gave scripts strange names that were not explained in the dialogue. Now, search engines revealed that Oleanna had been a utopian colony, set up in mid-nineteenth century Pennsylvania by a Norwegian idealist, Ole Bull, who had styled it with a combination of his own name and that of his mother, Anna. The experiment in non-disputatious living had rapidly failed but was immortalized in a Scandinavian folk-song, Americanized and recorded by Pete Seeger.

If Tom were not currently being so careful with money, he would search for 'Oleanna' on iTunes. Unlike Nod, he would never be on *Desert Island Discs*, but could play it in his unproductive study as a reminder of the attempted latter-day Arcadia from which he had just been exiled.

What Are You Celebrating?

First the waiter and then the maître d' asked: 'Are the rest of your party definitely coming?'

If Tom had been there, he would have corrected the verb to 'is'. But the pedant – the pedant, *though* – was absent, which was part of the problem.

Booking the table, Emma had enjoyed the chime of 'eight at eight'. At twenty-five minutes past, with three of the chairs still empty, the five who had arrived were being watched like shop-lifters. On a Friday night, turning away walk-up custom, the restaurant was as conscious of occupancy as a hospital.

Helen had texted that the Pimms were running late because Tom was *a bit wobbly*. Phee kept messaging her sister, who wasn't responding. Emma, who had only invited Dee from a sense of stepmaternal equality, had been surprised when she accepted and so was now uncertain whether to worry at her absence.

So four guests – Ned, to her impressed astonishment, was continuing his sobriety even tonight – were sharing a second bottle of champagne. With finger and thumb, Emma made the half-glass signal to Basham, who was pouring. She had been unable to concede to his frequent pleas to 'Call me Bash.' The ex-detective brimmed full Claire's and Phee's glasses and then his own. Angling the bottle towards Ned, he said: 'I really can't tempt you, Teach? Never had you figured as an Evianista.'

Ned defiantly sipped his elderflower spritzer. 'No, it's not an AA thing,' he lied.

Phee came to his aid: 'It's just if he gets Instagrammed drink-ing champagne, it might get the Twitterati going again.'

'Lines unlikely to be spoken in the nineteenth century,' Ned said. 'A joke which, if certain websites are monitoring my con-versation, I attribute to my absent friend Tom.'

Claire nodded. 'Probably sensible not to be pictured pissed.'

'Yeah. "Offensive" to the "victims" who aren't actually vic-tims,' said Basham. 'Tell me how that works? In my day, when we nicked serial killers, paedos, whatever, we got mullered. Drinking *to* the victims.'

This anecdote stopped the conversation. Emma had been unsure about including the copper in the dinner but he had become a sort of mascot to Ned, who, after reclaiming his phone at the police station, had found a congratulatory voice-mail from Basham, already tipped off by contacts about the outcome.

And Emma had an ulterior motive. Basham, who had become a telly regular telling news programmes why his successors were failing to find famously missing children, reviewed crime fiction for a Sunday tabloid.

Asking if she could send him a super-proof of *Your Love Always*, as soon as she secured the deal, she told him the premise, quoting the stonking opening sentence: *Two days after my beloved wife, Harper, was laid to rest in the earth of the Connecticut town where she had been born, married and killed, she sent me a message. It said: 'Scott, we need to talk. H xx'*

Basham took a big gulp of bubbly, swirled it like mouthwash. 'Okay. Harper is dead. The messages are coming from someone who has stolen her identity online and elsewhere. A chick who's in love with Scott, wants to be his wife, maybe an ex-girlfriend. No, *ex-mistress*. She set the fire that killed Harper. Gabriel is her brother, half-brother, stepbrother? Psycho. Thousand-yard stare, probably Vietnam vet. The chick who's stolen Harper's identity sent bruv to get close to Harper to kill her but he wrecked it all by falling in love with her so she had to be burned. When Scott eventually meets a woman who to all intents and purposes is his dead missus – hairstyle, utility bills, memories – he has to decide if it's the answer to his dreams or the start of his nightmares.'

The ex-cop beat a Hollywood thriller score on the table with his fingers.

'What the fuck?' Emma asked. 'Very funny. You got an American copy from somewhere.'

'What? No. Picking holes in murder stories was what I did for twenty years. It's like asking Pele to be impressed by the tactics in a playground kickabout.'

'Oh, God, I'm so sorry,' blurted Helen, arriving with the stumbling haste of the late, her long winter coat and trailing scarf threatening the drinks on the table. 'Tom's exhausted. He's been trying to write his book and not really sleeping. He thought he'd have a power nap but he woke up feeling groggy, so I've left him. Sorry sorry. I hope you've started.'

She wafted a kiss across the table at Ned, stooped towards Emma's cheek without contact – they had been wary with each other since Manchester – but hugged Phee, her goddaughter. Helen already knew Claire – who was representing Tom in his appeal against UME – but needed the heads-up on Basham, who handed her a glass of champagne as she gave a precis of who the Pimms were and why her husband wasn't here.

'Yeah. Teach told me some. I'm sorry for your bollocks. When it happens in our line, you set yourself up in private security. But I don't suppose in lecturing . . .'

'Not really. No.'

Across the table, Claire asked quietly how Tom was but Helen's answer was loud enough for Emma to hear: 'I think it's the thought of eating in public, to be honest. He gets the sweats, from the medication or the stress, whatever. You know, he has to actually have a towel at the table.'

Though aware of this upsetting symptom from Ned, Emma was pleased that Tom had wimped out. The evening had the feel of the family of a patient who had received a donor heart inviting to dinner the relatives of someone who had died while on the waiting list.

The manager of Luigi's came over and asked again about the missing diners.

'I'm terribly sorry but I think six is it,' Emma said. 'A lurgy and the M40. Sod's law.'

'Right. We will leave you for this moment.' Emma's liberal conscience struggled not to find a parallel between his manner and scenes in *Goodfellas* or *The Godfather*. 'But if we need big table we may move you to the annexe.'

The waiter, before taking their order, asked: 'What are you celebrating?'

In Winslow, apparently, champagne was still an aperitif for

special occasions. Ned looked agitated. Emma said: 'Oh, my husband' – the word was still new enough to make her stumble – 'has just had some good news at his work.'

'Cool.'

Too old to be a student but too young, well-spoken and (forgive her) English to have chosen to be serving food, how he must hate these smug rich people luxuriating in their success. If only he knew. Did he know? (The question that now shrouded everything they did.) If so, he gave no sign.

Emma had thought about proposing a toast but could not work out how to word it. *Clarity*, she considered. Or: *Normality*. And: *Getting Ned Back*. But all of these seemed either too simplistic, triumphalist or, in the last case, ambiguous. She had just rejected *Relief!* as overly two-edged when Phee lifted her glass and said: 'Common sense!'

These words – a neat enough solution – were murmured in a ragged round, followed by the sort of pause that is waiting to be filled with a speech. Emma threw a sympathetically encouraging glance at Ned, who equivocated facially, twitched his shoulders and began: 'As a supportive fellow academic once said in *History Today*: we could all sound smart if we were reading it from an Autocue. So I won't sound smart. But I hope I sound . . . grateful. Because I really am.'

It was audibly his television voice, though lower in both confidence and projection.

'The people here tonight' – his eyes wavered to the two empty chairs – 'The people I *invited* here tonight range from those I've . . . known for around thirty years' – looking at Helen – 'to someone I've worked with once' – a nod to the cop – 'and, of course, Emma, Phee and Claire who, in their different ways got me through it . . . and . . . and, of course . . .'

Ned was staring dumbly ahead. Emma was thinking of the banquet scene in *Macbeth* when, catching the line of Phee's anxious smile and following it across the room, she saw the ghost not of Banquo but Cordelia, shaking rain from her coat at the hole-in-wall cloakroom by the door.

'If Tom were here – and we now have to try to support him in the way that you have all sustained me – he would be as beady as ever for such solecisms as the misuse of the word *literally*. However, it is not a misuse to say that I literally wouldn't be here without all of you.'

In fact, Emma knew, Ned had wanted the assembly to be even more representative. Brimming again with ideas for books and documentaries, he had invited his publisher and producer, but Beane and Ogg both had clashing commitments.

Ned had stayed seated for the speech but now stood as Dee came towards them.

'Hey,' she said. It was a general greeting, meeting no eyes.

Because the earlier arrivals had arranged themselves to exclude gaps, the unoccupied seats were at the far end of the table. Father moved towards daughter in welcome but stopped as she took the space at the far end next to Claire. Ned, at the head of the table, now faced the one remaining social hole, where Tom should have been.

A Pinot Noir and a Sancerre had replaced the champagne. Basham held up both bottles as options to Dee, who smiled tensely and held a glass towards the white.

'I thought you were identical twins,' the detective said.

'We are.'

'Yeah? I've seen closer matches on an identity parade.'

'We needed our space.'

'You missed our toast to your dad for . . .' Again, Emma rejected several suggestions from her mental thesaurus. 'For getting through it.'

'Yes. Well done,' Dee said.

'And his speech thanking everyone for standing by him,' added her sister. Emma had never seen Phee so feline.

The disquieted silence was broken by Phee asking Emma: 'Tobes okay?'

'Yeah. I think so. He's flexi-boarding at Abbey Grove tonight. We'd never send him full-time but this gives him a bit of the best of both worlds.'

Basham had looked bored during the talk of children, as if weighing up whether to say something, which he now did: 'Teach, do you want to know how close it was?'

Claire leaned across to gloss the policeman's presence to Dee.

'I think we probably don't, do we?' said Emma.

Ned shrugged. 'A – sorry, absent friend, *an* – historian is supposed to want all the facts.'

The ex-cop aerated the wine in his glass, checking the legs by candle-flame, until he had the full attention of all six. 'The CPS was gung-ho for it to go before a jury. The Millpond play-book is Yewtree rules squared – better lose in court than risk being monstered for dropping it by people whose phones are smarter than they are. But, just as they were about to charge it, one of the women told them she wouldn't go into the box for them.'

Ned, previously quick to show his feelings vocally and facially, had recently taken on an almost Parkinsonian slowness (two of Emma's older writers had developed the condition), which, Google reassured her, was probably due to his medication for depression and insomnia. But something close to the old speed and needle returned as he asked: 'Really, which one?'

'No names. Just that they lost a witness.'

Sprung at once from recreational to professional mode, Claire challenged Basham: 'You guess that or you know it?'

'I know it. Leaving the job is the only divorce where you never stop talking to each other. I'm not saying you wouldn't have won anyway. But this is the better way to do it.'

After a colossal platter of antipasti to share – and a small vegetarian selection for Dee – Ned stood and said: 'Just going to . . .' Aware that *toilet* was supposed to be wrong, but finding *loo* awkward, people like them now generally left the word unspoken. Helen pushed back her chair and said: 'Snap. Can you show me?' Ned sat down again: 'No. I think they only have the one here. You go first.'

Working out that Ned was terrified of being alone in a

corridor even with Helen, Emma understood that this is what his life would be like now – always making sure that there were witnesses.

In Helen's absence, they talked about Tom, giving Basham a catch-up on what had happened.

'Accused and convicted in secret on the basis of anonymous gossip,' the retired policeman summarized. 'No trial followed by a show-appeal. It makes Millpond look like Solomon. Wouldn't last an afternoon in court.'

'And it may come to that,' Claire told him. 'But, first, we've got a hearing next week with – they all have these titles – the Group Divisional Director of Campus Happiness, or something.'

Helen, returning to the table, passed, in the lavatorial relay, by Ned who murmured: 'I'll call him tomorrow. Or should I pop round? How bad is he?'

'Not great. It's the not sleeping and effect of the pills when he does. I honestly think, if he was here, *were* here, he'd be face down in the bresaola by now.'

While Ned was away, Basham tried to pour wine into his water glass but Emma warned: 'No, he's genuinely off it.'

The fact that her husband wasn't drinking was good but, less happily, made a later attempt at sex (their marriage remained in a strict sense unconsummated) more likely.

During the main courses, the talk was of crime novels Emma was representing or Basham reviewing, Phee's progress on her Ph.D. and scandalous anecdotes about celebrities who had done interviews or shoots for Helen's magazine. The closest the conversation came to the two defendants connected to their number was Phee's mention of having taken a break from Twitter because of the threats of rape and death.

Even when telling her stories from work, Helen was busier on her phone than you expected from a woman of sixtysomething. And, despite ordering coffee, she stood and said, before it was served: 'I'd better go. Tom hasn't replied to my last two texts.'

'He's probably just taken a zonker,' Ned reassured her. He could still only sleep with pill assistance.

'I think you should go back now,' said Basham. His demeanour was immediately changed: sober, in both senses, an instilled skill at taking charge of situations. 'I'll fix you a taxi. Where to? Do you want me to come with you?'

Helen looked shocked and confused. 'Oh, er, no. No, I'll be fine.'

Emma glanced at her husband. He was too preoccupied to respond but she guessed that he was thinking about a world in which men and women had to treat each other with suspicion.

When Helen unfolded notes onto the table, Ned tried to insist it was on him. Since his phone call from the steps of the police station – Emma wept at once and had not stopped by the time he got home – Ned, confident about the resumption of his career, had abandoned his crisis economies. Helen, however, precisely divided the bill by seven and added a tip.

In the commotion of arrangements and goodbyes, Ned got himself next to Dee. When she didn't say anything, he tried a joke: 'I guess you probably expected it to be tea in Wormwood Scrubs, not dinner in Luigi's.'

This brought a scowl from his daughter, so Emma added: 'It means a lot to your dad for you to be here.'

'Sure. Why wouldn't I be?'

When Ned put his hand on Dee's arm, she shivered but accepted the touch.

'Cordy,' he said softly. 'You know, I do accept that this kind of stuff has to be investigated.'

'Well, bully for you. Or is that your friend Tom?'

Thrown off the always careful tread of a stepmother, Emma snapped: 'Oh, for God's sake. Why did you come if you're still being like that?'

Dee answered with the sulky superiority with which, as a teenager, she had regularly tormented her father's new love. 'Look, as far as I can tell from my sister, Daddy's line is that he wasn't a bad guy, he just couldn't keep his pants on . . .'

'Well . . . ,' began Ned.

'We're supposed to be celebrating the fact that he isn't actually going to jail. But you'd hardly raise a glass of champagne to the rest of it.'

Basham seemed not to be listening, which was probably a copper's trick. Helen, getting ready to leave, had stopped, tantalized, which concerned Emma because she thought the Pimms had been led to believe the allegations were malicious fantasy rather than conflicting narratives.

'I've forgiven him,' Emma told Dee. 'Why can't you?'

'Because, as far as I know, he's only done this to you once. He's done it to us twice.'

Helen was leaving.

'Let us know how Tom is,' Emma threw after her.

'Take care,' Ned said.

Ray (4)

Ellis shook the cider up again, making it as fizzy as possible, which, Toby knew from last time, made him even burpier and then more sick.

Wiping off the previous mark with a tissue, Ellis lifted the felt pen and drew a new black line, four or five centimetres below the old one, then shook the bottle again.

'Down to the line!' Ellis said.

As the liquid burned his throat, Toby felt some sick coming up, gulped it back down. As he spluttered and coughed, Oscar and Sweetman started the low whispering growl (so the patrolling prefect wouldn't hear): 'Drink! Drink! Drink!'

Because he had never drunk any until now, Toby couldn't know if what was in the bottle was really cider or only cider. The drink smelled like the jakes but he didn't want to think about why that would be.

Ellis grabbed the bottle and checked the line. 'Rubbish, Ray.'

He handed back the cider. Sweetman started up again the quiet growl. 'Drink! Drink! Drink!'

When Toby felt the hot horrible burning stuff at the back of his throat, he tried to choke it down, but there was too much and it was too late. Ellis held the wastebasket, lined with a supermarket plastic bag, and, as Toby chucked into it, pushed his head down into the mess.

'Pissed!' the ringleader hissed. 'Pissed again!'

Ellis, Sweetman and Oscar laughed, then started up the chant, as loud as they dare go: 'Ray Pissed! Ray Pissed! Ray Pissed! Ray Pissed!'

Ellis silenced them, making them wait for the last part of the game.

'Who does Ray know who's a ray pissed?' he asked.

Although he could not really see through his tears and the sting in his eyes that came with the sick, Toby knew that all three boys would be pointing at him. He felt Ellis grabbing his chin.

'Ray? Ray? Who do you know who's a Ray Pissed?'

His voice – high, sore, breaking – didn't sound like his own as he gave the only answer that would bring a stop until next time.

'Daddy,' Toby whisper-sobbed.

'Who, Ray? Who?'

'Daddy.'

What Minds Do (3)

She found him in the spare bedroom. There had been no answer to her shouts from the hall and on the stairs. When the bed was empty, she checked the bathroom, even though the door was open.

Her next hope was that, unable to sleep, he had tried Mind-fulness. Sometimes, she would get home late – on press day or after book group – and find him in his Tutankhamun cocoon,

397

snoring, with one headphone dislodged, spilling out the soothing tones of the guy who told you not to worry about your
mind wandering.

Nudging the dimmer switch to its lowest setting in case of
waking him suddenly, she smiled at the image she had anticipated, but then registered the differences, noting the absence of
sound at the same time as spotting the froth around his mouth.

With the unthinking instinct of an emergency stop – even
though this was a move she had never learned or rehearsed –
Helen dialled 999 on her mobile and answered the questions:
no, yes, I think so, yes, not sure.

Can you wake him? Is he breathing? If I tell you what to do,
would you be able to move him? Is there any sign of what he
might have taken? Can you tell how many?

The antidepressants were in blister packs, like when she was
on the pill, printed with the initial letters of the days:
S,S,M,T,W,T,F. All except the last three days of the pack were
punctured, which, as today was Friday, meant either that he had
stopped taking his medication or that he had swallowed up to
three and a half weeks of tablets.

Tom's wrist, where she was sure she could see a weak pulse,
felt warm to the touch. Curled beside him, she saw the white
envelope neatly lined up next to where the pills had been. In the
feeble light, desperate for her reading glasses but helpless to
locate them, she managed to make out the typed sentence
upside down: A Letter To My Family And Friends.

Non-Identical

People would often tell her that they had once read a really interesting book about identical twins, or seen an article in a
newspaper reporting the latest research on *them*. It was well-
meaning, an attempt to show sensitivity and interest, in much
the way that her black friends and colleagues in England had
endured months of being congratulated on the election of Presi-

dent Obama, but with the same objection that it reduced you to a single visual aspect.

Phee, anyway, tended to avoid the literature on her condition because she already knew as much as she wanted to about being permanently impersonated. Writers on the subject, she suspected, concentrated on the alleged psychological difficulties (eating disorders, relationship issues, the inevitable identity crises of adolescence horrifically multiplied) and the weird responses of others: the men who became obsessed with shagging the two of you alternately, or ideally simultaneously, in order to find out, in a joke they always thought they were the first to make, *whether everything's identical.*

Without reading the research, she guessed that matching sisters were more affected than doubled brothers. Although your bodies were genetic copies, you might expose them to different levels of stress, chocolate, alcohol or contraception. Self-conscious about gained weight or a zit erupting on your cheek, you came down to breakfast to face a trimmer, clear-skinned version of yourself, a bitchy Doreen Gray who hangs around the kitchen getting prettier. When a boy finds you unattractive, another guy – worse, sometimes, the same one – is drooling over your duplicate. It was a wonder that single-egg sisters didn't all turn out to be serial killers.

Except that the Marriott twins would be a perfect study for anyone seeking to disprove that personality and destiny were genetically determined. Since early in childhood, they had been uncut, cracked mirror images of each other. Dee, Phee assumed, had, unlike her, read every word ever published on the topic of identical twins. And her sister believed their father was a sex criminal.

At his funeral – their parents were in an age-range where you could not avoid imagining such an event – a joint eulogy would be expected from the sisters, a solemn version of their verse tribute at his sixtieth. Now, however, she imagined that they would follow each other to the altar – the speaking order decided, obviously, by Dee – and scowl through the other's account.

Was there some mystical link between writing and the night? Bed was the place where most people read and, from Claire's experience of writers both as friends and clients, the majority of books seemed to be written in spare bedrooms.

It would be impossible to sleep now in Tom's impromptu study, unless you were able somehow, snake-like, to coil yourself around the literature. Shelves filled every wall, the volumes squeezed so tightly that the spines distorted, blurring titles and writers. Trembling towers of hardbacks and paperbacks rose from the desk and the floor around it. In this wall of words was a hollowed-out space where Tom wrote and, on the books closest to him, two surnames recurred: *Days of Fire: Bush and Cheney in the White House, Hilary Clinton: Her Way, 41: A Portrait of My Father* by George W. Bush.

She was reading sideways the subtitle of a book about Bill Clinton when Tom entered. Letting Claire in, Helen had said that he was resting. The usual effects of shock and hospitalization – paleness and thinness – showed in his frame and face. She noticed the coldness of the hand he offered to be shaken.

The better of the two chairs was at the desk and he offered it to her but she feared death by published landslide. Tom wriggled himself into the gap as precisely as a racing driver fitting into the cockpit.

He lifted a finger gently towards the closest skyscraper of biographies. 'You can probably guess the book I'm not writing.'

'*Not* writing?'

'My concentration's shot. Halfway through every sentence, I start arguing with Special or Savlon or the Vice Chancellor. And I always thought the word *nap* was up there with jodhpurs among words I'd never need. But now I have one every afternoon. And it doesn't help that I keep imagining every presidential historian is already writing my book. Some bugger has to – I mean, to kick out George III and then use the Bushes and Clintons as two rotating Royal families.'

'Then that sort of answers the question about how you are. Tom, if we take them on, there are going to be a ton of meetings and a lot of bollocks.'

'And what's the point if I'm going to top myself and leave you to claw your fees from my estate?' She took his surviving bluntness as evidence of his recovery. 'Don't worry, I'm in it until the bill. You know my view on clichés. So can *I* be 110 per cent clear that this was not – I hate even to say it – a cry for help? It was that other, odder one – I did it to show them what they'd done to me. Which assumes the existence of an afterlife with viewing facilities, in which I don't actually believe. When I came round, all I thought was what a stupid selfish fucker I'd been, which seems to be the answer the head doctors want.'

'And Ned's . . . *outcome* – that isn't difficult for you?'

'Finland. If Nod had fallen off his horse, I'd come back for him. And vice versa. Although we're probably not supposed to mention that particular Australian pop hit any more.'

Pedantry (2)

Your correspondent [March 5] complains that the planned BBC historical series Who Was Who should correctly be titled Who Was Whom. He is wrong. As a useful rule, who is used when the word he/she could be substituted: i.e., 'it was Helen who found me.' (*She* found me.) However, whom is preferable if the alternative wording would be him/her: i.e., 'Helen is my wife, whom I have loved for 34 years.' (I have loved *her*.)

Following this formula, a possible other name for the retrospective documentaries would be Who Was He? / Who Was She? rather than Who Was Him? / Who Was Her? Therefore, Who Was Who is appropriate.

The luminaries included are likely to include more hes than shes, if the bias of history is followed; more shes than hes, if the selectors bow to current ideological pressures.

The series' name, however, is syntactically exact – an occurrence that may very well be historic. And not, incidentally, historical.

Dr Tom Pimm
Winslow, Bucks

The Network (2)

'Prof, you're looking very well. Percy's sorted your coffee. Good, good. If you move those scripts, you can sit there. So, settled out of court, which must be better for everyone in the end.'

'Er, well, hang on, Dom. If it works out this way, the innocent pay all the costs. Which you may bear in mind when Emma negotiates the next fees.'

'Whoah! Times is hard, Professor. And Emma's fine is she – you and Emma?'

'Yes. But can I just . . . Settled out of court implies some kind of deal. In this case, the CPS rejected the claims.'

'Decided not to bring them to court, yes. Look, Ned, I've had a meeting with the network.'

'Good. Since the verdict, I've had this burst of energy. I've brought you an episode breakdown on *The Bonfire of the Sanities* and I saw in the papers about the hundred hours . . .'

'Indeed.'

'. . . on historic, historical – historic and historical, I suppose – figures . . . is that happening?'

'We're still dotting the zeroes but it's happening . . .'

'Obviously, these days, it wouldn't be appropriate to have one voice – the *Civilisation* model is too monocultural – but I'd certainly like to make a pitch for some of the dead white males and even females . . .'

'Whoah!'

'No, I realize it's early days on that one.'

'Ned, I'm not going to hide behind my grandmother's skirts. As you know, the network has slightly reconfigured the pyramid recently, lines of responsibility and reporting have been redrawn. And I sense an energy to refresh the schedules, rest some established formats . . .'

'Dom, as you would say, whoah. I hope this isn't going where . . .'

'Ned, I can't lie to you on this one . . .'

'Oh, so you do on most other occasions, then?'

'What? The roundabout will turn. It will turn again. But, at the moment, there's a feeling from the network that, while the dust settles, it's a good opportunity to bring on some new blood.'

Bullying is Like Beauty

Because Workplace Harmony had ruled that Tom should not be forced to walk through History – a rare university stipulation with which he seemed happy to comply – the hearing had been arranged for a borrowed meeting room in Engineering, presumably on the basis that the traditional divide between the artistic and the scientific would avoid any risk of recognition.

All lawyers with a few years on the clock have dealt with suicidal clients. Discreetly watching Tom as he flicked distractedly through a metallurgy magazine in the waiting area, Claire wondered if she would have guessed, if unaware of it, his recent attempt at death. He was slightly less keen to see everything as a feed for a punchline but looked otherwise unchanged, which, she felt, might be misleading: he was the sort of person who hid his true feelings behind an armour of attitude. Even if you had met him in the minute before he tried to kill himself, you might not have guessed.

'Dr Pimm? Ms Ellen?'

They looked up and nodded.

'David Wellington.'

The disconcerting moment of a name and voice becoming flesh, like seeing a radio broadcaster on TV. Tom's parody of the

Friday suicide calls had been cruelly acute. Tall and deeply tanned, with thick dark hair containing a suggestion of gel, Wellington had the professional appearance more of PR than HR. They followed him along corridors to the institutional soundtrack of a necklaced lanyard rattling against his jacket buttons. Intermittently, he used the plastic card to green-light them through security doors. On almost every noticeboard were posters showing bright red telephones and a number to phone to report a colleague for an offence of some kind. The only alternative decoration advocated the banning of various speakers, allegedly pro-Zionist or trans-phobic, from campus.

With another swipe of his ID, Wellington admitted them to a steel and glass box with a label reading: Ferdinand de Lesseps.

'Suez Canal?' wondered Claire.

Wellington smiled, a frequent reflex: 'I'm pretty sure you're right.'

In a strip by the door, a shimmer of digital letters revealed that the room was reserved for two hours. The usual choices of bottled water and silver vacuum flasks stood on the table. Claire sometimes felt she spent her life checking her reflection in hot-drink pots. Tom volunteered to pour, but she took over when she saw his shaking hands making a mess of the peppermint tea.

'So,' Wellington began. 'This is a hearing, quite literally so. My role is mainly to listen. You have communicated your concerns about the process you underwent. I will listen to what you have to say and consider any next steps, going forward. This meeting will not be verbatimed' – Tom shuddered, at, she guessed, the irregular word – 'but I will make written notes, as may you. So – the time is yours.'

'Thank you, Mr Wellington,' Claire said.

'I'd hope I might be David.'

'You're not a Dave? Like our Prime Minister,' Tom asked.

'You know what? I actually don't think I am.'

The smile again, but as mechanical as a timer-light in an empty house.

Claire said, by prior agreement with Tom: 'I'd like to begin by setting on the record that Dr Pimm has recently been ill with a potentially life-threatening condition.'

Claire had formulated this phrase while representing a noxious entrepreneur who had launched defamation proceedings over claims of mistreating an ex-lover, but had tried to take his life after finding out how much dirt the prosecution had on him. For some reason, *life-threatening condition* always made people think cancer or cardiac, gilding the defendant as strong and brave, rather than suicidal depression, from which some judges and juries seemed to infer weakness and even guilt.

'I'm very sorry to hear that,' said Wellington, and, a credit to either his personality or profession, genuinely sounded so, although a corporate reflex added: 'The university regularly checked in with Dr Pimm during his suspension. He never mentioned illness.'

'Does that surprise you?' Tom asked.

'I can see why you would say that.'

'My first point,' Claire continued, 'is that the dismissal of Dr Pimm is the most serious abuse of legal process that I have seen outside of a developing world dictatorship.'

Wellington fiddled with his wrists, revealing cuff links, which he shuffled for a while like dice.

'So. On that,' he began. 'It can't be an abuse of legal process because we have never pretended that it *was* a legal process.'

Tom's laugh triggered the WH director's grin. Claire, contrastingly, frowned. 'Just run that by me again. It can't have been illegal because you were ignoring the law?'

'I don't think that's quite what I'm saying. It was an internal disciplinary process. Clearly the burden of proof is lower than in the judicial system.'

She had asked Tom to speak as little as possible, but her doubts about being obeyed were now confirmed.

'So, let me get this straight,' her client said. 'Suppose one of my students – one of my *former* students – were consistently late with essays or failed to attend class and, instead of talking to them or putting them on report, I placed them on trial in front of their classmates, they were found guilty and we executed them. You would say that their parents had no cause to complain because the university had never pretended it was a court of law?'

A passer-by catching sight of Wellington through the glass would have thought that he was struggling to dissolve an obdurate gobstopper. Having weighed the consequences of various responses, he said: 'So. On that. No, the difference is that, in that scenario, you would not have followed the correct disciplinary procedures of the university. Whereas, in your case, they were obeyed. I have personally checked that there were no faults in the process.'

From even her limited experience of pleading in court, Claire had to resist the temptation to stand up in objection. 'But – which is why we are here – we find the process full of faults from beginning to end . . .'

'So. On that,' Wellington interrupted, 'we are speaking at cross-purposes. What I am saying is that the agreed process was correctly carried out to the letter.'

Claire, as she wouldn't dare in court, laughed. 'But if a process is incompetent or inappropriate, then it's irrelevant if it was correctly carried out.'

A few more attempts to swallow the sweet. 'I can see why you might say that.'

'What I find most incomprehensible from a legal perspective is that, at a time when colleagues were being invited to make secret anonymous accusations against Dr Pimm, no one was ever invited to give evidence in defence of him.'

'So. On that, no evidence entered into his defence would have been relevant.'

Claire again had physically to resist the temptation to rise, turning the energy into a twist towards Tom, who trumped her own exaggerated double-take. Facing Wellington again, she asked: 'And a defence would be irrelevant because the process wasn't legal?'

'I don't think that's what I'm saying. Following a recent

root-and-branch review of the UME code of conduct, it was decided that a presumption of truth would be applied to complaints in this area.'

'This area being . . . ?'

'B & H. Yes.'

'Although my client . . .'

'Was accused only of B. Yes. And, of course, also Insubordination.'

'I'm not fucking having that,' Tom, from nowhere, declared.

Claire was about to refer again to her client's recently fragile health when Tom laughed and she understood what had happened, although the panic was only slightly reduced. 'Dr Pimm's sense of humour,' she reassured Wellington, 'has caught me out a few times as well.'

The bureaucrat's face was expressionless. 'Some people might argue that has been part of the problem.'

Scribbling a note about this comment possibly suggesting further bias in the process, Claire said: 'As far as I can see, you are saying that, if someone defined themselves as a victim, they were accepted as one?'

'So. On that, what I would say to you is – bullying is like beauty.'

In speech that consisted of administrative euphemisms, quotations from online modules and the anachronistically adolescent tic of *so on that*, this one phrase had the jagged poetry of a song lyric or the title of a film that won prizes at festivals.

'Wow,' said Tom. 'If I get nothing else from today, I've got the title of my memoirs.'

Wellington frowned. 'Are you writing them?'

'I don't have much else to do at the moment.'

Claire's raised hand advised a silence, which she filled with the bewildered echo: 'Like beauty?'

'So. On that. Bullying tends to be in the eye of the beholder. If someone thinks it's happened, then it has.'

Claire tried out in her mind a comment about how much cheaper and quicker the court system would be if justice adopted that principle, but dropped it when she remembered that there was a category of allegations – including those recently made against a member of this department – for which intelligent people did suggest that standard.

Her calculation left a gap, which Tom saw. 'That's interesting. So, if I happen to think that Dr Kevan Neades is a sycophantic mediocrity, then he is?'

Claire's grinning head-shake tried to pass this off as a waggishly lovable comment from her client. Wellington seemed to be struggling with his professionally required open-mindedness. 'Might that not be an example, Dr Pimm, of the type of personal comment that led here?'

'But there is a point there,' Claire said. 'If anyone who said anything about Dr Pimm was assumed to be telling the truth, then why would the same principle not apply to what Dr Pimm said about others?'

Unable to prevent a checkmate grimace, Wellington bought time by stirring and test-sipping his tea. 'So, on that, the university has instituted, in certain areas, a policy of sympathy towards the victim.'

'*Alleged* victim.' A flashback to the interview suite with Ned.

'Well, no, these allegations have been proved.'

'Really? When and how?'

'When we accepted them as true.'

Tom's mocking guffaw. 'It wouldn't surprise me if I stepped out of here into a street in Prague with corpses swinging from the lampposts.'

Claire got the reference; Wellington, if he did, made no acknowledgement, focusing on her as if to pretend Tom wasn't there. 'So. On that, er . . . er . . .' Eye-slide to her name on paper. 'Claire. Suppose someone were to call you a, er, er, *black* whatever. Or a, er, woman whatever. Surely the fact that you have felt offence makes irrelevant whether or not they intended it?'

Wellington had whispered the reference to race. He seemed terrified by her being black, the reactions of English liberals in this respect strangely indistinguishable from those of apartheid-era white South Africans.

'I don't understand,' she said, genuinely, rather than rhetorically. 'As far as I am aware, no allegation of sexism or racism has been made against my client.'

'So. On that, I was giving examples of sensitivities on which someone might be their own judge. The same could apply to a lack of professional respect or to resistance of authority, of which Dr Pimm was found guilty.'

'By a secret court on undeclared charges! And you still seem to be equating sexism and racism with – which is all this was – squabbling and ego-rattling between colleagues.'

'Who,' Tom added, 'were frequently useless, rude or otherwise infuriating.'

'In your opinion, Dr Pimm,' Wellington said.

'Yes, in my opinion. But you've just said that, if I found them stupid or rude or annoying, then they were.'

'I don't think that's quite what I said. But after what happened with Professor Padraig Allison, the University instituted a policy of zero tolerance on this kind of thing.'

'This kind of thing?' challenged Tom, all four words matchingly emphatic. Claire tried to moderate his volume and tone with a warning touch on the arm. 'Are you seriously suggesting a connection between sexually abusing and raping students and a bit of staff-room argy-bargy over how history should be taught?'

'So. On that, the University has recently actioned a root-and-branch overview of rules on duty of care.'

Approaching the conclusion that she could be no more use to Tom in this world of grandiloquent contradiction than a lawyer would have been to Alice in Wonderland, Claire let the dialogue of mutual incomprehension continue.

'And don't you have,' Tom asked the WH Director, 'a duty of care to avoid staff having to work with incompetent colleagues?'

Wellington smiled and nodded like a politician who has

been asked a hoped-for question. 'I can see why you would say that. So, on that, the University has no specific rules against incompetency, but it does have them in the area of B & H.'

'The University has no specific rules against incompetency,' Claire repeated to him with a sceptical tremolo. 'Isn't that like . . .' – she considered but abandoned *a church having no specific rules on faith* as the Church of England was such an example – ' . . . like a hospital having no specific rules on hygiene?'

'I can understand why you would think that.'

'Also, as Dr Pimm raised in his appeal . . .'

'To be exact, it was an informal hearing.'

'As my client raised in his hearing with Professor Gibson, this *process* of yours seems to assume a constant saintliness in the behaviour of the complainants in the workplace.'

'That observation has been noted. The University is learning hard lessons from this process.'

'You're admitting that the process was flawed?'

'I don't think that's what I'm saying.'

'So. On that,' Claire dared to say. 'I'm fascinated to know if you, Mr Wellington, have ever lost it with anyone in the office or, indeed, has anyone ever lost it with you?'

'So. On that, I myself recently had a 360.'

Claire and Tom bounced bemused looks between them. She could only imagine some variety of extreme manicure, probably intimate.

'That's a 360-degree management evaluation by colleagues who are encouraged by anonymity to speak frankly. And, when I got the feedback sheets, one member of the team had written: "David can be a bit tetchy sometimes." And you know what my thought was?'

'Was it, "Welcome to the workplace, you hyper-sensitive self-obsessive. You're probably no day at the beach yourself all the time so get over it"?' Tom disingenuously guessed.

'What? No. I told myself: "David, you need to be less tetchy." '

Claire saw the flaw in this. 'But you'd have to watch yourself with everyone, all the time, because the anonymity means that you don't know who it was who thinks you're short with them?'

'Yes, indeed. The benefit is that I've become less tetchy in general.'

'Mr Wellington,' Claire asked. 'Is it worth pointing out that Dr Pimm has recently finished in first place in most categories – for what I believe is the third year running – in the student feedback survey?'

Wellington looked puzzled, possibly because of no longer recognizing the word *student*. He unnecessarily smoothed his hair. 'So. On that, Dr Pimm's professional performance would not be a defence against this kind of thing. It's a frequent regret in our department that we have to let very good – even brilliant – people go.'

The Television of False Accusation

One night in the week that he was officially declared innocent – although he did not experience the expected physical sense of suspicion lifting – Ned watched a television programme alone. Emma was in her study, writing transatlantic e-mails. The deal on *Your Love Always* had apparently become more complex than expected.

During the adverts before the drama started, Ned meticulously tilted just half a glass of Crozes-Hermitage from the bottle on the coffee table. There had been too many nights of waking up at 2am, bone-frozen in front of a television showing an old film.

He had been drawn to *The Lost Honour of Christopher Jefferies* by the familiar chime of the title and a prurient memory of the name that had replaced Katharina Blum's. At the time when the Bristol landlord was arrested by police investigating the murder of a young architect who was one of his tenants – and then found guilty within hours by broadcasts and newspaper reports – Ned had been one of the mob, luxuriating in the details of the creepy bachelor schoolteacher (code for the crime that was the twenty-first century media's joint favourite with murder) who reputedly liked to read dodgy classical erotic verse to his pupils and collected French films. The clinching giveaways of a killer, though, were a blue-rinsed combover and grammatical pedantry dispensed in a campish drawl. As a sophisticated consumer of news, Ned knew that such stuff would not be printed unless it a) came from the police and b) was entirely true.

But, though the first qualification may have been in place, the second categorically wasn't. Jefferies had been completely innocent and received apologetic pay-outs from a railway station rack of newspapers. Another stage in his rehabilitation was this contrite bio-pic on peak-time TV. The programme was clearly supposed to make the accusing rabble repent their false conviction but Ned didn't have to. He was, by this time, no longer a member of the mob but one of its quarries.

As such a viewer, he found in the play reassuring proof that dark, tense, toxic smoke could billow with no spark beneath. And, whereas a Hollywood version of the same story would have made the central character an ex-marine headteacher married to the Secretary of State, Jefferies remained a slightly fey, strange, spiky loner, very well played by one of those English character actors who – after years of being cast in small roles as solicitors, minor diplomats and BBC managers – finally gets their chance when a casting director lines up a newspaper cutting with *Spotlight* and sees a similarity in the features.

But, although the Böll novella had been a favourite on his disgrace-related reading list, the allusion to it in the TV title seemed surprising, as Katharina was a murderer and the landlord wasn't. And, although Ned painfully identified with the scenes in which Jefferies was accused and interviewed, there was no comparison between their exonerations. In most cases – except for those men you read about who were inconclusively arrested every few years over the sudden death of an earlier wife – murder was something you either had or hadn't done, and, once you were not guilty, someone else was; dropped suspicion brought only sympathy and guilt from those who had distrusted you. With sexual allegations, you were the only suspect, and a declaration of innocence had no impact on some doubters, who could continue to believe that you had been the lucky beneficiary of the absence of evidence or competent prosecution.

What the Jefferies case consolingly showed, however, was that baseless, smokeless completely false accusation did occur. All the landlord had done was to be unmarried, with funny speech and hair and a liking for high culture and this was enough, in the times in which he lived, to be assumed likely to have killed a young woman.

During the last commercial break, he heard Emma going quietly to bed without coming in to say goodnight.

Cuttings (6)

UME TO SEEK NEW VC

The University of Middle England has pledged to 'scour the whole world – not just the world of education' to seek a successor to Sir Richard Agate, who has resigned as Vice Chancellor with immediate effect. Sir Richard, 64, has been appointed first President of the newly created Fair Finance Foundation, a body created and funded by the leading UK banks with the aim of 'improving the public image of the financial sector'.

In his three years at UME, the former senior Whitehall civil servant instituted a controversial policy summarized in his introductory address to staff as 'monetizing knowledge'. The phrase caused much concern across the Aylesbury and Coventry campuses and unrest also resulted from reductions in academic staff and budgets at the same time that the teaching loads of remaining staff were significantly increased. Sir Richard was also forced to deny a series of allegations that staff perceived as expensive or uncooperative were forced out through dubious disciplinary processes. He was embarrassed by the leaking of an e-mail demanding 'brand loyalty' and 'avoidance of dissent' from members of teaching staff.

Union leaders and other detractors further alleged that the quantity and salaries of non-teaching management multiplied significantly during the regime of a man who, after leaving the Civil Service, built up an impressive portfolio of public service and private sector posts. His positions have included being a non-executive board member at the BBC Trust, the weapons manufacturer International Peace Solutions Ltd, the bank HSBC and Arts Council England.

A representative of the UCU (University and College Union), a trade body representing professionals in further education, said: 'We urge the university to look now for an education specialist to fill the post. The brief and unsuccessful tenure of Sir Richard Agate was a perfect example of the danger of the fashion for inflicting on academic institutions those whose experience lies in other areas. It was not for nothing that a colleague nick-named him FUMO.'

Sources on campus explained that the acronym stands for: F*** Up, Move On.

Further Action

You can tell a lot about someone in England by what they offer you to drink. According to canteen chat, there were parts of London now where officers visiting victims of burglary were commonly asked: *red, white or craft beer?* Usually it was *tea or coffee?*, although you had to pace yourself when working through a witness list because even the clearly innocent seemed, for some reason, to become flustered when a police officer asked to use their loo.

Providing no choice, Mrs Hessendon Castle said *I've made*

us a pot of tea because that was what a woman of around sixty served at half-past four in the afternoon in a house in a Notting Hill mews. Heather was at least offered the option of milk or lemon in a drink that smelled like bath salts.

'If you're hoping I can remember anything else, I fear you've wasted a trip,' her hostess said. 'My daughter even got me one of those "box sets" of *I, Claudius* and sat me down through the opening episode but nothing else came back.'

'Thank you, that's great,' said Heather, taking a teacup, her hand feeling huge and clumsy against the fragile china. She noticed on the woman's tanned left fingers, as vivid as surgical scars, the white stripes where she had once worn rings. 'No, that isn't why I'm here today.'

'Oh, I see.'

The list of career development courses sent round by the training department included Breaking Bad News. Because the work of a detective may include telling a parent that the corpse of their child has been found by a morning dog-walker, Heather had signed up. Since transfer to Millpond, her refresher modules on Taking Sensitive Evidence had more often been relevant but she had soon discovered that this squad also sometimes had to deliver unwanted information.

'Mrs Hessendon Castle . . .' Heather left a space for an invitation to more casual address, which never came. 'As you know, we have investigated your complaint of historic serious sexual assault. We passed a file to the Crown Prosecution Service but they concluded that no prosecution should follow in this matter.'

'Oh. Oh, I see.'

In other cases of giving notice of non-pros, Heather had experienced angry crying or screaming but, with a woman of this sort, the absence of tears was as ingrained as the provision of tea.

'It's very important to understand, Mrs Hessendon Castle, that this doesn't mean that you were disbelieved or that anyone thought you were lying. But someone has to make a decision on whether there is what we call a "realistic prospect of conviction".'

'Well, I'm sure, but that doesn't seem to have applied to some of the cases one has read about in the newspapers. They seem sometimes to have gone to court with almost no evidence at all.'

'I can understand why you would say that. I suppose we would argue that the outcome of earlier cases could affect the decisions in later ones, so comparisons may not be exact.'

Her eye, professionally primed to seek revealing detail at the address of a suspect, instinctively swept these innocent premises as well. On a corner table was a shrine of pride, containing framed photographs of family members gathered around tiered or candled cakes, but the only adult males were of ages to be the woman's father (in a black and white snap), son or son-in-law. From this – and the Polo Mint lines above the knuckles – she deduced a divorcee rather than a widow, but one who had failed to meet anyone else. Half-bottles were precariously balanced in a wine rack in a corner of the room.

'I can understand your disappointment,' Heather said. 'But, as I said, no one is suggesting that you were not raped. Just that it is impossible to be sure of proving that you were in court.'

'My daughter says that I should have done something at the time. But it's lose–lose, isn't it? When there might have been evidence, the police wouldn't have listened to me. And, now that the police will listen to me, there isn't evidence.'

'Yes. That is often the issue in historic cases.'

'If you don't mind my asking, you're – what? – mid-twenties?'

'Up a bit.'

'Like my daughter.' A flicker of the eyes to one of the framed pictures. 'I think your generation's much luckier. The lines are clearer.'

A montage of moments, at most times forgotten, from a hostel, a hotel and a flat. There was one former boyfriend and plenty of men in pubs or at parties who could have been brought to court under the new Met and CPS thresholds, and she had been on the team of a DCI who treated female colleagues as if auditioning his next mistress. These men were scumbags but how far would she want to see them punished? She had refused her boss's advances but not reported them because of the concern that it would cost her promotion. She had gone on to have mainly good sex with men who were loving and faithful until they weren't. Was she a victim of crime or of life?

'It's a complex area,' Heather said, 'that remains a learning curve.'

At this meaningless sentence, Mrs Hessendon Castle nodded. Heather reassured her of her lifelong anonymity; she could choose to identify herself but, given the outcome of the investigation, must be aware of the risk of inviting an action for defamation by making any public allegations against her alleged attacker.

'I understand that, Detective Sergeant.'

'Is there anything else you want to ask?'

'Just that my solicitor was convinced that mine was not the only allegation against him.'

'I can only discuss your own case with you.'

They exchanged a frictionless handshake and stilted thanks.

Raîson d'être

Tom had seen marriages – Nod's an obvious example – in which the trust had gone. He and Hells, thank God, had avoided that but he learned – returning from the hospital, wan and hoarse from the intubation and emergency emetic – that he had introduced another sort of suspicion between them.

Sleeping late after taking one of the antidepressants now dispensed every few days in miniature plastic bottles – presumably containing a total dosage that would not prove fatal if swallowed together – he would feel his wife kicking him or raising the radio volume too loud in order to establish that he was dosing rather than comatose. In the interest of regular scrutiny, he had been allowed back into the main bedroom, his alternating spells of restlessness and snoring now welcomed as evidence of continued existence.

If showering or shitting took marginally longer than the time now obviously recorded somewhere as acceptable (constipation apparently an established complication of the uppers), Helen or (if back from one of her startlingly short college terms) Becky would tweak the handle repeatedly several times, like a frustrated defecator at a railway station. 'It's all right,' he shouted, when he guessed what was happening. 'I'm wanking, not hanging myself.' Should traffic or a phone call from Nod delay him at the supermarket, a text soon pinged in from Helen (who seemed increasingly to have a deal to work at home), checking that she had included on the shopping list an ingredient that they both knew she already had. If he failed to reply immediately, a phone call would follow. It felt too malicious to test what would happen if he failed to answer that. While he tried to work on the Bush–Clinton book in the spare bedroom, Helen was in and out like the maid in a Noël Coward play, offering another cup of coffee before the previous one had even cooled. It was a common observation that the geriatric becomes a second toddler, constantly watched as a protection against risk; but so, he had discovered, did the survivor of a suicide attempt.

After a week of this tender surveillance, as they lay in bed after Saturday morning sex that had felt like an act of medicinal charity from Helen, she said: 'I promise I'm not going to keep endlessly checking but tell me you won't ever try it again.'

He squeezed her hand where it rested on his chest. 'No.'

'Oh, Tom, I'm not stupid. I know you and your word games. *No* you can't promise me or *no* you won't do it again?'

'What. Oh, I wasn't trying to be clever . . .'

'Gosh. You are ill, then.'

'Ha ha. No, I meant: no, it's one pill at a time for me now and, hopefully, eventually, a tablet will just be something I play Angry Birds on. When they were making me sick in A & E, I suddenly understood what the consequence would have been.'

'Never seeing your gorgeous wife and two beautiful children again?'

Her playful tone held a serious meaning, as did his: 'Look, I have to be honest about this . . .'

'Tom Pimm, I'm warning you . . .'

She tweaked his nipple painfully, women oddly never suspecting how sensitive men's could be.

'Obviously, all that was a factor. But, actually, in the end, it was the thought of them putting out some statement about me on a press release. Special announcement. Although, at the beginning, I had that ridiculous fantasy of doing it to cause them trouble, I hadn't factored in their still being around. Before you ask, yes it is *their* not them . . .'

'You are getting better . . .'

'I'd left a letter barring them from the funeral but I'd never thought about the obituary quotes. So you never have to worry about me doing myself in again until I've outlived those stolid second-raters and career-creepers.'

England

Her Majesty The Queen has chosen to confer on the following the title of Knight Commander of the Most Excellent Order of the British Empire (KBE), the holder of which will be entitled to style himself Sir.

NEADES, Dr Kevan Michael, Vice Chancellor, University of Middle England. For Services to Business and to Further Education.

Further Action (2)

'Are you happy for me to call you Jess?'

'Yeah. And I call you Heather?'

'Sure. Jess, we explained to you when you decided not to be a participant in any court proceedings that there might be other investigations in progress that could still lead to the accused facing action?'

'Yeah. I got that.'

Like a walker plotting a course with a downhill finish, Heather had left the easier of the two non-pros conversations for second.

'So, in the circumstances, this is just a courtesy visit to tell you that, after consideration of a range of evidence by the Crown Prosecution Service, no further action will be taken against the accused.'

'Okay.'

The top-floor flat in Pimlico had the clean minimalism that only a kidless couple can achieve. Two pairs of Nikes – one twice the size of the other – were the only clutter beside the front door. His and hers toothbrushes and razors for face and legs stood in matching tumblers in the steel and glass bathroom she had to use when the mug of coffee pooled with the earlier cup of tea.

'Do you think it would have made a difference if I'd been willing to testify?'

'I can't answer that, Jess.'

Almost all the wall space was filled with shelves containing DVDs and, ageing the residents, CDs, but mainly books. A section behind Jess's head – *Charles I, Charles II, Elizabeth I, George III* – resembled a royal cemetery of gaudy gravestones.

'And you don't have to tell me this,' Heather continued. 'But would you be willing to say why you changed your mind?'

Jess caught a handful of long hair, scrunched and swung it, a nervous gesture that probably dated from childhood. 'I . . . had had to be talked into it . . . *originally* . . .'

'By us you mean?'

'What? No. What I'm saying is that I had been persuaded into coming forward.'

Heather glanced at running shoes that must have been at least a size eleven. 'By your partner?'

It was a common enough dynamic: instinctive jealousy of another man understandably multiplied by the violation.

'No. *No.* That would have been another reason for not wanting to go to court because then he'd have to know.'

Heather gave her wow-frown.

'No, I've never told Jeremy. He's away filming a lot, which helps. He's on a trip now. I told him the solicitors' letters are to do with a non-payment thing. Freelances have a lot of those. You think I should have told him?'

'A lot of women don't.'

'My BF, Bella, I did tell her, and she said: if you can avoid it, never let a bloke know that you've been . . . *assaulted.* Some of them it sort of weirdly turns on and others they suddenly won't touch you . . . or *daren't,* I don't know . . .'

The furthest Heather could go was: 'I've heard that.'

Jess swished a twitch of hair on the other side. 'No, it was someone in The Business, as we say, who persuaded me to do something. I can't exactly say he forced me – and, anyway, that phrase in these – but let's say he didn't seem to leave much choice . . .'

'So why did you change your mind?'

'That's where it gets . . . I began to suspect he had . . . another *agenda* is how I'll put it . . .'

Heather's next question was reflex, rather than thought. 'Do you need to talk to someone about . . . ?'

'What? Oh, I don't mean he . . . no, I think there needs to be a bit less talking to people about things, a bit more getting on with it. Look, I'm fine. I'm sorry I wasted everyone's time.'

'You haven't.' Heather was convinced that, even with two court-ready complainants, the same decision would have been made. 'Jess, it's very important you don't blame yourself for what happened to you.'

'What? Oh, no, I don't. But nor do I think my life was ruined forever. He was a guy who thought he could have whatever he wanted. I'd be very surprised if he thinks that now. I'm going to get on with my life.'

'Are you working on a programme at the moment?'

'Look, I'm sort of seeing what's around. I was working somewhere but then my contract came to an end. Occupational hazard. Still, Jeremy's got a job on this thing that's supposed to go on for years.'

Heather as well would be kept in long future employment by Millpond. There were rumours of hundreds of files piling up, the lives of two people redefined by an attempt to reconcile conflicting versions of a moment a lifetime ago. One complaint, corridor gossip claimed, related to an incident after a dance on VE Day.

As a detective, she followed the instructions that women alleging sex crimes should be given the sympathetic benefit of the doubt; privately, she was nervous of applying different evidential standards to one crime alone. How could you apply habeas corpus when the two bodies had walked away from the scene years or even decades before and now told contradictory stories?

Cuttings (7)

CONTROVERSIAL LECTURE GOES AHEAD

In the latest campus dispute over so-called 'no-platforming', UME officials have ruled that a planned lecture by a leading historian will go ahead.

Students had objected to the selection of Professor Ned Marriott to give the TB Macaulay Memorial Lecture, a prestigious event that has been hosted by the institution, based on twin sites in Buckinghamshire and Warwickshire, since 1969.

Marriott, 61, also a high-profile television presenter, recently faced two allegations of historic sexual offences, in non-academic contexts, but recently learned that no charges would be brought in either case. Student leaders complained, though, that the invitation to Marriott 'sends the wrong signals to victims of sexual violence.'

They also cited Marriott's admission of plagiarism in a case arising from a book based on one of his TV series, and his status as a former Rhodes Scholar, a postgraduate award named after Cecil John Rhodes, the British colonialist whose bequests and statues at several educational bodies have become a target for protestors who now condemn him as a racist.

There have been separate calls for the entire lecture series to be scrapped or renamed, on the basis that the historian and politician for whom it is named, Thomas Babington Macaulay (1800–1859), held official positions in India during the period of British colonial rule, and, in his writings, regularly differentiated the 'civilisation' of Britain from the 'barbarism' of other cultures.

But after a meeting of UME's board of management, the Vice Chancellor, Sir Kevan Neades, released this statement: 'The business acknowledges that there is a range of views on these issues. However, I am minded that the 2015 iteration of this lecture should go ahead. The business accepts that customers may continue to protest, but requests them to do so peacefully.'

Sir Kevan announced, however, the setting up of an inquiry into 'the possible impact on customers' of the TB Macaulay Memorial Lecture. Professor Andrea Traill of the Planet Directorate (a new department formed from the merging of Geography, Geology and Earth Sciences), will conduct the investigation, assisted by Jani Goswani, Senior Leader, Workplace Harmony and Joanna Rafferty, Director of History.

'. . . continues next Wednesday at 8pm. Now – don't go anywhere for the next five years because, over that time we'll be
broadcasting – starting tonight – one hundred documentaries in
our major new historical series, *Who Was Who* – written and
presented by Dominic Ogg . . .'

Confession

'Is it okay to call you Ned?'

'I've given up using the joke that I've been called worse.'

'Okay. Ned, do you want this to be an official or an un-
official confession?'

'Woh! What makes you think I'm going to confess anything?'

Ned sipped, wincing at the heat, the camomile tea that the
housekeeper had flutteringly discovered in a cupboard of the
presbytery kitchen.

'All I mean,' Tony said, 'is that you will always be speaking
to a priest but I can offer you degrees of formality. The sacrament of penance or just a sympathetic listening.'

'I'm a pretty terrible Catholic. I'm not sure I could, would
call myself one at all now.'

'Well, that can be part of the confession. It can be a way of
coming back.'

Ned lowered his head. The dark, heavy cloud of hair familiar from television was greying and thinning. From his frequent
appearances in documentaries to defend the Church's handling
of priestly paedophilia, Tony knew enough about make-up to
understand that this was more than the difference between on-
screen and off-screen appearances. The change must – shockingly
– be the effect of stress.

'I don't think that what I have in mind is quite a confession.'

'Okay. But you wanted to talk to me?'

'I agreed to. The only upside of all this has been the surprising acts of kindness from unexpected people – it seems churlish not to respond.'

'Well, let's just have a chat, then. Although, if it helps you, I can offer you the seal of the confessional on what we say.'

'Yes, I'd appreciate that. I've – probably unavoidably – become a bit paranoid.'

'Have you tried any of the talking therapies?'

'Not really. A friend gave me those tapes where a guy whispers at you about allowing yourself to admit how bad things are . . .'

'Ah.'

'In fact, your own voice is not unlike his. I don't mean that rudely.'

'I didn't take it so. In fact, you can partly blame Ignatius, patron saint of this parish. Some see a direct link from his Spiritual Exercises to something like Mindfulness. Did you find it helpful?'

'Not really. I think it's about submitting and I'm probably too stubborn. It seems to work for a lot of people, but not for my friend. His wife found him having taken an overdose, with the guy still murmuring at him.'

'Oh, I'm very sorry.'

'He survived. And he seems to be getting his fight back, as far as I can tell.'

'Ned, I'm interested that you used the words *stubborn* and *fight*. Ideally, you'd get through this on your own if you could?'

'Yes, I think so. My experience was of an actual moment of decision – that either I fought this or I went under and I was fucking . . . oh . . .'

'Before you say sorry, I think apologizing to clergymen for swearing is best left to the Edwardians.'

'Okay. I was *fucking* determined to survive it. What I can't know is if everyone who ends up in a mess gets to that choice or if seeing that there are two options is itself a sign that you can survive. Suicide must involve seeing no other solution.'

'Ned, I'm going to ask you the hardest question now.'

'Sure.'

'Regardless of what the police decided . . .'

'The CPS.'

'All right. Setting that aside, is there any aspect of your behaviour that you would have changed in retrospect?'

'Look, Father . . .'

'I've said: *call me Tony*. I know that phrase has a certain political . . .'

'The thing is that answering that question involves a certain amount of . . . *mechanical* detail . . .'

The perfectly chosen word. Tony still smarted at the memory of an early parishioner who had snarled, when urged to abandon an adulterous relationship: 'What do you know about love and sex? It's like taking your car to be fixed by a lifelong bicyclist.' During confession or counselling, he was always least at ease with sex.

Ned tested his tea again, found it cooler, took a procrastinating draught. 'I think, if they're honest, most guys of sixty, seventy, eighty could be hauled to court for something they've said or done to a woman. I suspect the younger are generally a bit better, although only in the way that, if you put up speed cameras, people will slow down. I think we know that sexual desire is hard to control – presumably *you* have to control it?'

Tony personally believed that the imposition of celibacy on the priesthood should be ended although, like a politician under cabinet responsibility, he continued publicly to support a policy to which he objected. He also, unlike many politicians and indeed priests, remained obedient to the strictures himself.

'Yes,' he said. He knew that this assertion was probably disbelieved – a consequence of the terrible transgressions by his brothers, and their cover-up by the Church.

'But many of your colleagues fail to restrain themselves,' Ned said. 'As do many people who are under no professional obligation, which is why there are so many unwanted pregnancies and, we have to assume, unwanted sex. I think, if you interviewed very many couples post-coitally, you'd get two different stories about what people wanted and got. I accept that. What I question is whether those competing versions can be settled in court – especially many years later. If you look at what juries are doing – Rolf Harris, Stuart Hall, Max Clifford, those DJs and prep school teachers – they're convicting if it obviously involved kids, stalling if it was over-age and it was he said-she said. I think, in the absence of forensic or documentary evidence, most of us would do the same, wouldn't we?'

Freed from the sacramental framework – not required to assess the severity of the sins and calculate the proportionate penance – Tony luxuriated in the lesser responsibility of a psychologist. 'Ned, I think – I'm not talking legally or even penitentially – but I think that's what we would describe as a partial admission?'

Cooling tea savoured as slowly as wine. 'Seal of the confessional?'

'Yes.'

'I treated women badly. Not criminally, I would insist, but thoughtlessly, stupidly. I learned to treat them better. I think, for the last decade, I've been, as they say, *clean*. I hope to get across to my son that you have to be beyond sure now that someone wants to. But, then, this awful word: *historic*.'

'Obviously, Ned, I'm not comparing you to a Nazi war criminal . . .'

'Well, I am known as The Hitler Man . . .'

'Really?'

'Office joke. No, I understand what you're going to say. We can't expect to escape our past – not even if we're ninety-six and living in Bolivia, not even if we're very sorry and haven't herded anyone into ovens for seventy years. But, A, I don't think this is quite in that league and, B, I realize I'm straying into your territory but what about redemption or forgiveness? The Americans speak a lot of guff but that phrase about the god of second chances makes sense to me.'

'And – some would say – that absolution – let's use that

word in a secular sense for the moment – can only follow penance, punishment . . .'

'I have punished myself.'

'*Yourself.*'

It was a standard pattern in penitents: the desire to be forgiven without quite confessing.

'The last year has been my penance. I have had condemnation without the possibility of any real absolution.'

'Yes. I see that. Ned, I can still, if you wish, make this a formal confession.'

'A part of me wants to . . .'

'And would it be trite to call that part your soul, your conscience?'

Ned grimaced. 'Yes, actually, I think it would be.'

'Sorry.'

'I forgive you.' Ned started a laugh, which Tony echoed. 'I'm afraid I couldn't resist that. Look, if you could absolve me and then ring my poor mum and tell her, that would be great. But, by definition, you can't. And anything you say wouldn't apply on Twitter or Google. One of the obligations on people in my line of work is to come up with adjectives for the decades: Roaring Forties, Nervous Nineties, and so on. And I think the only word for the one we're in – the Twentytens or whatever – is *censorious*. Someone takes offence at anything anyone says. One comment can lose you your job, your life. Excuse the sermon.'

'I've preached a version of it myself.'

'Look, actually, Father, *Tony*, there is something I want to tell you . . .'

Doctors said the same – that the real revelation often came late in the consultation.

'I've told you, Ned. Anything you say stays with me.'

'People knowing that I've hurt them is bad enough. But there's someone who doesn't know what I did to them.'

'Some would say that's better.'

'Yes, and I see that. But *I* know and – I see that it sounds as if it's all about me – find it hard to live with . . .'

One of the few useful things Tony had learned on ministerial refresher courses was the power of leaving a silence. He forced himself to say nothing.

'I betrayed – I suppose is the word – my best friend, who has been so good to me through all this . . .'

'Sexually?'

Pause. 'No. No.'

But the hesitation and then the repetition probably meant yes; a priest became as attuned to the tells of deceit as detectives and journalists presumably did. Ned's hands on his lap were twisted into entwined fists, fingers flushed by the tightness, at which tangle he stared as he spoke.

'What happened was – I gave evidence against him. There was some Savonarolan crackdown at work and I gave them stuff on him. The last thing the authorities would want would be for him to know it was me, so I'm safe in that sense, but I had to sit beside him while he read the stuff I'd said, hidden under a code-name . . . but *Jesus* . . .' It was a sign of how deep he was going that Ned did not apologize for the blasphemy. 'Or, more appositely, Judas . . .'

'Do you know why you did it?'

'Yes, I think so. Probably. Because, by the laws of both gratitude and statistics, it reduced the chances of the bastards coming for me. And because there's some awful human instinct to tell the soldiers what they want to know. We often think the really revealing historical what-if is: would I have been a Nazi? Or: would I have hidden Jews in my attic? And those are good enough tests. But I think the hardest one is: would I be an informer? Because it's something you can do – if you want to be any good, how you *have* to do it – without anyone knowing, unless there's a revolution later on and the filing cabinets are tipped out in the market square. I have raged in my head – obviously – about the people who spoke to the cops about me and the moral imbalance that must have driven them to it. But, the minute I got the chance, I – this word dates me – *grassed* on my best friend. From professional scruple, I'm always wary of the more explosive historical comparisons but let's say that, as certain leaders in certain periods have calculated, there's an almost genetic desire to be helpful to the authorities. It makes us feel useful, wanted, *pure*.'

'Have you thought about telling your friend?'

'Slightly. But I convince myself – as people probably did in those countries at those times – that the authorities would have done what they did to him anyway. I doubt my tittle-tattle tipped the balance.'

'I think that's a sensible way of looking at it. And can you do anything to help him now?'

'I try to be a better friend. I can't help him much because I'm damaged goods myself.'

It had become common for priests to describe confession as free therapy. Tony disliked the conceit because it was a cliché and because his suspicion was that the traffic went mainly in the other direction; people were drawn to therapy because it was confession free from the judgement of God.

'Ned, I still sense that you don't want the forgiveness I can give you?'

'No. No, I don't think I do.'

'But, from what I've heard, I can tell you that, over what you did to your friend, I sense genuine contrition. And so I think you can forgive yourself.'

Ned looked up and smiled. 'Thank you. You're good at this.'

'But you say we live in a world that's too unforgiving?'

'Yes.'

'Okay. Well, can you forgive the women who accused you?'

'Ah. Of course. I should have seen that coming. You're *too* good at this. What I'd say is that I understand that I have to try to.'

Why Them?

During unsuccessfully drugged nights, Tom tried to reconstruct the plot of his fall.

As the historian he was – was in two senses, *had been* – he re-examined conversations, documents, gossip. Special had pulled the trigger, but he had always seemed a natural patsy, someone else's heavy. So whose? The Vice Chancellor? Workplace Harmony, or Jolly Jobs, or whatever they were called this term? He imagined counter-histories in which he had beamed supportively through departmental meetings, or in which Professor Padraig Allison had been removed the first time that he abused a student. But each speculative route came back to the dead-end that it had somehow suited someone somewhere in the institution for him to go. Why, though, had they knocked on his door when more obvious culprits were left undisturbed? Tom feared that, ultimately, like Josef K, he would never know why They had come for him. *Someone must have been telling lies . . .*

Cuttings (8)

THE MOLE

Perverse Prof Strictly Off Limits

After learning that cops will take 'no further action' over two historic allegations of sexual assault against women, top TV historian Ned Marriott, 61, must have been keen to get back on the screen.

But The Mole hears that 'Professor Perverse', as the argumentative academic is called for defending Hitler and attacking Churchill in his work, has suffered a blow to his hopes of resuming his career. Widely tipped to be a contestant in the next series of *Strictly Come Dancing*, he has now apparently been dropped from the shortlist after concerns were expressed by some of those working on the ratings-buster BBC1 series.

A show source says: 'Everyone accepts that he is legally innocent but it's quite another matter to ask dancers to be pressed up against him in a waltz or samba. There was a feeling it would be tough for him to achieve the rapport and trust that a dance duo needs.'

Although legally in the clear, the presenter has faced separate controversy for having chosen, as one of his favourite pieces of music on *Desert Island Discs*, the pop song 'Delilah', in which a man celebrates having killed his lover for her infidelity. The academic was also involved in an earlier scandal after admitting to stealing a section from a history book by another writer and passing it off as his own work on TV and in a book.

Divorced Marriott, who has a 9-year-old son by his partner, 41-year-old literary agent Emma, has not been seen on TV since the sex investigation by Scotland Yard's Operation Millpond began. His legal representatives issued this statement last night: 'While there is no legal or other reason why Ned Marriott should not appear on any programmes that he wants to – and he is currently discussing a range of projects with different broadcasters – he has never been involved in any approach to or from this particular series and, although he enjoys watching the series, would never imagine himself appearing on it.'

A BBC spokesman said: 'It is our policy never to speculate on *Strictly* line-ups in advance.'

Pendulum

'How many times,' Ned asked Tom, 'have you – as an historian – struggled to avoid the metaphor of a pendulum? But the reason it's so tempting is that it's what always happens. We've gone from automatically disbelieving allegations to unquestioningly accepting them. Eventually, we'll settle in the middle with rigorous but sensitive investigation. But pity the poor buggers who get hit by the pendulum at either end of the swing.'

Cuttings (9)

MET CHIEF BACKS MILLPOND

'Operation Millpond' – the controversial police squad set up to investigate sexual allegations against celebrities – has been defended by London's top cop.

All of those quizzed by Millpond so far have been cleared without charge, and, after a two-year investigation, detectives admitted to finding 'no evidence' of a Satanic sexual abuse ring that one complainant claimed to involve senior politicians and clerics.

The Metropolitan Police Commissioner insisted in a speech yesterday: 'Millpond was fit for purpose.'

However, he announced the setting up of an independent inquiry into the perv probe, which will be headed by Sir Richard Agate, an education expert and business chief.

Transcript for Legal – Strictly Confidential

[NB: bleeped speech will also be pixelated to prevent lip-reading]

Narrator: Day 8 in the Big Brother House. 1.15am. Ned and Cassie are in the living room.

Ned: Do you want me to top that up for you?

Cassie: Say what?

Ned: The wine.

Cassie: Sick. So I'm gonna be, like, okay, right, here with you?

Ned: In what way?

Cassie: Well, no offence I don't like read the news and shit but Alex tell me in the hot tub you was like a [bleep]

Ned: No. No, I am absolutely not a [bleep]. Seriously, this is important. There were allegations but I was cleared.

Cassie: Yeah, well, so was [bleep bleep] but Alex says the judge just fancied him and shit.

Ned: Yes, well, I'm not actually sure that the legal system . . . anyway, my case never even went to court.

Cassie: Sure but Alex say that just because you knows people.

Ned: Cassie, I think you're a really sweet girl, person . . .

Cassie: Woh, grandad! Hope you aint gonna [bleep] me?

Ned: Oh, look, please. This is completely unfair.

Cassie: [imitation] 'Oh, look, please. This is completely unfair.' Sorry, Lord Grantham.

Ned: No, look we need to get this straight. Allegations were brought – as could happen to anyone, especially these days – but they were thrown out. I was never even charged.

Cassie: Well, half the cast of [bleep bleep bleep] aint been charged with doing blow but they was putting it in every hole when I was in it. Just saying.

Cassie: Aaaaargghh! What the [bleep] was that? Someone just touched my [bleep]

Narrator: Ned and Cassie realize they're not alone

Dave: Christ [bleep] me, I'm [bleep] [bleep]. Hello, darlin.

Cassie: [bleep], mate. Was you under those [bleep] cushions all the [bleep] time?

Dave: Yeah. But I was totally [bleep] out of it. Evening, Lord Grantham.

Ned: Hi, Dave. Should I pour you some wine?

Dave: Solid. Why you never drink, mate? You an alkie or is it antibionics [sic] or summat?

Ned: Neither, in fact. I just think I'm better without it, especially in some situations.

Dave: You mean like what you did to them girls? No offence.

Ned: Well, as it happens 'no offence' is the mot juste.

Cassie: Juiced? Is that like a drink?

Ned: Just to be clear, I was cleared of doing anything to them – or, as I'd say, *those* – girls, women actually.

Dave: No smoke without fire, though. Just saying.

Cassie: And them dancers on *Strictly* didn't want nothing to do with you.

Ned: Look, if someone from the company is watching, I really hope this isn't going out. I warn you I have very good lawyers.

Dave: [imitation] 'vair good lawyers' [sings] You're just a posh [bleep bleep]* You're just a posh [bleep bleep]*

Ned: Oh, for [bleep] sake. This is ridiculous.

Tannoy: Ned, will you come to the diary room please?

*Jimmy Savile

Shaky

Children, as their sense of identity develops, often want to know what other names they might have had. Dee, at eight or nine, once grabbed Ned's edition of *Tales from Shakespeare* (originally his dad's and so a treasured memento) from the shelves, ran to her room and at length returned to demand why she could not have been Olivia, Viola or Helena instead. Although Ned didn't tell her this, she might, if a single birth, have been Hermione and so had been spared immersion in the post-Rowling torrent by being a twin, which had led Ned to a chiming pair from *Hamlet* and *King Lear*.

Jenny, although she had agreed to carry on the Marriott tradition of Shakespearean naming, asked, hazily post-natal, 'Don't both of those, er, die at the end?' but he told her that the baptisms weren't meant literally. Edmund, after all, was a bastard in both the literal and metaphorical senses, but Ned's dad had presumably not intended either a confession or a prediction of his personality. Dee, later, set at A-level the play from which her name came, had raged on an access night, 'In this fucking boring play, you order me to be hanged. Thanks for that!' unrelenting when her father pointed out that Edmund changes his mind and tries to reprieve Cordelia. It seemed bad luck then – even more so now – to mention that their namesakes' attempted reconciliation comes only on the brink of the man's death, although, as he kept telling himself and relatives, the christenings were not predictions.

His brother, Timon, admittedly, had ended up a wealthy financier, though not in Athens but Australia with its large Greek diaspora. Emma had readily accepted Toby, one of the most secular male names in the canon, reassured by Googling, that, if they were condemning their son to anything, it would merely be mischievousness and indigestion.

Now, however, estranged from Cordelia and having betrayed Poor Tom, Edmund sometimes wondered if the superstitious had a point. He thought back to teaching his daughters to swim and feared that Phee had been the weaker.

Your Love Always (2)

Dear Ms Humpage, I am sorry to inform you that we will not now be licensing you to handle the European rights of *Your Love Always*. Melissa Plunkett-Grundy is a president of Safe Spaces and a trustee of POD (Protect Our Daughters) and, while making no judgement on your situation, fears that your involvement could create a distraction from both her novel and her pro bono activities.

Lessons from Recent History

The crowd of students protesting against Macaulay's racism was small but forceful, so it was a relief to reach the ticketed environs. There were inevitably flashbacks to Daddy's sixtieth, the night before it all began. Many of the same people were present. Looking through the door into the council chamber, she knew, from their faces or silhouettes: Emma, Tom and Helen, Granny and Grandpa Jack, the guy from the publishers, nice Ciara from the university.

It was a particular absence, however, that nagged at her; and she was soon reminded of it. Going into the room, she took a drink from the worryingly young-looking student, hesitating between apple juice and white wine before taking the alcoholic option which taunted by tasting like sour fruit juice.

As Phee reached the artificially cheerful semi-circle of her stepmother and the Pimms, Tom asked, 'Your other half?' his usual greeting when she was solo socially. Rebuked once by Daddy for resorting to the sort of recycled phrase he condemned from others, Tom had triumphantly insisted that he wasn't: in this case, it was conceptually precise.

'She texted me,' Phee said. 'To say she wouldn't be coming. She didn't want everyone waiting in suspense.'

'Well, that was thoughtful of her,' said Tom. 'I mean, the letting us know part, not missing her old man's Lazarus lecture. She's keeping bad company. Dom Odd is the other notable no-show. Did you see his debut as a TV presenter? An elephant joining the Royal Ballet would be a more natural transition.'

Phee had watched ten minutes of the opening programme and become depressed about human dispensability.

'Daddy *is* here?' she checked with Emma.

'Of course. He said he wanted to read through the speech quietly in a corner. TBH, I think he's gone to the Gents again. At their age, it's a vicious circle: thinking they might have a problem means they . . .'

Tom spun his head until he found the sign on the wall with an arrow and a male silhouette, and headed towards it. 'You're certainly not taking the piss when you say that.'

'Tom, are you . . . ?' asked Helen.

'Yes, I really do need a pee. I won't be found dangling in a cubicle.'

'Tom, I didn't . . .'

When he was too far away to hear and argue back, Phee asked Helen: 'How's he managing? And you, of course . . . ?'

Helen made a so-so face: 'I try to keep cheerful for him. But it just seems so . . . unfair . . .' The beginning of tears blinked away. 'He says it's like living as a criminal without having the nicety of a trial. I tell him it's not as bad as that but it probably is. I wanted to go over and say something to that gigantic waste of space but Tom doesn't want to spoil things for your dad.'

'He's been such a good friend to Ned,' said Emma. Phee asked her: 'You haven't brought Tobes?'

'No. He's flexi-boarding at Abbey Grove. He'll have a much better time there.'

'You'll be able to afford to send him to Eton soon?'

'Say again?'

'Daddy said there was some big American book about texts from the dead or . . .'

'Oh, that. Second time through, it didn't really live up to the title. I passed on it.'

Phee felt the familiar kiss on the top of her head and one of the two voices she had known longest: 'Cupcake.'

It was hard getting used to Daddy so much broader and bald. Last time Phee was round for Sunday lunch, Emma had been trying to persuade him to 'book an appointment' before the lecture, but he said: 'With this, you can't put the cat back in the bag without being ridiculed.' His appearance was still a shock; like it might be, Phee thought, if there were suddenly a world shortage of hair dye and you found out what older women really looked like.

There was a line of painted-gilt chairs along one wall, pre-sumably intended for those without the stamina for standing round for half an hour before the start-time, a courtesy of which Granny and Grandpa Jack had now taken advantage. Granny looked a little agitated – not who-am-I? bad but probably over-whelmed by the occasion and worried about her son – so Phee excused herself and went across to be granddaughterly.

After the greetings and cheek kisses: 'Just you tonight, darling?'

'Yes, Granny. She had a work thing she just couldn't get out of.'

'That's a shame. Your dad was singing your praises about what a rock you've been.'

'A rock chick,' said Grandpa Jack, weirdly.

'Jack thinks Edmund should bring a civil case against the lying little madams,' Granny said.

'There has to be a stand,' her stepgrandfather, or whatever he was, added. 'Too many good chaps being dragged down by this sort of thing.'

'I think to be honest, Granny, it's better to let it go. Daddy's policy is business as usual, like tonight.'

Students were circulating among the groups, asking guests to make their way to the Tuchman Lecture Theatre. Daddy was being ushered away by a tense-looking woman with a lanyard round her neck. When he tried to kiss Emma goodbye, she flicked her head aside so that he just brushed the side of her ear.

Heading for a precautionary wee, Phee passed Tom, coming in the opposite direction.

'Ophelia, has he given you his address?'

'What? Oh, his speech. No, he said it had to come from his heart not a committee.'

Claire, the black lawyer (no, the *lawyer*, her skin irrelevant) came out of the Ladies.

'Oh, hello, you two.' Greetings all round. 'Sorry, tiny bit of shop talk, Tom. Something I forgot to say, last time we met: you must never ever again use that word in print anywhere ever.'

'What word? You may not be familiar with the size of my vocabulary.'

'*The* word. The one in B & H that isn't Hedges.'

'Oh, that one. Well, I'm not sure I'd be *able* to write it.'

'No, seriously. From now on, you can't even write, I don't know, Napoleon was regarded by some of his soldiers as a *benson*. The President was accused of *bensoning* the Senate.'

'Really? What, in case some twitterer thinks I'm a *hypocrite*?'

'No. Because it increases the chances of a web-search coming up *tom pimm bensoning*. It's something to do with algorithms – a nephew explained it to me.'

Claire's eyes suddenly wandered. 'Don't look now,' she said.

But Tom followed her gaze, as Phee did, to a man – tall, tanned, dark hair greased back – who was going into the Gents. When Tom winced and turned away, Claire told him: 'I warned you.'

'Who's that?' Phee asked.

'The dude from Campus Karma, or whatever they call it, who heard Tom's appeal.'

'Oh. Daddy said it was rejected?'

'Not exactly,' Tom explained. 'They said that, as it wasn't officially an appeal, it could neither be rejected or upheld.'

'So, is that it?'

'Well, unless you turn out to be Portia rather than Ophelia.'

'I think we're going to sue the bottom off them,' said Claire.

'Subject to budget,' Tom added. 'Might ask your old man for a bung.'

Washing her hands, Phee found herself next to the nice professor, Ciara, who said: 'You must see a lot of Tom? I hope you can get across to him how much the students – the good students – miss him. This place is crazy. They're offering another round of redundancies and I think I'm going to take it.'

In the hall, there was the always satisfying frisson of picking up a Reserved notice and sitting on that chair. Phee, Tom, Emma, Helen, Granny and Grandpa Jack sat next to each other about ten rows back, a compromise between Daddy's fear of being able to see them and her grandparents' concern about being able to hear him. Ciara was just in front. A group of men who gave Daddy a thumbs up as he passed were, Tom explained, the five-a-side football team.

Daddy sat on a chair to the right of the stage, drumming the floor with one heel. With a rush of sympathetic nerves, she felt the reversal of the situation at school plays twenty years earlier.

At the back of the stage was a screen with the legend: TB Macaulay Memorial Lecture 2015. The dark-suited emcee for the evening – an Ulsterman with a grain-sack gut – stumbled up steps at the side of the stage, shuffled to the lectern and wheezed: 'My lords, ladies and gentlemen, good evening. I'm Sir Kevan Neades, Vice Chancellor of the University of Middle England. As you will see from the list in your programmes, this event has attracted a long – as it were – history' – his was the only laughter for the joke – 'of distinguished speakers.'

In an instinctive group-move, the audience, including Phee, found the page to which their host had alluded. Many of the names she knew from her father's conversation or TV series they had watched together: Barbara Tuchman, Robert A. Caro, Lady Antonia Fraser, Tristram Hunt, David Starkey, Kathryn Hughes, A. N. Wilson, Dominic Sandbrook, Amanda Foreman, Simon Schama, Mary Beard. As Daddy had pointed out when he e-mailed her invitation, alert readers would notice that the list of previous speakers jumped from 1971 to 1973. In the intervening year, the lecture had been delivered by Professor Padraig Allison.

She hadn't really been listening to the Irish guy but joined the applause triggered by the words 'Professor Ned Marriott'.

As the Vice Chancellor laboriously left the stage, Daddy came to the lectern, walking stiffly, she thought.

'Thank you for that very special introduction,' he said. Tom laughed as if something funny had been said.

'The question I'm addressing tonight,' Ned began, 'is: can the past be given a fair trial? It is not my intention to talk in detail about a recent well-publicized ordeal of my own: I am unable to do so for a combination of legal, medical and temperamental reasons. But these experiences provided the epigraphs that preface the printed text of this lecture. During my year of persecution and suspicion, I first read – and then saw a production of – Arthur Miller's great 1953 play *The Crucible*: written in response to his own suffering of false accusation and opprobrium during the McCarthyite anti-communist witch hunts in America but with wider – and escalating – relevance to other cultures in other times, up to this day in England. Two speeches from the play seemed to be speaking directly to me and, I think, now always will. In one scene, the protagonist, informed by the court that the claims against him have been accepted as fact, while his own case will not be heard, asks: "Is the accuser always holy now?" Later, when told that his life will return to normal if only he will give a signature to an apology for something he did not do, he explains why he cannot sign: "Because it is my name! How may I live without my name? I have given you my soul; leave me my name!" These, it seems to me, are phrases that we must emblazon on our highest buildings as a charm. Historians are familiar – even weary – with the desire to reduce each period of history to some pithy, alliterative summary. But it seems clear to me now that we are living through an Age of Accusation, a Culture of Comeuppance.'

In the silence of intense collective attention, Phee heard fierce whispering and, turning, located a muttering huddle – two elderly men and a pair of middle-aged women – several rows behind. Perhaps distracted by this kerfuffle, her father stopped to swallow almost two-thirds of the tumbler of water on the lectern.

His voice was slightly burpy as he resumed: 'I believe that we are living through a period that will be judged – in the near future – to have misapplied what it misunderstood to be the lessons of the recent past. Ours is a culture in which allegation is assumed to be fact and the bleating of the self-righteous equals justice. I am haunted by the fact that – in an era when most teachers and writers of History concur that it is unwise to aver with any certainty exactly what happened in the past – the CPS, the police, newspaper columnists, victim support groups and HR departments seem suddenly possessed by twenty-twenty hindsight, however thick the mists of time, doubt or confusion. I know of police forces – and HR departments – where the word *complainant* has officially been replaced by *victim*. This is presented as a small linguistic shift but it speaks volumes of a country that has substituted for objective justice the rule of mob orthodoxy and the appeasement of special interest groups.'

From behind the line of Ned's supporters came the sounds the public speaker most fears: the scrape of chair-leg on floor and the shuffling and mumbling of a disrupted row. Before she could turn round, Phee saw the four whisperers to her left, as they clomped towards their nearest fire exit.

'Do take it personally,' Tom said to Phee and Emma. 'Although they'd only have come in so that they could walk out. Savlon, Daggers, Horny, Quatermass.'

Daddy seemed equally laid-back about the reduction in numbers, pausing for a sip of the remaining drink while staring at his departed colleagues until the door rattled behind them.

'A culture in which some people literally cannot bear to hear opinions that challenge their received wisdoms,' he said.

That, Phee suspected, was an improvised put-down and Tom, seemingly feeling the same, started a round of applause that was taken up by others in the audience, including Ciara and the football team.

'This Age of Accusation,' the lecturer went on, 'has had necessary successes in its pursuit of child-abusers – or at least those in the lighter areas of 1970s Light Entertainment in television – who had escaped justice for decades. But against those placed in jail – or found guilty in their absence in their graves – we must balance the names that have been destroyed by whisper, innuendo, over-publicized arrest and excessively elongated bail before being let go without charge but never – for the rest of their lives – without shadow.'

On the screen behind the lectern, the title of the lecture blurred and was replaced by the word, its first symbol declaring twenty-first century as rapidly as the substitution of *f* for *s* signalled the 16th: *#tbmml2015*.

'Does he know they've got a live Twitterfeed?' whispered Helen.

'Another sentence unlikely in the eighteenth century,' said Tom.

Phee felt a presentiment of dread. 'I wouldn't think so. He can barely send a text.'

Her father's voice, un-broadcast for almost a year, was loudening and modulating as he luxuriated in performing publicly again. 'Apart from those whose lives and careers are interrupted temporarily – and their reputations permanently – by vague claims that never become charges, we read at least weekly – in footnotes rather than the headlines given to the few sent to prison – of schoolteachers suspended for a year or more before being cleared by juries in minutes – literally minutes – of assaults for which the only evidence was the claim of a pupil or former pupil with whom they had clashed over disciplinary or educational issues. Young men whose name will forever yield, on Google-searching, the word "rape" or the phrase "rape allegations", despite the fact that they were rapidly cleared by juries, while their female accuser receives legally protected anonymity for ever.'

R U watchin this victim blaming? appeared on the screen in giant italic script. The comments multiplied behind the lecturer:

Y they letting this raypist speak?

#raypist

#students boycott UME

 # UME = Useless Men Everywhere

'And, outside of these serious legal issues,' the TB Macaulay Memorial Lecture continued, 'are those who are prosecuted and convicted within seconds by the jurors in the global kangaroo court convened by those with a Twitter app and too much spare time. The politician, employee or university lecturer who offends – or is judged by others to have offended – some gender, racial or sexual grouping in society. The lives, careers and reputations of these unfortunate victims are also sacrificed on the pyre of wrong-headed self-righteousness. In a few decades, we have moved from a world in which any opinion, regardless of how harmful, could be dismissed as a "joke" to one in which even the most harmless remark is refused any defence of humour or fair comment.'

#paedo

#sackhim

#fucking psycholiberal

'I wish to stress as clearly as possible . . .' He paused, an increase in glances up from his text the only sign that he was disconcerted by the eyes increasingly focusing over his shoulders. 'I wish to stress that I am not in any way diminishing the horrific crimes of rape or child abuse or offering a judgement as to the accuracy of any specific claims made. The point I am making is that history and logic tell us that all such allegations must be rigorously questioned and tested and that this must be done in a way that does not result in the consequences of suspicion or even exoneration becoming indistinguishable from those of conviction.'

#kill this cunt

#victim-blamer

#deadwhitemale

#sack this guy

#resign

#gomeansgo

Even as Daddy attempted to clear his name, it was being further attacked, literally behind his back. As with so much that had happened in this year, the spectacle was at first shocking but then seemed almost instantly inevitable. Emma reached across a hand to try to hold Phee's but the sweat on both their palms meant that the attempted contact sheared off. Through the blur of tears, she saw that Tom was shaking almost uncontrollably, while Helen pressed her hands down on his shoulders. A bewildered Granny gazed at Grandpa Jack for explanation.

#this guy's history

The sudden slowness and emphasis of Daddy's voice signalled that he was reaching his conclusion. 'If I claim that I have been burgled, defrauded, defamed or even nearly murdered, my contention will be tested to destruction by a legal system that understands that an assumption that the accuser is telling the truth risks – even guarantees – corruption and injustice. This robustness cannot be suspended in any area of the law. Nor can justice be sub-let to media and social media whose operating principle so frequently seems to be: "Give me that stick so that I can get hold of the wrong end of it." Contemporary convention is that I should end by apologizing for any offence I have given but I cannot. History tells us that – if offence and debate become impossible – we will all ultimately be sorry. Although many of you won't thank me, I thank you.'

Aware that almost no one in the auditorium was looking at his face, he finally turned and stood with his back to the ragged applause that came from only sections of the audience as he read the surge of words down the screen.

#This guy's history
#History

Prefixed with its deconstructed swastika, the word rolled down the screen as the unseen mob took up the silent chant.

#History
#History
#History
#History
#History

AUTHOR'S NOTE

It is common enough in a coda of this kind to stress that what precedes it is a work of fiction; but especially so in this case.

This novel is informed by having had passing acquaintance with more than one of those publicly suspected (with huge career and financial consequences) of serious sexual offences for which they were never subsequently charged. However, it draws on no particular accuser or accused.

In regard to another plot-strand, it is also the case that – during a long, generally privileged and happy career in the media – I suffered one devastating experience of institutional group-think, baffling and contradictory management, false accusation and surreally sub-legal process.

As a result, I have personal knowledge of the damage to reputation, employability and health that can result from such an ordeal, and of its paradoxical outcome: silence or ostracism from some of those I had considered friends or close colleagues and – the poignant opposite – startling kindness and courageous support from others, including many from whom I had no reason to expect anything.

However, if I had wanted to tell that story directly, I would have published a memoir; and may yet one day do so. Though my own corporate experiences inevitably affected aspects of the atmosphere of the novel, the narrative and characters are specific to the circumstances of a fiction that mainly concerns a fictional university.

Crucially, *The Allegations* was not written as a *roman à clef* and narrative – and possibly legal – jeopardy could result from attempting to read it as such.

In this fiction, Ned Marriott's methods and beliefs as an historian owe much to the example of Lady Antonia Fraser Pinter, with whom I was lucky enough to have some illuminating exchanges on the subject. His documentary about seventeenth-century suspicion of women might have got him into even more trouble if he and I had not read with such instructive enjoyment *Witches: James I and the English Witch Hunts* by Tracy Borman (Jonathan Cape). As Professor Marriott acknowledges in the novel, his writing on moral crusades is significantly informed by Professor Donald Weinstein's *Savonarola: The Rise and Fall of a Renaissance Prophet* (Yale). Professor Marriott's historical writing has also clearly benefited from Peter Hennessey's *Never Again – Britain 1945–51* (Penguin) and *America: A Narrative History* by George Brown Tindall and David E. Shi (W.W. Norton).

Tom Pimm's approach to American political history is gratefully indebted to the work of Barbara Tuchman, Robert A. Caro and Doris Kearns Goodwin. My – and his – working knowledge of occupants of the White House was usefully fact-checked and amplified by Nigel Hamilton's *American Caesars* (The Bodley Head).

I read with great interest three articles about corporate branding and / or the suppression of dissent in modern universities: 'Diary: Why I Quit' by Marina Warner (*London Review of Books*, Volume 36, Number 17, 11 September 2014); 'Open-door Policy?' by Professor Thomas Docherty (*Index on Censorship*, Volume 44, Number 02, Summer 2015); and 'I'm a liberal professor, and my liberal students terrify me', published under the pseudonym 'Edward Schlosser' (www.vox.com, June 3, 2015). However, the staff and students of the fictional UME bear no resemblance to any actual figures in higher education.

My sense of the chronology and psychology of Britain's most notorious celebrity paedophile and sex-offender was usefully measured against Dan Davies' tremendous book: *In Plain Sight: The Life and Lies of Jimmy Savile* (Quercus). A technological aspect of the final scene in the novel was inspired by an actual event described in Chapter 3 of Jon Ronson's *So You've Been Pub-*

licly Shamed (Picador), a brilliant account of the social and moral consequences of inter-active advances.

Some of the technical and mental aspects of being under suspicion of sexual offences are drawn – though used to entirely fictional purpose – from *No Further Action: The Darkest Year of My Life* by Jim Davidson (John Blake), an eye-opening account of legal and reporting practices which, possibly due to the comedian's unpopularity with the liberal media, has not perhaps received the attention it deserved.

The literary texts that Ned Marriott and Tom Pimm read with such empathetic fascination during their suspensions are: Heinrich Böll – *The Lost Honour of Katharina Blum* (Vintage Classics); J. M. Coetzee – *Disgrace* (Vintage); Henrik Ibsen (translator Christopher Hampton) – *An Enemy of the People* (Faber); Franz Kafka – *The Trial* (Penguin Modern Classics); David Mamet – *Oleanna* in *Plays: Four* (Methuen); Arthur Miller – *The Crucible* (Penguin Modern Classics); Terence Rattigan – *The Winslow Boy* (Nick Hern Books); Philip Roth – *The Human Stain* (Vintage).

Tom Pimm listens to the audio-book version of *Mindfulness: A practical guide to finding peace in a frantic world* (Piatkus) by Mark Williams and Danny Penman, which I recommend to the tense or distressed.

The lines from 'It Was Good While It Lasted' by Blake Morrison appear in *Shingle Street* (Chatto). *The Lost Honour of Christopher Jefferies*, written by Peter Morgan, was broadcast by ITV in December, 2014.

The character of Dr (later Sir) Kevan Neades first appeared, working at a different institution and with completely different dialogue, in my radio play, *What Did I Say?* (BBC Radio 4, 2008).

Ciara Harrison and Elaine Benham bid to give their names to characters in this novel at charity auctions held respectively for The Sam Griffiths Foundation and Walk the Walk.

I am grateful to – apart from those in the initial dedication – Catherine Fehler for her legal brain and warm heart; Jonathan Moore for spiritual advice; Joanne Sharp for explaining flexiboarding and Colin Sharp for a knowledge of business that lives up to his surname. Many colleagues at the *Guardian* – especially Rosie Swash, Rebecca Nicholson, Chris Wiegand, Susanna Rustin and Michael Billington – did more than they will suspect to restore my confidence at the worst times and I will always be grateful for their support and kindness. At other places, Eoin O'Callaghan, Polly Thomas, Ben Preston, Ellie Austin, Fiona Hughes and Roy Williams were kind and wise.

The sympathetic interest and attention of Emma Bravo, Paul Baggaley, Kris Doyle and Camilla Elworthy at Picador also helped to save me from one possible outcome to the events. Nicole Foster's copy-editing was intelligent and sensitive.

Many others, in several institutions, who gave me great assistance – practically, psychologically, generously – know who they are, but would rather that their names are not mentioned here because, it pains me to say in the context of this novel, of fear of the consequences at their places of work.

MARK LAWSON
March 2016